Lunar Landscapes

Stories and Short Novels 1950–1963

John Hawkes

Lunar Landscapes

Stories & Short Novels 1949—1963

Charivari

The Owl

The Goose on the Grave

New Directions

SOME OF THESE STORIES AND NOVELS FIRST APPEARED IN MSS I, NEW
DIRECTIONS 11, 12, 17, AND 18 (ANTHOLOGIES), THE NOBLE SAVAGE, SAN
FRANCISCO REVIEW AND SAN FRANCISCO REVIEW ANNUAL.

PUBLISHED SIMULTANEOUSLY IN CANADA BY MCCLELLAND & STEWART
LIMITED.

NEW DIRECTIONS BOOKS ARE PUBLISHED FOR JAMES LAUGHLIN
BY NEW DIRECTIONS PUBLISHING CORPORATION,
333 SIXTH AVENUE, NEW YORK 10014.

Table of Contents

The Traveler (1962)   1

The Grandmother (1961)   12

A Little Bit of the Old Slap and Tickle (1962)   26

Death of an Airman (1950)   31

A Song Outside (1962)   38

The Nearest Cemetery (1963)   43

Charivari (1950)   51

The Owl (1954)   137

The Goose on the Grave (1954)   200

for Albert J. Guerard

Lunar Landscapes

Stories and Short Novels 1950–1963

The Traveler

Early one morning in a town famous for the growing of some grape, I arose from my bed in the inn and stepped outside alone to the automobile. I smelled the odor of flowers thirsting early for the sun; deep green fields stretched to either side of the road, wet and silent; it was the cold dawn of the traveler and I wished suddenly for a platter of home-cooked sausage. The car was covered with the same white dew as the grass, and when I opened the door I smelled the damp leather, the still cold oil and the gasoline that had been standing the night long. Soon the hot day would be upon us; the dust of driving would whirl us into villages, every hour or two whirl chickens and small children across the road like weeds.

Down the road came a young bent-backed girl. On her shoulders she carried a yoke from either end of which hung a milk can, and over her shoulders she wore a shawl. Her legs were bare and scratched by the thistle. Slowly she came into the inn yard and approached me, each step loudly sloshing the milk.

"Your name, Fräulein?"

"Just Milkmaid," she said.

"Well, Milkmaid, how many cows have you milked this morning?"

"Five, Mein Herr," she said. Her arms were pimpled with a curious raw color as if they had been sunburned the day before but now were cold. The girl tugged at her shawl, trying to hide the hump of her spine below the yoke. She seemed to know that I, Justus Kümmerlich, would miss nothing. She took the lid from one of her buckets—a steam rose from the white milk lying flat now inside—and offered me a ladleful small and thick.

"But it is still warm," I exclaimed.

"Yes," she laughed, "I have only now stripped it from them." And she made a milking motion with her hands and peered up at me.

I put the wood to my lips and quickly drank down the milk still raw with the warmth of the cows that gave suck to this community. I paid her and she walked again to the road, herself sloshing like a cow. Long and carefully I wiped my mouth.

Then, having drunk of the rich countryside, I climbed behind the wheel of my car and started the engine. I leaned from the door: "Auf Wiedersehen, Milkmaid!" I put my foot on the accelerator, once, twice, and the engine rocked full throttle in several explosions of cylinders and exhaust. Smoke filled the yard. I raced the engine again and took hold of the hand brake; the pressure of the automobile filled the dashboard; vibrations possessed the automobile in all its libertine mechanization, noise, and saliency.

"Wait!" At first I hardly heard the cry, "Wait, wait!" But from the inn ran my wife, calling loudly the word shaped in vapor, twisting her ankles with every step, and one could see she felt the possibility of being left behind, left all alone, so driven was she to run like a wasp across this strange and empty yard. I imagined how she must have been wakened from her country sleep and how she must have started, frightened at the roar of the racing engine.

"What, Sesemi," allowing the engine to cool down and idle, "no hat?" But she did not smile and did not stop her trembling until I had silenced the machine.

So we journeyed, bearing always south, bearing down upon the spike-helmeted policemen of small villages, coming abreast of flocks of geese by the road, driving toward some church spire in the distance, racing down our rich continent all that summer and settling ourselves to sleep each night in the spring-weakened hollows of familiar beds which, no matter how old we grow, tell us always of mother and father and sick child as we roll from side to side through the years.

"Justus, do you know what day this is?"

"No," I replied and kept my eyes to the road so flat now against the contour of the sea.

"They sent little Mauschel out of the house. . . ."

"No riddles, Sesemi. No riddles."

The sun was hot on the roof of the automobile and I sat with my chin lifted. Always I drove with my head raised slightly and looked clearly and relentlessly at the space ahead and now and then swabbed my neck, leaving the handkerchief to soak, so to speak, around my collar. That day the country-side was sunswept and a pale blue as if at any moment the earth itself might turn to water.

"Don't you recall it, Justus? Don't you recall the wreath?" Sesemi peered out of the window into the blue stratum of air spread over the sand. She was remembering, of course, and seemed to be washing her little eyes in that blue air, cleansing her sight if only to enjoy the scratching progress of the impurity across the conjunctiva. What memories she retained: only the unpleasant ones, the specks of gloom, the grains in the eye which, months later, she would tell me about. But the eyes of certain people are never without a redness inside the lids.

"I do not remember. Perhaps this is not a special day after all, Sesemi."

"It was evening, Justus."

"Then perhaps it was not a special evening, Sesemi."

"Oh, yes. How lonely your brother would be now, except for Metze and Mauschel. And you and me, Justus."

"Don't taunt me, Sesemi. Please."

Late that afternoon we approached a small city and I steered the automobile quickly as I could through the outskirts to the center of this traveler's resting place until I found the bank and parked in front of it. A group of children collected immediately around my automobile and began to touch the hood, the fenders, the spokes in the wheels.

There are banks all over the world and I am always at home in a bank. Nothing else is needed when one brushes off his coat and makes his appearance before the faceless tellers of these institutions. The clerk did not ask to see my credentials, sensing at once that his bank with its gold clock was my hostel, that some of my assets, a stranger's assets, were vaulted there waiting only upon my demand and my signature—Justus Kümmerlich. I noted that the pen trembled when he thrust it, his fingers pinching the wet point, through the grille.

"Thank you," I said shortly and raised my eyes.

There was a hair on the pen point. I handed it back to the clerk, indicating the dirt, and lit a cigar. I could not hurry bank business. I looked around the room—the same, all the same, this very bastion in Zurich, Paris, Milan, even small Tiergarten, retaining faithfully all one's fortunes, the scruples of one's piety and reserve.

"A traveler must be cautious, I imagine," came the sudden whisper.

"I beg pardon?"

"Cautious with money, Mein Herr. I imagine one does well to carry little." He dropped the pen, then reappeared, attempting to wipe dry that face and quiet those round eyes. "Traveling, sir, I should think one would take only the barest amount . . . thieves, chambermaids, accidents. Nicht wahr?"

I began to write. The round worried face hovered there behind the mesh.

"If one is ordained to have it, one's money is not stolen, my friend. If there is money in your pocket, it will stay. If money is your domesticity, you will have only to be a good house-keeper. When traveling, my friend, it is simple: one has merely to know how to pin one's pocketbook inside the pillow." I laughed and pushed the pen and the check into those reaching fingers.

He murmured something and then, smiling, sucking his breath, began to count with a terrible aimless dexterity, an inhuman possessiveness, confident but suffering while my money passed through his hands.

"Mein Herr," he whispered, "don't leave these bills in your hotel room."

I took the packet and counted it quickly myself. The grill-work closed without a sound.

I reached the automobile and wrenched open the door. "Mein Herr, Mein Herr," begged the children, "take us with you!" Against the hot leather seat I lay back my head and smiled though my eyes were shut. "Well, Sesemi. The Riviera?"

I paid the hotel manager in advance. I stared into his small French eyes carefully and signed my name on his register. I guessed immediately that there was no sand in his shoes and that he drank a good deal of wine.

"But the linen," staring at him again, "what of the linen?"

"Herr Kümmerlich, smooth and white, of course! Perfectly white!"

The room was small. It contained a white bed and a few white mats placed on the empty table and on the arms of the chair, a room facing the ocean and filled with that tomb odor of habitations built by the sea. Each time I entered there was the sensation of a mild loneliness, a realization that it was not one's own.

In the beginning I thought that if we tired of going to the beach, we might sun ourselves on the porch completely encir-cling our floor of the hotel. But those who walked the porch at night spoiled it for the day. It was not long before I moved my chair so that it blocked our own screened doors, which opened upon the rotting and down-sloping porch. The first night the sea was loud; we could hear it green and barbarous, having emptied itself of humans there below. The sun sank like a woman into a hot bath; it became dark and the night was suddenly singing with mosquitoes and violins.

Sesemi was at last done with her kneeling at the bedside and climbed in beside me. We lay in the dark. Someone, perhaps a child, had fastened two large starfish to the screens of our porch door and now I saw them, silhouetted in dead sea fashion, between the blue night outside and the blackness within, all around us. From the next room came a little voice:

"Mamma, a drink of water, bitte."

We lay still. The starfish rustled against the screen in a slight wind. The sea was beginning now to turn to foam, the hopeless separation of day and night, against all shores.

"Mamma. A drink of water, bitte."

"Sesemi," I said in the dark, "if the child will not be quiet and go to sleep, you must fetch some water."

"Ja, Justus."

My eyes would not close. Even an older man—I was pleased to count myself among them—watches the stars when he lies down in a strange place, watches them in their cold heaven as he wonders what he may find on the beach when next the sun rises and the sea grows calm. I reached out and reassured myself of the light switch, relaxed my arms straight by my sides, thought of the meal I should order at dawn, and subsided into that state of alertness which for those who have found the middle of life is called sleep.

But I woke and the violins, not the insects, were still. Some equatorial disturbance was reflected now in the sea, which mounted steadily upon the scales of the shore, that sea which drowned the midnight suicides. I lifted my head quickly. There were two in embrace. Together they leaned heedlessly into our screened doors as if they thought the room empty, the two become a single creature that rolled its back and haunches into the mesh, scraped its four feet now and then on the porch wood. Their single body moved, scratched the wire, intent upon the revealing introspection of the embrace, immobile, swept by the black sea breezes.

"Pfui! Pfui!" I cried, clutching at the top of my pajamas. And they were gone, drifting down the porch.

I got out of bed and trembled in the cold. Deftly, overcome with conscience, I pulled the billfold from my linen coat and opened my valise.

"Justus. What are you doing?"

"The pins," I hissed over my shoulder, "the pins!"

I did not eat heavily the next morning. But with the ringing of the gong and the screeching of a pack of gulls that early took flight from the roof of the hotel, Sesemi and I appeared among the first breakfasters and met, as we met morning and morning again, those old ladies who sat one to a table drinking their black coffee. It was said in the hotel that we Germans would not miss a meal, and that we even sat in the midst of the deaf ladies that we might eat the sooner. The old ladies were all grandmothers who had survived their young. All of them wore violet shawls over the quick irregular protrusions that were their backs and shoulder blades. They stayed in the dining room a precise time, each of them; and then, before the sun was fully risen, they retreated up to their drawn rooms to wait through the long day for sundown. They preferred the cool, they sought the shade like snails, and feared what they called the stroke.

Whenever we entered the dining room Sesemi helped one of them to sit; whenever we left the dining room Sesemi helped one of them to exit. Every morning the hotel manager came among the tables and spoke to each old woman and finally to myself, urging his guests to enjoy some special luxury, but knowing all too well the fruitlessness of his invitation. The dining room was a quiet place; the old women hardly tinkled spoon to cup until, in French, one of them would say, "Ladies, ladies, here comes the sun!" And, putting down their napkins, they would faintly stir, then flee.

And a moment later the beach would be turned to fire, scattered over with the burning bathers and their umbrellas, bathers who were as eager to lie in the violet rays as the ladies were to escape them. The young ate no breakfast but went directly from their beds to the beach as if their youthful bodies and anonymous lively figures needed no food, except the particles of sunshine, to exist upon. The Germans were good at volley ball. The others, the French, rarely played the game, but paired off, man and woman, woman and man, to lie on their bright blankets and hold hands, inert about the beach like couples of black and slender seals.

The sun was always upon its dial, sending down to the beach intangible rays of heat and fomenting over this area its dangerous diffusion of light. The world came to us behind shut eyes. A silent bombardment descended upon the women with dark glasses while old gentlemen stuck out their legs as for treatment, expecting the sun to excite those shrunken tendons. Feet ran close to our heads on the sand. The catchers of starfish came dangerously near and a small boy stepped on my arm at midmorning. The immensity of the sun was challenging, all the biology of myself, Justus, my lungs and liver, my blood-pumping system, cried out to meet the sun, to withstand the rising temperature, to survive the effects, the dehydration, of such a sun. We saw the child who had called for water in the darkness; well might it thirst.

When I went down to the water, Sesemi, sitting upon a towel, waved good-by and admonished me to return if the seas were too cold or if I felt cramps. Women have no place in the water. What is the sea if not for the washing of dead relatives and for the swimming of fish and men? On this trip, only a few steps, I left behind my wife, my housecoat, the muffler, the partially smoked cigar that marked me for this world, and then, feeling the sands go wet, braced myself for that plunge into the anonymous black.

When I began walking upon that nearer undersurface which can never breathe the air and upon which the less heroic sea creatures move, I saw the thirsty child standing knee-deep and not far off, watching me. The child did not wave or smile but merely watched as if its parents had perhaps told it something about Herr Kümmerlich. But no, as I splashed forward, I realized that the child was speculating, trying to calculate the moment when I should leave my feet and thrust myself to ride upon the waves. I shut my eyes and heard it calling suddenly for its papa to come and see.

I was an excellent floater. I could drift farther from shore than anyone, buoyed and perfectly calm, flat on my back, so unsinkable was my body, classic and yet round with age as my father's. Floating is a better test of character than swimming—creatures that float are indestructible and children beware of them. Their parents have only admiration for him who moves effortlessly, purposefully, out to sea.

"That is Herr Kümmerlich out there."

"What? That far?"

"Ja. Herr Kümmerlich. And, see, not a splash."

Now I was floating, perfectly proportioned, helmeted in my old bathing cap and rocking steadily. What a swim it was, what sport! The water carried me fathoms high and I lay on the surface, the plane, from which the winds started and across which grew the salt in its nautical gardens. I was the master and the ship. Now and then my breast went under, I rolled for a long while in the hollow of a swell. My feet cut the water like a killer shark's fins, I breathed deep—Justus Kümmerlich—in the world of less-than-blood temperature. The knees float, the head floats, the scrotum is awash; here is a man upon the sea, a rationalist thriving upon the great green spermary of the earth!

I might never have returned. The sea is made of male elements and I was vigorously contented there on the crest of it all. But at that instant there came suddenly the cutting of two sharp arms and the beating of a swimmer's legs. He made straight for me and at the last moment lifted his mouth to exclaim: "Mein Herr, Frau Kümmerlich is worried. She would be pleased if you returned to shore," and he shot by, racing, his head buried again in the foam of his blind channel. He was carrying on his back his little thin thirsty son, the boy sitting upright as on a dolphin and unconcerned with the violence of his father's strokes.

Sesemi was waiting on the dry sand with the towel. It was a noon sun, straight above us and near to the earth. I exposed myself to it and the thousand molecules of salt crystallized on my freshened skin. My hair was suddenly dry as straw. I heard her saying, "Justus, Justus," but I never moved and heard nothing but the swishing of the sun's tails. After all the peace of the ocean, now there was none; there was only the immoderate heat and a sudden blackness that fell upon me in the form of a great dead gull filled with fish. And so I stayed in the sun too long, and so I burned.

For three days I lay in our room occupying the bed alone, and blistered. A thick warm water swelled under the skin of my red body, my temperature would drop suddenly, chilled, and nausea would come in a storm. I knew the twilight of the sunburn, the sheet stuck to me like a crab. In the dead of night I would hear the speechless methodical striking of my compatriots' fists into the gasping sides of the volley ball. All memory, the entire line of my family, was destroyed in the roaring of the sea and the roaring of the sun. What horror when the bed turned and rocked gently out on the thick swells.

At last I woke. Like a gangrenous general waking from a stupor in his hot, fly-filled field tent, I peered through the sticky substance of eyeball and eyelid and saw the gray of the late afternoon, the gray of the dying window blinds tightly drawn. The room was disheveled and torn as if their attendance upon me had been a violent thing. But now they too were serene.

Sesemi and the child were huddled together in the corner in the half-turned chair. They were watching me and smiling. Wearily and happily they were hugging each other—little Frau Kümmerlich, her hair undone, was hugging the child about the waist. They came to the bed together; Sesemi held his hand.

"Justus," she said, and looked into the diffused parts of my eyes. "Justus," she whispered, "it has been a long while."

Then I was able to think of them and my lips slid open long enough for me to say, "Yes, Sesemi. Yes, it has."

"O die Fröhlichkeit!" she whispered, dropping her head to the tepid, sun-smelling sheet. The boy picked up the pan and went out the door, as habit had taught him, to empty it.

When I was able to travel, when I was able once more to hum the *Lorelei*, and we quit the town, I stopped the automobile before a butcher's shop and ordered the throat cut and the lamb packed whole with ice and rock salt in a wooden box.

"The whole lamb," I explained to Sesemi, "is for my brother. For Lebrecht! You see, Sesemi, I am the father after all."

We started home.

The Grandmother

"Lebrecht! I'm here, I'm here, Lebrecht!"

It was with all the old impatience that I cried to them, with all the old affection that I announced myself, and my hands were outstretched. A window slammed in the back of the house. How little it had changed; yet I seemed to bring with me the dust and aching of long travel and separation. At that moment, looking up the path, beating my jacket, waiting, I felt the wanderer come home.

"Why, look, Mauschel, it is your Uncle Justus!"

The door opened a crack, then it was wide, and suddenly the four of us intermingled in our confused and unexpected embrace. I shook my brother Lebrecht by the arm, bumped against Metze, his wife, and felt them gather about me.

"And do I smell the stove, Metze?" I threw my chin high, laughing.

"No," she replied in a low flat voice, "you do not. The stove is cold."

With clouds above us and a slight wind ballooning our trousers and sweeping away the summer, I caught hold of

Lebrecht Kümmerlich. He was not so much younger than his brother Justus now.

"Lebrecht, Lebrecht, it is so, nicht wahr?"

"Ja, ja, ja, Justus."

Our hands were on each other's shoulders, we faced each other and I cared nothing for the rest.

"Well, then," I whispered, "laugh, Lebrecht, laugh . . ."

And he did so.

The grass was long, the wind blew coldly among us. We all shook hands again, and I noticed that Metze had many wrinkles on her throat. Suddenly I pushed between them and ran back to the car. I pried loose the wooden box I had brought with me, and, though I was hardly able, carried it to them before the house.

"Lebrecht—for you, Lebrecht!"

Metze insisted that we put the box down immediately, there on the path, and open it. She scraped away the ice until they could see the white of fat and the redness of cold meat. Lebrecht began to thank me, he was serious and turned his face from side to side, but he was whispering so softly that I could not hear.

"Mauschel," said Metze, holding tightly to the edge of the box, "bring some coal, bitte."

"Metze," I smiled quickly, sure she would understand, "the lamb is for tomorrow's Mittagessen . . ."

"We will eat it tonight. And tomorrow also."

The three of them hurried inside with the box. I followed.

"Metze," I called, "the meat must season, it must hang in the open air!"

But she disappeared into the kitchen and began washing the pots.

We were silent a moment. Mauschel had climbed down into the darkened cellar, we heard him through the thin floor, moving slowly beneath us; suddenly there came from below, amid barrels and coal dust, a distinct and vituperative profanity as from the other side of Berlin. We sat still. What sort of boy was Mauschel now, shaking the coal scuttle by the throat? He grunted and drove the shovel deep again into the bin. Lebrecht walked softly to the door.

"Mauschel. Will Papa help you with the coal?"

The boy, man-sized, immeasurable, suddenly big in his shadow, emerged from the little stairwell and swung the sack of coal into view. Lebrecht stepped away quickly as Mauschel crashed his burden against the walls and to the kitchen. We could hear the two of them, mother and son, whispering.

"He is so big."

"Bigger than I," said Lebrecht softly.

"That is the way with you family men," I laughed, feeling my forehead, "you have your taxes, your dedication, the satisfaction of your big sons to wrestle with."

"Only one son, Justus."

"Ja. Remember how he needed a beating once, Lebrecht? He was always my favorite. Ah, he knows the character of his Uncle Justus." I smiled in the dark.

We began to smell the smoke of the roasting meat. And Mauschel was sharpening the knives. I noticed Lebrecht's slippers under the window, I was light-headed and content, sitting there, waiting for the meal to be served.

"And Metze, Lebrecht, has she overcome her grief for der Blumenstrauss?"

He lifted his eyes slowly. "Ja," he said.

I nodded.

"She talks to her mother some nights, Justus, but without grief, I assure you."

"So?"

"Ja. She talks. But there is Herr Popanz and the lady from Augenstrasse, neighbors in grief. And God forgives such things, Justus."

I did not answer. I was hungry and would eat a good meal.

"I have been ill, Lebrecht."

"Ill?"

"Ja, Lebrecht, seriously. Perhaps as sick as Papa when he died . . ."

But as soon as our father's name was mentioned, Metze called out that the lamb was done.

"Give the knives to your Uncle Justus, Liebling," said Metze as we entered the dining room, and Mauschel thrust the blades at me.

"In my brother's house . . ." I murmured and extended the knives to Lebrecht, and he was quick enough to take them. Pushing his arms out of his coat sleeves, he worked to free his shoulders.

There was a heavy, gasping, uncontainable sigh at the head of the table as Lebrecht raised his two hands—in one was the great carving fork, in the other a knife—and held them above the smoking lamb as in some kind of feverish dying benediction. His eyes looked straight down at the crackling skin, peering, taking aim at the roast which had been rushed to the table. Lebrecht's head became wet, and still the fork and still the knife hovered powerfully as if he could not bring himself to begin. But his nose was over the meat and he was sniffing it. And with the very smell of the fat and the meat, the juices were already filling his mouth and the acids seeping into his stomach's pit. He seemed so to be smelling that he could not bring his knife down, could not drive the point into the leg of the lamb. Then suddenly he sank back and half turned away, lowering his arms until the steel rested helplessly against the wood. He licked his lips and smiled.

"Ach, Metze, I've forgotten how . . ."

For answer, unable to wait longer, she reached out piercingly through the tumblers and from the platter snatched up a small potato which she immediately began to smash in the bottom of her plate.

"Pardon," he said softly and once more took up knife and fork.

"I'm not hungry," I said cheerfully, smoothing the napkin, "I'll take just a little of the skin, if you please, Lebrecht."

"Not hungry!" Mauschel pushed back his chair and rose menacingly on his big haunches. "Not hungry, Uncle!" He looked as if a fish had been smacked against his eyes. His hands clutched the empty plate. "Ah," he began to sit down again, "you are fooling me, Uncle Justus." Then, he put a large dirty finger into each corner of his mouth and pulled wide. After which he said, "Empty, you see, Uncle, hungry as all that!"

I smoothed my napkin. A shrill tinkle rang from one of the crystal glasses; at last it had been barely touched, nicked by Lebrecht's knife large as a scimitar. Lebrecht pushed his chair to one side of the table.

"Potato. Plenty of potato for me," said Mauschel loudly, peering at the carver. With a black finger he rubbed the bottom of the plate.

Lebrecht nodded, he had heard his son. Then, whispering, holding the knife up to the aging chandelier, "Mauschel. Give me a hair, Knabe."

"I'll give you my whole scalp if you'll cut us some meat . . ."

"Only a hair, Mauschel."

The coal carrier, the only child, pulled a hair from his head and Lebrecht, taking it, began testing the edge of the blade against it, cutting and swinging emptily in the air.

We watched. He leaned down and immersed himself in the delicate clutter of the table, and faced the lamb; obviously he wanted nothing more than to carve and eat.

"If you cannot do it," came the woman's hissing, "then give the knife to Justus."

So he began, as his wife coaxed him and his son leaned toward him salivating like a street dog. Lebrecht carved. But in the last pitiful instant he was unable to wield the fork— the knife alone was quite enough for him—and now one hand was clasped upon the lamb. That hand lay embedded in the fat, the fingers curled down the sides of the meat, squeezing their prints into the golden skin. He perspired, bit his lip, and with the very palm of his hand, and with the fingers—on one was a gold ring—pushed the roast firmly into its platter, despite the hot juice that trickled across the knuckles, the grease that splattered his white cuff. He began triumphantly to smile.

"Metze, you'll forgive me if I serve my brother Justus first . . ." And the plate was passed to me, heaped high.

Then Lebrecht sat and looked at the last filled dish, his own. But as he swung the knife down from its striking position, giving hardly a thought to the blood-covered blade, he brought another tinkling from a goblet, and now, after all his care and watchfulness, it fell over and emptied into his lap.

"Mauschel," said the boy's mother, "bring a cloth."

"Later. After we eat," came Mauschel's voice out of the deep and rattling plate.

"It's all right, Metze," whispered my brother, "eat your food, meine Herzliebste."

"Well," I said when the meal was half-done, at last spreading a piece of bread with preserves from a little pot, "well, I was sick."

"Ah," Lebrecht roused himself, "you were sick, Justus!"

"I was."

"Mama has been sick too, haven't you?" said Mauschel. He grinned at his mother, but Metze's eyes were toward me. Arching her brows and without thinking, she sat holding herself, the ache, under one breast. Her jaws chewed irrevocably and silently behind those pale lips.

"I have been nearly dead. Sick, yes, but worse, Mauschel, your Uncle Justus, mein Neffe, nearly died."

"Ah, Justus," Lebrecht apologized, pushing back his chair, "you had not made it clear. Ah, ah, was it bad as that?" He walked around the table, behind his wife, still carrying the full fork in one hand, and then returned quickly to the head of the table, smiling for their luck in having me that night, then frowning and shaking his shoulders.

"Yes, it was that bad," I said and tasted the jam which was quite sweet. "Yes. I did not think I would come out of it. But other than that I had my holiday . . ."

"Holiday?" Metze stopped chewing.

I nodded. "I stayed at the Gasthof. There was the beach, real sea water. All that."

"How then," her hard yet almost tearful eyes turned sharp

like the sights on the end of a gun, and from the twisting of her hand beneath the heart, the pain must have been growing. "How, then, did you nearly die?"

"Sunstroke," I said calmly. "Lebrecht," raising my voice, "I was nearly burned to death by the sun down there."

"Were you, Justus!" he exclaimed, plunging the fork into his mouth and looking from his wife to his son and back again to his plate. "Scheusslich, scheusslich!" he faltered and banged his knife handle on the table.

I took a mouthful of potato. Then I pushed the dinner away.

"There is nothing worse than sunstroke!" exclaimed Lebrecht, wiping his mouth thoroughly.

"Ja. Nothing so bad, Lebrecht, I could actually hear the hoarse cries of the angels, my brother."

"Is that true?" he asked.

"True, Lebrecht. True indeed. And the blisters were big as pullet eggs. It is true: near death, near death."

I glanced at Metze. She was lifting the breast now to probe at her pain. All of a woman's hurt collects there, all of the nerves seem to end there under the breast.

"Did you," turning the wrinkles of her forehead into a cold smile, "did you enjoy swimming in the ocean, Justus?"

"It was perfect," I said briefly.

"Poor Justus, poor Justus," sighed my brother, clacking again at his food, pausing again to stare at me as at a man in his coffin. "How many days did you lie there, Justus?"

"Well taken, Lebrecht. I don't know. It was long enough for that burned body of mine to cool off, long enough for it to cool down like a comet that plunges into the shore and steams in agony for weeks, until the night air and sea breezes cool it a little, and the fires die out. Then, my skin turned to water. And, of course, there was the odor, Lebrecht."

"But you should have called me, Justus. You should have communicated. Metze," turning suddenly upon his wife, "didn't you dream, didn't you get a message? Didn't you know that Justus was slipping from us? Metze never fails, Justus, she is a receiver of the sparks from beyond. We rely

on her, Mauschel and I, to interpret for us, to tell us . . . Didn't
you know, Metze?"

"I did not," she said.

"You must not have been listening for me, Metze!" I
laughed. "Yes," I went on, leaning back to pluck off the end
of my cigar as they poked in the debris of gristle and cutlery,
"I was red as the lamb's tongue. Red and rather yellow too,
I believe. Metze," I held out my glass, "may I have some
more water? Sunstroke leaves a man dehydrated, leaves him
with a thirst in every cell of the flesh. May I have some water,
bitte?"

Mauschel watched his mother. She said nothing and did not
move. She simply remained white and perhaps trembling, as
if that mechanism inside her bosom had missed a revolution
or two.

"How restful it must have been for your Uncle Justus on
the beach, Mauschel," she murmured at last.

Mauschel looked at her a moment more, then drew back
his elbows, relinquished his massive guard over his plate, got
to his feet and fetched the water pitcher from the kitchen.

"Ja, Justus," his mother began, without looking at me,
"I have been ill."

"What, Metze! You, too?"

"Ja, Justus. We shall accompany each other," and she
touched my hand with one of her frozen fingers.

"Ah, too bad," I answered. "But then, Lebrecht," I looked
down the table, "Metze had no blisters after all!" We laughed.
"Here, Mauschel," I said, holding out a cigar, "give this to
your father."

"Thank you, Justus," my brother said softly and felt in
his pockets for a match. I thought that he was going to eat
more, but no, he could not and began instead to smoke.

Metze suddenly pulled her fingers away from the breast—
gone the pain!—and laughed like a charming mother.

"Mauschel," leaning forward, "Mauschel, my son, go put
on your swimming suit. Let us see you in it, Mauschel."

"What? Has Mauschel a swimming suit also?"

"Ja," said Metze proudly. "Hurry, Mauschel!"

It was as if she had asked him to play a piece on the flute or to recite Goethe. His head hung like a sheep dog. He kicked the legs of the table a moment, then left us.

We remained waiting around the drafty and ruined table. Metze smiled. But her eyes were blank and white as the knucklebones of an old woman. Lebrecht Kümmerlich was no longer hungry, he held the burning cigar in his teeth and sent the smoke up into the blue of the ceiling.

"Tell me, Lebrecht," I said out of the silence, pushing back from the table and crossing my knees, "how is the old wireless?"

He did not answer. His mouth made only a small, violent puffing gesture, like a noiseless engine. I watched my cigar ash grow, and sat with them in this room suddenly cold for summer, filled with shadow and plaster, this world full of family dinners and Mauschel's growing pains, far from the sea.

"Come in, Liebling," said Metze toward the dark door, "don't be shy." Then I saw one of Mauschel's bare feet dangling, showing itself just over the edge of the jamb, feeling its way timidly as if into a pool of cold water.

"Gut, gut," exclaimed his mother and smiled upon him.

Mauschel was naked except for a pair of bright black trunks which fit his loins tight as the skin of a melon. They were cut high on the buttocks. He was white, grinning, and came around the table to stand beside Metze. He had large legs and enormous arms; and every section of arm, of leg, was nipped tightly at the joint where it ended, but was otherwise fat. I noticed a few babyish freckles on the white slopes of his shoulders.

"Is he quite fully grown yet, Lebrecht?" I asked.

"Oh, indeed yes. We can get no more out of him. You're not going to grow any bigger, are you, Mauschel."

The boy shook his head. He grinned and slapped his arms loudly.

"Next year," Metze pronounced, trying to twist about to see him, "we're going to take Mauschel to the beach."

"Fine, fine," I answered.

"And you won't get sunstroke, will you, Mauschel?"

"No," he said, "not me." Then, taking courage from the laughter: "This is the way I shall dive!" he exclaimed and suddenly thrust his arms above his head and shook his very gelatinous soul into the swimmer's fishlike form.

"Ah," Metze reached and touched his flesh.

"Mauschel," I spoke softly and drew out my purse. "Come here, Mauschel." Feeling him close by, suddenly obedient, I gave him the bank note. "Don't spend it, Mauschel. It is to bring you good luck."

I heard the earliest sounds of birds outside and, louder than the birds, a woman's sharp voice. I pulled on my trousers, went into the bathroom, carefully raised the green glass window, thrust my head through the opening and looked down. Metze was standing below on the stoop talking loudly. A market boy, leaning on an iron cart filled with food, watched her, grinned, but made no move to unload his packages.

Against the fence that bordered the yard stood Lebrecht's row of birdhouses, and the sun lighted the houses while the birds hopped in and out, quickly, noisily, fluttering and ill-prepared for the morning.

"Put the food in the kitchen," Metze commanded. The boy laughed and scraped one of his muddy boots on the iron spokes. He had only one eye and wore no patch to hide the withered empty bed of the other. His fingers were red from handling wet carrots and sides of beef, his leather apron was splashed from the road; he pulled a green stalk from a bundle in the cart and began to eat, scratched his blood-stained cheek, under the skin his jaws moved sideways back and forth. He looked at Metze. The birds sang loudly.

"No, Frau Kümmerlich. I might leave you this little bag, but no more."

"The kitchen!" Her voice rose to my window. "The whole wagon load goes into my kitchen!"

"No, Frau Kümmerlich," eating more of the green, "why

only yesterday the butcher said, 'The Kümmerlichs have stopped eating meat. And they eat no garden produce either. When Herr Kümmerlich's wife grows thin,' he told me, 'leave them a box of meal.' You don't look thin to me, Frau Kümmerlich."

Still leaning on the cart, he began slowly to push his weight on it, swinging and moving it in Metze's direction, and the iron wheels ground slowly with a muddy, metallic noise, slipping, clanging, the cart turning as if to run her down. The boy's bent uncombed shape—I could see that he had brushed against dead fowl and smoked half-cigarettes in the butcher's meat locker—sidled close to Metze. He lifted up a package, shook loose the paper exposing a large beef heart and dropped it again into the wagon.

"Have you a good fire, Frau Kümmerlich?" he whispered and, reaching out stubby fingers, tweaked her arm.

"I want the food," she said, "all of it!"

He stood straight up and with both hands took hold of the cart's pushbar, wheeled the iron-walled vehicle around and ran off, laughing and bouncing the wagon so that a few soft oranges flew from it and fell to the roadside. I shut the window and washed myself.

Downstairs Metze was trying to build a fire in the kitchen stove. The shades were pulled tight in the living room. During the day we ate in the kitchen and there was a plate—a sausage, a piece of bread—for each of us. Metze kept Mauschel's meal on the stove in a large double pot with a black lid.

"Where is the boy?" asked Lebrecht after a long silence.

"He is not late," said Metze. "Mauschel is never late."

Then I saw my nephew's face at the kitchen window: only the head, the face, staring at me over his father's shoulder. He had taken a bit of yellow leaf and wadded it into one eye socket. He winked his visible eye and raised one hand. Satisfied that we were already at the table, he must have walked around the house, for we heard him tramping near the front entrance and the door banged. Lebrecht nodded and smiled.

We waited. The forks lingered in the broken skin of our sausages.

"Come in, Mauschel," his mother called, "we've only been eating a moment!" Lebrecht stood up and took the pot off the flame, filled the dish at Mauschel's place and blew lightly on it. Lebrecht sat down. Our heads—Lebrecht's contented, Metze's starched, mine massive—turned toward the door.

Mauschel was leaning there. His belly swayed sleepily, his shoulders massed themselves against the wood, a jacket hung over one arm, the seeds of his eyes were black.

"Welcome, Mauschel," murmured Lebrecht. "Monday's greeting, Mauschel." Lebrecht lowered his eyes and began spreading a piece of bread for his son. The boy said nothing. At the top of his shirt I could see the broad expanse of thick flesh white and damp as a drake's breast.

"Wouldn't you like to eat just a spoonful or two?" his mother asked him.

"You had better join us," I agreed quickly, laughing, "or I will eat your portion, Mauschel!"

Mauschel then started forward. He was fat, he seemed more ready to burst a clod of earth than to rest at the table. His hair was wild and his shirt wet, his bulk cut off the sunlight from the window.

Mauschel walked around the table and stood for a moment beside Metze, letting the jacket slide off his arm. He put his arm like a dead reptile across her shoulders and pushed his face into her hair; his free hand crept to a pocket in the tight trousers and, while Lebrecht and I watched, the fat fingers produced a single bank note and stealthily placed it in the middle of his mother's plate, draped it over the two split sausages.

When he moved, the sun danced thoughtlessly across the kitchen tiles and poured itself into the empty potato bin, swam in the empty sink, cast our four shadows on the white wall. The morning seemed to flow forward and backward, flooding the day with its light and the smell of hungry children, as if all our lives had come here to rest, to stop, and our fortunes were to be found in Mauschel's untouched plate. I heard the sound of a far-off dog, heard the bark that bites into life itself. We sat still and straight.

Then Metze saw the bank note, there on her plate and already soaking up the sausage fat. How she looked! How wide the eyes! To be kissed, yes, but then to find this tender money on the tip of her fork! Metze at that very moment must have felt this bit of paper safe in her bosom, finding a meager breakfast flowered to a fortune. A strand of hair came loose and scraped at her neck, the blue veins sang on the backs of her hands and she reached out, trying to pick up the bill with calm, trying to take it at last between icy fingers.

But Mauschel was quicker than Metze. He snatched the bank note from under her eyes, caught it, leaned and turned in front of her. And then, clicking his teeth in a moment of joy, he stretched the bank note wide, pulled it suddenly until it measured a good foot, elongating the rubber bill wide as his smile, and let one end go, snapped it in Metze's face.

"What shall we buy, Mamma?" he cried. "Look, it is bigger than that even!" And he stretched the hundred marks again. "What do you want, Mamma? A leg of lamb?" He laughed and stuffed the piece of rubber counterfeit into his hip pocket. "It is a good joke," he said flatly as if to himself and walked from the room, leaving his coat on the floor.

"Ach, Mauschel," whispered Lebrecht, hanging his head, "ach, my dangerous son," and slowly emptied the plate into the waiting pot.

With a cold gliding motion Metze went straight to the living-room couch, still tumbled and stale as it was when Mauschel roused himself at dawn. She lay down but did not close her eyes. I saw her ear, a kind of muscular shell, quite separate from the head; I saw the mole on her throat; I saw the line where the hair grew upon the scalp. I watched her, making no sound, and waited to see what she would do. Her wedding hand hung down forgotten. Then, like die Leichenfrau who cares for the dead, her lips moved, her eyelids narrowed, and she began to talk to her dead mother.

"Mamma?"

"Metze?"

"Shall we speak to him, Mamma?"

"Natürlich, Metze!"

"Mamma, we must be firm with him."

"Bring him to me, Metze. Bring him to his Grossmutter . . ."

"Oh, he loves you, Mamma!"

"He is a good boy baby, Metze. Bring him to me . . ."

"Mamma?"

"Ja, Metze?"

"Talk to him, Mamma, talk to him . . ."

When Mauschel stood in the doorway, his mother groaned from the couch. I pushed past him and up the stairs.

A Little Bit of the Old
Slap and Tickle

Sparrow the Lance Corporal knew he would find his family by the sea.

Now through the underground and in a public bus with wooden seats and on foot he traveled until under the dusty tree tops he smelled the surf and brine and stood at last atop the great cliff's chalky edge. On the upward footpath the trees had fallen away and at the head of the ascent he was alone, windswept, with the sun in his eyes and a view of the whole stretch of coast before him. It was a peaceful sea, worn down by flotillas of landing boats forever beached. And away to either side of him the cliffs were crumbling, these desolate black promontories into which gun batteries had once been built. Now it was all won, all lost, all over, and he himself—a tiny figure—stood on the crest with the seawrack and the breeze of an ocean around him. He was wearing his old battle-dress and a red beret.

The war-worn flotillas lay a hundred feet below. Down there, spread at the cliff's bottom, was the mud, that softly heaved between the line of water and the first uprisings of dry stone: and down there lay the iron fleet half-sunk in the mud. For ten miles in either direction from the stump on the cliff's high windy lip—a flat tin helmet was nailed to the stump and it was Sparrow's sign, marking the steep descent he had found for himself—he could see once more the wreckage and this low mud of the coast, washed with foam, slick, cleaving to the sky. Terns sat with ruffled, white, still faces on the spars; the ends of cables sucked up rust from the low pools; the stripped hull of a destroyer rose bow first from the muck.

Here was Sparrow, come back unannounced. Leaning forward, resting his kit, grass tangling up about his boots and the wind blowing tight wads of cloud in his direction, he gazed down upon the scene and knew it was home after all. His own spot was there, the sweeper lying straight and true in the mud up to her water-line, his salt and iron house with chicken wire round one portion of the deck where the children played, the tin pipe at the stern with a breath of smoke coming up, the plank run out from her bow to a sandy place ashore. It was like living in a war memorial, and letting his eyes swing back from his own ten windy miles of devastation, fixing upon the tiny figure of a scrubby black dog that was barking at the abandoned shape of a carrier listing not fifty yards to the lea; seeing the dog at her game, and seeing a handful of slops come suddenly from one porthole, now he knew that his sweeper was inhabited and that, once aboard, he was father of this household respectable as a lighthouse keeper's station.

The terns set up a terrible cry that afternoon as he made his way down the cliff, and the dog—Sparrow loved her bent tail, the sea lice about her eyes, loved the mangy scruff of her neck—the dog leaped, then floundered out of the mud to meet him. So with kit and cane, red beret hanging off the tip of his skull and dripping dog in arm, he climbed the plank and shouted the names of his kiddies, limped round the capstan to see that the rain-water pan was full.

"You back?" The woman stepped out of the companion-way and stopped, her eyes already simmering down on Sparrow, sharp fingers unfastening the first three buttons of her khaki shirt. "Well, it *is* a good day." And then, coming no closer, speaking in the hard voice wreathed with little trails of smoke, standing with the dirty ocean and derelicts behind her: "The boys have been wanting to search the *Coventry* again. We'll let them go. And we'll put the other buggers in the brig for an hour. Funny . . . I've had it on my mind all day."

"Good girl," said Sparrow. "Good old girl."

It was the home air that he breathed, smells of mid-ocean, a steady and familiar breeze pungent on the deck with the woman, a sweeter fragrance of grass and white bones on the cliff top, an air in which he sometimes caught the burnt vapors of a far-off freighter or, closer at hand, the smells of his own small dog. Scraping paint or splicing rope, or sitting and holding a half cup of rum in the sun on the bow, or following the boys down the idleness of the beach, he smelled what the woman washed or what a hundred-foot wave discharged into that whole long coastal atmosphere. In the dawn the red sun stretched thin across the line of the eye; throughout the day there was some davit swinging and creaking; and at supper they all ate black beans together and drank their ale.

There were old ammunition boxes for Sparrow and the woman to sit on at dusk when at last the terns grew quiet. Man and wife smoked together while the night blew in across the cold slickness of the sea. A bucket of old rags at her side, her legs no more than two white streaks, the starlight making the sock or shirt turn silver, she hunched forward then and sewed, and he liked her best in the beginning of the blue night when she was thin and preoccupied and without children, digesting her meal and letting him sit with his arm across the shoulder hard as a rocker-arm. No park benches, no dancing or walking out for the woman and Sparrow. They turned to a great pile of anchor chain or to the deck when the sewing was done. In union their scars, their pieces of flat and no longer youthful flesh touched and merged. He liked her to leave the impression of damp potatoes on his belly, he liked to feel the clasp-knife in the pocket of her skirt. And love was even better when they were sick, the heart of it more true with aching arms and legs. It was a good red nose that pleased him, or the chance to kiss the water from her eyes. Love, not beauty, was what he wanted.

In the beginning of night—the time when at last the woman leaned far forward so that the shoulders disappeared from under his arm and his hand traveled down until the four glossy tips of his fingers were thrust into the crevice between her flesh and the lid of the ammunition box, feeling her more desirable than the girls he had seen in Chisling or Squadron Up —in this beginning of the night, Sparrow knew the privacy of marriage and the comfort to be taken with a woman worn to thinness, wiry and tough as the titlings on the cliff.

And the second night, after the moon had gone into the sea and after the woman had returned from helping Arthur out of a bad dream: "You're a proper fire-stick, little cock," she said. "You could spend more time at home, I should think. It's been on my mind."

He nodded, taking the offered cup of rum and the cigarette. "I could do that." He put the cup to his mouth as if the burn of the rum and the fire of his own lip and loin could bring to life the great amphibious shadow around them. In the dark he looked at the bridge wings and dipping masts. "I could stay home rightly enough. No doubt of that."

The woman took the cigarette from between his lips, put it to hers and spoke while exhaling: "Why not set up for yourself?"

He shook his head. "I'm not big enough for that."

"I've thought you were. Like the old girl with the glass ball said."

He nodded. "It's the risks, that's all. You take them alone if you try it alone." And after a moment, shifting, wetting his lips for the cigarette: "Shall I sent down a packet of skivvies for Arthur?"

"Oh, give us a kiss," she answered, and she was not laughing.

For the two days and nights that was all they said. Sparrow watched the woman throwing out her slops, putting the youngest to play under the cover of chicken wire, or smoking at the rail with broom in hand and eyes coming down to him. In a few old jars she put up wild berries picked from the cliff.

Once, wearing a short mended garment styled before the war, she stepped slowly into the deeper brown water off the stern, pushed her chest down into the warmth of the water while the boys clapped and Arthur, the oldest, cried: "Coo, Sparrow, why don't you teach her to swim?" Until he saw the look on his father's face and his mother's own humorless eyes and soaking wet hair turned up to him. The dog, that often lay panting in a little black hole in the mud against the carrier's enormous side, danced in after the woman and pulled abreast of her with spongy paws. While Sparrow, toes dangling in the silt and the faded old red beret tilted sharply forward on his brow, found everything in the woman that the boys were unable to see. The awkward movement of her hands and legs, the faded blue of the suit tied carefully across the narrow back but wrinkling over the stomach and stretching loose from the legs, the clot of seaweed stuck to her shoulder, the warnings she gave the dog, all this made Sparrow pause and lift himself slightly for a better view.

"Arthur," he called. "Show more respect for your mother."

At that moment he took in the swimming woman and paddling dog and sighed. For beyond those two, beyond the sweeper with its number still faintly stenciled on the bow, there lay in muddy suspension the entire field of ships, encrusted guns. and vehicles. And he thought of the work it would take to set the whole thing afloat again—seeing the splash, the snort of the dog—and knew it could not be done, and smiled, clasping his knees, sucking the sun. All won, all lost, all over. But he had his.

So the leave passed. He shook Arthur's hands and the woman went with him to the end of the plank. "Send the skivvies along," she said.

Then Sparrow stood on the cliff with home flashing through his head. Then he was gone, leaving small footprints below in the mud. He chucked his cigarette as he limped back into the world from which he had come.

Death of an Airman

On a white mile of fine sand breaking a foreign shore, Cecil
Bodington gently lay down his shovel and looked to sea. He
squinted once at the officer and carefully, as if reaching for
the spade, stooped and sat down in the sand. He gripped his
thick hands across his knees and the single, loose chevron
hanging from his rolled sleeve never fluttered. The officer
looked up from his book: "Lance, this man's due to come up
today. I'd keep with it."

Even when he stopped digging in the shallow trench and
concentrated without moving on the dark wet sand—it was
hot beneath the white top layer—he could not hear any
sound. Day and night, there was no breaking of waves nor the
slightest ripple of changing tide, no sound of wind across the
Air Force blue water. Since he did not know how to swim
and since swimming was prohibited, the sea was only something that hour on hour changed color slightly to a man who,
staked on the beach, grows parched and blinded to the black
of his own skin. He scraped again with the tip of the shovel.
If he stared long enough toward the narrow beach road he

could see their small, desert-painted lorry and beyond it, over the gray sand, the salty branches of a few burned pines that marked the area collecting lot, an unguarded flat acre of clay. And to his left, the pink-tanned officer sat on the flotsam barrel in shorts and dark glasses, read his book, and borrowed matches from the corporal to light his pipe as the mosquito swarms grew larger with the opening of the trench.

Bodington slipped a soiled khaki handkerchief over his mouth. He had been assigned to a Graves Recording Post. It consisted of registrar, sometimes a clerk, a vehicle, several sets of spades and a non-commissioned digger. These units, bad for morale, were segregated from the troops and from each other; faces turned away when the trucks with the black flags on the doors drove past, rattling, lurching, never sent to the fitters.

He worked in the open sun, moving a few feet up the beach each day, opening the unmarked traps, driving to the collecting lot and digging again. But the tide did change, though he could hear only the turning pages. And occasionally he found bits of kelp on the sand, dried hard and crisp by the time he unloaded his tools soon after sunrise. Some burials had occurred below the water mark. There the sand, once free of ocean and even before he turned it down, was cooler to his feet.

When he discovered where the head direction was, but before uncovering the man himself, he dug without care hoping only to hit the breast pocket, to find the pilot lying on his back. Once fallen into the ocean, they were not seen again along its surface until discovered rolled, dark and pierced, singly on the flat beach.

He felt a button. But there was no pocket, simply the bare outline of the papers he sought, somewhat the color of the body itself. He pulled them out. They tore, were quickly taken by the officer and he scraped again for throat and wrists, for rings and chain tags. Cecil paused and looked at a few bathers; they arrived, but as usual did not go into the still water, rather took turns under an old, faded umbrella. He sat on the edge of the trench and tried to loosen his heavy woolen trousers, brushing off the sharp grains of sand. The officer glanced at him from behind dark glasses and again he raised the shovel. As he emptied the sand—not into any one pile—he saw that all the bathers were crowding the umbrella together. One of their children carried a white cloth to the edge of the water, dipped it, and back at the umbrella was wrapped in it by his mother.

Later Cecil fried the officer some sardines over a small fire on the beach, strolled close to the bathers out of water and returned to work. The sun stayed at the same degree the whole day until it fell below the uncertain line of the sea. If squinted at, it burned the eyes a moment before hiding itself in its own sails, shadows and whitening aurora. He dropped the spade— its head was crusted and stopped at the strike of iron or bone— and tried to get a grip under the man's shoulders. The officer moved away and raised the book before his face. Disinterment Officer, his duty kept him on the beach—never in the collecting lot—and he saw their faces only as they came up, never as they went back down. This man was known as the most skillful D. O. in the entire sector.

Cecil raised the pilot's head to the level of the grave, held it with one hand and felt about with the other in the sand. He looked at the officer who thought: "He's forgotten it again. He's forgotten to bring down the blanket." Cecil breathed heavily through the handkerchief.

"Well," thought the D. O., "the odor's the same behind any army cook house." And he peered over the book. "Out of an old can or from the sand, the smell's still the same." He stared at the black figure in the soldier's arms. "They're coming out together." The D. O., seeing that he was unwatched, looked quickly at the still wet papers he had stuffed in the back of the book. "Number twelve, twenty-two, ten, sixty-six, coming up for the last time," he thought. "When you go down now, you'll stay." He wiped his face.

Cecil, needing the blanket, slid the body back into the pit. "Wait! You'll never get him out again!" The D. O. dropped the book and leaned forward, doing the work himself, perspiring at the hands of the novice. "I've just hauled my own body up from the pit," he thought, "and let it down again."

The child walked slowly toward the water, kicking up scoops of sand, to drench his sheet. It was hard for such a man as the D. O.—who had worked up from a shoveler himself, who had begun the trade as a boy carrying the sexton's pick and a candle-lit lantern, who had studied every feature of the dead and could gauge their position—it was hard for such a man, up from the flowered rows, to keep his eyes away from a trench that should be neatly opened with a precise three inches around the corpse. The dark glasses could not hide the old craftsman's look on his face.

Cecil wiped his hands on his battle jacket—he was used to the oil that preserved the dead—and started for the lorry.

"They should never be left open to the light of day." The D. O. shook his head. "Bodington," he called, "don't forget the decoration."

"Right, sir." The corporal walked toward the little car with the same slow pace as his old father. They used to walk the fields together, the old man first with his staff, Cecil next, glancing over his shoulder to see that the younger boys stayed in line. They walked through clumps of new forest, laid out by the owner of the land, and over pasturage, green and deep, that had not been touched since the first monk collected dues and sullen tillers thought they had a righteous cause. The only thing Cecil had ever buried—and that when a grown man— was a tough swan, wrenched from a poacher he labored on the head with a wooden fork.

He opened the back door of the wagon leaning on the slant of the road and felt about until he found the cutters in their leather thongs, a tangled coil of wire and one of the less stained blankets, all of which, requisitioned by the Graves Recording Group from the medical battalions, were too heavily darkened with iodine and stiff with salt solution to be used again on wounded men. From a dusty spark-plug box he picked one of the decoration ribbons and from the tool compartment, filled with bottles, he pulled the billing pad.

"This isn't a man's work," he thought. For a moment the heat inside the lorry—the wrinkled canvas top was hot to touch—made him think of the Graves Depot, where he had trained a fortnight and eaten his two meals a day by a practice pit. All diggers were drilled between rows of crosses, which though bearing names and numbers, marked no actual bodies. He pinned the decoration to his shirt front for safekeeping and left the truck.

"This is the real thing," thought the D. O., frowning at the trudging corporal, "and not for heavy peasants either." The D. O. had made mistakes himself when he started—a pick would get out of control and hit always the least likely arm or leg.

Cecil could handle the wire well from mending rakes and binding hay, but his folds in the blanket were loose and bulging, the flap over the flyer's feet came loose again and again. He put the spade across the ankles and stooped over and around the short body stretched on the sand. The officer wiped his brow and finally held the blanket himself: "All right now, string it up." And then, after Cecil had shipped the wire ends, the officer sat again on the barrel with the pad on his knee to fill in what he could. In section eight, he had no clerk and did such things himself, writing in the open sun, scratching his pen through the sand dust. He adjusted his broad, dark glasses and looked to the horizon away from the water where, silhouetted, stood a gray stone remnant of a Catholic tower, in which the bathers lived.

Cecil had learned to drive in the forces and never well. Hauling a dummy about the depot wasn't the same as carrying a pilot washed to shore across an ox track never as smooth and shaded as those over the sea. He heard the body rolling behind him, knocking into the tools, gear, and thudding against his bedding. The wheels shivered and caught as the path changed from sand to clay, the truck slipped down a slight shoulder and for a moment he lost sight of the sea, blue as an apothecary's flame. The lorry barely ground into the collecting lot. He left the body, sealed with a few mosquitos, in the back. He picked his spot and broke clay, the pick striking lost chips of a pink marble garden seat.

The saluters, with their rifles, black armbands and one with a standard, stood about waiting as he dug. It was an honored corps, but small, the last admission of an old custom, and its members mixed freely and went home on leave, were told to walk the streets, to impress saddened survivors with the honor, the excellence of military last rites.

The clay was hard, like packed fodder in his father's yard, and as he swung the pick he had no time to look at the cool tower behind him. Once he had seen the golden dome. He felt them at his back, perhaps impatient to get on to more important burials, and he pitched into the clay, rolling his sleeves higher. Though the sun spread itself immediately over a few dusty trees on the brick-like plain, the clay still smelled of the seashore, the undivided vacant place for the tide.

Beyond the old horse against the hill, below the thatch and poles turning black at dusk, among the soft birds in the valley, there, near his mother's hearth, was the only cemetery Cecil had ever known. He expected the shaded plot and deep grass. There was always moisture on the heavy leaves, the hedgerow was untrimmed and where a man lay beneath the earth that earth was undisturbed except for the careful shuffle of an old caretaker. He expected to see a darkened church by any resting place. He expected shadows and mementos on the stones, a stile, a gate rusted open and thick with foliage, a light burning far in the distance and, as he stooped in the damp weeds, he expected to find dates impressed on the leaning stones.

Cecil climbed from the hole and scanned the lot. They were hard to see, but luckily the turned-over clay did not reflect too highly the glare of the sun. The graves could be made out. He was expert, from long early days, at one thing: furrows. And up and down, from one sparse bordering dune to the other the new pilots lay in even lines, straight, gray, with not a grapevine to scratch the dust between them. The saluters lined up and shot their volley. As he had learned at the Depot, he signed the chit. They left.

The D. O. knew the sun was about to set and that there was

time for no more. He waved the corporal back to the lorry and wearily climbed in beside him. "To the base."

When night had come and the bathers left the beach, when the heat still drifted in from the sea and the D. O. was settled in his small tent, he was glad to take off the dark glasses, after securing the flap. He smelled the clay. Cecil tossed and turned in the back of his lorry, pushing the shovels out of the way, rearranging the blankets under his head. He had no idea how long these days would last, but he was just as tired at the end of each. He put his hand on his heart and felt the decoration. He had forgotten to pin it to the corpse.

A Song Outside

The vulture wheeled and bumped briefly against an invisible disturbance in the air and, surveying the desert, let fall some bitter discard from its curving unsheathed beak. Down below, its shadow rode uneasily and erratically on the sand. The bird sat up in the air, glaring, pushed and pulled in the palms of the sky, black and indigent. Now it hovered and turned, as if it had a quaking one-way rudder, in guardian flight over the whole desert and over the small motionless outcropping of white adobe buildings below as well. The vulture was not high, it glided, strayed only several hundred feet above the earth; yet, peering bottomward through its pinched red eye, it saw that it had a long way to fall.

It paused with a grinding of bare bone and watched something hop out of one hole in the desert and escape down another, crossing the hot red strata in a glance. But the vulture rested where it was as if it could not bear to drop its ballast and descend. It jerked its pointed head toward the mountains, seeming to fly in the face of the far-off blue and white of the peaks. And it leaned steeply over, circling, looking over the edge of this altitude and leaning into the dry wind, trusting its ragged heavy self on high.

The vulture approached over the buildings now from the southeast, flying until hunger should come to it, and hung its head limply on its breast for a good look at the village, staring down slowly and covertly at the small white figure of a naked man who lay on one of the flat roofs in the morning sun. The vulture twisted suddenly from the grasp of the air currents and calmly returned, slightly lower, to pass again over the roof and man. Then, watching, poised as steadily as it could, having dropped one aged glassy foot, it shuddered, closed its eyes and began to float straight up, unappeased and rasping.

The vulture drifted high enough to enter a current of cold air off the ice of the mountains, the crest of the sleeping lady. It quickly stretched out a wing and beat its way down to a softer, warmer zone. The desert turned like a circle of red clay. The vulture drew around again, flapping forward through the sun until it could see the bare road which did not enter the village but curved to pass away a good distance from the buildings. Once more the vulture spiraled, venturing to manoeuvre its split wings in the wind, head hanging always forward, loathing and apprehensive, as the serrated sand running with red and brown dipped and fell away. This vulture waited over the world; then, seeing the low humps of cacti moving faster, while the air passed clearly and harmlessly by, it began to make an almost undetectable noise, a mere sullen rattle in the throat. Then it was done, and in panic, squeezing its claws, the vulture suddenly began to fall. It did not glide serenely down but dropped with its red neck burning and its pale undercarriage shriveling for the crash. Momentarily the image of the naked man rose up, then disappeared, and the vulture landed.

It hit the sand with the dust of a volcano all around it, the heat of the earth covered it in the first instance of its return; and still prostrate, still settling, before it could feel that all its ugliness was safely removed from the air, a boot struck heavily into its side, and the vulture, square and hollow and feathered, rolled over, righted, drew back and exposed its black and white poisonous parts to the laughing men. It waited, then slowly retreated, trembling and dragging of tail.

"I see it," said one of the men, "I see right through it."

"Let's give it the boot again," said the other.

"It was hovering over us," said the first, laughing.

"Talking to us," said the other. "How would you like that thing making down on your grave, man."

The two men—they had left the adobe buildings and come out upon the desert merely to await the vulture's landing— moved side by side, their hands touching now and then as they walked back across the sand toward the shadows of empty doors and roof poles. Neither wore shirts. They were dressed in black trousers and to their bare feet were strapped identical pairs of large brown Indian sandals carved with images of bulls and serpents. On their bodies lay no fat or muscle, only the suggestion of shoulders and thin, barely jointed arms, all slender and white as if they, together, had cracked their way out from some large dry shell deposited on the sand. One of them was bald and had a small hard naked skull with a suggestion of lace across the forehead. The other's head was covered with hair, black hair greased and cut so that it drew to a sharp edge from the top of his brain to the bottom of his neck. A head of feathered black cultivated hair.

"Is it a vulture?" asked the man with the black hair. "That hot bird, is it a vulture?"

"It's a taboo," answered the man with the lace drawn gently apart for his eyes. "It's a mistake." He looked away to the mountains without blinking.

"Do you see it, man? Do you see it?"

"Sure. I see it."

Then, stopping, "I want to ride on it. You look at it, man, but I want to ride on it." The other turned toward him a face wrapped perfectly around the skull to which clung two small waxen ears.

"Don't get carried away, man."

They reached the buildings and side by side went under the

arch like two figures into a tangled wood. They stooped and, neither standing aside, reluctant to part even at the entrance to a narrow way, brushed aside a drapery of black netting and climbed through a low door into a patio which was walled with rock and which radiated the white sun. A dry empty pool lay sunken in the middle of the patio. The native children had told them that if an ear was pressed to the drain hole of the pool, dead ladies could be heard singing and dancing in the pits of the earth. Now the men sat cross-legged against opposite walls and stared at each other across the narrow patio. Slowly their white shoulders began to burn.

They sat in the patio and breathed heavily, soricine and white, thin and light-headed under the pulseless sun and high on the altitude of the plain. Their razor-edged knees were crossed and they watched each other, while the sun made the floor of the patio glisten, turn brown or pink, and drew some faint odor from the dry manure falling to dust in the abandoned stable just over the wall. And the sun, the adobe, the plateau of the desert—out there squatted the vulture—and the buildings, the black holes of windows like cannon ports, the cornices of white and the silence: for the men all this was the mere end of a bus ride, the space for which there was no rent.

They lived in the patio—and in a small adjoining room which was connected to the patio by a door and an iron-barred window—like tropical birds, except that they ate beans and a kind of red soup and scrubbed their plates with sand after dark. They bathed one at a time at dusk, stood each alone by the pool and tipped a leather water bottle up on its trickling end. A pair of blue suspenders and a shirt in the corner of the patio and a few cigarettes hidden beneath an orange earthen jar were the only signs they left to tell that they were, or had been, in the village.

"*Lazy River*," said one, "*Lazy River!*" He leaned forward to see the movement on the other's lips or to catch the heartbeat. He put both hands to the sides of his head, cupping the palms around the greased sweepback of the hair, and watched his companion as if he himself might be intoxicated by the message of the sound. He whispered, *"Lazy River,"* and his fingers slipped from his head to his shoulders and dragged down his chest until they lay in his lap, leaving long red lines down the length of the white skin.

He was humming. His lips were set, his cheekbones were motionless, the sun shone on top of the pompadour, rounded and contoured like something to be kept in a box of green grass. There was a rhythmic jerking in one of the crossed black legs. And immobile under the sun, shielded from the desert by the close wall, hard of eye and fluttering his hands, thinking— but not of wicker baskets drying in the sun, nor of the silver peaks, nor of the women dancing with golden moons pinned to their ears—this man who had been pulled by timid donkey from where the bus had stopped to the village, merely sat and hummed.

All at once he appeared to need more air; the mouth opened, snapped shut again; and the chest, though the white ribs had not moved, was satisfied. He hummed, and without melody, planting one harmonic structure upon another, evoked a bitter terrifying image of the vulture landing and sliding head first across the sand to devour its prey.

The Nearest Cemetery

Scene of narration: a small state penitentiary in New England.
Characters:

THE PRINCESS: summer visitor to Bloody Clam Shell
Island; unhappy wife of a New York meat packer; woman
of beauty; victim of the local barber.

MILDRED: The barber's wife.

CAPTAIN RED: lobsterman in his fiftieth year; first lover
of the Princess.

BLUD: lighthouse keeper; Mildred's brother; second lover
of the Princess.

JOMO: off-island gas station attendant and vicious small-
town sport; third lover of the Princess.

THE BARBER: narrator; fourth and final lover of the
Princess. He loved her from afar and killed her.

I remember the day—blue, puffy white, orange—and that I
was smiling until we passed a hot dog stand and a shingled
church with windows as bright and painful as some of my own
dreams. In the darkness my eyes began to heal. But the car

was twisting over a torn-up section of the road or pushing between the pines or darkening the corner of a plowed field, and I couldn't smile. I remember the smell of upholstery and gasoline and vomit and the sound of the Marshal talking to himself the whole way. He looked like Vinny who wore a poppy in his cap. Suddenly I blinked and through the window I saw Blud's lighthouse standing in a plot of dry yellow sod, Blud's lighthouse by the side of the road and rising up from dead ground and sand instead of the bright wet rocks that always looked as if they had been freshly painted with black tar. But it was a hot dog stand. Another hot dog stand and closed for the season.

We drove through Jomo City and there, in the door of the trailer, was Jomo's mother husking an early ear of corn. A heap of pop bottle caps was sparkling out of the tall grass at her feet, and Jomo's mother made me think of Mildred, except my Mildred lives in an unpainted clapboard house on Bloody Clam Shell Island instead of in Jomo City in a trailer with flat tires and propped on concrete blocks in the tall grass. The old woman did not look away and did not wave, though she recognized the car and shadow that fell within twenty feet of her and swallowed the three gasoline pumps—two were dry—and even though she knew I was the only passenger that day. But between the trailer and the pumps was an overturned rowboat with a hole ripped in the bottom and, before the dust settled and we passed once more into the damp pines, a small dog thrust his head and paws out of the hole in the rowboat and barked as he might at a great crow flying across the woman's head. There was sun in the dog's mouth, sun reflecting from the bottle caps and from the antennas Jomo had rigged on the trailer's roof.

The Princess always stopped in Jomo City to fuel her car. The old woman worked the pump while Jomo brought bottles of orange pop for the Princess and her little boy, Jomo whose brown arms bare to the shoulder were washed with gasoline and whose hair is still a wavy cap of pitch, Jomo who sometimes let the little boy shoot at the rowboat with an old .22

calibre rifle hung inside over the trailer door, or at a piece of window glass propped against a stump while the Princess leaned out of the white Cadillac and laughed and smelled the salt in the air. Princess always brought Jomo's mother a bottle of perfume from New York and next Saturday at three o'clock, when the old woman comes in with the rest, Jomo and Captain Red and Blud and I will smell the odor of that perfume again and think, each in turn, of culvert or open sea or the town hall or the Princess coming down the rocks like a little plume fluttering in the sun or the pinging of the rifle and the smash of glass (all of us will remember that the Princess had a mouth the color of the orange pop Jomo gave her in the cold wet bottles he wiped with his undershirt)—and all because of a few drops of scent daubed behind the ears of an old woman who sits heavily on her trailer steps in weeds and wears a corset, Jomo says, which she repaired with pieces of a black inner tube.

Like an island. In the first sunset that prison was an island without rock or spume or salt, an island without buried barns and sea air pollinated and apples that fall from fractured boughs to rot on the shore line with the periwinkles—island almost the size of Bloody Clam but with gongs and siren instead of buoys and twenty-eight miles inland from the sea. So that day I only went from one island, Bloody Clam, to another island lying in a white valley across which move not boats, orange and black, but a few muddy dump trucks and, occasionally, the Marshal's car.

Each of us has his Venus—four men and four women who are either mothers or wives—Venus at least in memory. And if there is no seaspray here, no Crooked Finger Rock, there is at least the wind, though wind over watch towers and down lengths of walls makes other sounds, whether moan or sough or shriek, than it does through the wormholes in unpainted clapboard or when it is bending the tops of pines that ring the burning town dump of a little island town. With the wind, on which I smell the blood of fish, and with masonry and with fixed perimeter that is nonetheless fluid rather than geometric,

the walls buttressed against open fields, road and village in a
circumference vaguely but not perfectly circular, the prison is
in itself an island (and time is the calm, or time the hurricane)
but further it brings to mind the lighthouse because of the
white painted stone, the metal underfoot thick with coatings
of gray heavily-leaded paint, lighthouse because of the narrow
walks and odors of fresh paint and oil and half-inch sheets
of glass blinding, at sunset, high above our heads and behind
bars. Island of men; lighthouse large enough to contain so
many men each with his own Venus (though in memory;
though only some approximation of her who charmed, each
to her liking. Blud and me and Jomo and the Captain) and
each with denim pants and coat and face like that of the keeper
and the kept combined, since in his tower at dusk the lighthouse keeper shows his enchantment in his white stubbled
jaw and eye that looks and looks nowhere except down the
three-mile path of his silent light toward a sea from which no
ship may rise and approach because of the very nature of that
eye's desire, the very nature of that light's dangerous beam.
It is the lure that warns away the catch.

My shop is empty on Bloody Clam, empty and boarded up,
and the hair will grow long on Bloody Clam Shell Island.
But here I keep most of the heads of hair cut short, and every
day I shave the allotted number of white jaws and cheeks the
texture of a field of lice. Among so many men, week by week.
I wait until it is their turn and they come to me; and I smile,
knowing that first this neck and ear and hairless scalp—it is
forever speckled red and white with sunburn and bears a scar
—and this temple-pulse of the oldest man of them all belong
to the captain of the *Peter Poor*. And next I find that I am
lathering the swollen cheek of Blud, my own brother-in-law.
(Isn't he like Mildred? Mildred to a tit?) Jomo still has his
curls, the blue-green hair sticky with pine sap. Then one day
I notice my hands are becoming sticky. And I turn the chair
and my razor shapes those sideburns—they are the color of
trees in gloom, the color of water at high tide—and I remember
the black T-shirt with the sleeves cut off at the tight shoulder

seams, and I remember the bleached purple baseball cap he wore high and tight and perfectly horizontal on the living hair. A faded baseball cap he wore for Princess. And I reach for the hot towel and on the end of my finger see the little red line as bright and delicate as something you might see wriggling in the eyepiece of a microscope. I stop for a minute and suck it clean. Then with the towel in my hand I see again that he has a chin, rounded to a point and firm and white as a duck's egg, and that he has a mouth unmistakable and two lips bowed and dry and faintly red and capable of moistening or smile. He has all this, the hair and chin and lip. He had them for Princess. Carefully I brush on the powder and sometimes, holding the talcum flask in one hand and, in the other, the silver shears—sometimes I wonder if all those features won't suddenly disappear when I wipe off the powder. There is no talking in this barber shop; I talk with none of them. But I know their heads, their hair, I know what they did. And each of them knows me. And our eyes meet in the glass.

They—these three—were waiting for me when I arrived. I knew that despite the identical denim pants and shirts and coats and despite these numbers of men, they would find me, or I them. I knew that they were waiting and, in shoe factory or corner of the yard or high on a catwalk, would be standing or walking slowly or gesturing together out of their common dream. And now I wait for them. There is no talking in the barber shop, or in the yard or factory; no talking here, except for a single half-hour after dinner at noon and yet during all the hours measured by the moving shadow of a tilting shotgun's barrel and on through the dark hours when the men lie on their backs asleep or smoking—during all this time the forbidden word goes around from tier to tier, from one end of our state's island to the other. Only a joke (about Johnny in the privy, about the old white horse) or a plan to steal knives (I listen in such cases but never reply). But whatever word it is, it goes around among us like temper shooting down a row of quickening hands or the laugh that only we can see on faces expressionless and cold. Talking is against the rules and you have to be able to read the tongue still thrust into a cheek or hear the drag of the foot or the sound hissing from between two front teeth. No talking here. And yet for most of them, for me, there has been no talking all their lives (or mine). At least there is no talking on Bloody Clam Shell Island, very little requiring actual speech or anything more than the slow ceremonial of the dumb, the daily slow hustling of the island's dumb. But honor and piety or desire and stealth create different silences, and the child learns to hold out his cup, the waitress to set down the plate, a man his money. The child learns to get from the cemetery to the barber shop without a word, from the wild still competition and gainless amusement of the single bowling alley to the salt and blood and danger of the fish-bait bench without a word. The man has already learned his silences. Through habit. Through years of practice. Through contempt or love or inability or weeks and months of long days when the wind is too high to talk, the sea too rough.

The wordless life. The lifting of his chin for a fight, the tossing of his head for a kiss. And everything is in the lift of an eye, a hitching of the hips, the tossing of his head after a bottle of beer drunk under the herring boat docks in the mud at low tide or the way spring daisies appear wordlessly bound into a bun of hair. One sentence will sell boats, nets, house and land; one sentence will serve for a whole night and get a child. Nobody talks more than that. But everybody knows. Like Johnny in the privy or the white horse. There are six hundred and fifty people on Bloody Clam and three thousand convicts here. And none of them are talkers. They never were.

But the Princess talked. Each summer from the moment her yacht first came flashing into the green harbor and she stood on the bow in sunglasses and silk trousers cut like a man's and waved, with her little boy propped in a deck chair behind her and the husband buried away in the pilot house, until the day she left (always last to board the white boat with the crew and child and husband looking up at her and waiting to cast off) the Princess talked—talked all over the island—and on a clear day it would be the only voice to hear, the foreign tongue and fairy-tale accent coming down from the hill in a lilting continuum we knew was words (so many she might have been reading aloud or singing aloud the pages of a book) and someone rolling a cigarette or someone holding a knife with a hand slimy and silvery would hear that voice and listen, not stopping the fingers or staying the hand, but listen and nod perhaps if there was anyone else nearby. But the Princess would be too far away for the old men to hear and they would go on looking at their feet or sleeping with their backs dusty and humped in the sun. Sleeping, not knowing what they missed.

I lie on my back just waiting to hear it all again, just listening. Because the ear is already packed with sound like the hollow tree or the dog's skull in the dump or the coffin Vinny carries out of town in his garbage truck. Every object—length of wood, weight of bone—and every place already contains its fill of sound and the ear is its own coffin, its own little reverberating casket that hears everything it was ever meant to hear at any moment of the night and even though sometimes you want to sleep and so lie there holding it beneath your trembling hand. Your ear. The barber's ear.

The ear is the coffin that can't be closed or nailed or buried —it is forever warped with so much sound—and through the snoring and scraping of the old men in the sun I hear the girlish floating of words rounded in peculiar tingling accent (*Good morning, boys*) or among the picking of the rats in the dark Town Hall I hear it again (*Poor Blud, poor Blud*) and through the rumble of the captain pulling on his boots, fishing for the patched rubber, feeling about and then jamming in a foot like a cannonball puffing into a mountain of used car tires I hear it still clear and round and insistent at five o'clock in the morning (*Take me out on the water with you, Red*) and sometimes I can make out what she said to Jomo and sometimes I can't, and then (despite the singing of the larches and the rote of the sea and the wind and the clattering of Vinny's truck outside) she talks just to me.

So the mind lies between the echoing coffins of the ears—a

barber's ears—and you try to calm it in the midst of all that roar and whisper while a shadow falls through the bars and sweeps your chest. But then I raise my hands; I hold one ear; I hold both of them; I press with my palms. Because then it is not Mildred's voice I hear—not the voice, though I hear it often enough—but rather Mildred playing steadily on the church organ, Mildred pumping her feet, Mildred pushing the keys and Mildred making the reeds and seagulls shriek. And in each of Mildred's chords is the heavy harmony of the Lord and bass voice of Mildred's other brother who died from drink. And I cannot bear to listen. The barber cannot bear to listen to Mildred pumping and marching with the Lord at the town's church organ. The Lord and Mildred deafen me. They make me think of lying dead and naked beside the body of the shipwrecked woman on Crooked Finger Rock at the height of the gale.

Short as the watch that ends the night is what I hear, and *Time, like an ever-rolling stream, Bears all its sons away* is what I hear, the phrases filling the mind with their monotony and fear, and *They fly, forgotten, as a dream Dies at the opening of day*—all of it this booming, this beating of hymn on slick shingles and empty beach, and the Lord and Mildred are bearing me away to the Rock. Singing. Bearing off the naked barber to the heart of the hymn that is the gate, carrying me away at the center, easily, while the plankton spurts aloft into the dark of the storm, and I fly, fly, while Vinny cranks his truck in the wind and Mildred sings with the lost brother.

The barber. But even the barber has his tongue and toes and fingers, his hidden hair. The barber too has his lungs of twisted and dampened paper, his ears in which the islands float, his eyes that gleam, his sensitivity to skin, his touch. And sometimes I think I am all water. Hair and water. What the crack leaps upon, leaping to deform the image further, is nothing and my shop is on Bloody Clam Shell Island—closed, safely boarded up—while I am here.

Charivari

COURTSHIP

I

They slept in separate rooms. A massive dog patrolled the space between. His big eyes glimmered in the darkness, sniffing from door to door, a weak growl.

Henry curled in one corner of the four-poster. He dreamed fitfully beneath the sagging unwashed curtains overhead.

    Expositor: What time is it, Henry?
    Henry: Four o'clock.
    Expositor: What should you be doing?
    Henry: I should be counting my gold.
    Expositor: Nonsense. You should be out cleaning the stables.
                Come on; we'll take you to clean the stables.
    Henry: Must I do it with my hands?
    Expositor: Certainly. What do you see lying over there in
                the hay?
    Henry: A woman.

Expositor: What is she doing?

Henry: Making love to the stable boy while I do his work.

Expositor: Do you notice anything different?

Henry: Yes, she has a baby in her arms.

Expositor: What do you have to do now?

Henry: I have to put it in a bucket of water and keep it there so she can go on making love.

Expositor: Do you think you can keep it from jumping out and biting you?

Henry: I can't. It's going to bite, it's going to bite! I'll run away. I'm going to run, run. . .

Expositor: I'll turn *you* into the drowning baby if you do, Henry. . .

Henry: I'm drowning. Help me, help me. . .

The dream continued off and on the rest of the night. The dog began to howl.

In her room she slept soundly, muffled up to the chin in a fuzzy quilt. A small light burned in a corner of the room as she didn't like the dark. She rubbed her feet together. They reached almost to the middle of the bed and had been that long since she had been eleven years old.

A cock took to crowing where the dog left off, a tiny fowl bedraggled in the morning mist.

Daybreak, warm and bright.

When Henry, the parson's son, got up, he thought how much he hated shaving.

When Emily, the general's daughter, got up, she thought it would be a wonderful day for a parade. She had been brought up on parades.

They said good morning in the area of the big dog. It was always chained up in the daylight.

He kissed her.

The parson's son and the general's daughter sat at breakfast, he with a spiteful irritation in his eye, glancing once, twice, unable to stop, at her meagre glass of juice, the rim stained unevenly with lipstick and the pieces of unpleasant straw-like material lying in suspension in the green emulsion. The spiteful eyes still hung together in the rude awakening of sleep, still burned. She, on the other hand, the impersonal, everlasting she, watched his heaping plate decline with a strained pleasure, watched his fingers lift the thick-lipped coffee cup to his mouth. The sun on her shoulders, she felt a pleasing depression, the warm sensation of being ignored; she brushed a fleck of powder from her nose. If either of these forty-year-old jackdaws had looked up over the crest of the hill and out of the window, they would have seen acres of close-clipped lawn rolling down to the boundaries of the apple country; they might have remarked, of course inwardly, on the beauty of the blossoms, or they might, at least prosa-ically, by looking at the sky, determined the costume for the day. Instead, and more prosaically, they seemed irresistibly drawn into the negative contemplation of each other. The room contained the helter-skelter conglomeration of toeless shoes, round pared nails and Chaucerian plumpness reminiscent of a general's board. Gigantic maps on the walls still outlined in minute lines, details and descriptions the general's various and multitudinous campaigns. Plus a few locks of graying hair, butter melting on the already hardening toast, crumbs caught in a trouser cuff, and a soft perfume suggestive of many by-gone springs. She rose unsteadily, walked in tiny steps to a dusty writing desk. Her lips pursed, she wrote. He looked harder into the trough of food. Finished, she tacked the piece of paper to the wall. It read, "dinner at one." She considered a moment, put her hand on her hip, pulled at something, then with a violent little twist of the wrist, put a question mark at the end of the phrase. He heard the door closing in the utmost of caution and deliberate consideration.

Down went the napkin in a fragile neglected heap. The last bit of stubborn sausage rind left disturbing savage testimony. The fork hung in a mentally deficient angle on the plate. He felt in his pocket, the deep catchall of good taste and felt with warmth the assertion of the paper that his fingers found, a to-whom-it-may-concern graph and history of his intelligence quotient in good standing at one hundred and thirty. He lit a cigarette, and in his own impeccable manner, made his way across the floor of bric-a-brac. Old college dogs with twenty years of age, and Papal dolls stuffed with cotton were sad at having been daunted in one glorious almost forgotten day. His toe disturbed a little faded bag of pine scent and trod on an ivory god. He found the door he was looking for, let his fingers slip a few moments on the brassy knob, then descended into the frictional paradise of his own room.

She stood before the glass, puff in hand, desperately unhappy and desperately pretty, face to face with all the peeking, denouncing photographs on the three walls. If only daddy could see her now, his stern lip would quiver at the injustice, his completely beribboned chest would heave in consternation. She could forgive him now, poor petty dear. And her mother's jade eyes looked out, not up, in sure unrelenting hostility. After all, she saw as she focused on the Egyptian dame of herself in the mirror, she had sacrificed all this libido and all this beauty on the incriminator in the other room, and could not ask, and hated herself for wanting, to be spared.

He messed with a spotted, endlessly cumbersome cravat. He thought of her, the resistless feline eyes, the phlegmatic voice, the smallish bundle of uncompromising mental ways, thin hair piled on the head, throwing the picnic scraps upon the ground.

She thought of him, brute. Unknowing, egoistic man. A burst of pity.

He longed to go into her room and make it up, to show her all the other things he felt.

She wanted to ruffle his hair and hold his head on her mothering bosom.

They met, near one, two different people.

2

They stood receiving at the door, he trying to hide, and at the same time excuse, his amazement at the dapples, piebalds,

grays, and blacks who streamed pretentiously past his outstretched hand. He stood uncertainly beside his dear bright
wife who tried to keep a garbled account of the fleeting uninteresting faces: Mr. and Mrs. Gaylor Basistini of the short
height, Dr. and companion Smith with a monocle, little Man
and Lady Wheeling Rice, a ruddy monster from South America, impeccable Mister and Madame Bird, a determined un-
named adventuress in green, Sir Dewitt-Jones in blue, the
Ottoes and their young son, restless Mr. and Mrs. White, an
ungracious daughter, the Demonoes, the Burgesses, shy Mr.
and Mrs. Young, an unmentionable bevy. At the very last
minute, enter bubbling, vicious little Noel in glory. Awkwardly, and in a hurry, they sat down. Then came her parents,
followed by his. The butler began to serve.

Fingers sought, amid the gross confusion of heavy, disturbed
silverware, to separate a knife or spoon, to tuck an unsoiled
napkin beneath a powdered chin. "Oh, Mama, how could
you?" followed by an unsteady blush, circling up beneath
young pointed ears. "Yes, sir, we won all right." And have
you heard, or do you think we are likely to hear what very
private shames and resentments and misgivings these people
are harboring? May we be cruel enough? He managed to
convey a solid frontier while waiting to drop the fork into the
beef, then felt his casualness wither away at all the provisional
commands for proper cuts, accompanied by gestures, anec-
dotes, and grimaces that echoed and rebounded from his right
and left. She felt a pantalooned and properly pressed knee
graze her own. What would Papa think, what *can* he think?
"Regular good stuff," the old man thought, his private orderly
standing stiffly, unconsciously, unhelpfully behind his chair.
Somewhere, someone's forgotten misbehaving baby howled.
Calmly Mrs. Rice's tongue lashed about inside her red cheeks
and with a calculated movement, dislodged a stringy unrecognizable left-over. Her eyes sought out the hidden glass of ruby
port in an anxious appeal. A fattish man, completely unaware,
with a sudden desire for enlightenment, turned a question
at a coquettish, aged head. "Who are they?" he asked. The

head turned slightly towards him, a side of the face merely moving as a muscle twitched. The gray eyes looked back into the plate. The fat man grunted, began to finger his well-concealed belt.

Henry was still carving. His fingers trembled deliciously. He cast his eye down the cluttered expanse until he found the decayed form of the general and fixed him in a mean feminine gaze, "sending all those poor chaps up to be cannon fodder, unforgiveable." Back to the meat. She was laboring under her heavy secret. "How awful," she thought, "not to be able to confide even in Mama. And something like this could be dangerous at my age. What would Henry say? Perhaps he would be proud." A shudder. *Thing* inside of her! He felt the butterflies under his shirt, but continued to pass the plates down to Gaylor Basistini. Good old Gaylor, his one real friend, mousey little man, how good he was, his steady face, reaching up hand after hand to take the plates. Reassurance from the mousey man, a knowing look. She excused herself, please, from the table. The butterflies flapped violent wings.

3

Henry Van, perturbed, his stomach still unsettled, his mouth forewarned of gastronomical acidity, crept into the den through the noiseless underfoot protection of a polar bear rug. He inched his way into the darkness. Beneath the steel, concrete, and mahogany floor, the guests were clattering in great pomposity in the game room. Under cover of glittering and seductive exhibitions, internal abdominal rollings, machinations, and exertions were oilingly at work. Above the game room and her fortunately estranged spouse, Emily sat happily arrayed among septic bottles, silver tubes, rubber tubes, and bunny slippers, confronted on all sides by mirrors decorated with hearts and flowers. She dipped her fingers into cream and listened to the running water. She was joyful in her lonely vigil and in making her painstakingly thorough examination of herself. Henry sat dwarfed by the radio, which reared itself to six full feet, a present from his general-in-law of the medaled set. On his right, Henry found himself under the scrutiny of the solid eyes peering from his photographed handsome father's clerical head. At the moment, possessed of no recourse, having neither the sense to run nor the goodness to resent, nor the ability to withstand these not-too-well meaning troops of guests that pushed and stayed, Henry simply turned himself over to the rapid tic-tapping of his foot, and the slight discomfort of a headache. He welcomed the release of a short doze.

An inward consciousness of his inopportune match with the little, physically-preoccupied woman up above drove him into a sleeping activity. He had bills to contend with, even though there was an endless supply of money. He had awnings stored in the basement that had to be put up. He had dogs to be spayed and ponds to be stocked with silver fish. He had dental plates that were absolutely worthless. He had a priestly father who resented almost everything, who rode sometimes upon a mule, and who disliked Henry most of all, a man with whom Henry would have to speak before the afternoon was ended. The sleeping, dyspeptic body began to move. Suddenly there was a blaze of lights; someone was shoving a drink into his face; another proffered a bunch of flowers; someone held a golden cigarette case and a match popped before the startled eyes. The violent voices descended upon him in unkempt joviality, eager arms clutched and stuck to his shaking shoulders. On the periphery of the agitated circle and uncontrolled laughter he could almost discern the helpless feeble face of his feeling friend, Basistini. Lost . . .

Upstairs, she was thinking, fanned by the fluttering pairs of drying stockings. She was going to have a child. She was afraid. All our neighbors lean on physical oddities, but I will not be odd, I will not let them leer at my progeny, she thought. She dabbed at perspiration with a tiny cloth. How could Henry do such a thing? If only she could get off into the mountains. Suddenly, without thinking, without knowing what it was all about, she *was* afraid. Quickly, she pulled on her shoes.

She reached the middle of the giant staircase just in time to see Henry being carried off by the great host of friends, off like an adulterer riding out of town on a rail in front of the vast guffawing crowd. She saw his hopeless eyes for a moment, not even conscious enough to make appeal, Henry in tar and feathers and so completely miserable. And all at once she felt herself succumbing to unburdening peals of wild laughter as the last of the group disappeared through the French doors, Basistini trailing behind.

Henry looked from one unrecognizable face to another, felt a suspender-snap pull loose from his trousers, groped in his hip pocket for a damp handkerchief. He felt the murmuring wind through the game room windows, and became conscious of the adventuress in green, idly and unspiritedly commanding his attention. All of a sudden the arms let him go, the mob dispersed in little wrangling groups, and there was the girl. Absently, he at least had presence of mind to notice her.

"Having a good time?" he asked.

"Why, sure, I suppose so," she said, reaching his spirit of the thing which he, of all people, noticed. Her popularity is a pity, he thought. He himself had dropped, in thought, into that prosody and ununiqueness of his disturbed kind, straightening his tie, smoothing the jacket. He thought her eyes had an angry tilt.

"May I get you a drink?" Another try, unimportant, forced, without meaning.

"No, I don't think so. Feeling a little empty."

They walked upstairs in the direction of the kitchen, her fingers lightly on his arm.

I'll have to speak to father *sometime*, he was thinking.

They discovered a platter of odd-size celery stalks, the centers carelessly lined with cheese, slightly discolored with red pepper. Although it was only four in the afternoon, the celery stalks had the withered, after-party look, dismal and lifeless. Henry, now increasingly nervous for no reason, snatched one of the more blossoming bodies and offered it, with his great eyes wide, to the girl. She opened her mouth. He stuck the oval end between her lips, the spongy stalk protruding out with its drooping, yellow leaves.

"Thanks," between mouthfuls.

"I don't suppose I'm a very good host," he said.

"Why not, Vanny? I think you're doing very well," she said, brushing the hair away from her enormous throat, "taking care of Emily's intruder nicely. All progressing as I'd like to think you'll let it. Haven't you got anything besides celery?" Henry looked for a moment: coldness in her green eyes. Then pushing and pulling inside of the refrigerator, he emerged with a frosted bottle of thick tomato juice.

"Now if I can find the glasses," he said, and began to rummage through shallow, secret cupboards. Methodically looking, piles of aluminum pots, another wrong closet. He felt her behind him. Because of her smiling knees, her mannish voice, and acquired rouge, she reminded him of "Christabel's" friend; similar, though not in desire, at least in spiritual mystery and saintly odor. He could see her, long-limbed in the dark forest.

"Here we are," he said and poured two potions.

"Skoal," she said, the glasses touched, and for the first time she smiled, a bashful, yet satisfied, womanly, momentary grin; perhaps as the regal friend of Christabel would smile at the peak of the moment in the middle of the night. Her eyes grew brighter with faint intoxication. Then she lapsed back into her sad-eyed implicating act. "Healthy boy and healthy girl." She emphasized the word 'girl.' Henry made a gurgling sound and sipped the juice, aperitif of a gray-eyed fawn. She lolled complacently in green on a kitchen chair. She raised her head in a devouring gesture.

The sounds of the party were no longer confined to the game room, but seemed to start and jar uncontrollably from every conceivable hole and cranny in the house. Hearing the high-pitched marauding voices, Henry felt an uncomfortable anger in the pit of his stomach and a desire to lash back.

The adventuress's breath had been made to grow a little stronger, her shoulders tilted back.

"Wouldn't you like to sit down?"

"What? Oh, no, I really think I should go and find my father. Have you had enough to eat?"

"Certainement, my Vanny," she said and collected herself. She accepted defeat and unrecognition as easily as if they were going up to his plush master bedroom instead of into the drafty hall.

"The moving finger writes," she said, and Henry's writing was choppy from habit. They left the isolated kitchen ward.

4

Parting in the semi-darkness, he stood alone, and though he couldn't see it, he faced a full-jawed daguerreotype of the general, his hair trimmed down in a Prussian cut. Henry hit the doorjamb, recovered and placed a retaining hand against the wall. The small wires, hung dangerously across the air to strike unwitting men beneath the chin, began to hum menacingly. Childhood goblins arose: "Sister Ann, sister Ann, do you see any Saviour at all coming?" "I see only donkeys raising dust in the evening and dust in the morning, and the pugilistic form of Noel chasing *femme* to *femme*, only the little nervous wife sitting on Caesar's bust preening her black wings." "Oh, dear sister Ann, what *can* I do?" as he felt the shadow of the sword above his head. He stood alone in this hallway that seemed like an underpass, passing below the antics of those in hell's seventh circle up above. Henry heard the buzzing bees, the long-billed tapping of a kiwi bird, the pizzicati in his eyes and ears. The frayed wires slipped from his fingers. He went reeling on, standing still, his arm just brushing a black vase, just missing a potted plant that hung tensely on a chain from the ceiling. All his fingers crossed and uncrossed in anonymous expectation, as he had learned to do as a child. He felt a delicate sensation among his vertebrae, a macabre delight, an overall, bewildered, ecstatic fear. He partly reconnoitred with a humdrum glance; no suspicions were aroused, but as he heard a Herculean guest bellow in ribaldry, he felt the powdered gnashing of his custom teeth. He adjusted his rimless spectacles, clenched his doubting fists, and hovered over the black cliffs. Impersonality clutched at the largest and smallest of his blind spots with a clear grip and shoved his anger deeper; he whipped at the filmy egg with a constant beater. The adventuress, and Emily too, were as far from his mind as the wind he had heard, or his rough, degrading ride of the previous hour on the backs of his plebeian, cross-bred, plunging guests. Now he must whip and find his father. He began to retrace, over the path of his violent exit, his steps to the half-safe den.

The general's wife was a lean woman who had adopted her husband's stature and calibre. Her calling cards were printed, "General and Generaless Soris Smithson Valentine," and she carried them in a small, black leather case. The generaless now sat, with the sleeping general, in one corner of the den, visiting with the parson and the parson's wife who sat in the opposite corner. The parson rolled his big blue eyes, and smoked a clerical cigar. Henry's dame mother sat quietly at his feet. The generaless commanded the room in unfriendliness by her clear green stare. They waited, unknowingly, for Henry with some sort of determination.

In the growing darkness, people tittered back and forth from crevices to kitchen, broke glasses, soiled the rug, and made lewd exclusive demonstrations. Two unclaimed canaries were fighting in a gilded cage.

Emily sat in a yellow chair, her stubby calves drawn up beneath her, not quite the center of attraction. Noel was running around her little throne, talking at her, but glancing vivaciously outwards, afraid to give her all of his complete and undivided exhibitionism. Each time he passed, he tweaked her knee or slapped her ear, and looked from side to side for laughing male corroboration or exotic female indulgence. His cantering became more suggestive.

The monster from South America was taking it all in with suave approval.

The ungracious daughter left the room for intimate, private purposes, in haste.

Emily guarded only her stomach, which she thought was

swelling, from Noel's explorations; she suffered his other insinuations with innocent hospitality, never for a moment doubting what she considered to be corpulent sincerity, but what was actually nakedness of intent, gross body with the girdle wound about the stomach, unelectrical, and hidden beneath dusty layers of flesh. She bobbed to and fro in the wind of his gyrations and contortions. The monster rubbed his thighs; the ungracious daughter looked disturbed; and Mr. and Mrs. White sat mutely talking. Noel's pose was flawless, very loud; it was all a joke, but one sustained on a serious, determined, biological level. Each gesture of his hands grew deeper. He fitted in a tighter, more insistent sphere with each advance, soft and airy in his tights, seeking hopefully fine areas of sensitivity, overestimating Emily.

One by one the audience disappeared: one to the stables because he liked the smell of hay, another crawling down the stairs because he couldn't walk, another with his tail between his teeth, the ungracious daughter back to the lavender retreat. Six o'clock and the room was shadowed, guests were dropping off to sleep throughout the house; the apple blossoms at the end of the lawn breathed an artificial nostalgia. Emily and Noel were two round, pink ghosts. He flung himself on the arm of her chair. His nostrils flared. He fidgeted.

Emily felt his numbed fingers tickling her throughout her senses, felt them only as a coarse foreign matter. Noel worked to arouse that gigantic passion that was only in his own imagination. His hand slipped and slid over flat smooth surfaces. He teetered on the arm. Behind his comedy he planned; it would be a difficult thing curled in the chair, perhaps the floor.

She was just as bad on the floor as she was in the chair.

Noel's scope was enormous, pathetically phallic, whether in partnership or not. But his emotional pattern was always loveless. He had insidious and uncomfortable talents for satisfaction and exuberance. He was never daunted, but always too unsubtle, too pugnacious, too jolly, too stimulated, too ready and quick. Always ready, willing or not. He was the life of the party, but had to be beaten off with a stick.

He crouched above, beside, below, and around Emily. He looked for a light in the little eyes, tried to make her fingers move. He pinched.

Emily lay quietly on the floor, head propped on an arm, thinking of little sweaters and things. Didn't they teach something about it in school nowadays? How unpleasant. She plucked at her skirt's hem that casually tarried on the middle of her thigh. Several of her friends had children and didn't make out too well with them either, conceived in eating, born in the bathroom. Over Noel's frowzled head she could see, out of the impersonal window, the nightly blue sky. How peaceful. All at once she remembered her mother's words, "Don't ever let a man do *that* to you!" The generaless had looked very stern. Quickly Emily climbed to her feet and without a backward glance, trotted out of the room. She left Noel wriggling, wriggling all by himself.

She went to find Henry, to see what he was doing that she wouldn't like. Him! And possibly she would approach the generaless.

All of them are elders, bawdy old-folks, clustered around the water hole. In succession they peer down milk-white shoulders to seek and relish the sight of younger elders. They chatter among the reeds. They shake their linen vestige and scatter saline calling cards. They ride in *petit* leather saddles to the hunt and are entirely harmless. Though they peek. And they worry. Beneath all of their eyes, beneath indifference, and fish and wine, is a humorless apathy. They are stately and gruff; they wear laurels. Their ankles sink in the water by the bathing pond. They stare.

The general woke with a heavy start to the prodding of the generaless's slender swaggerstick between his blunted ribs.

"Really, my dear," the poor old man complained.

"Come, come, Soris, none of your terms of affection. Up, up," she ordered in her best clipped sergeant major's tone, "up on your feet. I believe the fire needs attention." The general arose, trying to conceal the stinging tears and discreetly smoothed his coat. Beneath the coat was a soft shirt, beneath the shirt a wide thin undershirt attached to a pair of flaming blue shorts. In the last few years, the general had grown to well over seven feet and had expanded, and the brilliant shorts were so constructed.

"Faster, Soris," a curt command. He turned, bristling with effort toward the fireplace. As he stooped, his face was caught for a moment in the round, concave mirror over the stones, and was twisted into a red-eyed drawn distortion.

"Heavy," he grunted in his most childish tone. "Awkward," and he slipped. Rough, green logs fumbled over the dead coals.

The straight-backed militant spoke: "Enough!" The general seated himself again, may I?, at last.

The generaless continued, "Parson, Beady, draw your chairs over here. There is something we should discuss." The parson and his wife clawed to life, looked about, then together dragged the parson's heavy chair across the floor of the cold room. They seated themselves, Beady again at the parson's feet. The generaless took a deep breath, threw back her head, stood up on the chair, and began:

"The general has forwarded some information to me that is of vital concern to us all." Her tongue clucked and hissed, she swayed and felt an itching on the underside of her gaunt thigh. Suddenly her voice jumped a half tone, she shifted her slippery eyes. "It's a damned folly for anyone to let her go on like this," the general thought.

"As you all know," her glance included the farthest isolated corners of the empty room, "Henry has been speculating in something or other, I know not what, for the most part of his life. You, as his parents, and we, as his parents-in-law, must hear, and act upon, this report. . ." The parson's jolly fingers stopped playing with the pleats in his gown, Beady huddled closer to his knees. "Damn," said the general, "damn," and the generaless continued, "Henry has suffered a loss." She stood stonily in triumph, and her fish eyes bright in a glaze of glory. Then she fumbled.

"I feel that it's up to us to say something . . ." she paused, all at once slightly agitated, an embarrassment that was difficult to

meet, to comprehend with her tactical wall broken for a moment. She blinked her eyes, no longer fish-like. Silence.

These poor people. We should pet them; we should take care
of them. But we must not make an obligation of it. Send them
a painted teapot, perhaps, listen as attentively as possible, be
prepared to write a simple postcard, nothing more. They are so
flimsy, apt at any moment to be blown away forever. And we
too, perhaps, with them if we are not careful, over the Via del
Rosa, Street of Whores.

The generaless tried to collect her skeleton of prose again,
tried to gather in the stock phrases that had been split under the
slight emotion. She colored visibly.

"Of course, I don't want to interfere," she said.

"For my part," the parson interrupted, "I've done everything
I can for the boy, trying to instill in him the principles of sta-
bility, honor, faith, piety, sobriety, sensibility, manhood, and a
respect for his father. . ."

"I believe," said the generaless, "that we should try to relieve
the moroseness that is probably weighing on his mind, and also
try to encourage him to attempt business ventures that are less
unsure; perhaps a slight admonishment is called for."

"An ugly little bit of nonsense," thought the general.

"I don't see how he could do such a thing," whispered
Beady. "My poor dear boy." She lowered her head, the weight
of motherhood wringing tears from her small eyes.

"Why, I remember," the general mumbled, "used to lose
money on girls, all the time, never meant a thing. . ."

"Please be quiet, Soris," the generaless's calmest voice, "and
of course this is quite a different matter. Henry is, I think we
should remember, forty years old."

That sobered the judges into a miserable silence, a thought
about the passing, denuding years, not for Henry's sake but
for their own. They became conscious-stricken of gray hairs
and kidney pains, not destined to habitate forever, palpitation,
palpitation, sleep.

Beady tucked her paling legs further beneath the youth-
fully cut velvet. The parson squared his head and fingered a

two-inch key that hung from a corroded copper-green chain. The general snorted. The generaless spoke, "I feel greatly for the boy. It is not easy to resist the temptation of an 'easy deal.'" Sometimes she shocked the general. He stirred, uncomfortably. "Certainly not," they echoed in unison, like classroom children repeating dull lessons, stricken, leaning against the wailing wall, mastodons protesting. Now there were glances of hypocritical pity and agreement with each other, long faces. The general struck a match on the creamy flank of a marble cherub who clung fly-like and precariously to the fireplace.

"A little discipline, then laughter, always helps," he said and sat again on the plush uncomfortable chair.

"It is my opinion," the generaless began, "that we should wring a confession from the boy. . ." At these words Beady collapsed inside and the parson was unable to conceal a vicious snarl of "now, really." He had never liked the way that woman stood up anyway, never liked her incisive odor. "I merely mean," she continued, "that we should make him bare his guilt out loud, and then we may give him all our aid." A pause.

"Agreed," said Beady with a tiny voice, and she looked out into the dead of night.

"He's a rather crumbly sort," the general tried, a murmur of dissent, not from any loyalty but just a threat against their only target. He did not finish the sentence. The generaless tossed her head in contempt, then hissed a slant-eyed narrow look at Beady. She returned a bilious glance.

At that moment, Henry's head entered out of the black opening of the door. A general, hurried confusion.

"Hello, mother," Henry whispered.

A thousand hands reached out for him at once.

He was a gaunt, cut-up, timid little boy, his mouth awry. Henry entered the room in an arc, curving over to the far wall, behind his father's chair, then slowly drew nearer to the group, his face at the mercy of dismay. He never really knew how to act before these people, and always felt that he was expected to act *somehow*. He looked down over his father's shoulder, "It's been very long since I've seen you. I thought we might have a chance to talk." The old man didn't seem to hear. Each one of the group thought that he was the one imposed upon by this embarrassment, thought that he should never be a part of scenes like these. Black magic. Contempt. The fire flickered testily, making not the slightest impression on the chill that arose.

The generaless cleared her throat, looked about for any signaling eye, and finding none, began: "Henry. We'd like to talk to you." Her voice was stimulated by a fleeting pathos. She was enjoying herself.

"I don't understand," thought Henry, "how I always manage to allow myself to be talked *to*." He scowled.

The generaless resumed, "It has come to our attention that some of your speculations have proved unprofitable. In fact your last is a great loss, and hence a danger to yourself, and of course to your family. We cannot take these things lightly."

All at once Henry understood. A loss. "My God," he thought, "is that all?" He hadn't known anything about his business failure. "This is the first I've heard of it," he said. "Of course, I'm sorry." He wiped away dampness from under his collar. He was irritated that they should bring the matter up. "I'm sorry." He wilted.

The generaless immediately took up the flag. "We are too, dear child, nothing hurts us more than your unhappiness. We only want to help."

"Thank you," he said. "Thank you all."

Emily announced herself by striding through the French doors, and statuesquely still, she stood, her body hallowed in a sheet of light, all her inner character chained and thrust to the surface. She caught the words of the chorus, "Oh Henry dear, accept our sympathies, you know you can count on us." She saw him fidget. What on earth was he doing there: they should be waiting for her. Emily felt her careful little body shake. She loathed his silky-lined complexion, resented his downcast eyes, and burned to smite them all with her unhealthy burden. It was so unfair. But now before this impersonal aged tribunal she could speak with a proud anger that was only meant to shock.

"I'm going to have a baby," she blurted out in a strained unnatural daughter's voice, and tears welled up. Her little speech gathered fragments of anxiety, self-pity, hostility, and indifference. A slight patter of rain was heard. Beady mumbled incoherently. The general sat bolt upright and the parson looked piously at cracks in the ceiling, deepening fissures.

The generaless spoke, quite becalmed: "My dear, we are so happy. . ."

Emily began to weep, her round face caught fitfully between her hands.

Henry left the room in slow strides, his eyes straight forward. He felt a yell mounting to his lips. Behind him he heard a sudden burst of chattering voices and the drastic sobs.

He escaped.

5

Gaylor Basistini was waiting beyond the French doors, under the rug. His small round hands were held furtively in front of his chest. His fragile mouth smiled a welcome of condolence. In the dark this little centenarian reached for Henry's hand and tossed away the black shawl, exposing to view steadfast short shoulders, trim tapering lines of a gray suit, a rose in his hair. He buzzed with muffled phrases and held his master's horse of sorrowful words.

"Henry, here I am," he said.

"Ah, Gaylor," a voice coming outward from the jurystand, then a change, charged words, "I can't stand this any longer . . . she's going to have a child . . . spying." Then his angry voice was gilded: "Come along, Gaylor."

The two men sat under the basement stairs, the bottle propped between them in the dust. Light from knotholes shone from the liquor to their studs, to rings, and to their eyes, like diamonds of fire-points, rainbow cat-eyes. Gaylor Basistini's knowing fingers repeatedly pinched the bottle neck and filled two clear cocktail glasses with the brandy siphoned from the saddle-flasks. A tardy grin settled on his head.

"I quite sympathize with you, you know. I never was able to stand unpleasantness at all." Gaylor's voice was confiding.

The more Henry drank, the more free he was of anger, the quieter became his slender hands, the more empty were his eyes.

"I simply don't understand," he said, "I feel as if there were a hundred persuasions, attachments, curried and combed asses, all tangling themselves about my neck, all people I have never seen before, but there is nothing I can put my finger on." Gaylor adjusted his bonnet.

"Have another drink, Henry." The liquid slid over the bottle's lips and stained the doilies Gaylor had carefully spread out on their knees.

"Thank you, my friend." They stooped and drank together. Henry spoke. "My home is a microcosm of the world to me; I'm afraid I cannot name it. Perhaps I should say microbes, or mercuries running to a bar, fleet-winged marmosets, poisonous mushrooms in a Victorian age. The mam'selle of my old heart —I'm buying her up for my own death."

"Now, Henry, don't worry, mustn't give't a thought—let's have some awful cute fun—come on." Gaylor had a bad taste in his mouth, a film before his eyes; his fingers crawled up and down Henry's sleeve. His teeth had a distinctly yellow taste. The stairs and cobwebs moved. Basistini's neck seemed to grow larger, his head gyrating on its pointed end. His shirt was dirty.

"I simply do not understand,' said Henry. He put an arm around his sagging friend, could feel the ribs. The stairs dropped off at a dangerous angle, thousands of candles burning at the bottom. Then Henry heard them singing up above— something about rolling eyes and on the floor. He stood up, dropping Gaylor's head, and with a set determined face, began to climb the stairs. The head lolled against the wall, then became sick.

He climbed the second flight of stairs acutely sensitive of the noise. The gathering had hauled itself out of the comatose realm of stupor, sleep, and strained love-making—but he didn't resent it.

"I say that we must have decentralization, an overall technology for the good of mankind. . ."

"Of course capitalism is still the backbone of the civilized classes, *and* of the others. . ."

"Indeed it is an art of mutual satisfaction, an objective ritual. . ."

"Bunch of old men over there in Rome. . ."

His ears alert, his temples tightly drawn, he did not hear the prophetic grasping conversation of the four, nor the gasps of Gaylor, nor Emily weeping.

"Pardon me," he brushed past an outstretched arm, visiting plunderers. He found his own room and set to weaving his tapestry, methodically preserving odds and ends, awaiting the return of his warrior soul.

He smoothed the sheet of paper before him and wrote; a man who even in his most childish moments had never seen a star to wish upon, but who had smelled the blood of an Englishman many times, who had been reared on a penny wafer and a glass of wine, who had placated and argued, never greatly disturbed.

Henry to Emily, 10:30 *PM.*

(He undid his collar.)

"I am not sure what has happened to me this evening, my dear, but I feel somehow concerned and want to write to you. Perhaps nothing has happened, but I believe this insecurity must be expressed.

"It is simply as if they have taken everything from me; Gaylor's understanding, love for our parents, closeness to you, even those memories, which I do not find particularly pleasant, of childhood; all gone. The house itself has become a secretive, unfamiliar place, hatching many subterfuges and maddening familiarities. I find Gaylor's fondness deeply depressing; I wouldn't know my father if I saw him; you, I'm afraid, have left. I know nothing of children; I have no memories; people in this house simply disregard me, and I cannot see them. I know it is no great calamity; no blow has fallen, except your charming but frightening news—what kind of a father would I make?—and yet I am distressed. Perhaps I would throw the baby over the parapet. Why must I always play the feminine role? Why don't they come and change my pants—forgive me please, I realize this meanness is uncalled for. We must protect ourselves from each other. It seems we haven't even got the decency to quarrel openly. But then we have nothing to quarrel about—"

Over his desk the Christ Child's face was gray in the lamplight. Beady's face shone down beside it. Near the blotting pad his eye fell on a slip of paper: "Dinner at one?" He must have unknowingly taken it from the dining room. For a moment he saw the kimonoed figure. He wrote again.

"At any rate, I suppose it is unjust of me to judge or criticize our lives together, especially when there doesn't seem to be anything to judge. Gaylor got very sick tonight. I was rather ashamed of him. Still the old oppression; I'll say goodnight."

He put the letter in an envelope to slip under her door.

They wrote notes like this to each other all the time.

He put the letter under the door, walked downstairs, said, "I've had a lovely time," to a shadow, smiled, and walked out of the house.

He went slowly down the lane, still smiling.

6

Mocked and scorned, she fled—but, darling, what delightful news, come sit—quickly as an angry water-fowl rushes into the air and cheeks blush. No longer had she this one very intimate, private possession that kept her different from all the others, no longer could she lick her wounds alone, no longer would she be able to look forward to the day of utmost confidence. Her secret was grossly illuminated with social pleasantry and parental goodwill, openly bandied about. It was no longer a precious, delicate, striking detail of the minor, inner life that was her own. She had been driven to this divulgence, not led, or coaxed, or loved into it. She simply smelled the odor of dying lilacs. Are we never going to be happy, little woman? Mother had always been a military man, that was that. She felt her hair unruffling and getting thin. Oh, it was messy.

She had stopped crying long ago, about the time she was tramping heavily up the stairs. Her face was tearstreaked, wrinkled.

Emily lay still; she would have kissed.

She didn't have very much that was her own. She had a kewpie doll for every happy party; it sat old and depleted and hypocritical near the sewing basket. It was a pretty doll though.

She listened. She heard the nightbirds singing their only language, voices up from the terrace beneath her window.

Noel's croak, "And you know what that damn little farmer's daughter did? She got out of there just as fast as her little legs could take her."

"How disappointing!"

Drunk Dr. Smith's, hoarse and provocative, "And they castrated Abelard for that, absolutely castrated."

"Shhh, darling, be quiet, got a match?"

Emily heard these words as she never heard them before.

"The whole w-o-r-l-d's singing my song. . ."

She felt knife blades running through her heart. She turned to face the wall.

She heard a timid knock on the door. Fumbling for the key, just a minute, please, and then quickly jumping back on the bed.

Beady came in.

"Are you all right, Emily?"

"Yes, of course I am."

"I was a little worried about you, dear."

"Don't worry, please."

A thin cold hand scraped Emily's. That terrible perfume.

"I'm very happy for you." Whispers in the dark.

"Thank you."

"It's the most beautiful thing I've heard for a long time. I'm going to begin to knit. I remember knitting before Henry was born. I'll make you something really nice. And small."

"You're very kind."

"Oh, my dear, please don't be so cold. I know what you're going through."

"Beady?"

"Yes?"

"Will you do something for me?" A tight voice.

"Of course, anything." An eager answer.

Silence. Then, under a quick pressure of the cold fingers: *"Go get Mother."*

Beady groped through the doorway. Her shallow footsteps sounded down the stairs. Emily smiled to herself with satisfaction.

The cat's jaw broke the wings of the thin bird.

The generaless came in and put on all the lights! She strode quickly from one small globe to another and finally sat, good evening, mother, in a flowered chair, eyes focused above the bed, on the far wall.

"Beady said you weren't feeling well," crossing her legs.

"Oh, of course I'm well. I just wanted to talk. . . I wanted to see you. . ." Emily made no pretense of smiling.

The generaless was paling.

"You mustn't worry. I'll handle the whole thing. Perhaps you'd like Dr. Smith."

"Yes, mother." A whimper.

The generaless rose and began to collect the scattered magazines, picked a skirt up off the floor, one by one replaced bobby pins into their carved wooden box. Her shoulder blades hunched back and forth beneath her gown.

"Your father is very happy. He's counting on a grandson." Words from the face that could not be seen. Powder showed in synthetic layers under the white lights. She had a thin speckled bosom.

"I'm glad." An indecisive tone.

The generaless took some flowers from an old green vase,
walked to the daughter on the bed, and tucked the blossoms in
the crook of her arm. Emily lay there, young and round, the
flowers on her arc-lamp burned shoulders, smiling her prettiest
reward, a tumble-stomach little doll. It spoke, "Good night,
Mummy."

"Yes, yes, my dear. Sleep well." And the door closed on
the dangling mother. A second more and Emily crouched near
the door, flowers hanging from her fist:

"Now you can *go*. You can *go*." She slapped the flowers
against the door and dropped them all. She did an odd dance,
smacking from side to side on solid feet across the rug. She got
back into bed and was sorry.

Again she was up, putting out the lights.

The lack of genes, the lack of a ganglion, the lack of a seed;
the moon was not right, or the baby was dropped, or the chem-
ist was wrong, or the teacher untaught, or the night air bad, or
the witch was around, but something concocted these dis-
creditable results; something gave the little woman a bad temper, made her lonely and kept her eyes open in the darkness.

Emily watched the shadows on the ceiling, thought of a
highwayman glittering out on the night road. She dozed and
woke again.

Beady encountered the mastiff in front of Henry's door.
"Go away," she said. It slunk off. Softly she called his name.
No answer. She walked all the way down to the game room.
The curtains flopped. She tried the upstairs sittingroom. She
walked faster. She thought she saw a shadow and ran from
it. A spiral of cigarette smoke. An owl's eye. She followed
the pebbles; they did not lead to Henry. Darkness. She
stumbled over a stockinged leg. "Henry?" No answer. She
raced down again to face the other incarnate three: "He's
gone!" Out of breath. The two men hunched forward and the
generaless spoke quickly:

"Who?"

"Henry. I can't find him anywhere."

"He's probably out getting a little air, taking a walk. Don't worry, we'll find him tomorrow."

The generaless spoke again, "I wouldn't say anything to Emily."

Beady squatted in a rank position on the floor. She worried.

Emily spoke for herself, "Henry? Henry? Now where can he be?" She rolled over.

1:30 *A.M. Emily's dream.*

She was a little girl, nine years old, walking through the forest.

Expositor: Where are you going, little girl?

Emily: I'm going to grandmother's funeral.

Expositor: And what will you do there?

Emily: I'll say goodbye.

The archetypes stood around the room in black and white, the moon shone through the window, red trees surrounded the house. Father was a stern man with shiny insignia on his shoulders, and mother looked as if she would cry. The organ was caroling very softly.

Expositor: You have come a long way.

Emily: Yes. But now I am here to see grandmother. She is a very lovely lady. I would like to give her a kiss.

The little girl crept up to the bier, pushing her way through gardens of flowers. She held one of the cool hands as the minister's sonorous voice began the farewell. All of the people lost their names in tribute to beautiful grandmother. All of their quiet breaths together seemed like the breathing of the sleeping woman. She waxed and waned. I leave all my children.

Then a little bell tinkled and everyone began to put on their hats.

Expositor: She is gone. It is time for you to leave too.

Emily: No. Please let me stay, please. I don't want to go away.

A voice spoke to them all: "*We are mourned only by children.*"

Emily began to cry: Please, grandma, don't go away.

Expositor: You are almost a live thing. Come.

He picked her up and carried her outside into the quiet vale.
She felt very cold fingers against her own. Then the Expositor's face, under his black mantle, began to resemble the woman's face that had slept on the satin pillow. The voice was the wind over the organ reeds.

Expositor: You must come with me.

The face grew drawn and plastic; the eyes closed.

Emily awoke and listened for sounds in the darkness, in the vale.

The generaless walked through a maze of lights, glancing from bulbs to china figurines. The light careened in pinks, grays, and brilliant white from window panes, brass rails, whorled glass and candleholders. She carried a little tomcat at her breast, and moved through the islands of festivities to try to find the creature milk.

The adventuress in green, on the monster's back, thought she was riding a dromedary over the sand. Hand to forehead she urged her beast, and scanned the horizon for a sheik. . .

Dr. Smith had cornered the ungracious daughter, who was sleepy but frightened. He was talking of sutures and instruments, and an oval abdomen.

The Burgesses were drinking beer, remarkably content.

Mr. and Mrs. Young looked at photographs.

Mrs. Wheeling Rice slept soundly on the sofa, her gown undone.

They carried bamboo sticks and cellophane to build their nests.

The generaless walked, the cat buried its head at her breast. Suddenly Noel jumped at her; he stood in her path, his boy's face beaming up, his head wagging. He looked straight at the cat who poked at the low-cut gown.

"That's all right," said Noel to the cat, "you won't get anything," and he ran on his way. The generaless couldn't, how awful, speak. The rain came down harder.

THE BACHELORS

7

Hatless Henry flagged the bus. Its yellow eyes bore down in the mist with steaming silhouettes behind the smoked glass. The silhouettes were clothed in blue and gray. No one talked to the driver. A few looked up at the new passenger; he smiled and reached to the cash box.

"Look at da babe in da corner."

"Look at da babe."

"Look at *dat* babe."

A young woman holding a wet bundle sat in the corner. Her eyes were shaded by a little black hat, a hat above the pointed skull of a Jezebel.

Henry dropped his coin into the box and braced himself against the steel stanchions. He heard the wheels churning the mud. He looked in the direction of the woman with the little hat. For a moment, she looked like Emily, then he looked away.

Only the splash of water on the radiator, the faint odor of gasoline, a carousel of advertisements up near the roof in the shadows, and the bus stopped. The folding doors banged, the rain sang. Then the tires rolled, blurred lights coasted by and they moved again, with the sudden sensation of wet feet. Henry jingled the change in his pocket and stared at his own reflection in the glass, difficult to recognize amid the others. When he was a little boy he went to the ugly town of Ghent, to see the fat man at the fair, and all the funny animals there. He looked back again at the woman with the black hat.

Emily?

He almost wanted to go and speak to her, to sit and chat. A red glow in the sky ahead, a pleasure dome, drifted off to the left and was lost like a cloud. He looked at the neck that protruded up before him; it was large, it was bulky, it was shaven. Scraps of paper and tiny stones clung to his shoes. No smoking. He was taking himself for a ride. Once he met the hostile eyes of the driver in the streaked mirror over the wheel and they became enemies with the whine and sigh, whine and sigh of the engine between them. Cockeyed roadmarks hurried past.

"The Saviour is coming. Do you see Him?"

"Marsh's for Fine Funerals."

"Come and see our Wedding Rings."

The bus swerved around a curve and rain beat on the windward side. Henry noticed her head nodding, the black hat falling lower and lower. Before he could go back to her, he was blocked by unanimated talking faces, gathering all around him. Again he looked out of the window. She slept.

Morning. Henry rang the doorbell, straightened his spotted cravat, and looked at the shaded windows. The sun was just behind the gabled rooftops and he could hear the sea still pounding down on the beach and around the wharf, could hear the cries of a few scattered gulls. He smelled the salt air and his eyes moved back and forth following the movements of a rusted inn lamp swinging in the wind. He looked closer at the card over the bell-buzzer, faded by rain: "Mrs. Mahoney. Rooms." He rang again. He heard the clatter of broken glass, the cry of a baby above the wind, and the rattling of an automobile starting down at the end of the street. Then he heard the padding of slippers on the other side of the door and the scratching of a key.

Madame Mahoney opened the door and she clutched at her gown as the wind swirled around her ankles. She faced a man in a wrinkled gray suit with thinning light hair and rimless spectacles. She herself was a demure-looking lady, extremely short and extremely thin. Her gown was frilled and had a collar that ruffled high about her throat. Her gray hair was up, hooked and held together with stays, pins, pieces of paper, and other foreign matter. She wore a dominant heavy perfume and small gold earrings that pierced the lobes of her ears. She was prim and pretty, delicate and old, and had a straightforward masculine voice. She never blinked. She never drank tea without smoking a cigarette and only smoked during teatime. Madame Mahoney was young in heart but she had, in the past, known the pains and seen the midwife many times. Now she looked the effort.

Henry smiled at the mannikin: "Good morning, I was wondering if you had a room to let."

"Please come in." Utter graciousness.

The door closed to. The hallway was dark.

"I've only one room. It's rather small. I don't know." Her a's were very broad, her lips tight and darkly painted.

"Oh, anything will do. I'm not particular. I really would just appreciate a place to sleep. Of course I'll pay you something now. . ."

"Well," she paused, "I suppose I'll be able to accommodate you." She crumbled the bill up into a ball and carried it in her fist.

"Would you like a bit of tea before we go up to your room?"

"No. No, I think I'd like to go right up if you don't mind."

They climbed two carpeted flights of stairs. Waste baskets were toppled over in the hall, an old fur coat was draped across the bannister, cushions were scattered on the floors, dim lights burned overhead. Pieces of newspaper were stuffed in the chinks around the windows. At one place the carpeting left off to give way to linoleum only to commence again, a more ragged, faded-looking piece of cloth. A broken pot was lying in one dark corner. At the top of the second flight of stairs they came to a bare wooden-runged ladder, straight up into the blackness, high in the old provincial house. Madame Mahoney went first, her silver slippers disappearing into the inverted pit. Henry got a splinter in his hand. At the top of the ladder there was a low door, opening into Henry's tower room where a single window looked across the main street and out to sea. The sun had never gotten any higher than the rooftops before it had been lost in descending storm-clouds. The sea was turning rough and black. Extra wads of paper were considerately crammed in the turret windows as they were up so high, but still the window shade was torn and it flapped. The shingles fluttered on the roof, tree branches brushed against the window.

"I think this will be comfortable," said the Madame. "It's very private, you know." In a single moment she grabbed the broom, swept, and dropped it back again into the corner of the bridal chamber.

"It will do very well." Henry smiled. He was beginning to wish she would go.

"If there's anything I can get you, just you come out and call. I'll come up, Mr. er. . ."

"Van." Henry said the word and nothing more. The old woman took a handkerchief from her sleeve and blew loudly, a foreign sound, a cry, in the room that smelled and felt like the inside of a clock.

The sounds of a bell were carried to them by the wind, nine mournful notes that whirled and fell.

"I must go down now and finish my tea, Mr. Van."

"Of course." She slammed the door in her wake.

Henry draped the cravat over the back of the single chair and stood in the middle of the clock. It contained a bed, a wooden table covered with cheesecloth, the broom, a gaunt chest-of-drawers and a closet with a skeleton in it. He took off his shirt, then his shoes; Susannah entered the icy waters. He stood by the window watching the sea when his eye was caught by a movement in the street below; a woman was entering a low building holding a small black hat from the wind and carrying a bundle of fruit—she, a bartered, mythical bride, vaporous Emily. It was a slanting sea-green house with a steep-pitched roof, and she went in through the back door. Henry pulled the blind and flung his body on the bed. He pulled the lumpy quilt up over his head, brought his knees up to his stomach and fell asleep.

Madame Mahoney sat enthroned in the kitchen, smoke curling from her nostrils, sipping her tea with Millie, the midwife, to her left.

"He's a rawther interesting man," the Madame said. "It appears to me as he's suffered some sort of catastrophe. I think he's probably lost his wife."

"Poor man," the midwife said.

"He's got soft gray eyes, I couldn't help noticing."

"Poor man."

"A very quiet person with a heart of gold, I 'magine. But I think he is a gentleman who takes his due, I rawther like him."

"Poor man."

"Millie, I'll have some more tea, if you please."

"Yes, mum."

The fire sputtered, steam on the iron, old paper and coals. The smells of beads, cloth, peppermint, cinnamon and seashells filled the room. The wind grew stronger. The two old ladies talked.

The storm lashed the piers, pitched crawling sea-life to the shore, covered the nets with brine, and smothered, breath after breath, the planks in foam. Aged bull-shouldered men smoked their pipes in spiced, aged rooms throughout the town. The storm hurled itself on old brick chimneys and sent the shingles flying.

"Another toddy, Jim."

"Aye, aye, Capt'n."

"And my dear," sewing lace, "you should have seen the look on that man's face."

The smell of burning logs.

The groan of old stuffed rockers.

A garden gate banged its head.

The terrible crescendo of the sea, the gigantic breakers rocked old dead hulls.

Clustered around the oil lamps, "Another, Jim."

Storm clouds and rain between the paintless houses, and they mended a little rip or sewed a button.

The howling wind.

Henry awoke at one in the afternoon in darkness and to the crash of thunder. The scent of marshland flowers was in the air and he felt an exhilaration—in the pitch of love and in the face of death. The weeds beat around the bottom of the house, doves cowered in the belfry of the church. Madame Mahoney pulled taffy, Millie stole a sip of gin. There was smiling all around and the wind smashed the ominous and joyous word of storm into every room. Henry shivered and fumbled about inside the gray clock. He washed himself in cold water in the sink off the hallway where the ladder was. He scrubbed until his skin was red, he rinsed his mouth many times. Back in the room he spent an endless and pleasurable time carefully tying the cravat, pasting his hair down with the flat of his hand, picking pieces of lint from his trousers, and trying to polish his muddy shoes. The air grew darker, a crash of thunder, until the day was gone. He went to the window and let the shade up; it stuck, got out of hand, went up with a bang and rolled angrily for a moment. Excitement. He was not sure whether Emily was across the street or not. He peered through the wet glass, go out, go out to play he thought, and his forehead touched the cold surface. Then he saw the lighted window. She sat looking out, still wearing the little black hat, a phantom bride-elect. She simply sat motionless watching the rain. Henry felt that the time was fast approaching when his eyes would fasten onto her and hold, when he would speak. The life-giving color of the sea turned deeper and spray flew high from the slimy rocks. One more look at her in the window, her hands awaiting the calla lilies, and he went downstairs. He missed a rung in his impatience and nearly fell. He straightened the cravat, more stairs, and he heard the noise of the wind.

He joined the ladies at their festive board.

"Do have some marmalade on your toast, Mr. Van."

"Thank you. I believe I might." Madame ladled a dripping orange spoon of jam onto his gold-rimmed plate.

"I made this jam myself, you know. Have you got a light?"

"What?" Henry looked up. Sure enough, a cigarette. "Oh, of course." He held the match, a puff of smoke.

Millie poured the tea, hot and dark. The house shook, the drab little chintz curtains hung by the kitchen windows cascading in water. The three old people, with the unpleasant attributes of youth, all smiled, sharing an imagined secret in the heart of the storm. These cronies with the beaming eyes reminded Henry of two other mothers.

"Here's to you, Madame Mahoney, Millie."

"And to you, dear boy," in chorus, this elated tribunal. They drank together. Since their first meeting, Madame had pinned a few violets to her gown and now they were crumpled.

"This is one of the happiest days of my life," said Henry. His little trip, the house, the tea, charming old women, and the beautiful storm, the dame across the street, they showered him with gifts. He inhaled deeply.

"We're so happy for you; we know you'll have a pleasant stay here."

"Thank you," he pushed back his chair, "it's time I went to pay my call."

"Try to get home for supper and have a good time!"

"Surely."

The two women grinned after his retreating blushing form. He stepped out into the rain and the light went out of the window across the street.

He walked toward her house.

8

Revelry fluctuated all night long; a single laugh would ring out; someone would become temporarily excited, and so stir the whole party awake again. Then silence, water running, the sound of "Sleepytime Gal," "The Lambeth Walk," "That's My Baby," the sound of flesh, oh, get out, and back to silence, with the curtain of rain. They were celebrating, though they never knew it, of course, while Henry wandered far and Emily stayed alone. She managed to sleep through the last hours of the night. The general, parson, Beady, and generaless never went to bed at all, but hung dizzily and doggedly on to the end of the celebration, dodging rainbow streamers and tipping drinks, bearing up under toasts.

"Here's to old Vannie, wherever his happiness is. . ."

"To the couple, for a nice life in a cave, ha, ha. . ."

"May the old hunter bring home lots of bison. . ."

"That means friends to drink," someone added.

"Soris, wake up now," a violent shake.

"Here's to the lord of the castle, may he stick to one queenie. . ."

"I guess he *will*," a tense squeak, choking with laughter.

The ungracious daughter thought to take herself apart, away from the completely uninteresting life, hot, sticky, muggy with rain, and absolutely worthless people who brought the beer to tap, to foam, so flat.

They lost the last redeeming grace of manners, stifled irritating pygmies, who tried to make and make, and coughed no longer behind their hands but coughed. In the darkness they picked carloads of roses, brought them in for sweetheart's decoration, strewed them about, and never noticed them again.

A plaster nymph teetered on a table, fell, and shattered wildly on the floor. The head rolled under the piano legs.

"Hurrah, hurrah, hurrah. . ."

They were a little worse than intolerant of each other; they minimized all but themselves; everything was seen in a minor light through minor eyes. They moved in and out to water.

Drunken morning arose from a drunken night.

"Toast and coffee, dear. Wake up," the adventuress in green stood by Emily's bed, tray in hand, not too much the worse for her long night.

"Come on, darling, have breakfast."

Emily sat bolt upright. She smiled.

"Oh, thank you. How good you are."

"Think nothing of it, darling. But take the tray so I can have coffee too."

They fussed, straightening the tray. Thin wisps of steam arose from the coffee cups. Emily began to eat, quickly, a crisp piece of toast.

"I'm ashamed of myself for leaving the party last night. I was just worn out." Mouth full of toast, crumbs on the pink sheets.

"Why, that's all right, dear. We didn't even miss you." A plum between two fingers and dark lips moist.

Emily sipped her coffee in rapid thimblesful. The whole world seemed brighter somehow.

"What's going on this morning?" she asked.

"Not a damn thing now. Most of them are still half dead. . ." She pulled her skirt up to scrutinize a run, poked at it with a broken fingernail, holding the coffee cup in the other hand.

Gaylor Basistini held his ringing head down in the darkness under the cellar stairs.

The ungracious daughter slept beneath her mother's wing.

The monster from South America was cold.

One of the Burgesses had begun to weep.

Dr. Smith was telling a story.

The fat gentleman was fast asleep.

A bathroom window was open and rain covered the floor.

"Some more coffee, darling?" The adventuress held the little pot.

"Thank you. My, what a beautiful morning." Emily's head kept pointing back and forth from one sunny corner of the blue room to another, from the toy chest to the book of paper dolls, to the radio, to the corset on the chair, to the bar of cream jars. Her eyes lit up, "It *is* a nice morning. Have you seen Henry?"

"Who?" A pause. "Oh, Vanny. He went out for a walk last night, a long one. He's still gone." The maid of honor-elect went back to her coffee. Then: "He's pretty cute. But I never saw a man so completely uninterested. I was rather surprised."

"What do you mean?" The jaw stopped working. The adventuress raised her eyes.

"Why, darling, don't you understand me? I just mean that he wasn't attracted to me. That's all." Another bite.

Emily looked hurt. She picked at the crusts left on the saucer. It would have been nicer if Henry had been a trifle unfaithful.

"He'll probably come back soon. But he's never done this

before. Oh, well, I won't worry." She looked up brightly. "Today we'll have fun."

"Sure, dear." The adventuress looked at that cracked nail. "By the way," she said, "have you got any shorts? I'm supposed to play tennis with that character from South America, and I haven't got a thing to wear."

"Certainly, I have; I'll get them for you."

"Of course, they'll be a little large for me, but they'll probably be all the more appealing. Don't bother now, I'll be back for them. Must go. . ."

"Thanks you for the breakfast. . ." but the door had already closed.

Emily sank back on the pillows. Then quickly up again, and her body down over the edge of the bed to reach for a magazine hidden under it. When she settled back with a sigh she looked at the cover—a man was wearing a golden loin cloth, slim girdle, and a woman a green. She sighed again.

Joe Ottoe, a guest who had last been seen at the dinner table and who had been busy the whole night out in the summer house, even in the rain, now walked up and down the living room between the prostrate forms.

"Sma't piples," he kept repeating, "sma't piples," shaking his head. A short cigarette. He wore a wrinkled bright green tie. "Sma't piples." His wife was beginning the day out in the kitchen, trying to make a cool drink badly needed.

Emily, having passed the cover, flipped the pages quickly. "Oh, why doesn't he come back," she thought. Irritated. Oh, that beautiful morning, streaming with gold.

Tired of the magazine, anxious to get up but much too comfortable to move, she relaxed and gave herself over to the sun; consciously she rested each muscle, felt herself pressing into the warm sheets. It was so pleasant, so really nice to be alone. What a nice luxury. Nothing could be wrong this morning. She could hear the stamping of a horse's hoof, the steady pulling of a rake. Ducks fluttered their wings on the pond, fat yellow bills; throw them crumbs. Now if she got up, she could wear that pretty white dress. Yes, she would in a minute. A bluebottle fly buzzed, then lumbered off. She pressed her cheek against the pillow. Oh dear, sometimes things were just too much to think about, but then everything changed, somebody said something nice, you could give them a present, come for tea, dear. A small crib, she thought, with rattles and counting beads. Indeed, it would be a beautiful baby. A beautiful day with water dripping on the small pointed leaves.

How comfortable. How very comfortable.

She closed her eyes, opened them and heard the harlequins arguing downstairs. Quickly she jumped out of bed and barefooted, hopped to the bathroom door.

Gaylor Basistini struggled up the stairs.

The adventuress and South American linked arms and stood in a corner to discuss their coming game.

Flowers turned a delicate purple.

Joe Ottoe's young son had been snared by Sir Dewitt-Jones. Dewitt-Jones was saying. "We sort of collect young boys. We lost two sons of our own, so we like to get to know you young fellows." The young son blinked.

Mr. Bird was out for a morning walk.

Someone struck up a tune on the mandolin.

"Oh dear," said Emily standing at the head of the stairs, "oh dear, this *is* going to be a good day." Her stomach was getting a little rounder, she thought.

"Say dearie, what do you say you and I go out in the moonlight. . ." A recumbent figure in the dark hall.

Emily didn't notice what he said and continued down the stairs. They had put too much starch in her dress again. She heard the radio, very, very soft harp music. A beginning day.

9

The wind shot down the main street, oscillating, shimmering from side to side, pulling with its giant tail armfuls of driving rain from the doldrums; it broke off in tangents to be drawn into a chimney flu, to swirl madly, trapped in a dead end, or to fly swiftly and vertically up the crevice between two houses, to be spent in the still aimless air high above. The main blow beat its way down the narrow street, tearing leaves from trees and rattling windows, smashed between two warehouses and jumped out to sea, tearing frantically at the waves. The rain was almost impenetrable; it beat like nail heads on the rotting wood, and covered cobblestones with a running slime.

Henry lost his nerve. Pummeled he stood heaving to and fro, floundering, flapping wildly, in the middle of the street before her house. His hands shifted and beat the air, thrusting outward to clutch at lost supports, to maintain a precarious balance; he hung by the good graces of the wind. He laughed and felt himself shoving off at last, but he simply couldn't go to the house.

The door opened and she came out and walked easily into the storm. For a moment she was but thirty feet from him. Miraculously the black hat stayed in place. He could almost see the features of the face, oh, Emily, yes, yes, the howling wind, the shadowed mouth open to gasp for air behind that wind, the eyes covered by a constant veil, the hair beating upon the open throat. Fish were being hammered against the logs, clouds collided with mountains of water, the fishing nets tore loose, and wandering, flying, flung themselves on teak-wood ribs, sky, and rocks.

For one brief moment his hope and desire came together, to walk up to her, hold her, speak to her, hold the blowing hair. The taste of salt was on his lips. Then he turned and was carried off down the street. Once he turned back and saw that she was following.

This was his gigantic hold, the town of water. He noticed each blurred metallic color or lack of color, each gray and black, each wet shadow, salt and iron of the sea and blood. Drawn to her, he fled from her, happier in each dolphin-winged spasm, careening along with pillaging, battling black birds. To catch fish. To catch grain. To shed the strengthening water. He bent his body and ran disjointedly for cover. The inn door. Pieces of driftwood were pounding on the shore; a deep loud voice from the doldrums. Sailors from Madagascar,

ships from the Caribbean, the Puritan, iron hulks from Liver-
pool, plunging their crimson sails and tarred lines through the
surf, they hovered in the harbor. No sun, no moon, only hurl-
ing starfish and fine foam, water hauling in the wizened lives.

Leather rots; rubber comes alive; the beach erodes; the fun-
gus grows; the sound of the wailing bell. And always that
barely remembered woman behind him, the faint flush of youth
and scrubbed cheeks.

The wind pulled the door from his hands and slammed it
shut. Conversation died. He stood facing the fire, trying to collect his excitement, to hold his spirit down here in the *Sea
Horse*, a timeless inn. Wooden tables and benches were worn
smooth and white and around them were massive red flickering
faces.

"How d'ya do. A rum for the gentleman, Jim."

He sat down next to the big capt'n with the silver mug. The
heat of the fire curled round his ankles. The ship's bell tolled
five bells; it was dark outside.

There were no women at the inn. Absence of long hair, pale
skin, tapering legs, and Piccadilly voices; no childish heads in
dusting caps, no Eve dressed in leaves or slinking in spangles,
no perfume, nothing for the bees to buzz about.

Quite the contrary, it was a place of stags. Fat men had their
vests unbuttoned, gray wrinkled shirttails crumpled out from
the tight waistlines, toothless or even gumless, jowls were
stained with the iodine tint of nicotine. A few of the very old
wore pairs of small, round, gold eyeglasses; they constantly
squinted and wiped their heavy faces with their hands. The
masculine chamber, with spittle, beef and beer, the roaring fire,
stench of drying cloth, the pungent odor of burnt-out pipes,
and a boar's head on the wall, moth-eaten. Here models of ships
were hung in dirty bottles, a keg of ale with a brass spigot was
green, the paintings of fish and fisherman hung crooked in the
shadows. Coat tails high, backs to the flames, in forgotten
rough voices the old bucks grumbled. Stags. Out of the storm.

Stags. The work, stuck in Henry's mind. Men, gathered con-
genially to talk, to smoke, fat hands holding the claws of chairs,

grew old; and plans, experiences, masters, clustered together now for protection. And one was an old black dog, scratching, to listen to the talking. Clustered together. Stags. Henry noticed the curtains drawn over the windows. The fire crackled, a log slipped down and he tasted the odor of smoke.

Gaylor had thrown a party for him the night before his wedding. Giant candelabra, evening dress, thin cigarettes, leaders of the western world, they came to a private dining room in a large hotel. Slender glasses, medals on black lapels, discreet waiters and they told their jokes. "That was a good one. Hear! Hear!" Red beef, cut with a sword-like carving knife for the fops, grew cold. Men together only for the show.

"Here's to Henry as he starts out on the sea."

"We'll drink to that!" Dinner jackets open, cigars, they tried to be informal with bald heads and tales of espionage. Henry had felt rather shy, Gaylor was very happy, claret, white wine, brandy, stories of first nights, the hunting of the virgin, expensive and false, glittering.

"To the master, may he rule with an iron fist."

Loud laughter.

"Beat her if you have to, Henry," more laughter.

Hand-shaking. Pomp. Good fellow.

He had felt terrible the next day and couldn't remember very much but millions on millions of lights.

"But," thought Henry, "this is my stag party." An old man fell to snoring. It was the party of a few healthy chuckles and grunted cackles. In the silence these oldsters seemed to say, "Be of good cheer, be of good cheer, lad, your wedding night is still to come." It was all for him, the old granddads were giving him this, a stag party. Survivors of the sea, a little group of Ulysses' men with albatrosses hung round their necks. Henry felt as if the bouquet and sword were in his hand. He, the man with the returned spirit, would find her waiting, dressed in rose, a simple rosary around her throat.

The big man with the silver mug took another drink.

"C'mon, lad, drink up."

Henry gulped the hot liquor. "Thanks," he said.

The rain came down harder, but the wind was letting up. Rain coming mournfully down. A stag party. Another drink. Happiness.

Suddenly the door flew open with a gust of rain. A little white, frightened, wet face, partly hidden under a large sou'wester, poked in.

"Drowned," it yelled.

"Drowned," in a high voice above the sound of the rain.

"Drowned. A girl is drowned." The head bobbed out of sight and scurried away in the rain. There was an unhurried rustling of oilskins. Girls might have been pinning flowers in their hair for all the noise they made. Rubber boots were heavily pulled over woolen feet, snaps were fastened by clumsy fingers and hats pulled down and tied by old bearded sailors dressed in black.

Another head popped in, excited:

"C'mon, down by the pier. Girl dead." He ran off. The door had been left open and puddles of rainwater were forming on the floor. The stag party for the groom-to-be was robed with black, but none of them seemed bereaved. A last large tumbler of rum, or blowing the foam off beer, slowly with pale blue eyes over the mugs. Then they filed out of the door. Henry turned up his collar and, flanked by stoop-shouldered figures, trudged out into the rain.

The wind had completely died, an ode, but it was still dark with heavy clouds. They moved toward the shore, their boots sloshing in the steady drizzle. He put his hands in his pockets. He could smell the sea animals and fish, strong wood and tar and noticed, for the first time, that all the shades were drawn in the gray houses. One or two windows showed a soft yellow from a hidden lantern. The sea was still running high. They walked slowly, their motion obscured by the flapping skins.

One by one they climbed down the rusted iron rungs of a ladder on the pier. It was darker below, a thin stretch of shore around the massive pilings, then the earth was lost into the water. A dark underground world, and here the smell was overpowering; dead marine life, carbuncles, blue jellyfish in pools, mounds and mats of congested seaweed, huge silver fins and dark green tongues, transparent bulbous forms, soft egg-like stones, thick black-blue devil crawling grass, and ancient pieces of encrusted iron. Shivering species and dead bones. A few dim lanterns cast uncanny shadows and pierced back into the inkiness beneath the soaked pier. Staunch, tilted piling, wrapped in gray, jagged and rough. Henry ripped his trousers on the vertical ladder.

A small knot of black ghosts stood in the middle of the pit of sea; water drizzled down their backs. A basket stretcher was at their feet. Coils of new rope, stiff hemp, fish eyes left from bait. A sweet-sour stench.

"Who is she?"

"I dunno. Just got into town."

"Must have been out on the end of the pier. Probably slipped and got washed back under here. Gimme a hand."

The figures bent, hands running with water. Soaked, mushy cloth, tangled hair. An axe blade glittered dully by lantern light. A shuffling of feet in the rubbery weeds. Someone puffed on a cigarette, an acid smell.

"Do ya think she jumped in?"

"I dunno. Mebe. Mebe got caught in a wave."

Hands touched a slippery surface, then got a better hold. Smell of fish.

Her black hat was caught under her head. The body was half twisted around one of the piles. She was put into the stretcher and rope was laced, criss-cross, up the front like a jacket. The face was pushed down under an arm. Pounding of the surf. They began to pull the ropes from up on the pier.

Henry stood ankle deep in water. The rain blurred his glasses until he could hardly see; his nostrils stung. He was wet through. Gulls circled overhead and cawed unmercifully. Black shiny arms and burned hands labored with the burden and with the ropes, guiding and hauling it up. He was calm; he had the utmost capacity for calmness. The storm was a whimper. A long flat shoal stretched out under the water. He passed two rescuers.

"Seems someone always is caught in these storms."

A nod. "My missus jumps to them shutters mighty quick. Don't even want me t'get outa doors. *Like* a good blow m'self. I been wrecked twice a'fore. No more sailin'."

"I can still see that face down in the weeds, all white. Ya know, it's a funny thing, for such a sprite of a girl she shore weighed a plenty, jus' made o' lead, could hardly lift 'er. A dead weight. . ."

The conversation was lost. Henry thought he would go back home. First to the room and then home. It was his own decision; he would go home.

He opened the door of Madame Mahoney's establishment. The Madame herself greeted him with a flourish.

"We've been waiting," she said. "Do come for some tea." Her pointed eyes were inquisitive, the face zebra-striped with shadows.

"I'm afraid I'm in a hurry, Madame Mahoney. And I must leave now."

"So soon? Oh dear." Her tone was coaxing. They heard Millie sweeping up pieces of eight and glass in the kitchen.

"Yes. I must go." He started up the stairs. "I have biscuits," she said, but it was hopeless. If you want to try my wares, follow me. She started for the back of the house. On an impulse she wheeled around, as if in spite; her voice was vehement, "there's someone up there to *see* you." But he didn't hear.

He climbed higher and higher, could only faintly hear the rain. It would be nice to get home. The little town was more tranquil and more desolate than ever. Clip, clip, clip, of scissors, the brushing of a broom.

The parson sat waiting, stiffbacked and with a scowl on his face. He held his hat in his lap.

"Hello, Father, what a pleasant surprise."

"I've come to take you back, Henry."

"Yes, sir." There was nothing he could do.

Together they left. It was dark. Mile after mile they drove, uneven trees and lighted houses slipping by. The headlights spotted enormous cows, then only the black edge of the road. Sweet smell, sour smell, blown into the darkness. Henry remembered long vague journeys, when as a child he had slept curled on the back seat, sleeping and dreaming, half awake, never knowing where they had come from or where they were going. The gentle rocking of the carriage, not to know either direction. He closed his eyes and saw myriads of color. The parson dozed, still straight backed. The chauffeur drove at a steady pace, a figure in purple livery. The flowers they passed were dead. The father relaxed in his armor of years, the lover relaxed in his armor. A thick pond, gone. He saw the stars, then looked out again into the vista of the headlights. Everything was moving, even sleep. Moving sleep. He smelled the dust of the upholstery, the taste of tar, the night air. Troubadour, troubadour, playing his guitar to a lady love, speeding tires. He slumped off, awoke with a start, then settled again. No people. No barriers. No people. A lonely bird.

When they drove up the long driveway and neared the brightly lit house, Henry could hear the loud noise of a progressing party. He was bewildered, for they were there, the voices and the dancing feet.

They walked up the front steps out of the darkness towards the monstrous pale reflection.

THE WEDDING

10

Standing before the mirror in her mended shift, the collier's wife could hear the terrible noise below. Horns clattered in the cold smoky air and streamers of orange paper flew past the window. A boy, muffled up to his chin in a flannel bandage, beat upon a kettle with a stick, crying "macaroons, macaroons." Her fingers worked quickly, coiling the single braid of hair that fell to the floor. She heard the sharp cries of another boy stuck in the chimney who struggled downwards inside the wall, showering soot before him. Large encrusted ladles lay on the hearth. A row of thicksoled boots by the bedroom wall was scraped and bright with water and soap. Her hair was finally wound, left half undone, when she spied a little pot of idiot pennies hidden in the unwashed linen in the low-boy. The coppers were black and burned, toppled over under bundles of cloth. A turtle slowly moved his arms in a porcelain dish. Long needles were lightly left in the bundles of cloth, and bitten-off lengths of colored thread were in the eyes. So skillful was she, her fingers were never pricked as they rummaged beneath the needles and cloth, ribbons and pins, to find a comb, or brush, or coin. She could see the eyes of the needles in the dark and loved the bright points. The collier himself was often stuck. There were needles in the shoulders of his coats, in the rug, on the curtains, and in the drying socks.

Quickly she put the coins in her apron pocket, wrapped an odd shawl over the shift, listened for a moment to hear the short breathing of the chimney sweep, and ran into the other room where the fire burned. A wrinkled dress was hung to dry before the open window; pieces of rag covered the floor and in the corner was the black iron bust, a plumed hat on the neck. The tumult grew worse as children wrestled beneath the feet of men with hollow laughing eyes, and drivers cracked their whips above the village crowd. "Ah, lovely, this is surely a fine day. C'mon now, dearie, let's you and I just take a walk." The collier's wife hummed to herself. Her arm was scarred with a triangular iron burn; her shawl was a livid red. Suddenly she scooped all the pieces of cloth from the floor and dropped them into a tub by the hearth, and the dirt came to the surface of the boiling water. Steam filled the woolen-and-clove scented room. She stooped to buckle her shoe, she smelled the odor of evergreens, wine, and morning rain that came in around the edges of the hanging dress. Shingles on the steep roofs outside the window were wet and bright and one after another they appeared crooked in the morning sun.

Children dragged large green limbs through the streets, and the cold bark of the forest scraped on the cobblestones. Frost clung to crumbling doorways and red ribbons were hung to the tavern signs. The collier's wife sang louder.

This was the day when the end of May joined the beginning of December. Sleigh runners cut through trembling grass, fires burned in the white streets and the Maypole dancers of early spring were carolers under lantern light. "Dearie, I traveled a bed and bairn," sang the wife and put last minute bent pins into the loosening shawl. The crowd yelled louder, and the fair, that had come with its bright tents and dashing horses, dubbed every one of them a clown. She banked the fire, listened for a moment to the ringing bells and screaming blackbirds, and having collected her measure, beaver satchel and long scissors, she fluffed her hair once and went out to the landing and down the stairs. The black iron bust grew larger as the sun rose. She pushed the boy off the bottom step and joined the crowd. A processional of children marched by in the street, their faces painted black, calling, in their high sharp voices, the banns.

Too-la-la, too-la-la went the organ at the fair. A prize porker grunted behind mud-spattered beards and stared out at the passing feet with murderous red eyes. Walking with the furry satchel held in both hands, the collier's wife muttered, "Come now, don't you push me," "Well, you're a big fellar," "Now that's a sweet bonnet for such a nice day." The old woman was carried along, past the post where they had hung the thieving man, past apples soaked in honey, and past the lane where couples walked arm in arm.

Henry was fitted for only one pair of trousers at the tailor's shop. He had been in the shop many times before with the parson and the parson's friends, but never to have his own clothes made. And now he found himself between the fitting and the finish, with a high price placed on his end. Giant silver shears lay gaping on the long counter. Through the broad dusty windows he could see the bobbing caps, the trailing skirts. An old woman with a big satchel hurrying by, and little

boys with bundles of newspapers going in and out of the building across the street. He could feel the probing fingers of the
head fitter, the dissatisfied white fingers with the long dangling
tape measure. He concentrated on the window, tried not to
move. An old gentleman sat asleep in a gilded chair, asleep with
gout, fat with pain, his heavy arms hanging towards the floor.
A few thin flies buzzed up near the ceiling. Young men in
black aprons, hair parted in the middle, idled about the rear
of the shop, laughing, smoked rolled cigarettes, started and
stopped the sewing machines, and looked out of the rear
window at row upon row of flapping sheets. Henry tried to
withdraw from the wretched precise fingers, felt his mouth go
dry. Over and over the tailor wrote on his little pad, a laugh
from the black-eyed men in the back. It was necessary to order
the flowers. And since she didn't like that ring, he'd have
to go after another. Spindle upon spindle of colorless cloth
waited to unroll about majesty's back, or drape the forms in
frozen biers. The fingers were insect's wings in the crotch of
his trousers, hummingbird wings in the crotch of a young tree.
He looked down upon the bald head of the kneeling tailor
and then out into the street. It was cold and it was bright. He
saw the old woman pass in front of the window again. He
smelled the odor of fine clothes.

"A little bit tight, sir?"

"No, no, Alfred, that's all right."

The sun was suddenly blocked in the door. The general
entered.

"Morning, Henry."

"Sir." Henry smiled.

"And are you doing well by my future son-in-law, Alfred?
I trust nothing exorbitant."

"Oh, I'm doing well, sir, well indeed." Alfred, sitting on the
floor, his thin knees resting against the little podium where
Henry stood, grinned up at the reddening face.

"That's all right, Alfred," said Henry, "please just hurry
up." The little tailor jumped to his feet. A piece of thumbnail

chalk in hand, he scribbled hieroglyphics about the trouser seat.

"There you are, and a fine specimen it is." He beamed.

The general stood patiently by in his old khakis while groups of carolers passed the window leading fighting cocks on strings. The trousers and the morning coat cost Henry a great deal of money.

The general and Henry hurried along the street. "Have a flower, mister, have a flower for ya missus." It grew colder, Henry covered his pointed ears.

Suddenly he was startled by a grunting snort that protruded through the beards. He saw the red eyes and quickly looked into the crowd to see if the old woman was there—

"I suppose you'll meet your father now? Then I'll leave you," said the general.

—She was not.

The collier's wife entered Mr. Alfred Beetle's tailor-dry-goods shop. It was dark and a few candles were lit in waxen brackets on the wall. The beer was strong. Fat-necked men and women with baskets of eggs were rummaging through mounds of cloth. A young girl, her calves white in the candle light, was eating from a box of figs. Tables were piled high with patched jackets, wrinkled shoes, sows' ears and discarded feathers. A stuffed peacock stood by the head fitter's chair. One glass eye surveyed the mob.

"One of my sister's young was an idiot, 'e plays with a spoon. Funny creature never says a word."

"Aye, Flo has a whole flock of 'em, lets 'em play in the yard. They say the doctor's hurtin' 'em is the cause of some."

A bell rang as the door opened and closed.

A smell of dust hung on the galatea. Petals fell from a pot of old flowers.

"Now, Mr. Beetle, I've come for you ta help me," said the collier's wife. Her fingers touched the rolls of satin.

"To be sure, anything I can do," he said. He eyed the old woman through thick glasses, stooped his shoulders a little more. He puffed on a short weed. His bald head shone. Canaries sang in the apartment overhead; one of the shoppers sneezed. Mr. Beetle quickly chewed a piece of matzoth.

"We know you're the queen of the seamstresses," he said, "we'll try to be worthy of your trade." He smoothed one of the rolls that she had touched.

"This is a very important mission," she said, looking down at her chapped hands. "I been commissioned ta make the weddin' gown of a yun 'ooman, daughter to a very prominent general."

"Ah, I see how it is. That what you're lookin' at is fine material," he said. His shell was covered with black and purple spots.

Carefully she turned the faded price-tag over. Her eye was caught by a flaming orange scarf. Her nostrils waited a moment as she smelled the Christmas smoke.

"Mr. Beetle, it's outrageous the price for a bit of cloth. Between you and me, who's old friends, I think we could make a slight agreement, seein' as my customer is such an important yun lady."

"Business ain't easy." His fingers stayed longer on the cloth. He hitched his trousers.

"I can't pay such a domm amount!" The old head bent down and looked into his.

"Then take *that* stuff," he cried, his hair on end.

The collier's wife turned to the new roll with a witchery look at the little man. The cloth was very cheap, thin, and covered with a glossy sheen.

"Now, at half the price of this, I might do some business wi' ya fer a few yards," as her eyes lit up.

Beetle bit his thin lip, pressed a finger against his nose.

"Aw right, dam woman, I'll give it ya for a quarter under, but no better."

Grinning, she walked from the Beetle's shop, the gaudy cloth beneath her arm, the extra coins in her apron pocket, and with the satchel bobbing. She mixed with the crowd on their way to the fair. She laughed at the bearded men with tarts and caps made from newspapers. She clicked across the street in her thin boots.

A young man, high silk hat cocked upon his head, played the organ and a fat child worked the bellows. Behind them, on a stand of planks, danced the girl. Her veils trailed above the boards around her thumping feet. Still, uplifted faces watched her move, while a bottle of stout was passed from mouth to mouth.

Hands on hips, bundles by her feet, the collier's wife surveyed the group of men pressed against the stage, the waterhole, staring at the lean calves. Faces were covered with soot; hard thick thumbs were hooked into waistcoats. The smell of taffy, boiling over open fires, drifted across the stage. The collier's wife watched a figurative movement of the dancer's knee. "Ah, ya big men," she said, "go on home!" And gathering up her satin and bag, she made her way back to her rooms.

She heard the children's giddy screams as they watched the dancing bear at the fair.

Henry stood on the street corner, the carnation on his coat jiggling in the wind. He looked for the old woman among the passing, merry faces. The gray wind swept by his legs. He could still feel the fingers. Automobiles swerved and jammed, lights wavered on and off, and a heavy man, dressed in red, slowly shook a bell on the opposite corner. Henry tapped with his cane and started to cross the street.

The eyes of the mob were ringed in black. Bowler hats and caps, peaks and sticks, carrying split pumpkins, they pulled Henry along. They screeched and cawed, waved pennants of the fair. *Too-la-la* went the organ, *puff-puff* the little boy. "Now you're going to get it," said the young man in the black hat, and using his high-heeled foot he jabbed the struggling boy at the bellows. Henry was slowly wedged through the rind of men until, amid their silent breathing, his body was pressed against the edge of the stage, and he stood by the collier. Moving unrhythmically from side to side, the dancer tapped her palms against her hips. Henry saw that the bottoms of her bare feet were black. Slowly those rising and falling black soles worked their way towards the front of the stage and closer and closer to Henry's eyes. The collier pressed forward, his knees and heavy hands blocked by the upright boards. His eyes moved to follow as she moved. The veils fluttered; round rough thighs were taut. The woman's hocks sank in the mud. Her eyes strained. The driver flecked her with a switch of brush. Her nostrils were red, the horns lowered. Henry heard the clanking of chains, the suck of hoofs covered with water. The haunches swayed, moved forward and stopped. She mooed.

And at that moment, the men began to cheer, clapped each other on the back, their heads motionless, throats opened. The deep bass clamor for more swung up over the woman's head. She breathed hard; the muscles went limp. Henry rested his forehead against the boards. The organ began, and again she danced, moving backwards. In a wild effort Henry looked around and, for a moment, saw the old woman behind the men. Using his arms, his head, his chest and elbows, he pushed and squirmed, and free of the staring faces, he ran. The organ thumped; the dancer calmly retreated. In another step she reached the curtain. She disappeared.

The cheers broke out again.

11

Slowly the pieces formed a pattern on the bust. The cellophane-satin doll, half-made faceless bride, waited upright, cold, for the hour to come. Twilight. A full moon was over the crooked chimneys, a silver plate over the highway. Low coals shone, burning brightly, on the collier's wife, a wrinkled red Indian beneath the eyes. Her head was full of springtime. The single coil of hair had come undone and, alive, the braid hung over her red shoulders. She sat on a threelegged stool watching the corner where in the shadows, in the aisle, stood the helpless, silent bust, peering back. Large sections of the gown were still unsewn and were held by bitter, glittering pins. The bust waited impatiently and the collier's wife watched with a wary eye. Neither spoke. But again the old woman commenced, heaved herself to life and grinning, poked the needle and snow-white thread in and out of the gown on the bust. "Emily, Emily, this is your own, a gown to be married in, made of stone." She worked quickly, as the room became filled with needle-eyes and arms and hands, filled with smoke. She towered above the dress and roughly pulled it and pinched.

Panda-like, a cat who had lost his whiskers and part of his tail swung across the clothesline out of the window and dropped into the room. "Good evening, Mr. Cuddles," said the old woman. Stitch, stitch. The cat walked to a dish and began to drink. "Ya don't 'ave too much to say, do ya?" She bit a piece of thread, squinted at the light.

"How are ya doing tonight, 'ooman?"

"Healthful, Mr. Cuddles. But I've lots of work."

"It's a lame old sufferer you are."

"Mind your tongue, or you'll find yourself back outa the winda."

"That's all right, now, you'll hear from me later on tonight. I might do a bit of singin', ya know. There's poisonous people who comes to hear me sing."

"All right, drink up. But give me no foul play."

The scissors stuck upright in the table. The cat's eyes, the wife's eyes, and the bust's fell on them. The coals rustled. She eyed her handiwork. The cat scooped in the dish with his paw. Nothing. He sat down, dropping his hat on the floor. "Who's yer friend?" Yellow eyes peering into the corner, grinning. "Just don't bother me," answered the collier's wife. She scowled, looked darkly down at the tired cat, "It's none of *your* affair, whoever she be. Not a bit, I tell ya." She rubbed her damp chin. The bust in the satin gown moved with the breeze. The empty face turned more demurely into the blackness. The dagger flashed on the table. "Why don't she speak?" asked the cat. He pushed the gray dish away from his chair. The wife stood still, hearing the soft wind. She held the needle poised, the lips quivered. "If you don't stop yer whinin' questions. . ." The thread was whispered into the steam over the hearth, hung above the boiling percolator, was lost on slimy aluminum kettles. The cat's eyes were closed, his tie fell over his throat, two short black ribbons. A lorry rolled by in the street below. The scissors cut quickly, the knife moved in and out, an arm appeared through the hole in the satin, a thin white arm. The wife's cold fingers smoothed the bodice where the flowers would be. The pale arm swayed to and fro, weak and alive. The shears and needles darted faster; blue shadows rose and fell from the rotting chairs. The hair on the cat's spine slowly bristled. The collier's wife left her sewing for a moment, swept across the room and stirred the simmering pot. An acid smell of herbs filled the room. The ruffled cape, perched above the wedding gown, shifted back and forth. The old woman stirred the pot and eyed the slender figure across the room. The hard coral fingers began to tremble; the dozing cat moaned to himself. A bug crept out of his fiery lair, stared for a moment and scurried across the floor. The wife chased him with her stamping foot, monstrous beastie, and rested, panting, against the bare wall. She heard the breathing of the bust, pulled the red shawl tighter about her shoulders. She began to work. "C'mon," mumbled the cat in his sleep, "give us a kiss."

He awoke with a start, slowly flicked his tail. He saw the old woman bending over the body in the corner, saw the unfinished, fluttering, wedding gown. A green light filled the room with the depth of the sea. The old woman hovered silently at work, her shift through the loosening shawl. He heard the scuffling of her slippers. With a grunt he heaved himself from the little chair and walked across the room on his hind feet. Reaching the cupboard, he climbed and the room, the rags, the eyes, began to swirl. He held his breath, his claws dug deeper. Almost to the top, almost to the jug of wine. He sucked the breath into his purring chest, extended his left paw over the right, was conscious of the bride's white arms. Then the scissors smashed passed him, the windmill dagger blades whirling the air, and hit the pyramid of cans over his head. Amid the vicious outraged yells of the wife, he and the cans fell clattering and screaming to the floor. In a single leap the old woman scattered bundles of rags and buttons into the air; a table hit the wall and collapsed. The cat bolted to the door. Locked. He looked up in horror at the descending maenadic wife. The door flew open and at that moment he felt the impact of the iron foot; his mouth still open and eyes glazed, he careened down the stairs. The door slammed. Cans rolled on the floor.

The collier's wife leaned against the door, her ear pressed to the panel, her hands at her throat and she heard the heavy pounding of her heart. Then the anger twisted her eyes again. "Twist," she screamed, and ran to the window. Up and down the street, no one there. No cat. Everyone was at the fair. Nothing moved. "Nubbins," she cried, "Nubbins, come back here." The blue street was still. A shadow moved under the lamppost, then was gone. She leaned her head out into the cool evening, leaned on her heavy arms and the cool air brushed past her face. Slowly she felt the throbbing pain in her finger. Up to the light she saw the spot of blood, the needle's point, and she felt the pain. She looked in disbelief, her face became white, and stealthily she turned her back to the window. She peered into the corner. The bust, white-robed and slender, moved. The breeze touched the back of her neck. She shivered. Holding the long pearl-headed hatpin, the collier's wife crept towards the bust, her eyes never leaving her prey. She inched forward. Then she leapt. The pin plunged in and out of the abdomen, quicker and quicker, in and out above the thighs. Small drops of blood appeared on the satin. Her breathing was strong.

Outside the cat returned, cried under the window once, then limped away.

The dress was finished.

"I do wisht 'ed come 'ome instead o' leavin' me 'ere alone like this," thought the collier's wife as she stirred the soup.

At precisely the proper moment Beady knocked on the parson's door. Everything was timed by the little silver watch that hung from her breast. Old cassocks were tossed about the room, black beneath dust. A white collar sat in the middle of the rug.

"How many are expected at the ceremony?" asked the parson. He stood in his shirtsleeves behind the marble desk, prayer book in hand.

"Five hundred, I believe, dearest."

The parson grunted. He never appeared before a group of less than three hundred. All of his choir boys had his initials stitched on the collars of their gowns.

The room was dark, most of the light shut out by thick window bars that protected the ground-floor room from vandals. And since the parson didn't think the bars enough, heavy iron-mesh gratings had been added to the bars. A picture of the Christ Child was on the desk, one of Beady was in the drawer, face down. The parson walked up and down behind the desk in short footsteps. His fingernails were polished white, his forehead straight, and his hair black and sleek. "Dearly beloved," he intoned, stopped, continued his walk. His voice was smooth and rich like the imported bells that rang somewhere high above in the gray air. The room was warm. "Please shut the door," said the parson. The lights that burned around the dressing-table mirror were dim and yellow. The grease paint in pots was sticky from the heat, the crumpled pieces of tissue and cotton warm and used. Beady stooped by the oil heater, shielded her face, and turned the knob. The flame went out with a pop. She jumped back.

Small and aloof, she again stood by the desk, humming, waiting. "Dearly beloved," he said again. "Well, how does it sound?" Before she could answer, he said, "Never quite right. Not quite." She spoke, "Henry will arrive soon." "I perform so many of these ceremonies. I feel as if I'm participating in world union. As if I add something to their happiness, the bliss of young couples. You might help me with this." She stepped to his side. For a moment his head, shoulders, and waist were a fumbling black mass. Beady pinched and pulled until his flushed face appeared. At the mirror he combed his hair over again. She caught specks of hair and lint from the gown. Pigeons fluttered high over the steeple, beat their wings against the parson's barred windows; they could not reach the ledges to roost or walk. Beady admired his fine figure. He plucked some of the lint from the gown himself and smoothed it around the collar.

Out in the kitchen the cook wept. The cake was covered with frosty curlycues. She looked at it, wept again. The little man in black at the frosting altar had no face.

Passersby walked with their heads down.

A short boy reached up to light the candles. His stiff collar rubbed.

The organist practiced his scales.

A few scattered people sat in reserved pews. They whispered back and forth, nodding and smiling. The faces were pale blue in the dim light.

A mother fumbled underneath the dress of a flower-girl, the little girl talked incessantly. A pigeon walked up and down in front of the high doors, hopping quickly as feet approached.

Two white ribbons extended up the aisle. Adults stepped over, children crawled under, and they laughed or stared but none untied the knots. Flowers hung from the ribbons.

The parson looked once more in the mirror, fluffed out the creases in the gown, studied his reflection. "You'll be sure to prompt me?" he queried. "Of course," she quickly answered, "of course." Abruptly he turned to the desk and slid some scraps of paper into the prayer book. He always inserted fragments of a sermon into the service and made special announcements.

Outside the door her watch showed ten minutes had elapsed. Soon it would be over. She started upstairs to dress, dabbing at her eyes with a handkerchief. The organist went up and down the keyboard.

The collier's wife carried the rolled-up wedding gown beneath the shawl, next to her shift. Through the rips and holes it
touched her skin and the small bodice rubbed against goose
flesh. She walked quickly and held her bandaged finger up to
the wind. A thin dried line of blood traveled down her wrist
and crossed the burn. Her eyes watered. "Wretched, wretched
cat. I'd a' broke is back with me own foot if I'd only thought."
She passed a dark doorway. "Keep away, I want no truck
with ya, old cross-eyed devil." She shifted the gown against
her breast with her uninjured hand. The gown wrinkled. She
walked faster, hobnails clattering on the stones, her finger
throbbing. A one-legged crane was black against the sky,
perched in his nest on a chimney top. Tears started from the
old woman's eyes and slipped down the yellow cheeks; she
caught them with her tongue.

The crooked street became gradually more narrow until it
was only an alley between high, unbroken walls. Chickens
hunted around the bottoms of rain barrels, padded feet
knocked against tin cans and darkness drifted out of barred
cellar windows. The collier's wife climbed over an orange
crate, her feet crunched in broken glass. "Fool," she said. Her
foot sloshed through a puddle of water; she dodged a loose
dangling iron wire. She ran along a slippery plank like an old
fat mouse, peering into the darkness. She stopped, listened,
ears twitching as she heard dull unrhythmic footsteps on the
other side of the wall. Water dripping from her matted coat
left an uneven trail on the plank and she stumbled beneath
stone arches and overheads, passed cavernous sewers and tasted
the damp, rotted bricks and concrete dust. Her white fangs
glittered, the hobnails caught a mouldy gunny sack. She
smelled the lime and rusting wainscots. "If I catch ya," she
mumbled, "I'll cut the curling hide right from yer bones." A
can rattled. "Poke at yer eyes," pebbles rattling on the iron
roofs, "cut yer mouth right off," she shook her finger, "boil
yer carcus," and breathing quicker she rubbed her chest
through the wedding gown. Her face became wizened and
blanched and when she lost a tooth she stopped to search for

it. "God beat me, if ever such luck. . ." Then she ran on, feeling for it with her tongue.

The alley narrowed until it was a tunnel through shingles, plaster, corrugated walls, barred wooden doors, gables, endless pipes, and overhanging beams studded with crooked nails. Angular rough corners caught her unawares and tore at the shawl. With wooden shavings clinging to her socks, she made her way through stonehenge. From the other end of the tunnel, the dull half-pitched note of a bell swung towards her and drifted past. A dog staggered across her path and growled from one hole to another. And as the sharp steam from a whistle on the other side of town shot up into the evening, she reached the house. A chill came out of the clay. The house was in a crevice of windowless brick walls, squat and black beneath the rising tile roofs and blackening sky. A blue marble birdbath was tilted against the stoop, and bundles of gray weeds coiled about its base. The empty windows of the house were streaked with candle wax; smoke poured from the chimney.

She coughed, abomnible e'enings, into a rag and clumped up the steps. She pulled the chain and waited, sitting in front of the door on the wet steps. Unfastening the shawl, she withdrew the wedding gown and shook it over her knees in the wind. She dropped it on the steps beside her. She waited.

"What do *you* want?"

Gathering up the dress she turned and looked at the high voice in the doorway. "Well?" said the generaless's chamber boy. His purple livery was stained with spots of jam and his sleek black puttees were covered with dust. The hair stood up in a cowlick in the back, his hands were in his pockets. There were faded gold stripes down the trousers. A pencil was stuck cross-wise between his teeth, like a bit, to perfect his pronunciation.

"Don't know I want nuthin' from you," she said. He looked placidly into her red eyes, looked up and down. Past him in the cold light, the old woman could see frail gilded chairs and many-colored campaign flags stacked against the walls.

"There aren't any handouts. . ." he grinned, his mouth a loose red bow.

Her scar turned a chalk white, knees knocked. "I'm here ta deliver this weddin' gown." She shook it in his face. The pretty red mouth drew away, the cowlick went higher and he wiped his cheek with a soft cloth. He took a small apple from his pocket, tossed it, caught it, and held it up to his eye. Emily sat alone in her bare room and listened to the voices at the door.

"Well, deliver it and be off." He looked at the apple.

The old woman dropped the dress at his feet. She stepped from the porch, and turning, yelled, "Ya fresh yun' screw!" She went back into the alley. With a quick movement, he retrieved the dress, went into the house, and shut the door. Emily heard the far-off voices of the carolers and began to weep. Taking the pencil from his mouth, the boy took a bite of the apple. It began to snow, small flakes that were like raindrops.

As she stumbled through the alley and the snow wet her shoulders, the old woman thought of the fair and the dancing girl. "The idee," she thought, "him leavin' me all alone to face them insults." And suddenly she knew where to find the collier.

The chamber boy hung the wedding dress on Emily's door knob. Carefully, in secret, she retrieved the gown and laid it on the bed.

In the middle of the procession, the flower girl's shoe came undone. While her mother left her pew and stooped to tie it, the organist repeated two notes over and over again. Snow banked against the windows and people coughed, while the pigeon left the steps and walked up and down inside the vestibule. Chauffeurs talked outside and beat their arms; a few went in to watch.

Wind blew through the cold chancellery and the candles jumped. The flowers were numb, ears red.

"Gore, 'ow long dese t'ings last," said a driver near the doors. He put his collar up and watched the long white line and shivering girl move up the aisle. They blew on their cold fingers. The old women buried their faces in black muffs, tight white curls on wigs of ice.

"*Maledicat illum sancta Dei genetrix et perpetua Virgo Maria*," prompted Beady in a sharp whisper. Her head strained forward, hands cupped about the mouth. Words droned on and on and snow lit the windows with the sound of spattering sand.

The driver in the back began to stamp his feet.

A few carefully calculated handfuls of rice were thrown—but fell short.

The collier's wife kicked at the thick ankles and jabbed her fists into blunted ribs: "Outa my way, feller, outa th' way." She worked towards the tough, coal-dust covered collier. The dancing girl stayed almost motionless on the edge of the stage in front of the men, just to be seen, dancing as little as possible. The white flesh that Henry had gazed upon barely quivered. The face was rigid, dumb, a ring through the nose. The collier's mouth was open, the gray collar of his shirt open, his heart thumping steadily.

When she reached him she sank her iron fingers deep into the muscle of his wooden arm. She tugged at it.

"Ya ought ta be ashamed," she said. "A grown married mun standin' 'ere in the cold ta feast 'is eyes on that bare 'ooman, leavin' 'is wife ta 'ome." He looked steadily at the girl, raised his chin as she came closer.

"Ashamed! Me 'avin' terribul fights wit that vulgar inquisitif mun and a 'orrible, insultin' boy. Cum wi' me now, and get yer eyes from off them sinful legs." The men strained closer to see the snow was white on the tops of their caps, fell on the wife's uncovered head. The girl shivered. The wife tugged harder on his arm, the fingers closed.

Suddenly he turned, "Awe, gawd a'mighty, I dun't know wat yer peevin' aboot. . ."

She led him home through the wet snow.

RHYTHM

12

Henry shook the snow out of his eyes, swept past the violet chauffeurs and into the house. The monstrous pale reflection was a glandular bell-jar above the revelers, reflecting white light from towels, tiles, and bones to their white heads. Hiding his head under his arm, Henry put the geranium into his mouth and with a quick swooping movement struck the match on the wall, watched the flame for a moment and inhaled deeply. He was dizzy. Emily laughed, twisted the paper flowers in her hair and pulled at the elastic in her frilled pantaloons. She waved, her mouth full of pins; he acknowledged the wave with dumb-sign over the crowd, hitting his cheek with his fist, touching his ears and nose and throat with his long fingers, tapping his elbows against his knees. Emily left the room.

Upstairs she looked for a long while into the empty bassinette, a basket propped between two chairs, covered with a handkerchief and filled with cotton. Midnight crept continuously up from the apple country and leaned against the window. Emily sat on a stool peering at the wads of cotton, looked at the glittering axe in the waiting pap and sniffed an unopened powder box. She had already had the new small shoes cast in bronze as keepsakes for the mantelpiece. Quickly she put on the little blue bonnet and the tassels hung down to her ears. "Now you must be a good boy," she said, "and love mother. Grow up to be a fine handsome man." Her gaze, wriggling in the bassinette, became afraid and, very slowly the white transparent face began to cry. Long bristling sideburns grew down the cheeks. The gaze, small, old and parched, answered her, helpless on its back. "You must never do a thing without consulting me, you must always come and see that I am well and not crying." Her heart, the size of an egg, began to tap, and slowly turning over, stuck under her tongue. "You better give me another kiss, you better give me another kiss, you better give me another kiss!" The gaze in the bassinette held out its hands. Emily stared at the fat fingers. "You better know how," the little blue face coughed, choked, "to take care of me." It gasped. "You better know what to do." It laughed and choked again. Midnight covered more and more of the window, slowly lifted the silver shawl from her bare knees. There was only one bead on the counting board, one red bead and she pushed it back and forth. "The first, a little round first, first, first." She looked into the open dripping mouth. It was like a bird's. Its high whistle pierced louder and louder in her ears. The fingers worked rapidly and aimlessly towards her face. A giant silver pin popped open in the oblong pouch with a twang of sprung steel. She hopped to her feet. The eyes were as white as the cotton wads, rolled upwards to the beginning nose. The sideburns withered and died. The frail peeping voice grew more excited, the toes curled. She heard the low, persistent, burning rattle. Midnight fled, leaving the bassinette bare and cool. Carefully Emily picked up the miniature comb and brush and little silver mug and one by one flung them into the bassinette. Tap, tap went her heart. She reached the door and heard the startled gasps of anger. "You better give me another kiss!"

She slammed the door and tore the baby cap from her head. She listened, short and fat in her blue jumper, her bare feet touching cold smooth boards and the violent ribbons in her hair spinning tightly in a color-wheel. Kiss, kiss, kiss.

The roses are frozen like frozen huddled pigeons. The feathers and petals are smooth and round, shine dully covered with frost. Only their heads move, bending gradually in the chilled air, eyes moving, startled short movement. Mother's hands are hard and cold. The pigeons watch. The red brick house and house with the slanting roof are very big; the tree is bare and the swing hangs straight. The woman is at the other end of the street and as she nears, her black hat hangs down to her shoulders. Closer as falling temperature, the blood pressure from its high peak quickly falls, and a gather gray cloud of cotton descends. As the woman passes, her hip brushes the child's eye.

On tiptoe Emily went back into the room and powdered her throat.

Dr. Smith tugged at the long cord tied around his stomach as a belt. He felt the rope slowly choking him in half, looked at the loose ends hanging below his knees. The knot held. The ungracious daughter perched on the back of a chair and shielded her face with both hands. The ivory necklace about her neck flicked its tail and collected itself to squeeze. A knot of men encircled them, golden nooses hanging from their vests. Henry brushed the melting snow from his shoulders as the necklace twitched on her breast, and the white chandelier hanging from the ceiling swayed to and fro, its feet lifeless and still. Long sharp wires ran under the rug and through the walls; the window cords were weighted with lead. The doctor played with the string dangling from his monocle. Henry fingered his tight collar. Gaylor Basistini undid his shirt.

"Time," said Dr. Smith, "is a nutcracker. Get what I mean? A nutcracker." The ungracious daughter trembled and the little pekinese, whose basket Emily had upstairs, sneezed fitfully in the corner. Joe Ottoe, who had pushed himself into the group, swirled the ice in his drink. His eyebrows arched.

"You're a *bull*-a'tist, Doc. M'own term. A bull-a'tist." A long twisting thread hung from his coat sleeve. He tried to brush it away.

"Be that as it may. O. K. Joe, but you're the typical man who feels the rough cracking jaws of time, and right where it hurts most." He adjusted the glass in his eye. "A man who's always on the bicycle-bar."

"Yeah," Joe grinned, "I guess I know what you mean. Pritty sma't." His eye circled the huddle of men.

"You do know, on a certain level, Joe. Below the belt. But after she squeezes for a long time, there's nothing left." The doctor threaded a long tough suture into the needle, focused on his head the reflector that shone like a locomotive search-light. Joe pulled at the thread. Dr. Smith looked for a moment at the tendons in the daughter's long legs.

"Man tries. . ."

"Man plays. . ."

"At first with himself. . ."

"Finally grows. . ."

"He's sm'at, he knows. . ."

"Then he dies," said Henry. The heads turned to look at him.

The doctor burst out laughing and took a drink from Joe's glass. "It's a nutcracker, boys." With two fingers, Henry plucked at his damp shirt. His necktie grew tighter.

"Everybody wants to kiss, kiss, kiss," said Dr. Smith. The ungracious daughter looked up, eyes starting from her head.

"Hell, we all gotta have our fling," said Joe.

His wife sat on the floor in the bathroom, her stockings rolled, her hair undone, smoke curling from her nostrils. "It's a wonderful pa'ty, Beady," she said. "You don't mind if I call ya Beady?" Beady fumbled. A long wire from a little dim lamp caught around her foot. "Not at all." Quickly she rinsed her mouth with cool water. "Ya know," said the woman on the floor, "Joe's gettin' kinder hard to hold." She took another drag, wiped her eye. "You better know," said Beady, "what to do. You better know what to do."

"Yeah."

"Excuse me a minute, boys," said Dr. Smith. He turned away, leaned over. "You better give me another kiss," he said. The head turned sharply. Henry's finger stuck between his collar and throat. The music of a harp and its long vibrating strings filled the room, plucked strings and struck strings, wires and chords, tinkled together. "Hey, who's got de ear?" said Joe. The windows softly rattled with the music, a kiss in the dark, a good tune, floated along the ceilings. Noel grew fatter and fatter under the piano, beer cans piled around his feet. His ears pricked up when he heard light tripping footsteps out in the hall, footsteps coming down the rope ladder.

Emily walked carefully down the stairs, holding the baby as far from her as she could. "Now, remember," it said, "I don't want anyone to see me." Emily turned her nose from the dripping form. Joe Ottoe's wife, who had come out to find a towel, met her at the bottom of the rope. "Hi, Emily! You don't mind if I call ya Em'ly?" "Not at all." Quickly she put the baby in her pocket and, skirt split up the side, she danced into the bright room.

The adventuress in green had lost her green and with her hands under her head she lay like marble along one wall, cigarette holder clenched between her teeth. The harp strings ran through her hair. Yawning, the monster from South America sat by her side, painting his nails. His shoe laces were knotted and hung over the sides of his yellow shoes, floated in the tepid water like strangling water moccasins. The cigarette holder bobbed up and down, empty, and as she drew pictures on the wall with the black end of the butt, she was dimly conscious of the voices.

Dr. Smith had the ungracious daughter perched on his knee. It answered "yes" to everything he said.

"I once had a girl about your age," he said. "She was riding down the street on a bicycle one day and got tangled up with a wire from a smashed telephone pole. After the sparks stopped flying, she was as black as an Indian mummy."

"Yes," said the girl.

"Gee, that's tough, Doc."

His slender fingers ran over the mummy's knee.

"Boys," said Dr. Smith, and looked up at them, "have you ever looked at a blonde head like this, an' ever thought what was inside it?" He nodded at the head. She blinked.

"It's something for an old man to think about," he said. "I just hope to hell she doesn't see what's in mine," he added. "She's time's little helper," he laughed and dropped her on the floor. The circle of eyes looked coldly on. She began to pick up the string of broken beads, picked one like magic from the doctor's cuff. He took off his coat and shirt and turned around.

"See this back?" he said. "It's still a strong one." They all laughed. A long scar with a noose at the end of it ran down the thin white flesh. "It'll make 'em or break me," he said. Henry watched the jiggling noose.

No one saw Emily dance.

First she whirled to the right, then to the left, and stopped. She flew around and around, elbows bent over her head, hopping on one foot after the other.

"It never seems to lose its charm," said Dr. Smith. He smoothed his rubber gloves, cracked a piece of ice between his teeth. "All starts with a baby's little pink. . ."

"Aw, Doc, that's gettin' pretty raw," said Joe.

"Joe," the doctor said, "when you've seen as many of those things, both on the old and on the young, as I have, you won't worry about whether they're raw or cooked. And you'll find out they're all cooked anyway." He reached down and slapped the thin white haunch. One by one she dropped the beads into her mouth.

"Bull," said Joe.

Emily was conscious of the eyeless faces and laughing gayly, she spun around once more and sat down amid waves of applause, her tail wagging.

"It's all glan's," said Joe, "all glan's."

The white walls were covered with long black lines, finger marks, telephone numbers and little drawings, games of tic-tac-toe, in pencil or ink, and filthy words, left by people who were waiting for the telephone or piano, or radio. Emily's mouth hung open, she gasped for breath, breathing through a handkerchief to escape the germs.

Upstairs in the master suite the generaless opened her mouth and swallowed a black pill. The general pounded her shoulder blades, as she coughed, and when he stopped, his orderly took his place.

"Oh, God," she gasped, "get this animal off me, Soris."

"Yes, my dear. Stand off," he cried, and the orderly shrank back.

The parson, his chin on his cane, glared at them all. "More hot milk?" he asked. He was in charge of the round gold samovar from which spurted the steaming colorless milk.

"I might have some for the cat," ordered the generaless. It still clung to her bosom.

"Here, use my cup," said the general. It squirmed.

"You better give me a kiss," said the generaless and, its tongue still wet with milk, it licked her cheek.

Beady came fumbling into the room, her eyes not used to the dark, her hands wet. The orderly tried to push her out again, quickly, with a single heaving motion. "It's me," she cried, "it's only me. I want to *stay*."

"Stand off," shouted the general.

"Milk," said Beady, "how nice. I smell it."

"Well, you can't be underfoot," said the orderly, and pulling a ball of twine from his pocket, he tied her to the foot of the bed. The long sharp cord bit into her ankle and she heard the breathing of the samovar that rumbled like an anesthetizer. The parson clapped the mask over his nose. Drinking from the cat's cup. She spilled the milk down the front of her dress and felt it seeping through the silk. "Don't you think," she said, "we should do something about Emily?"

The parson sank into the ether. "I think they can tell when it's expected. Right down to the size, I think."

"You might let *me* handle this," said the generaless, "*I* know what to do." The orderly, feeling his way, helped her, trembling, to a chair. She dabbed at the scratches from the cat's claws. Beady's yellow eyes blinked in the dark. The parson's cane hit the spigot as he dreamed, and the milk poured out into the darkness and onto the rug in an endless stream.

"Damn," said the general and pushed the orderly away from his side.

"My goodness," said Lady Wheeling-Rice to Noel's advances, "I haven't done it in years." She peered over the top of an enormous fan.

Henry looked up at the single white bulb that blazed down from the chandelier. The cord from which it hung was a straight black rope behind the brilliant light, that swung like a paralytic metronome. He tried to remember something about a seacoast town but could not. He felt the milk seeping through his shirt. His eyes converged on the unshaded light, the bell-jar breathed in muscular undulations, the parson slept. Ether arose from the bassinette.

Emily knew that the baby had been shaken up by her dancing and, sitting on the edge of the sofa, she waited for it to emerge into full view. She kicked off her shoes.

The arm swung back and forth across Henry's face as Dr. Smith talked and gestured to the ungracious daughter.

"Well," said the doctor, "now you know how it all works. Your mother should have told you long ago, but now you know the whole story."

Henry was sorry he had missed what the doctor said.

Dr. Smith closed the medical handbook.

"Pulse, a hundred and twelve. Let me have that sponge," commanded the doctor. The samovar gurgled.

He wiped his rubber hand over his forehead. She opened the fat plaid purse, dropped in the rest of the beads and produced the sponge. He pounded it with a mallet until it was flat and soft and shapeless on the butcher's block and quickly he crammed it into the wound. "It hurt a little, didn't it?" he said. The sponge puffed out to its normal shape. She said nothing. He showed her the extracted splinter.

"Nutcracker, nurse," said the ungracious daughter, in her turn, and holding the ether can under his nose she went to work.

"You're a funny kid," said Dr. Smith through the enveloping fumes.

She hacked furiously.

Pain shot up his spine and bright and sharp as the light overhead, Henry felt it strike behind his ears. The masked nodding heads and muffled words, the steel chandelier and gurgling pekinese, spools of gut and pounding bull, all rushed upon him to melt away each vertebra. He tried to pull the fingers from his arms, to tear the hands from his throat. But he could not remember. The bodies of the guests were made of glass and every time he tried to look at them they wrapped themselves in great black slickers so he couldn't see. He was eaten by the blinding pain and searing light and was consumed with curiosity. He felt layers of cracked ice packed about his spine.

"God, it's cold in here," said Dr. Smith and tore the sweater from the girl's back. The seams split open over his pointed shoulder blades.

Henry shivered. Out in the garage the chauffeur worked by candlelight jacking the middycar up, pumping grease into the nipples. Henry heard the steel hammer-head beating the diaphragm, striking the warped fire-wall, and felt the pain of gas on his stomach.

Emily touched her landscaped abdomen, felt the twisting scars like a rough starfish. Every few years she liked to have an operation, be careful, please, and the starfish grew larger and larger with fat stitched tentacles. She felt it move. At any moment she expected Dr. Smith to say, "A boy. Nine pounds five ounces. Nice work." She waited fidgeting with her toes.

"You're quite a little girl," the doctor said. The ungracious daughter didn't answer but leaned her back against his knees, trying to keep warm.

Emily frowned.

The chauffeur scratched his ear and looked at the large black body and jumbled tubes. It was dark.

The generaless's voice rang out in the darkness. "We'll take her in for an inspection tomorrow. I'm sure Emily will feel better when things are more certain." The parson muttered in his sleep; Beady bit through the cord with her teeth and started downstairs for some more milk. "That's a wise decision," she whispered.

Her white dress was unsoiled, the bows on her braids immaculate and as she walked she twisted the rings on her fingers. Wings of marquisette trailed behind her in the suspended dust and the hem of her dress barely swept the balustrade. The smell of hemlock fell from her evening hair as she circled downwards over the stairs of glass, a rosary falling almost to her feet. Below her swirled the river and she heard the children laugh as they parted the waves. She heard the feathers of a bird stirred in its slumber and shadows followed her in the marble wall. A veil covered half her face and bosom and a little crown was on her head. A lamplighter lit each wick as she approached. She took two steps forward and one back, two forward and one back, gamely and triumphantly, the children laughing, until she finally reached the bottom, the steel milkcan tilting her to one side.

Henry jumped when Beady, dear mother, touched his arm and dropped the milkcan at his feet.

13

"Wait," he said, "don't do that." Calmly he took the handkerchief from Beady's hand so she wouldn't wipe the cold tears from the corner of her eye. He stuffed the handkerchief into his pocket.

"Henry," she said, "would you go fill the milk pitcher for me? That's a good boy." He stooped to pick up the heavy can. Beady saw that his eyes were filled with little black crooked lines of sleeplessness. She frowned.

"Certainly, Mother," he said. As he stooped he peered closer into her eyes for a moment to see if he could find one small red flower. He could not. She drew away from him and frowned again. A bead of perspiration dropped in a long cold thread down his leg and twined in rivulets around his garter. He heard a glass fall and smash on the floor and the pieces showered in flashes of artificial color in the boudoir, on the tiles, across the dining-room table. He started toward the kitchen and heard the solitary crunching of his shoes.

"Hurry up, dear," she called after him and sat down beside Emily.

"Now I'm going to tell you all a story," said Dr. Smith.

Henry dragged his shoulder along the wall as he slid down the hallway and his padded jacket left a lengthening smear in the white dust. His fingers and shoulder dragged as useless paws through the dust, the steel milk can swung between his legs, striking first one knee then the other with a hollow painful sound.

"It all began," said Dr. Smith, "like this. . . ." He coughed, his chunky red face shaking from side to side and the venom shot from his incongruousuly small mouth.

Henry tried to reach the kitchen, but the note said one and it wasn't one at all. The guests would be waiting, he should make the pie. He coughed.

"A pretty girl," said Smith, "came into the office and said, 'Doc, I'm going to have a baby. But I don't want it.' She was a cute little thing with a plain white face and a little black hat cocked on one side of her head. I had a hard time seeing her over the bundle of groceries she put on the desk, but you could see she was cute." He chewed quickly on the end of his cigarette. Emily leaned forward to listen.

"You better get some sleep, dear. We have a big day to-morrow," said Beady. But Emily stared at Dr. Smith and dimly felt the squirming new being beneath her fingers. Already the generaless held the field telephone close to her face in the bed-room and, polishing each brass button down her tunic with a scrap of handkerchief, she spoke; "Have the middycar by the side door just before dawn. Be prepared for a long drive." The chauffeur in the barn saluted at the mouthpiece and heard the machine click off. The generaless, her head on her fist, stared coldly into space.

"I felt sorry for this girl, understand," he said. Smith looked around at his audience. "But it's not my job to feel sorry. There just wasn't anything I could do." Emily looked down into her lap. "I had my nurse give her a drink and then we sent her over to a classmate of mine who hadn't made the grade. Give him a hatchet and he was happy." Dr. Smith's eye was caught by some leaves, pieces of cloth, silver buttons and a rusty dagger pinned to the white wall. "Say, what's all this?" he asked. Emily wanted to say that they were Daddy's cam-paign collection, brought from many foreign fields in a care-fully locked steel trunk, but she could not speak. The words were vapid circles that labored hollowly up through her dry throat. They rang emptily against the roof of her brain and vibrated over and over around her eyes and ears, as if she had actually spoken, with the monotony of sleep. "Well," said the doctor, "that's the way they get stung, stuck and undeceived. They lose it, drop it, throw it away before it's big enough to name or be a bastard in the family circle." He laughed. "Sometimes, though," he laughed again, "it's all a mistake, a dream and there isn't any roe at all; and they end up just as dry as ever."

The monster from South America and the adventuress hung together and waltzed about the room, her eyes closed, his trousers rolled to the knees. His garters hung down like little sets of suspenders and red and yellow they bulged over the shoulders of his block-like calves.

Beady dozed.

Henry reached the middle of the room and knew he was finally near, dear Sister Ann, the kitchen. The French doors, ajar at the far end of the dining-room, swung to and fro into the blackness over the terrace outside, and every time the moon struck them through the trees, their many little stained-glass panes shot up in blurred and jumbled light. Over and over he rubbed his fists into his eyes, but each time he looked he caught a glimpse of Gaylor Basistini, hanging just beyond the swinging doors, a monstrous knot jammed partway through his broken neck, his feet almost resting on the flagstones of the terrace. The mirror beyond the doors flashed on and off broken by showers of color from the panes and the sound of leaves scraping over the stones. Henry thrust his mother's cambric handkerchief into his mouth and clenched his jaws. Over and over he saw the black taut rope. Gulls toppled over about his feet and still he watched, dry taste of dust and perfume in his mouth, white light shimmering on the walls. The black body moved, struck a match and flicked it into a potted shrub. The head, mouth open, tongue hanging out, turned and glanced through the open doors. "C'mon out, Henry," Gaylor said, puffing on the cigarette. Henry tugged at his necktie, felt the sand in his stockings. "I can't," he mumbled, "have to go on an errand for mother." His words came angry and trembling through his handkerchief. Crawling with the legs of a centipede he struggled forward and dragged the can over the last few Persian feet and reached the narrow coral arch of the kitchen door. "Ah, now, dear," said some old woman who was sitting at the littered table, "have some tea." Then she was gone. Leaving the can in the center of the clear bone floor, he tried to find the handle of the refrigerator door. He reached farther with his fingers, trying to get the milk, the cool green earthen jar of milk. He clutched, tried to speak and as the party filled his head and he sank back on his knees in the brilliant, white, empty sleep, he heard a voice calling, "Goodnight, Henry, goodnight, goodnight. . ."

14

The middycar roared through space. A long dark stream of soot and cinders settled in its wake and its high black wooden body swayed from side to side. Middyhead, the chauffeur, dressed in faded purple livery and wearing a wrinkled white cap, clutched the stocky steering-wheel and whistled through his teeth. The three old ladies, veils down and bearskin across their knees, sat in the back seat, heads barely high enough to see through the flashing windows. Each wore a black bandana across her mouth and nose, beneath the veil, against the dust and wind, and as they rode in silence they kept their eyes on the back of Middyhead's neck. The noise from the great engine pounded in their ears along with the clattering of a bell which Middyhead pounded each time he shifted gears. They sat in silence, small pointed shoes resting on the straw-covered floor boards which jiggled and lurched above the gravel road. Ahead of the flying car the sky was dark and gray, and sheets of cold morning air cut past the sides of the sleek machine. Emily, in the middle, felt gusts of cold air climbing up her back, bent her head to escape the wind that swept through the cracks in the celluloid windshield. She wanted to scratch her nose beneath the veil, but each of her wrists was pinioned at her side by firm unrelaxing fingers. The blindfold pressed into her eyes and the little ribbons in her hair were squashed down under the black hat. Beady, to her left, was softly weeping, the tears draining onto her high starched collar. The generaless, on the right, called instructions through the microphone, her sharp head thrust forward.

"Take this turn, Middyhead. More acceleration, man. Watch that dog!"

The car swerved, the dog leapt from beneath the frail wheels of the middycar and scurried, yelping, to the side of the road. Wheeling, the generaless watched through her field glasses and saw him running off over the hills. The car accelerated, on and on. When they stopped for fuel the generaless pulled down a'l the little black shades and even when they were in the open country, she never ceased her vigilance. Emily was stiff and cried in horror when she was bounced up and down on the springless seat and to the right and left as they bounded along, throttle wide. Fumes from the smoking engine filled the cab, the horn rang out, long and low. Dew-covered hedges and twisted trees flew by. Rotting fence rails lined the road; deep ruts and puddles were filled with cracking ice and sand that was flung up behind the whirling wheels. They crossed dry river beds, lurched through gullies, or sped over narrow wooden single-laned bridges, the wheels skidding on narrow-gauge rusty trolley tracks. A thin mist hung above the dump yard for a brief moment; an abandoned moss-covered mill shot by. Gray and black guinea hens struggled from the way of the onrushing car. Middyhead pulled the whistle cord and a long scream floated over the desolate country and across charred acres of burned-out forest land. Far ahead, against the cold pink horizon, they saw the black finger of a smoke stack and a thin line of heavy smoke that drifted against the shingled, frost-covered roofs. Middyhead swung the bow of the car dead against the faraway stack and pulled on the thin vibrating throttle with his white-gloved fingers. Emily felt herself thrown backward and felt the fingers hold tighter to her wrists. When the sun had swollen to a dirty red behind the smoke stack, Middyhead flicked the switch that cut off the piercing searchlight, adjusted his frog-like goggles and crouched forward. With a violent effort the middycar left the ground. They hung above the deep black gorge streaked with dirty swabs of snow and thumped across the railway trestle, the wheels banging on the ties. Frost-covered clumps of weeds grew from the crooked rusted elbows of the spindly girders and the steel wheels of the middycar pulverized glass bottles left on the bridge. In the middle of the trestle the engine choked and Middyhead, his eyes pressing rigidly forward, kicked at the long electric lead wire that ran, like a fat hose, from under his seat, between his legs, to the single chunky sparkplug in the red-hot block. The engine banged, caught, fired and they sped onto the wagon tracks beyond the bridge. They hurtled through the air, wind whipping past the ribs of the old car and little bugs struck and crashed against the massive brass radiator. The smoke stack loomed in the distance, the faint sun lighted moist broken windows of tool sheds and caved-in shacks smeared with red clay, that beat past. Emily's heart pounded to the violent rhythm of the engine, one and two and three and, and her head rocked to the heavy pulse of the flat spot in the wheel as it beat into the sand, thump, thump. The generaless leaned over and adjusted the knotted cord that tied Emily's feet. Wisps of hay and pellets of oats were tossed into her face by the oily wind that zoomed over the floorboards of the car. They passed a windowless trolley car, warped and gray, covered with bits of rusted wire and surrounded by glittering bits of broken glass, that lay overturned in a vacant field. The generaless lifted the microphone: "Faster, Middyhead."

Click, click. He heard the croquet balls and mallets ticking out on the green lawn, heard shrill little shrieks of girlish laughter and a few small birds singing on the bare branches. The sun cut downward through the ivied window and covered him with a cold, early morning light. Henry's shoulders and back were twisted and cold on the hard linoleum of the kitchen floor and the sunlight pierced through his eyelids in a painful red haze. Click, click. His eardrums sent pain penetrat-

ing deep to the back of his skull. His mouth was full of dry
powdery breakfast cereal and his cracking feet were numb
and cold. A white fly buzzed over the heaps of dishes and
tangled spoons and knives and a faint odor of gas drifted
across the floor. Spat. A hard drop of water fell on his forehead, and for a moment he opened his eyes and saw the
spread legs of the parson standing over him with a carefully
tilted can of water. Another drop hit Henry's head. He tried
to move but could not. Tendons running down his foot were
hooked and cramped by the tongue of his shoe. His shirt, tight,
shrunk, the tails high above his waistline, gripped his arms,
strapped securely to his side. His upper arms ached and
groaned, stiff crusts of muscles standing stripped and torn.
Over the motion of the gently revolving floor, and beyond the
drops of water pounding on his head and trickling down his
face, he heard the soft rubber-soled shoes and the gentle clicking of the balls, the cry of a lively girl and the flash of hair
ribbons. His throat was long and closed and the sun grew
hotter on his eyes.

"Get up, Henry," the parson said, and peered closer to watch
the water splash on his face.

The smokestack reared itself high above the hospital's glass
walls, its steel terraces and concrete yards, and slowly filled the
air above with a black porridge smoke which dulled the sunrise. Sharp angular beds, weights, pulleys, trays and tubes, were
pushed to thin open windows, or pushed from room to room
and golden-calfed girls clicked down the aisles or scribbled in
red crayon on the charts. The front doors were two enormous
hammered sheets of aluminum, studded with star-shaped heads
of brass spikes, gleaming and heavy above the copper steps.
The entire giant structure was made of cubes and tremendous
oblong bricks of brass, solid glass squares, all heaped together
about a few off-center globes and blinking lights. High with
mountains of ice a river ran along the lower face of the hospital, churning with heavy, tar-covered tugs and wrecked
bridges. Several strips of trimmed lawn covered the front and a

few thin strips of vine tried to climb the vast clear white wall. A head peered from a window here and there and high overhead the smoke billowed the sky with blackness.

With a swooping rush the middycar settled to earth and rolled noisily up to the steps of the hospital, chugging, rattling. Middyhead cut the engine, pulled off his rubber gloves and lit a cigarette. Quickly they untied Emily's feet, took the gag from her mouth and pushed her out of the car door. "Please hurry, dear," said the generaless, and she and Beady settled back against the lumpy seat to wait. Emily walked up the copper steps alone, facing her distorted tall reflection in the aluminum. She tripped, caught herself and putting her shoulders to the door, pushed through.

Behind the littered desk was the enameled pig, peaked white cap topping red hair, a gold pen tucked behind her ear. As she thumbed page after page of the register, she tapped her little toes on the white uneven floor. Emily lifted her veil and coughed. A thin girl, gold medal pinned to her chest below a purple handkerchief, ran past them down the corridor, her hands held forth beneath a covered pan and chipped cosmetic set, a black rubber tube dangling from her pocket. Behind the desk a blank-faced steeple clock on the wall chimed each Catholic quarter hour in code, and the pig's red fingers smudged over the print.

She looked up. "Name?"

"Emily."

Red rose from the stool, pulled down her skirt and going to the large vault doors beside the clock she vigorously spun the silver wheel, first to the right, then the left, over and over. A red light flashed on. She walked down the black hallway of the vault, stooped to search through row upon row of orange drawers, dress drawn tight around her back. Finally Red came out, a little black card in her hand. "What's the trouble, kid?" "Oh nothing, really." Emily put her hand over her stomach as a short white-coated orderly sauntered by with narrow, gleaming eyes and rust-soiled trousers. "This way, then," said the nurse and Emily followed her down the narrowing broken tiles. The corridor was long, narrow and high, and black tunnels shot diagonally off from it every hundred feet. Red took Emily by the hand, pulling her along through the dim pink light, brushing their shoulders against long lines of single-filed patients with shaved heads and stiff white gowns. At each tunnel entrance stood an earphoned man who, listening to the voice of the central office, sang forth instructions to surgeons, messengers, florists and pages, and by the side of each of these men was a smoking iron trash receptacle. Wet lime slithered along the floors and down the walls, large keys rattled on Red's wooden hoop. As they walked, nozzles in the floor blew up their skirts. A sharp voice, "Sit here, young woman." "Well," said Red, "I'll leave you now," and turning, she trotted away. The desk was in a small hole in the wall and Emily crouched before it. The man's head, the size of a tennis ball, bobbed up and down, gold-rimmed midget glasses shaking on his nose. He asked questions: bust, shoulders, glove size, hips.

"Ever worn glasses before?"

"No."

"Well, come on," he said, "take all those ribbons out of your hair and look into this machine."

He lit the sputtering burner, twisted dials, spun plastic knobs, watched needles jump, marked six crosses on her scalp, and laughing wildly, swung the machine into position. He forced her eyes against the forked lenses and timed the number of buttons down her blouse. After fastening a piece of garden hose around her arm and poking needles into each of the crosses on her scalp, he hunched over the desk and rapidly wrote with his chicken quill, blinking at the faces on the dials. An assistant kept hitting the back of her head with a mallet. The ball-headed man wrote his calculations on a large white card and hanging it around her neck from a loop of steel wire he pushed her again down the corridor. It split and split again, each segment lined with stacked pine boxes and a pungent smoke, rubber-wheeled carts glided by, stacks of crumbling eye charts piled in corners. The muscles across her abdomen flexed and unflexed and she crouched, as she wandered, to hide herself from view. Long rows of skulls were hung on pegs from the scrubbed walls, candles burning behind the eyes— part of an experiment, skulls that were still growing, and a short fat man climbed up and down on a wicker chair to measure them, steel tape measure dangling from his fingers, a pair of iron ice tongs as calipers. The steady industrious whirl of the hospital was broken by men who loped along the corridors, tin buckets on their arms, ladling out solutions of iodine and foaming water, and by structural inspectors who beat along the walls with their short heavy hammers.

"Stop, young woman," shouted a thin matron with spotted white coat and stringy hair, and holding Emily's arm she peered closely at the white card. "I thought so," she said, and drawing back she leveled a large atomizer into Emily's face. A harsh red liquid squirted into her eyes and immediately a cotton fuzz grew about the skulls, covered the walls and floors and sealed her eyeballs in a filmy crust. One hand over her stomach, the other over her burning eyes, she ran on until, above the grinding of dynamos and the hiss of steam, she heard a faint rising and falling wave of squalls. She stopped and squinted. Behind an open iron mesh, slung in row upon row of canvas hammocks, were the new babies, each head covered with a shock of black hair, all the cheeks covered with matted black sideburns. From each hammock hung a tin cup and a haggard woman in a blue apron passed up and down between them, doling out the gruel. Emily watched the twisting shut eyes, fingers trying to clutch at the cups, and the laughing hag lumbering between the bobbing bodies, her thick legs spread wide.

Henry twisted and again opened his eyes. He saw the parson's rearing pillared legs, saw the planted thicknosed shoes. Henry tried to remember black legs running with water. He could not. His head close to the steel milk can, he heard the hum of the ocean from the giant shell and heard, from its winding depths, the shifting of sand.

"Get up," said the parson. The words crashed through with

terrifying light and he felt, with his numb tongue, the green taste of the day before.

"Havin' trouble wit' de kid?" asked Joe, who was slouched over the kitchen sink sloshing water around inside his mouth, spitting through his teeth over the piles of dishes. The parson said nothing. Over the frosted air came the muffled sound of beating wings and the slow scraping of a rake in a frozen flower bed, the squeaking of an empty swing blown back and forth in the morning breeze. Henry, sprawled tightly on the floor in a waking sleep, painfully rolled his head again and stared dizzily upwards at the massive clerical form. Beneath one black stolid arm was a bulky yellow ledger, packed with envelopes and debts, columns of red quavering figures. Henry waited for the book to fall and crush him, but the parson's fat hand was glazed, straight, and still.

The general leaned against the doorjamb, a large white pipe hanging below his jaw, faded campaign ribbons askew on his chest, rolls of white hair falling below the beaver hat. He looked at the distorted body of his son-in-law and watched the impressive figure of the parson, mitre thrown aside on the kitchen table. "Throw him in the glasshouse. Damn good place for him," mumbled the general through the pipestem, focusing his stern, red, sleepless eyes. Henry's eyes were watering, crossed, glasses hanging from one ear and still asleep he heard the chilled ticking of a clock and the rustling of leaves.

"Get up. I want to go over your accounts with you." Henry coughed, his red skeletal chest heaving between the parson's legs. He shut his eyes.

Emily tried to shut the babies from her mind, but, her eyes closed, the black heads multiplied, bobbed faster, and swarmed over her from behind the mesh. She ran, white card smacking against her chest, bumping breathlessly past blurred white coats and kicking up flurries of sawdust, wads of cotton, and tufts of clipped blond hair. She smelled the sour alcohol of hair tonic and long greasy working shears and heard the hot whir of electric blades. Running she waved to and fro, her eyes burned almost shut from the red liquid, her damp hair hanging behind her. Holding her nose she passed the emergency stations, towel-covered pans beneath red ominous lights, passed open pigeonholes containing stretchers propped on sawhorses. A senile old man, his head gashed open, shrieked at her and she ran faster. Finally, chest constricted, she leaned against a low green door. Floors above her the smoke stack breathed quicker and the black smoke, striking against a low thick ceiling of clouds, pressed downwards about the hospital. Throughout the building a low rumble of hacked coughing started up. Tissues were brought to gasping mouths; corded throats, with knives in hand, coughed through wrinkled unwashed masks. The green door jerked open, leather fingers wound about Emily's arm and a coughing man, spasmodic face below a bright reflector, spoke in her ear. "Come in, Emily," said Dr. Smith.

The room was empty except for a narrow angular white table, a dull overhead light, and a few belts, trusses, and bulbs piled below a dark grilled window. Girders, riveters, and a red sky were muraled on the walls, and the shrill whistle of tugs struck her ears. Light, broken through the grillwork, shot in frenzied beams over the scraped floors, and the glare of acetylene torches flashed from the curving hook in the doctor's hand. "What seems to be the trouble?" he asked.

"Christ," said one of the riveters, "Spike catches dem red hot hunks in his bare hands, pounds 'em inta de box wit his fist."

Below rushed the screaming chains, frothing river, and tardressed figures with glittering hatchets. Dr. Smith pulled a rope and hot streaming air poured into the room. The second red riveter wiped sweat from his black bull neck. The doctor stropped a scalpel, looked at the woman from the side of his head.

"A child," said Emily, "I'm going to have a baby. With a black head. I want to know when. . ." She saw the first riveter look at her in contempt, black glaring eyes. She wept.

"Now, now," said Dr. Smith, "it's not as bad as all that."

"Smack the god damned thing wi' a hammer, quick," shouted the second riveter. The steam hissed.

"Here," said Smith, "Let me take a look."

"Oh, no," she said. She put her hands over her skirt. The furnace roared, flames leapt from the hot box, parched tongues shriveled over the molten steel.

"Let me see."

"Oh, no." A whistle screeched.

With a violent effort he heaved her onto the table and Emily felt the broad flat straps falling over her body, needles jabbing into her arms.

"Drive the damn thing in," screamed the riveter.

The examination began.

15

Shaving brush and mug, soap cake, comb and rusty blade swirled together in the rose-colored basin beneath a torrent of hot water and billowing steam. Henry rubbed his finger on the misty mirror until one eye glared out, then extended the line through the damp haze until he saw both eyes. As he watched, the eyes began to fade, covered with beads of dampness. With a quick movement he smeared a circle on the glass with his palm so that his whole face shone through and leaning forward, hands gripping the pink edges of the bowl, the scented smell of soap, powder, and dry steam rising against his nostrils and throat, he peered closely at his short yellow beard and reddening crown. The razor hung loosely from his fingers, his mouth tasted of soap. His shirt and undershirt were tangled on the floor under his stockinged feet and a cold shaft of air cut from the open stained-glass window through the heat to rake across his thin shivering back. He burned his fingers in the bubbling water, hot water scorched his cheeks and scratched neck, and the yellow beard matted and caught in the trembling razor. He heard sharp clear voices, the swish of skirts, through the open window.

"Beautiful shot. My God, what an eye, darling."

"I think we deserve a cigarete for that one, partner."

The modest laughter of the South American rang out. The dull stamping of a horse rang from the barn across the driveway.

Henry slowly pulled the rough blade from the lobe of his ear down to his chin and dabbed at his cheek with a damp red-blotched piece of tissue paper. The room was littered with tissue; damp pieces crumpled on the tiles, hung from the blue mica seat, stuck to the flowered shower curtain and filled the new pink baby's duck-covered pot. His trousers were spattered with suds and water, his hands were raw, his mouth twisted. He shivered with anger. He slipped, dabbed again. Amid the wet towels on the floor lay his electric razor, shining red case cracked, the gears gummed. He kicked it from under foot. In the row of rotted family toothbrushes, bristles worn, handles stained, hung the newly purchased miniature baby's brush, ribbons dangling below its rubber teeth. A glob of soap fell on its head, it teetered and slipped into the boiling basin. Water poured from his face, trickled around his waist and he tried to listen for the pounding surf.

"Oh, you awful man!" The adventuress's voice, laughter.

His ears twitched. The scent of coagulated gutter leaves and green pine soap, the smell of insecticide and lichen-covered trunks, the brittleness of morning air and glittering slate, the muffled stench of boiling towels, frosty grass below and trembling mirror, swirled about him, flushed and drawn as a stranger's face. He pulled his face up over his shoulder, drew the flesh tight between his fingers. In the distance he heard the fluttering unhappy cries of a hundred spaniels, bushes wagging, faces scratching at cold wire. Morning. The pack cried out. Quickly he slapped a towel against his cheek and, head wrapped in fumes of steam, he waited for the hand to steady itself.

Noel leaned on his croquet mallet, soft dirty hands beneath his chin, tie-ends hanging from his rumpled collar. Close-set eyes stared out over the thin white shining fields, stared bleakly at the distant film of river ice. His saddle shoes were wet.

"Hey, it's your turn!"

"C'mon, play!"

With an effort he righted his pudgy tousled form, shot and missed.

Gaylor Basistini, alone on the terrace, watched critically, then chalked a giant zero on the slate.

Specks of hair, like grains of sand, stuck to his wrists and white speckled halfmoons curled round his nails. Head still empty, temples cold, he forced himself to wait, continue, burn his flesh, throwing towel after towel into the loaded hamper. The violet water burned his cheeks in hard red planes and his hands wrinkled and turned white.

The bolt shot from the door, a toweled figure leapt from the steam bath, and sweltering, red face wet and turbaned, stood near the mica seat. Henry paused, water dripping from the jug, and looked at the wrapped man.

Expositor: You brought it all on yourself, Henry.

Henry: No. You're wrong, because I'm too old. I couldn't.

Expositor: It's too late to be old. You'll take it for walks and play with it in the snow.

Henry: I don't like the snow. And it's not my fault, because I never was capable. Never, you see. It's all a mistake.

Expositor: It happened in a dream. It happened in one of those dazzling dreams, a dream of your omnipotence, when you lost track of time, when you were caught and fooled by space, by a shadow of perfume.

Henry: Stop! I was too old.

Expositor: You'll catch your death of cold when you walk in the snow. It will want to play and run but your hands will be blue, scarves over your nose will not be enough. Your voice will die out in the ice. It will toddle and babble but you will be lost in cracking shelves of ice. It is your fault. Beware the snow,

Henry. Beware of the cold days when you must walk with the child. It will take away your old age and you will fall in the snow. Beware winter.

Slowly Henry's voice repeated: "Beware winter, beware the snow and the child. Look out for dreams. Beware." The old man closed the door into the steam room. Eyes shut, motionless, he wiped the lather from his face with a blown-up towel and ran it round the crown of his head. The young dogs yelped, beads frozen on the whiskers from their snouts, the pads of the paws slashed with thin red lines, coats pasted to their gaunt sides. The gardener with his striped trainman's cap and mudcaked coveralls eyed the dogs, put the horn to his mouth and sent shrill strains over the morning countryside, calling the pack. The water ran hotter. He heard the blasts of the trumpet, the cold sharp alcoholic smell of sound and the pounding of horses' hoofs. They clattered by, brandy bottles banging on leather, fat red riders rolling in laughter. He heard them float past the house, heard the spattering of spurs. He leaned against the radiator until red welts shot up his white leg, until he smelled burning cloth.

In his room, with the door closed, he could hear nothing. All about him was the silence of frost when the chattering has ceased and the walls turn faintly blue. The chill of a room mapped in squares, and he thought that later he would fix the furnace. He thought that he would bolt the gates and walk along by the crumbling walls, his face hidden in a blue cowl, and as the red sun rose he would make a sign, lonely in the open vestibule, that peace had come. He fumbled with the buttons, turning from the mirror so he wouldn't watch himself. He brushed the golden tassels on his robe. He would stand in the door and watch the sun rise on an empty land.

The parson sat still, the ledger on his knees. He waited.

"Ah," said Joe Ottoe, "let's take a break." The mallets were left propped against the trees.

The adventuress threw her pool coat over her shoulders, listened for a moment, but heard nothing.

Holding his thick white flannels doubled about his waist, he walked down the driveway to the fence by the barns and looked over the briar-covered hills. The mules pulled at their tethers, the bony ageless horse lay in the weeds. The sun was a dull red in the morning mist and nearby his brothers rattled ice in empty glasses. The car came slowly down the hill and stopped at the side door, engine slowly turning over, cold dust settling on the hood.

When she ran across the lawn, hair loose and flying, colored skirt whirling about her knees, he knew that she was not going to have a child. The flowers around her neck were white with dew, and as she ran she laughed, and her face was momentarily bright.

"My goodness," thought Henry, "she *does* look young." She ran quickly towards him.

Gaylor blew loudly on his whistle. "All right," he called, "it's time to play."

The Owl

"Him?

Think not of him for your daughter, Signore, nor for her sister either. There will be none for him. Not him. He has taken his gallows, the noose and knot, to marry."

The fathers of Sasso Fetore, their chins in hand, let me by and stuffed away the dowries, squinting at the shadow of the tall lady at my side. Though I was named Il Gufo, the owl, I was tall as she. One by one they deliberated, and well they might, for Sasso Fetore had few left who could walk on the cold stone in the morning without clutching their knees, curling their toes, bending their bare narrow backs, who could wake and anticipate the cry of guai! on the cold air. Few enviable as I. If a father had once seen Il Gufo, sucked in his breath when I was pointed out to him, he might climb again to the fortress for another look, alone. Theirs were the wobbling legs and, at the last minute rubbing tobacco under their lips and turning to flee, they had no word for the hangman. Not one had thought to put his daughter's hand into mine or expected mine to fall on hers. Now they were tempted.

But with each new day the old fathers of Sasso Fetore returned to the field, pressing here and there the suit of a Teresa, Lucia, Antonina, Ginevra. The woman Antonina accompanied her father and if his task, hasty, catholic, were not impossible, she made it easier. Even when passing the bodies of the foot soldiers, blackened chimney boys, collected in the ravines like thin logs with blackened shields or visors turned up to the weather, they devised second-best plans for making husband of the prisoner held captive in the hangman's fortress. And at the time when light rain or storm quickly darked the fortress any hour, my ward Pucento was begging for a wife.

The prisoner, delivered into altitude where there was time and silence to devour him, was the hangman's. The fortress which kept him safe was cleft in two parts on the pinnacle of the city, high tower and low tower, and from either battlement there was an iron-edged view of the world, its cliff, the tilted slopes at the bottom, the sunrise and sunset, and, not so far off, the border itself of a definite black and white. To the east it was possible to find a thin white horizon, the sea. If any in Sasso Fetore saw out there a Venetian sail, they pretended it was a dream.

The fortress was property willed to Sasso Fetore's hangman; his also the road winding from the valley, the produce of the fair set up summers at the foot of the mountain, the remains of the monastery and Campo Santo, and the barrenness of the wasted descents below covered with briar and rose campions. To the hangman went the souls of death's peasants, to him were bonded the lineage of a few artisans and not least the clarity of such a high place, a long firm line of rule. If there was decay, it was only in the walls falling away from proclamations hundreds of years old, still readable, still clear and binding.

The sun reached the mountain first and finally the valley. Each morning I waited for the light, and from the high tower, back to the steady winds, I watched the border until I saw the white skeletons of horses and men with hanging heads,

the white bones of the legs sinking into the sand, the pistols
swinging against pumiced hip bones. An order kept them
ever moving around the mountain clock.

"Mi scusi, Hangman," the first deputy would shout, "it
is time to assemble!"

Leaving, taking another good breath as I turned, my boot
might kick a stone from the battlement and down it would
fall until I heard it land with a breaking of shells in one of
the rooks' nests that littered the golden vertical cuts of the
cliff. My boots were the heaviest of all, black, laced under
the knee. The birds made no sound but suffered these accidents in silence as if natural. The cloud formations over
Sasso Fetore were consistent of color, large and geometric,
the clear head of a Roman heaven.

By a decree dating to the Council of Bishops and Gaolers,
the heart of the hangman's escutcheon burst and became an
owl: with wisdom, horns, and field rodent half-destroyed,
hardly visible under the talons. The bird, the scholar with
his hunger clamped exactingly to the rudimental prey, peered
from his shield tacit, powerful, bits of ruff and gut caught
to his savage bill. The owl. And the hangmen, as they came
down the inviolable line, sat or hooked the demanding winged
beasts upon their necks and shoulders, lordly claws digging
into lordly men, and assumed rule to the archaic slow drumming of the nocturnal thick wings against their ears, bearing
instantaneously the pain of authority injected directly into
their blood streams, as the owl clutched and hooted of old
upon the darkened tree tops.

The owl kept watch on peasant and prefect alike. He
sat erect, taking keen sanctuary among the stones of the
campanile, unmoved while slitting the thin stomach of some
gray animal with his beak or dusting with his low matted
feathers our rubrics. On a cold throne, twisted branch, he
kept a mute, tenacious, arbitrary peace, fit with little exercise, thirsting quietly for the scrap of ligament or skin needed
to keep him cloaked above the city another hundred years.
He had a foul breath, a deadly hold, and was quick; his eyes,

and the trembling in the short armor feathers, the beak that when sated remained locked, were for the cold law and sermon that came out of the forest to make the husbandman quake. To some he brought this surety of judgment and the vision, challenging, of the broken neck. I am speaking of myself, Il Gufo.

To the hangman also went a senatorial apartment and a donkey. Faggots for the cold of winter were supplied on the hunched back of a creature, Monco, who had in his youth fallen from a parapet of the fortress and survived.

They in Sasso Fetore said that I rubbed soot on my face before sleep, that I possessed a lock of every hanged man's hair, that I confessed once a year to a Jesuit exiled from the Holy See, and that I collected about me varieties of stinging insects. None of this: my walls, ceilings, and stairwells were painted often with a white chalk, fresh and sharp as bone, and not a shadow went undetected. The sun was urged down the spires of the scaffold. But the old men of Sasso Fetore needed to talk of their hangman.

Up and down the cleared streets they went, peering overhead lest the bough break, spoke of young women in wait at home, every day combing their hair in a different style, each villa, town house, hut become an urgent convent. Most, like Antonina, were mistresses of bridal chests filled with seven years' accumulation of lace and white bodices, linen, and trinkets that were bolted from the rain. Their fathers plied for them by day, toured the countryside, down on the rocks they beat their hands under the prison windows. The girls were not merely virgin, those unseen propagated a sense of the timelessness of denial, of death hung rocking around and around on the broken-spoked wheel atop a pole. Little Ginevra was kept at home; Antonina, with compressed jaws, came to see for herself the smoke rising from the mass, the even rows of old women paddling their wash, the air of vigil and continuance over the bridled province.

"He hangs them until dead. Will we have a race of executioners, Signore? Let her be still."

However, they turned to stare, to speculate on Il Gufo with or without hopes of conjugation even though the custom of ribaldry and carousing during the season of the summer fair fell more and more into disuse. The men now alive, remaining, had not often seen me in a black hood and waited for the sight.

Storms came from the prohibited east of the ocean. Green and sudden and, sometimes mixed with snow, they battered first the fortress, tearing the bartizans, dislodging and rolling into the air the rooks incapable of opening their wings. For kilometers the rose campions were pierced under the hail and the vineyards bodingly destroyed. Rain scrubbed the high cobblestones, made the straw roofs swell and doors swell, imprisoning Sasso Fetore behind the thickened jambs. Nowhere could a man walk without seeing through the rain the city's virginal design, the plan of its builders: the sheer blackness of stone intended to resist and put tooth to the howl and sluice of water, intact as it was, echoing, beset with the constant fall of the rain, unviolated and dark as in the Holy Day curfew of the year twelve hundred. No storm could dislodge those early grimly smelted chains but rather gave the city its victory in its architecture fixed, steeply pitched, weatherbeaten. Not a bolt rang. As a prosecuted law with the ashes of suffering and memory carried off on the wind, Sasso Fetore was a judgment passed upon the lava, long out of date, was the more intolerant and severe. Only the absolute wheel is known, old as it is, and I looked for the first exacting laws in the archaic, listened for the skidding of an obsolete machine on the narrow driving streets.

"He shall be dead, by means described hereafter, on the first sunless day to come, and his soul shall be said to exist no more." The census of Sasso Fetore was set with the great seal of depuration—jugglers, actors, lame soldiers, all condemned and hanged.

The snow, falling morning and night upon the head and arms of the Donna, inevitably ended in an hour brighter than any season's and one, two, but no more, children and

perhaps my ward Pucento slid down the slopes on their bare
haunches. Hatless, without sweaters, one or three black mer-
rymakers scaled down the white field kicking against the
snow, careful to make no noise, each figure far apart and a
speck black as a devil's finger. Then Signor Barabo, Antonina's father, would climb into the town, up the narrow
street with his brief under his arm and head bent as if looking
for a drop of blood on the snow. He stopped to read every
proclamation again. He had some divination into the past,
for he knew that a hanged man's legs were bound at the
ankles, that once the body is on the rope, it is at the executioner's disposal to hang it as long as he wished, a week or a
day. And while thinking of this ritual, Signor Barabo thought
at the same time of the ritual in which the groom and grooms-
men were about to fall upon his Antonina, corset, mantilla,
and all.

The road up the valley was almost impassable in the snow.
A thin fox, the old man might traverse it but the way was
unbroken as if the forbidden horizon of the sea had crept
during the night to our walls and pickets. My donkey's hoofs
split in winter, still I drove him each day under the seven-foot
arches of Sasso Fetore burdened with a saddle built of wood
and iron and bound to him by a girth that froze and cut the
belly. The tips of the donkey's ears were cut through and a
small rusted bell permanently fixed to each that jangled to
his uneven gait and high station. Astride him early in the cold
and short-breathed brilliant morning—the pinnacle of Sasso
Fetore was like a crag summoned from the Alpine assizes—
I sometimes heard the prefect's voice piping our drawn
streets: "Permesso. Countrymen, good morning!" I would
pull sharply on the bridle.

In Sasso Fetore all but the prefect welcomed the communi-
cation of interdicts whether cried or posted, "Blaspheme
no more. Il Gufo." During the rain, or after one of the determined snowfalls, this injunction met the eye of every man
and boy and was obeyed. The fox was traditionally the blas-
phemer, and the white length of the idle valley road was lit-

tered with the red carcass trapped in winter by a few terrified
children blowing on their fingers. My ward Pucento cut the
tail off close as he could. I saw Signor Barabo cover the fox
hastily with snow. A dead fox meant another wedless day.

Signor Barabo forever carried with him some item intimate to the nuptial, the garter, the soldi the bride tucks
against her bosom, some aphrodisiac trinket he had spirited
from Antonina's seven-year store. One of the articles often
in his possession was the private purse she carried under her
skirts. And this he displayed under the priest's window as
if a lucky impregnation might come between the secular
nectary and the sacred. Signor Barabo's heart, consciousness,
and ambition ended in an appendage that housed the kidney
and overhung his groin like a tapir's snout—blind sack he
lightly rubbed while discoursing and guardedly measuring
the passers-by. He had a large flap hanging from the shoulder
under cover of his coat. On winter evenings when his old
wife massaged it with liniment, he struck her and, enraged,
leaned over again so that the deformity rose up with uncanny
liveliness to be oiled. Outside he was a peasant, inside a fish
whose concealed pouches could inflate to considerable size
until he groaned in his own monstrous dimensions.

"My Antonina, my daughter Antonina, will be ready to
take her husband immediately after the Pentecost."

Antonina was a woman with a narrow girdle and face the
soft color of an olive. It gave me the same strong feeling of
satisfaction to see her as it did to spy my ward Pucento
falling about in the snow, the western gradation of white
marred by the far-off kicking and helpless salutes of his
lengthy arms and legs, an autonomous and senseless play before the afternoon closed to the rising of the wind. It pleased
me to watch him attempting to steady himself, the black
straw on his head rolling across the snow field, one at least
from whom the owl could snatch a river fish without trouble,
so valueless was he. Idyllic his thin trunk, woman's voice, his
pranks in which he exposed his shivery loins unwittingly to
the power around him. Pucento as my ward remained to

hurtle himself against Sasso Fetore's grave unrestored stones, a jest of flesh, angular, laughing, incompetent.

"Pucento," early in the morning I leaned over his bed, "Pucento," I said until he opened his eyes. And, but a moment awake, flat on his back and face to face with Il Gufo, he would try to answer, fall to twisting from side to side, clutching at the gray shirt he slept in and grimacing. He little thought of jesting if I caught him with the dream still on his fingertips and if I broke in upon his disarray and refuge. "Buon giorno, Pucento." As soon as I moved, he lapsed into sleep again. Waking later, he his own medium, he would bolt for the cold street shouting, "Faggots, faggots!" heels skipping high as his knee and wailing as if the wood might crawl to him at a slow-moving pace.

The parochial owl hooted and Pucento made a good deal of noise before he thought better. At night he sat in front of the wintry red brazier and I put him to work kneading my virgin rope coils. He ate cheese cut from a large white tub. The owl stood above us like a thick-chested, legless, disciplined commandant facing, between torn forests, a ragged enemy of Austerlitz.

I watched the coming of dark from the high tower. Sasso Fetore, its roofs sharply crumpled and pitted below me, grew dark but never completely invisible, always some fragment of thatch or colored glass withstanding the night. There was only part shelter in the tower; I stood with my shoulders hidden in the damp and one fist and my face raised, exposed to the rush of air, the long fall away to the villas and water wheel lost below—that curious feeling in the fortress of half human, half mildew of history, a precarious high post with the open night in front and a wet niche in the stones behind. I gripped one of the cornices. And the moon passed, small, cold, flying between the dead trees. The ordeal of older tribunals, the plagues that attended the newborn and the roof of black stoop-shouldered angels that awaited them, the fiber and the crack of the ferrule amongst the population, these I thought of in the evening when my boot heel ground under a bit of fortress rock scum.

Down, in the dark, the peasants were eating their macaroni, flat bread, and a paste made of sheep gut. On each wooden table was a liter flask; the wine was new as sap. It was as if I saw them all, corselet, benches, arms and legs, Garibaldis burning in a cold and windy piazza, so certainly were they in the outer and lower spaces, peaceful. And behind the huts, near the mouth of the cave marked by a white statue of the Donna on a pedestal, lay Sasso Fetore's forests, barbed and stripped to order. Here the female owl scratched at her blue egg with a diamond.

"Signore. He sleeps in black sheets. Black straw lies in his stable. I would not give him my daughter—no, Master—not even if he does eat, I've heard said, the pulp of freshly crushed deer antlers. Cross yourself, Signore. Take my advice."

Like oxmen huddled around a milk cart in a dry rut, they had their opinions. But whether the issue that gave shape to the head and bulged the eyes was the catechism, the death of a prized boar, or a remark about little Ginevra's beauty, the old men soaked their hands in warmed oil and all their thoughts and feelings, the very grayness of hair, vanished when the hangman put on his black cape.

It was the prefect who kept the streets picked clean. I could urge my donkey to a gallop until his shoulder blades rubbed and the bells tinkled unnaturally at the tips of his long white ears, and from one end of Sasso Fetore to the other I could see dry gutters, not a dead raven or a cat, no new piling of dung, and, down below the captive sewerage. The small man, fastidious only in size and weight, scourged the lice; short, thin, his bones so many that they formed, instead of a skeleton, a mesh. Across his chest were belted two thin straps pulled to the last hole. The prefect inspected cupboard and water closet, descended into foundations hunting for ripened curd, wielding his torch and four-headed pike. His badge bore the wolves at the dugs, his brief epaulettes, his black hair hewn to the narrow side, and he obeyed, though not without pinching his little lip until it became white. He lived alone below the fortress within shouting distance of the dungeon, sleeping on a cot like a field commander. Martial drum and thin trunks of plants were hung about the walls and obscured the windows.

Of all the prefect's belongings, only his stately ganders seemed descended from Sasso Fetore's own lofty impartiality. His four red-eyed birds, though they had little to eat, covered the countryside in good regiment, their tense hungry step marching over sand, ashes, trampling the rose campions. No girl could drive these white creatures in such formation, and one behind the other, making no noise, they hunted small game and insects. To see them in single file atop the fortress —even I looked up. Or below, in the ravines, winding their way among the dead, always white, sharp-billed, not so beautiful that they would keep from scavenging. Sometimes only the necks were visible, long white necks that might be broken in a dozen places; fierceness and starvation were evident in the ganders' windpipes unreasonably stretched in God's dark and genic pillory. The fowl survived, now holding their flat honed bills high asway against the horizon. The four of them, Sasso Fetore's flock, never emitted the shrill crabbing sounds of their species but appeared on the steep slippery cobblestones in silence, checking themselves, and it was with precision, quickly, that they pecked anyone who crossed their path, thrust forward the snowy Netherlandish throats like serpents. Sometimes I tempted them with my fingers, but they did not bite and continued their marching.

Perhaps Sasso Fetore was most lofty when no one was in sight, when the owl was at his instruction and outside the ganders were poised, making little headway against the sunset, the blue wind ruffling their single file, when the rope swaying from the tall lady dangled idly like a ship cable in the middle of the voyage, and the province, sloping upward, was burnished red and gold, like a Florentine coin, before night. Faintly, in his knotty ears, the donkey's bells would jangle. And the fortress with its rocky view showed its temporary darkling life of lanterns. "Buona notte, Hangman. Good shelter," whispered the last to leave the streets. The clapper hung silent in the campanile, while it was still day, the curfew formidable over sagging bellies, over the aged coveting their anchovies in the dark, out of sight. I looked up, down, Sasso Fetore held the spirit, the law of the swift leg, stones reddening above a country that had no marsh.

At the last moment, before the windy collapse of the day —swiftly it deserted, sinking to another meridian—I myself took the road down toward the ravines and stakes of shriveling berries, keeping to the center of the way, holding firmly the donkey's jaw. A little dust rose some feet behind. And from the cliff, huddled under the balistraria far overhead, I might hear old men playing the viola da gamba, their black coats sawing musically to the left and right in the very position of skirmishers.

Many ravines were empty, offering at most a bit of crackling skin cast off from the snake, a dark spot where moisture was working up from the center of the earth; but in others sat the foot fighters who would run no more, the burned bodies listing into the sand. I rode on the edge of these pits and then through them. I counted the backs of the heads. I looked at them lying upon the earth like assassinated sheep. The remains of a water-cooled cannon were driven deep into the sand. The trenches were filled with letters, in the moonlight I looked at them, letters dropped during the summer and again the next summer on the faces of the dead. The letters were strewn upon the cinders and some had been torn open by animals. And some stuck to my boot heel. I pulled the donkey after me and could not control where he stepped.

The dead were lieges to Sasso Fetore's hangman, a chary parliament with which he met at dusk, having no voices to raise and unable to tell which limbs were lost or which ribs had been staved in the process of death's accomplishment, what weight of marrow and gut given. The numbers I stumbled on, pitifully small, did accrue in some historic calculation, out of their tangle raising an arithmetic council that gave more body to their subservience than the hair, cloth, and tissue withering. I climbed through the ashes hearing my foot turn over a trench knife or wooden shoe; and the contortions, the shrinking about the knees, the unexpected oddments I found poking in the soot, in a Roman fire, were symmetrical, ordered, suitable as the leaning masts topped by slowly turning wheels that were implanted—some signaling device, not monument—in their midst.

It was here I thought of Antonina going to her bed.

Night. I was a lonely rider who urged his donkey into an overheated aged canter on the lesser slopes, and fast even as we returned up the mountain, the road became straight and high, bleak with hoarfrost. My boots, protecting as jambeaux, rubbed his hide back near the tender joining of haunches, the spurs rang. Behind I was followed by speechless adventure, the impersonal ganders. Below, the foot soldiers must wait another inspection, thoughtlessly camped in the hollows where the summer fairs were pitched. Balcony, turret, cloister, arcade, the stones immobile in tempest, all silent and austere, the city descended a few hundred meters and stopped, formidable even to me. A city through the center of which grappled the prefect's four hooks, a place part chalet, part slaughterhouse, with scrollwork upon the gables and brass crowns upon the chimneys, a province whose wooden coffins were lined with porcelain, whose garrets were filled with ransacked portraits of dignitaries and half-eaten goose. Without mass violence, Sasso Fetore was still unmerciful, it was visible in the moonlight, purposeful as the avalanche of rock and snow. Here in the cellars and under roofs far as the boundary, the old men slept in their stockings and the others, confident wives, warmed wedding bands in their armpits. Politically, historically, Sasso Fetore was an eternal Sabbath.

Using flint, iron, and tinder, I struck a flame to the candle at the base of the white statue of the Donna to whom was attributed tolerable beauty and humility and who was thought to destroy dreams. Perhaps to her could be laid the spirit of black and white in the peasant, that suited their soft flesh in both valediction and penalty. Surely the Donna made the scaffold majestic. Week after week of Sabbaths attested to this, when the regimen set down for the citizens was not perfectly autonomous and in the blue night some worshipped object was accountable to the spirit, or the spirit for a moment was awed in some simple fashion; when the law gave bony strength to the lover of Donna and legend. The character and the code, right upon right, crashed into the pale heart when the culprit hanged, her prayers for him so soft as hardly to be heard. She saved none—salvation not being to the purpose—yet, like the virgins, stood off with low head and waited for movement from him bound on the gibbet. Her statue was placed before the cave near the forest and owl's tree.

And the prisoner: perhaps he too had his Donna or some lady to accompany him to captivity. Perhaps he too had his fragile witness in another language and blessed in that outlandish tongue. And if so, perhaps she lent him an untouchable comfort in the cell, peace, his angelo keeping him quiet as he kissed her feet or paid whatever was her homage. Perhaps she assured him of clemency and calmed him. But I would think not.

Guai! Guai!

The sound made my ward Pucento pull his hands and wince about the eyes and mouth. It was Pucento who started the rumor that I would hang him immediately after the Pentecost. How could he know the day!

Several paths led to the fortress. The approaches to the prison that appeared so inaccessible from the slopes below or from the boundaries—on some mornings the patrol raised their skeletal hands—were ready, easy, and at one turning there was even an abandoned pump as if it was here that visitors were expected to drag their mounts, here that they should naturally stop to drink, being able to climb little further. All men wanted to reach quickly, to see for themselves, either the high tower or the low, bloodying their fingers if necessary, sparing not their heart valves or horse. At a bend in the high path there were loose stones that, along with nature's debris deposited in the ruin, fell down upon the rocks. Antonina let her hair drape against the rotted pump the wood of which concealed in its grain a hundred eyes; the ganders favored the low path with their rhythmic scuttling, their search for food out of the rocky air. There was a place in the middle path, steepest and most direct way to the fortification, where from an irregular hole in the rock no larger than three fingers flowed a constant trickle of water, always to be found stirring, always seeping down, draining, from the dungeons— on the brightest of days and though it had not rained for weeks. It was water they said that cooled the ardor.

In the morning, early, the unshaved prefect climbed to the prisoner with unusual speed, as if to put to his lips the treacherous and unruly ram's horn. Bloodshot, hurrying when it was not yet his hour to come to the streets, he avoided my eye, a nightmare still fresh in his head, and as he passed he covered his eye nearest me with the glove that pinched the fingers and left the wrist bare, hardly saluting, carrying his water quickly along in a rat's sack. And already the prisoner studied the lines in his hands and picked at his incomprehensible tin insignia, the badge of those about to die in public.

And still Signor Barabo tried to speak to the prisoner. He petitioned to husband him. He asked for his name. Promising him—sure of my pardon—consigning his very procreative parts to this daughter or that and joining him to his otherwise fruitless family. And Signor Barabo was not alone. The men, oldest of all, with lids falling away from canine eyes, with clay pipes wrapped around their fingers, could be seen every day dusting, dusting the studs, the iron, the boot toes, a long and tenuous bell pull, hook-backed and hard at work polishing the war horse. They uncorked bottles of spumante. The prefect talked; and in the excitement some suppliant thought to smear the face of the Donna with blood. There was more spumante.

I, hangman of Sasso Fetore, prepared in another manner to give them a spectacle that would bring a laugh, a cry, and an upsurge even from my confessor, the Jesuit.

I washed down the scaffolding brought from the seventh hill.

I, hangman of Sasso Fetore, set in motion the proceedings that drew ledgers from their vaults and inkpots to the oak table, pushing the rafters, the spokes, the axle cold and thick with bear grease, touching these ancient parts in the law's carriage house—and through the city I had justice dragged on a hundred wheels roped to the distended body.

I went to see if they also were ready.

"But he has a fine stand, has he not?" The other, bowing his head, answered, *"He has, Signore."*

And the old man, muttering to himself, would set off as if to settle the matter immediately, jogging his proposals and senility, muttering in Sasso Fetore's pantomime, smiling down the hill and moving his lips.

THE PRISONER COMES

"Permetta che le presenti mia figlia. Permetta che le presenti mia figlia Antonina."

It was the feeling in Sasso Fetore that after this introduction, she—be she Teresa or Antonina—would say, "Quando potrò riverderla?" hiding hair and throat in a tight veil. During the warm weather they stood out on the rocks to watch, a young woman standing white as the Donna upon each stone below the cliff. The romantic gambados of all such as Signor Barabo—these aging courtiers—tempered the season, and the cockle cap, the red noses, turned to home greatly astir. The devil sat between Signor Barabo's shoulders and breathed heat down his neck. There was an air about Sasso Fetore—it was felt in the council, near the pump, or behind a stained glass—that one wretched mass of the sex was about to rise to the temptation.

What one of them did not expect to husband my prisoner?

Signora Barabo, with fiery arms, bathed her daughters in an alcove behind the farmhouse and the water ran from under the bristling swine, seeping across the yard from the bath: first little Ginevra and then Antonina, sparing neither, the shouts of the three women loud as slaves naked in their stockade. And not a word from Antonina when, accompanying her father, she carried pressed to her bosom a book from whose foot hung a flower, the Spinster's Needle, hardly moving under the clasp of her hand. In Sasso Fetore female fingers were powdered and ringed, were driven carelessly into dough or the common crush of blood apples, or took the axe to the pig.

It was at the time of the bath one day, when the owl also spit and picked his front, that my ward Pucento led a small column of soldiers, and amid them the prisoner, up the hangman's road. Pucento, the lictor, was well ahead and he was covered with the camouflage of torn coat, berretta, and dusty face. Pucento led his band past the girls' shifts drying on the barbed wire and forward to the steeper grade at the same moment Signora Barabo splashed Antonina from the bucket.

Pucento brandished the Roman fasces over his head. The bundle of straw and the scythe blade, arms of authority, these he kept thrusting left to right at the open road so that the rushes whistled and the blade hooked into the air. It was an instrument he might shake at the path of a fiend or rattle on the day of excoriation. Every few feet Pucento, still on his toes, suddenly crashed the jacketed axe head down upon the earth savagely as he could. I felt also his extravagance and I too the compulsion in his various steps. And as this small figure flexed his legs, his arms, even from the tower I could see that he was capable of cutting down the bush and huts as he passed.

The marchers that he led huddled together and tramped up the hill. They had been joined by one, two, members of that outermost patrol whose skulls were cavernous and whose muskets were covered with the bleach of bare collarbones. They walked heavily and clung to earth, often making a cordon out of their arms, knapsacks and blackened eyes; their greatcoats billowed and exposed the home-sewn sleeping shirts grained with lice. A rifle raised, I saw the black expulsion of shot and ball signaling their arrival.

They had come far. Still, close as they were to the end of the march, they crowded together, menacing their prisoner as if they could not bear to give him up.

A small child ran from a sty and threw grit into the midst of spiked boots, perspiration, and white lips. It was not long before those few figures old and bent out in the fields—accustomed as they were to till from light to dark without looking up from the furrow, so alike and so menial they could not be picked out from the clay and pinch of seed they attempted to sow—dropped their rakes. From several corners they hurried toward the road to stare after the band smelling of the capture. A foreign crow glided above them and watched for refuse. An old man shouted: "Come si chiama? Come si chiama?" excitedly, squeezing his hands. But if the prisoner understood, he dared not answer.

The wind tore to shreds the clouds about me, the taste of morning coffee and cognac was on my tongue, and so high on the fortress walk one could hardly imagine the burnished air and the moisture that lay in the beds of the bullocks at the foot of the valley. The rooks cowered in their nests. A spirit bottle had smashed on the stones in this deserted niche of the fortress and back and forth my boots ground the glass. It was a cold vigilant place. As I watched the progress of Pucento and his patrol, my mind measured off the fields like parallel rules: a hundred kilos would be reaped from that one, another hundred from that, in the middle field there was nothing except the grave of a peasant's small boy. The earth looked like the mud holes of rice flats, it stretched away only to provide a surface in which to hide excrement. On the eastern horizon, on the sea, a lone sail leaned down skirting the salt caps.

Then Pucento was nearer. They approached the gate that was proud only of its immunity after a past of doges, conservatories, learning and brotheldom—the Renaissance driven from our garrets and streets. The foot soldiers were close, the green skullcaps, the rusted saber, the empty sacks. They disappeared into the arches and piazzas and the smell of burning twigs.

I was spared the sight of the women holding their bosoms to the window in welcome. Sasso Fetore gave them its unlatching of shutters, and they were followed by an old woman offering them a hot pullet. As the soldiers passed the coffin maker's shop, the old fellow poured a drop of spumante into the tin cup of each and tried to detain them.

"Where is your daughter, coffin maker?" growled one, taking his draught and flattening his boots on the stone.

"Inside, inside," was the quick answer. And, "Lucia! Come down, daughter!"

But they were gone and he drank a bit himself and sat upon the curb. Two children, dressed only in shirts, ran ahead and pounded on the doors, and their running feet sounded like a monkey clapping his hands. "La, la, la, la," were the exclamations within.

They went through the streets barely catching the pieces of bread and meat thrust at them, and they turned the corners all at once like a band no longer familiar with avenues and pedestrian courtesies, took large strides, men just come from marching in the snow. They were conscious of the weapons, the powder bags hanging to their bodies. They were poorly shaved, having cut at their faces out of doors and in cold water. But even those in Sasso Fetore had gray cheeks and oily hair, the marks of their Latin, circumspect temperament. Even Signor Barabo had inherited his weakness.

And men as well as women appeared at the windows to wave stockings or a wooden fork, wiping the wine from their lips and sleep from their eyes. "Che cosa, cosa?" whispered the very young until they were lifted to see. Pucento led his men upward through Sasso Fetore.

From the roofs below me rose a crematorial smoke which they had fanned to fire in the middle of their stone floors early that morning. The first awake had shaken the second in his blanket and then the third; with the confusion of dawn still upon them, they lifted dirty heads from their arms and a vocabulary humble as the sounds of animals was put to use again. All of them wanted to touch the prisoner who had not a moment before been brought from the fields and ditches into the streets and bolted structures of Sasso Fetore, past the sagging figure of Signor Barabo himself gripping aloft a handkerchief and shouting: "Viva il prigioniero!"

From the absolute clarity of my vantage above—the wind was strong enough to prickle one's skin but leave the eyes starting from the head—I surveyed the slate roofs and beneath them those who hurried in anticipation through the morning.

The band emerged from the edge of the city and faltered a moment upon the plateau of the last back houses and over-toppled fountain, shouldering their arms before crossing the graveyard from which started the paths to the fortress. The eager crowd did not follow them from under the pitch of roofs and balconies, but the women and children went indoors again. Two old men tipped their heads together, held their arms up in excited tremor-boned salute, and went their separate ways, listening with their ears to the lock holes for what was to come.

Pucento thrust high the fasces and twisted them around and around in helpless signal, unable to move further, paralyzed with wine. The others pulled their coat collars over their mouths. But even paralyzed, Pucento's standstill was tormented with the sound of dogs leaping with torches in their jaws, his indecision comic and fearful as a clown's.

I leaned over the parapet. "Avanti!" I shouted, and at the command they rattled forward, striking their pennant staffs into the ruts. The owl hooted. The climbers in their bulky clothes tried to balance by clutching the blue and black scrub trees that twisted horizontally from the cliff. The hidden villagers sent up a low-lying olive smoke. Then I saw the prefect come out, finish his piece of dried pepper, hastily tuck his shirt into his trousers, and descend to meet the prisoner. He was short and wiry in the light. On his belt he carried a ring of keys and in his hand a pair of wrought-iron pincers. He poked his sharp tongue against his cheek thoughtfully.

The ganders cut between the prefect and the prisoner. The birds, dragoons of the farmyard, precariously trod the sheer ledge, and continued unswervingly, keeping formation in unlikely crags and watches, pointing their sails, languid but regimented and stately despite webbed feet. White and silent was their propulsion. Between the prefect and Pucento, the ganders sailed with prohibitive bodies the shape of vindictive Flemish women's headgear wide and crackling beyond their backs.

I stood tall, shoulders hard against the round of the high tower, surveying the radii of earth not quite a maremma. And far, far off some low women beat their loaves upon an ox's haunch. All about was the deceptive blue sky. In, out, to the chest and extended, I breathed deeply of the air the wind hath frozen in his belly. I hardly noticed the black tiles on the roofs directly below and did not know whether all were impassioned of the prisoner thinking he would escape the scaffold or, more likely, thinking I would hang him. But I did not concern myself with the whispering women or with the deceptive plans of Signor Barabo. Nor with the prefect's temporary arrangements for the captive, for he existed only for this, the torture that demanded no strength from his own arms, the turn of ratchets, and a blowing of bellows into live coals, his activity confined to the adjusting of his four hooks —a cunning that grew in the dark, that filled his lungs with the smut of burning hair and oil.

But I would sooner my boots pick up fresh dung by the hour, the rain splatter my bald skull, the ice stiffen my red cape, and the dwarf trees lash my shoulders at a run, than sit

bent over, afraid to injure my windpipe, studying the silent
drops of moisture on the aquiline nose of one being garroted
in a cellar thick as a furnace. Signor Barabo could recite the
canticles: 'the hangman shall be four cubits tall or more, shall
have a head of prominent bones and smooth on the top so
that all admire the irrevocable round of the bone and largeness of brain, and he shall be bareheaded except on each day
preceding the Sabbath named in advance by the hangman
when he shall wear a pointed black cap the better to see him
and to make the grimness of his nature apparent by contrast
with the conical black peak, in the manner in which the
fiercest animals are fashioned with some unnatural largeness
of hindquarters, stripes on their sides, or horn.'

Between the high tower and the low was a rampart of moss
and stone, a catwalk connecting the two as stolid as a Roman
battlemound. It led one at a level with the chimneys and un-
earthly shrubs. There was no handrail, here the rock was soft
and sloped toward the drop to the valley, narrow and red
with the iron secreted in the crevices. I walked out upon this
ledge, the wind swept it with his frost. As I moved, a large
barren nest, insulated with old feathers, was suddenly flung
into the air where it hovered a moment, a round tangle of black
briar, and, striking an invisible pit, fell down heavy as a de-
mon's iron halo.

The low tower barely held one man. I was able to look
over its edge into the silence below. It was a mere turret fashioned from the silence of the fortress, protected from the wind,
and covered with drops of moisture like the hollow of a tree
trunk. To wait here and to watch, confined in the lookout
overhanging the quiet court, made my crossed arms patient
and the eyes dilate as through the gray of the dark. The stone
that came to my chest hampered even the intake of breath,
yet at that moment I might have already fallen, stepped into
the beating air.

The tall lady stood below in the court almost as if she were
taking the sun. Now she had no rope. Her place had been
appointed by men who with trepidation paced off the earth

and tasted it upon their knees under her shadow, a shadow taken to the earth and remaining there. The scaffold itself, shaped like a tool of castigation, was constructed to support the dead weight of an ox if we came to hang oxen. She was of wood and black as a black ark, calm by nature, conceived by old men with beards and velvet caps, simple and geometric as frescoes of the creation of the world. She offered no retraction or leniency once death was in motion. Much about Sasso Fetore was told in the idleness of the gallows. And idle, without her tongue, how stolid, permanent, and quick she was, still ready as the roots of ancient speech for the outcry. Her shadow changed sides while I watched and it became more cold. The sun did not come too close to her.

"Grace to you, grace to you, Hangman," shouted the citizens of Sasso Fetore and put flame to their torches though it was still light. The faces in the crowd that formed on the swept cobblestones when the prisoner was hurried into the fortress, the faces whose noses, cheeks, foreheads—of a greedy man, sullen man, obedient man, choleric serf—struggled to free themselves from the caricature putty and paint of their daily look. There was a murmur, the press of the people, in expectation.

If Signor Barabo had come upon me then, he would not have bothered with his long practiced and formal 'Permetta che le presenti mia figlia' nor bothered to bow or hide the worn patch in his official cummerbund—he was flushed and might only have shaken his head at the obvious color and fulsomeness of his daughter's arm. But he remained now behind closed doors in the caffè and the glass before him was kept brimming.

"My eldest daughter—gentlemen, Antonina—has become the belle. Let us be bold: the word is *appassionato*. Already, sirs, I seek to hire two backs at least to carry the dowry, two more her gowns and the rest of it.

"Let us call her 'respected bride.' Donna, but we can agree, every bone in her body is true, the knuckles are hard, and the

heart does not flutter needlessly. Put your coats down, gentlemen, for my daughter.

"She has been standing these seven years—confident the
while—in a pasture of chilly reeds and not once has the wind
spied her ankles. Have you seen them, gentlemen, the virgins
touching each other's cheeks by the mill or the lonely south
crèche?

"But, gentlemen, even the little girls titter when my daughter passes. The children suspect something, my friends! Will
it be the white gown or the gown the color of pearl? The
embroidered linen or the plain? Shall we order radiant dignity?
Will we serve pheasant and fish or goose? What sort of rings?
I ask you. I ask you to think of Antonina. . . ."

"There is Lucia, also, Signore."

". . . Yes. And of Lucia also if I may ask it. Think, gentlemen, for your pleasure and make your decisions. The baking
must begin at once. For I tell you, the weddings will sweep
us like grass fires. . . ."

Signor Barabo rubbed his hands as if he were rolling a great
ball of unleavened dough, the fathers of Sasso Fetore raised
the bowls to their lips in salute. A small lizard ran across the
floor and the coffin maker reached out his boot and destroyed
it against the beam. There were two narrow windows in the
caffè, each filled with small thick cubes of purple glass sealed
by lead into the frame, through which, thick, opaque, the
street and the world beyond were dimmed.

And out in the street thronged the crowd. A few, grinning
uncontrollably, rapped on the glass, an aimless communica-
tion of the drift of their mood. The emotion went among them,
possessing their hands and feet, making them noisy. Those
who had been asleep asked, "When did he come?" "Citizen,
only one of them?" "When will we see him again?" Some,
with uncomprehending eyes and jaws slack, shouted, "The
hangman has taken his wife, he has taken his wife!" knowing
not what they said.

They put their hands upon Antonina, crying, "Fortunate,
fortunate, she here will not have her purse for long. . . ." The

women dropped combs from their hair. Now two, now three, fell from the crowd and stood looking at each other with wonder. Signor Barabo's wellborn eldest daughter, Antonina, was no more able than they to resist the street crowds. She walked in the direction of the Jesuit's chapel, but she did not enter it. She was reluctant, yet Antonina, also, was not to be denied and climbed to the heights of Sasso Fetore, as women will when they have heard of a disemboweling or other fascination. She did not shudder seeing her sisters with the cloth off their shoulders.

Antonina was one of the virgins who have grown knowledgeable as an old wife, select at nursing fires or calling back the dead with circles and chalk. Up she came through the rose campions and sourweed, having refused the accompaniment of little Ginevra, and the tears of the brisk wind were impersonal upon her cheeks still olive with the pigment of generations.

"Antonina, Antonina, this way," hailed Signor Barabo from the door of the caffè and waved the handkerchief he had lately shaken at the prisoner. His daughter gave him the rare crow's wing of her smile. "Gentlemen," shouted the father, "behold!" And they gathered behind him in the door frame, a dozen pairs of eyes and a dozen goblets.

In a curious manner, with intoxicated bravado and a fear lest the words not be said at all, Signor Barabo shouted his daughter's banns loudly, each time incomplete: "Antonina, respected and loved of father and mother, has become betrothed by law and by permission of her father, soul, spirit, and good temperament to Signore . . ." "Gather the white flowers, gather the white flowers, Antonina shall marry . . ." "It is declared, this woman's betrothal has been fixed on earth and I, the father, give her, I give her . . ." And these speeches —he was clutched by his compatriots in the doorway—were addressed to the oglers nearest him, the red noses and scar cheeks of the women who replied by opening their mouths as if hearing a proclamation of punishment instead of the banns. Then he freed himself and pushed a way toward his daughter. "Will of the Donna that she marry, will of the Donna that she enter the rooms of the tall booted hunter; no daughter shall refuse to give herself and her father asks it. All the public shall see her enter the stranger's house, none see her return. Begone to wedlock, then!"

He took her arm and stepped forward, bowing to the left and right, low, and the integument wriggled under the coat between his shoulders. Antonina was a head taller.

"Un momento, per favore," muttered the coffin maker, catching up with them and pulling after him his daughter Lucia. The two pairs climbed the black and white streets. Black rings and bolts, white stones once washed by the sanctimonious noviates, how the wind whistled in them, preparatory to thundering down the mountain. The two old men held tight their virgins. Antonina, despite disbelief and the black band fastened about her throat, walked sternly a little in front of her father, hastening to see for herself. Her face was like the Donna's. Already she knew what propriety was lost—but Antonina's heart made public would perhaps put them to silence. Her mother, deftly, had pinned a small male figure of silver to her hip and there it caught the sun.

The red and the gold were gone from the fortress. Signor Barabo took his daughter in Pucento's late footsteps, grimacing as the shrubs slipped through his hands and he tottered, wiping his face. The fortress was black and white with age, the rooks screamed the cry of a dying species.

Signor Barabo stared up at the grated window of the fortress and as soon as he got near, he bellowed: "My son-in-law, future son-in-law, look here!" stamping his foot and shaking his black hat in the evening, unconscious of the shadow at his side.

I, on the other hand, took my usual ride that evening. Despite the disturbance among the people, the graveyard was still and softly grained as an etching. Since some had worked this day, I passed the trees still smoldering, the stunted pines whose roots they labored to destroy by burning. I rode across their farms and through the middle of Signor Barabo's villa as well. There were no signs of the young women waiting out upon the rocks. Perhaps their mothers were plying them with mulled wine. Certainly they were not teaching them any matter of weights and measures—even the women of Sasso Fetore were acute in the practice of weighing sin in their hands like a pound of oats—the sciences of law and balance being this twilight abandoned for the plaits of the true lover's knot.

I did not stop. My donkey trotted jangling past the very light from their windows, so close his hoofs shook the earth of their floors, but there was not a question of my dismounting, not a movement to detain me though the donkey brushed the sides of their gates. One would hardly know what they were thinking, except that I saw a creature leaning over a hooded well and, through the dark, laughed at her reflection in the green water. And in front of a hut there fluttered a fresh veil on a tilting weather-beaten post. The women of good station and poor were distracted from the bedrails, the pitchers, the pillows grown small and brittle under their heads. Large women such as Antonina now fitted their bodices in the moonlight.

The farther I rode from the city of Sasso Fetore, the better was the view of the fortress, large and silhouetted, black and irregular up there as the multi-prisoned bastile town of Granada. What fate had it to offer the husband hunters! Or the fathers also who, had they the stock, would have busily slaughtered the hogs and cut from them the delicacies of the viscera to be served black and steaming as roasted chestnuts.

To turn one's eye from the immediate rock, the cannibal briar crouched under cover ·of some phosphorescent leafy plant, from the immediate valley road crooked and hard to the rider, to twist about in the saddle and back there, high, far away, see the white fortress and its stripes and shadows, black with its secrets, terraces, barred apertures: the landmark forever there, from which formerly flew pennants of the 'festa,' now sporting crows' nests and rooks' nests over the smell of dead lions in the arena.

The forest was full of activity; on all the trees the small twigs were newly broken and some trunks were still aglow with sparks. The donkey took me heavily through the underbrush, not starting at the fired tree trunks but shying testily when we neared the mouth of the cave. The tunnel, polluted during the time of the fairs, was now lit by torches, pitch sticks wedged deep in the rocks. They had picked the forest bare, dancing a quadrille almost extinct in Sasso Fetore.

The Donna stood before the cave, an idol whose nights were spent with a few small deer and speechless animals. The donkey turned a sharp foot, the lumbering saddle creaked, and even this far I saw the defamation, the Donna's face smeared with blood. I galloped. As I passed her I raised my boot and, ramming her chest, dislodged her so that she fell and rolled upon the crackle of the clearing. And there came the peculiar rush and windmilling, the sound of a bird striking in the dark the outermost protective net of leaves, as the owl first beat his wings attempting to penetrate to his roost at dusk.

THE SYNOD AND THE SENTENCE

"Mi scusi, Hangman," cried the deputy, "it is time to assemble!"

The hunchback went first with his load of faggots and after him, one by one, the council entered, folding their way into the dark, the draft of the senatorial chamber. The old men took their places at the table and awaited the burning of the fire which was preceded by a cold unsuccessful time of acrid smoke. The hunchback kneeled and blew, twisting the faggots with a bare hand, poking his tongs.

"You too then, Hunchback, you have a daughter." Monco peered up and grinned at me, splintering a twig with his knife, and I at him, for Teresa was a girl who should have been burned in Sasso Fetore. He tore a bit of rotted cloth from his sleeve and fed it to the sparks; nothing burned so well for the firekeeper as what he wore. But it was a slow fire and there was whispering at the table.

"A man with a daughter, your honor—Grace to you for having none—cannot think of cutting wood!" grinned he again, lifting his lamed back like a tortoise.

There were twelve seated at the table, far apart and separated by such broad wood that now and then they put their bellies upon it, stretching the whispers. About their throats they had tied the traditional magisterial ruffs, collars like honeycombs of rag paper. The uncomfortable ruffs scratched as they talked, louder and louder with the hurry of the words. Each had a gavel fashioned of rolled calf's skin.

I took my place at the head under the tester blazoned with the escutcheon of a burst fess, a black leathern tapestry from which the dust was never blown, reputed to have once been the skirt of a barbarian conqueror. To conquer without going to field, this spirit of mettle was vested with predaciousness in the hangman.

"Grace to you, grace, grace," said each as I sat and the first deputy posted himself at the door, carrying athwart his broad sword. The fire sprang up and the hunchback and my ward— Pucento was weary and laughed the more—both on their knees pushed and knocked the live coals across the flagging.

"How does the prisoner sleep this first night, is he cared for?" asked Signor Barabo. Before the question was done, Pucento shouted, "Hooks!" and put his forehead down to the stone like a frothing jester. The reeds from the fasces were still bound about his thighs and ankles and some, catching a spark from the embers, smoked, shriveled to black char.

The judgment supper was served, a formality that appeased the instincts of the council, food thought to bind the officials to the hangman and to perpetuate the feast of the law body which preceded Sasso Fetore's original compulsory execution. Before each place was set a platter containing a fish, as long as a hand and thin, speckled green and served whole with the tail and head gray-black in color, bright and opal. I cut my portion with a three-tined fork and a dull knife, but it was customary for the councilmen to take the fish, and its slight dressing of oil, up in their fingers. The river diet was never changed, each day the hunchback wedged his sieve traps into the rocks of a vapid waterfall and awaited his catch, relishing most the moment when it was time to pile the fish together on a peeled stick, thrust the point through their blinking gills.

The thirteen waxen fish, lying straight on the porcelain platters, were devoured again; the councilmen once more broke the tough skin and immobile, formidable under their broad brims, separated the white from the myriad hair-sharp bones. The fish was bitter, its meat came apart with the elasticity of muscle instead of flakes. Occasionally there was a portion of small black roe. This was the cuisine of justice, by firelight the minute fish and the pointed fins were illumined, sticky, each one silver and half-picked against the great black of the benches and under the gray hands of the councilmen. The fish was the fare of all the verdicts delivered and with its complicity of bone and deathly metallic flesh, it had the character of a set jaw and seal ring. It was by the fish that the jurists earned their title Mongers. The season of salting the furrows with the fresh water's spawn was the season of many bells when the Mongers brooded upon those to die.

A food of no sweetness, small pleasure, but the same distributed at the council of Bishops and Gaolers, the same that stuck painfully in the throat of the past—Signor Barabo ate his share quickly enough. He was heard to mutter, "Bella, bella," between mouthfuls though the meal was declared a period for silence. He was tired of seeing each morning begin with the scrubbing of his daughters, was glad now his wife might put aside the wet bundle, her broom. Signor Barabo was volatile and held the fish up by its tail, the shadows taking dark hold of the ragged cavalier cut to his uniform.

I rapped my knife on the table and passed it twice sharply in front of my face, blade toward the lips. Signor Barabo, fat as he was, pugnacious as he was, kept himself quiet after that. The twelve old men concentrated until the last of the fish was gone. The hunchback went down the left side then the right, taking the plate from each as he was supposed—

assuming the familiarity that might be expected from the serfs with their rock plows or from the wine pressers—tapped each councilman on the shoulder so that the citizen should be represented and their fraternal feelings, like the tipping of a hat or the offering of swine for mercy, should be expressed. But he did not touch the hangman. When he took my plate, setting down the tall stack of the rest, he pulled a crust from his pocket and rubbed it in the remnants of the fish oil. Then ate the crust.

The moon appeared beyond the high windows criss-crossed with iron. The moon, having suffered in the heavens some voracious attack by night-migratory flocks, its face having been picked by the wind, drifted low past us now in shreds of yellow against the darkness, and disseminated the cold of its center over the roof tops, the priory buildings of the fortress. Inside, the fire took some of the chill from the room. Yet it was cold with the damp smell of their boots, beards, brown hands, and with the machinations within the councilmen's heads, each one thinking his own daughter the kindest of tongue, the best of proportion, and the keenest to do marital bidding.

The old men were dressed alike. The men of Sasso Fetore, and the Mongers with them, at a distance could not be told one from the other except by shape or peculiarity of walk, and these marks too were not obvious when they were gathered in crowds. The brown shirt and the wide-brimmed black hat covered all of them. There was hardly a variation, earthen cloth for the back and a headgear adopted from the primitive monastic order whose members worked in strict obedience and were the first inhabitants of the province. So the shirts were still the brown color of the lay members' robes and the black hats unmistakably derived from those creatures who chanted while fighting on the early slopes of Sasso Fetore, pair by pair beating each other with hard fists under the watch of Superiors—these same fighters who during the matin scrubbed the garments of the sick and diseased on the rocks by the river where the councilmen's fish swam.

Despite Signor Barabo's sash, the twelve Mongers sat before me in such lowness and humility, the fattest and oldest for all their years and their daughters still covered only by the cloth brown as the furrows and dead grapes, the brown that flooded far as the black and white posts of the border. The hunchback's fire and the cold-smoked walls of the chamber allowed no other uniform for the tribunal: by common dress the disparity of their height and features should be shown trivial and in no way belying the meanness of men.

The first man to rise, rip open his hempen shirt, and expose his breast was allowed to speak, the rest thereafter not needing to perform this ritual. That night it was Signor Barabo who could not tear at the buttons quickly enough, scratching the white skin in his haste. The others, who remained seated, buried his first words with the crash of their gavels. Antonina's father revealed greater and greater portions of his chest, appealing to that which he was not and could not hope to be.

"Hangman. *Boia savio*. I asked if he was well cared for," he began. "There was no answer. I sought to learn if he slept and was not gratified. And I climbed to the fortress, *Boia*. Yes, straight up without admiring the view and risking myself to the steepest path. I called "Son-in-law!" using that familiar term. His face was easily seen between the bars and brambles but even from him there was no answer. It is boding. What has been done to him already? Are we not to welcome him when the sun warms us?

"Look at me. I show my chest and part of the belly also, and I ask: *Boia savio*, what is to be done with him? Are the dead to be made jealous for nought? Who would make Antonina—think for a moment that she is not mine—who would make Antonina shudder again? Must our young women walk with their faces forward and forever scanning as if they be the figures with salty bosoms leading ships by iron noses into the gales? *Boia savio*. Not she.

"Should not my son-in-law walk freely? What have I but to take his fecundating germs like pieces of eight for my daughter? And to let him build some cradle, gentleman's cradle, if he can, out of the deep. I've thought of it, so I might lean myself between the two of them when my old wife is dead, and hang to the arm of each when they take me airing. I'd hurry my decrepitude for that. No one else, Hangman, has come or here offered himself as yet. . . .

"And yet my knuckle, with the rest, has surely tapped their breastbones, and in the past we've hung them. Rather you have hung them, *Boia*. What will our justice be? If it is a white card—a white card, *Boia savio*, what mercy!—think how my son-in-law will sleep with his snoring and rise early to stretch his white legs, while I sleep late! Think how Antonina will lift her eyes! Who knows what his inheritance might be.

"I would have it so she will her husband, one to whip the hostlers when the hostlers return, and be regenerative after she has collected a thousand lire of his passion.

"That. Or hang' him high by the law?

"Which?"

I gave him my answer. He shook once and attempted to button his shirt. It was as if I had ordered his soul bled from the arm, and Signor Barabo sat down. It was impossible for the old man not to betray himself, his disappointment physical and evident as the rings round the owl's eyes. He looked at his fingers, thinking vaguely there should have been large blood-gems set upon them. I gave him my answer again, adjuring him, and the Mongers listened on either side of him with faces like millstones, turned to profile and blinking. There was the coffin whose face was nailed together, the cart with his elbows resting upon his wheels, the wealth of land and his earth belly, and Signor Barabo who was not loath in his heart to see the prisoner die. This oligarchy—the mud of their thighs no better or surer to last than that of the old man who left his rake to watch the prisoner pass—was yet familiar enough with the ancient tongue to understand me, these old masters having in their histories sentenced not a few.

High over our heads there was a rustling, a tearing as of a sailsheet, and from a nest suspended by the beams dropped a half-stripped bone to clatter upon the table. Signor Barabo asked to excuse himself. Monco the hunchback burned the last of the fish in a heap on his tall fire. The air of longevity was strong, the Mongers sat straight as those before them, it was a hall in which the lizards in summer, the rats in winter, peered at the justice of Sasso Fetore captured in oil paint, the noses and downturned months preserved by the sculpting twist of the palette knife. The building had a flat roof and was surrounded with arcade and flagstaffs and marred by the slings of barbarians. It was the only white building in Sasso Fetore. Here, this night, we conducted our business despite the look on Signor Barabo's face and while he trod through his dreams keeping one hand on the pocket where he carried a curl of Antonina's hair.

How long shall be the length of rope? That was decided. And the braid of the rope, fine or coarse? That was decided. Was blood to be drawn first from the throat or not? That was decided.

And who shall be witness? Also decided.

At last Signor Barabo began to wake and to his brothers' voices added his own yea or nay. Still he interrupted to murmur, 'The respected bride, the respected bride,' and sharpen his eyes as if to contemplate the beneficence of this title, yet envisaging a wedding summons of four quaint pages.

The firelight seemed to come out of its hiding, their faces became white and more round. There was a cut to their lips and a leathern round to the knees beneath the table. The hunchback—the rock that bowed him rose on his spine higher than the head—waited upon each old man with an iron pot and from it doled half a hand of ash on the wood itself in front of each; to each he gave a quill and poured water over the ash, the writing fluid thick and black and staining the wood. They commenced to scratch and blot the document as it passed up and down their row.

"*Attenzione,*" they again would read along with the rest from the northern wall, "*Attenzione . . .*" I could see the rain beating the shoulders of those who depended upon nothing so much as the formality, stringency, the trueness of ring, the

evidence of the Death Decree. "*Attenzione!*" Always the Decree contained the name of the condemned. It was the task of
the citizenry on hands and knees to scrub the piazza after
the execution.

"*Boio savio.* Antonina would wear twelve skirts to her
wedding." And he wrote his full illegible name in the script
that once flowered in this country. But Signor Barabo was
also a cruel man, as his daughters told.

"My daughter, Altezza," grimaced the hunchback, "would
wear none!"

My face showed nothing. Like long trained and impounded
clerks, the old men dropped their quills and took up the
gavels: "Grace. Grace to thee, Gufo." And they followed
me into the night, leaving the faggot-gatherer to quiet his
flames. The Mongers huddled together and waited to see
me depart before dispersing, before touching each other's
shoulders silently and descending alone to their several rooms,
knocking secretly on the thick doors in narrow streets. Think
of them then finding their way about among their personal
belongings, correctly choosing the bed, the roughened walls,
and those who have kept awake for them. How unsearchable
is the law whose sentence they subscribe to and which leads
each home and to a sleep that continues while the chimney
cools! We left them, Pucento and I making a hard noise up
the slope.

We went the way from the senatorial chamber to the
square of the tall lady, past the hangman's leaning house and
stable, and up the highest rampart broad enough to permit a
cart of fifteen unfortunates to travel—before dawn and with
hands roped—to the gallows. A few posts like black briar still
remained driven into the rampart; from these Pucento hung
out, peering, a bare-headed silhouette, toward the nightly star-
spaced distance that drifted over the whole of the valley.

"Padrone," my ward pointed and whispered, "the prisoner."

Up there was a window and two thick bars, a window
secreted in the crevices of the fortress, an opening eaten

through the stone so small as to hide the features of the prisoner and stop his cries from passing to the air.

The portcullis was only an arm's length over the prefect's head. There he stood idly, a truncheon dangling from his wrist, and smoking a short butt of cigarette.

"Buona sera," he whispered and made a gesture to straighten the two straps snarled across his breast. "A respite, *Boia*," he said softly and shook the fingers of his truncheon hand as if they were stiff and pained him. He had oiled the keys and they glistened at his belt, those that opened the locks of coffins as well as the fortress door. He smoked and the thin substance of his cheeks stretched over the bones to the mouth. He shifted, the rotted pumps on his feet scratching the ice and gravel, and he glanced between the teeth of the portcullis toward the clouds.

"Will it storm, Hangman?"

"Prefect, I will see my prisoner."

Still he put no life into his marionette arms and legs, thin akimbo creature resting, inclining, bedraggled in his official position. Then he began to study his keys as if he did not know them well. Sullenly he thrust them toward me.

"Can you choose, Hangman?"

I chose the large bull-headed key. Yet he did not move. To the west stretched the topography of our lowlands—the snow was collected in the pits and gullies and with the flat white shape of salt encrustations gave tooth and rib to the night, dimly providing a body for the dark. The low possessions were there, wind-swept, across which barked Pucento's fox. The prefect's name would never be scratched on the floor of the senatorial chamber, nor would he have so much as a tombstone to slant abjectly through the lean centuries to come. He existed as at the mouth of the drainpipe to Sasso Fetore. But the prisoner was, for the moment, in his custody.

"I will need a lantern, Prefect."

"Carnefice. Eater-of-deer-horn. Will he not have a term of servitude? I should care for him, Hangman, as he deserves."

The prefect made this plaint and leaned more heavily, refastened the keys to the leathern girdle beneath his tunic. His kepi, with its battered top, was ill-fitting and crooked; it slipped far forward, giving outlandish shadow to the shape of his head. There was no sword in the scabbard which he still dutifully wore where most men in Sasso Fetore would carry a good hip.

"If he has not escaped, Prefetto, I will look at him."

The bolts fell. Pucento began a soft excited keening as we entered and, before we reached the dungeon, was calling ahead *prigioniero! prigioniero!* The prefect faltered with the lantern. I walked slowly, my footsteps paced. But Pucento ran suddenly, flung his body against the bars of the cell, and shouted loud as he could: "If we free you! If we free you, Mostro, will you not ask for the hand of little Ginevra!" And Pucento panted, the straw on his wrists and ankles rushed against the wooden bars.

"Look now, Hangman," the prefect swung the light at arm's length, "and decide, per favore, to leave him with me."

For now the prefect was the proprietor, knowing only too well of the young girls who were ready to bribe unmercifully for a sight of his charge: malignant, with a show of pride, he turned the best possible light upon the prisoner.

The floor was dirt. Through the high window I saw a cold star, then a few flecks of snow. The cell was short, the eastern wall a ledge, stony and down-sloping, upon which the prisoner was to sleep. A large wooden spoon and fork lay there and black thistles shedding pollen dust. At first the prisoner tried to protect his eyes from the lantern glare, then slowly he got to his feet.

"Mio prigioniero," I addressed him simply and said no more. He looked at me; and the prefect also, with Pucento, looked at me. In the recessed eyes was a worn pleasure and, in this fortress cell, expectancy. Here the prisoner was detained in Sasso Fetore's highest stronghold, a man with two hands, feet, and all the past we can remember, our captured image, a foreigner. He blinked less in the rusty light.

"Little Ginevra," muttered Pucento, kneeling, peering first at the prisoner, then at myself.

"Shall he take off his coat, Hangman, that you see him better?"

Every now and then the prefect shook the lantern as if to shake it into other focus. Nothing was the prisoner's but what was about him, little remaining yet all, the hair on his head, the gray of the skin around his mouth, the coat.

"No, Prefect. But unlock the cell."

"Donna. He is used to no one except me."

Pucento's round head, the round head of the prefect, the lantern's head were at my back in the doorway, and I faced him with nothing between us but the air which we did not turn to intelligible sound. He wore a gray trenchcoat that buried his legs; he was hatless, and on his face was an expression of wistfulness. His collar was damp as if he had been breathing quickly all his life, on the collar silver insignia of a skull and crossed bones. The features, the teeth pressing against the lips, the eyes which had failed in his calculations now lay pale and aged with pupils in semi-focus. And yet all about him was the smell of earth, as if earth had been packed into his helmet, ferns packed in his sleeve, and the buttons, catches, and chevrons had rusted away.

I took his two arms and lifted. They remained outstretched, and I took hold of his lapels and pulled. I put my hands on his ribs and felt with care high as his armpits, slowly, and he remained standing despite evidences of the prefect's hooks. There was a lump on one rib as if it had mended of its own strength. He endured this inspection: and the while his attention, his form of halted intelligence, was upon me as if to find some information for his own welfare in a gesture of mine.

I was that close to him. And did not intend to be so near him again until the Pentecost was past. Still there was not a word from him, only the accumulation of strangeness, the signs that he would never be at home in the cell before we removed him. Never again quite locate himself, he who had lost his battalion of all things familiar and banal, his comrades. I suddenly found that it was with curiosity I searched him.

Under the coat, hanging from one shoulder, I discovered the black grained map case, much out of shape since he had slept on it, and across the front of the case were loops containing two thick writing instruments and a steel calipers. This I took and opened. A thin sheaf of maps was tied inside, a packet on thin paper and wrinkled with constant exposure to water. They were of our province, the details, landmarks of Sasso Fetore recorded precisely, the perimeter clearly indicated, the place of the charred foot soldiers, the forest, and there was the fortress. I looked closely. Then handed the case to the prefect. There was nothing else. Only that he had known his way to us by these directions, the work of an old and shrewd cartographer.

The cell was narrow, the ceiling low, and the earthen floor was covered with the many sharp prints of boots wide and thin, pointed or blunt. The red light honed the bars, and the two bars also in the window beyond reach. I wondered what ruse he might try to get his head up to the window, what efforts he had already made. He was perhaps sensible enough to catch a glimpse of the night and to remember his homeland. Beneath the natural height of the cranial cavity were the skull and bones and the enveloping wrap of the coat with its accumulation from long roads, and the great collar which had protected him from the winds when he followed behind the laborious gun carriage of his century. He was the embodiment of caution, the human form endeavoring for obedience and sustenance. I felt the beating of his heart and in that instant he too seemed aware of it and ashamed of it.

Had the women in the streets seen him at all? And Signor Barabo, paused in the caffè, sleepless, he too had overlooked the submission, the fated attitude of the prisoner who might yet be beaten to violence.

"Altezza." The prefect interrupted me and handed me a document that had been carried with the maps. It was written in the language of Sasso Fetore, faded and washed:

If I have fallen into your hands, treat me with humanity. While in your captivity, I should receive half pay in your own currency. No outmoded punishment should be practiced upon me in the name of the Spirit. The agreement is that I shall not be maltreated. You who take me abide by the charter. I am to have no fear for your charity. I will not give up hope. Regularly give me water and a ration. Honor, publish abroad a notification of my surrender that I may keep my place in the world, even in the separated ranks.

"Primo Boia," shrieked Pucento from his knees, making some sense of the paper, "tell him the truth! Tell him he will receive no visitors but these!" Pucento, my ward, reached up for the document, and I gave it him, with its notions of temperance and gothic print.

I stepped back suddenly from the prisoner and saw him sacrificing his last days to conversations with insects, growing a beard, and fasting without recognizing hunger. He would study his fingers closely, the expression of consequence would pass from his face until he was carried to the piazza of the tall lady. I saw a curious crudeness around his mouth. I looked at him, at the shape of his jaw, his height, standing with all the turmoil of his senses guarded, his knowledge serrated, and the skull and crossed bones were his last insignia.

I stepped away from him. That one human might inspect another, I peered at him and was aware of the declarations and betrothals within him. But, as he raised and bent his arms, I saw only the white tips of his elbows protruding from the sleeves in the coat. Signor Barabo's son-in-law! He was ragged! I would not remember him for long. Nor certainly would Antonina. I would not see him in such calm again. And then I shouted at him: "What is your name, *immediatemente!* Your name . . ."

He did not answer, and we left him in the darkness.

Pucento and I wound our way bottomward, both of us silhouetted at the rim of the cliff and against Sasso Fetore, its obstructing roofs and chimneys through which no one dared to call the watch of the night. The last lock closed behind us.

It was late, the doors appearing in the darkness were not plumb. The nosegays of the welcoming crowd had been swept from the streets and they were deserted. The immense king's evil of history lay over the territory, and it waked me, as in the dawn, to breathe deeply, and I raised my hands at each doorway putting the seal upon them. Pucento careened ahead of me. Had it not been for the curfew, we would have been approached by those out of the dark begging their fortune. But the noose of night was drawn.

At my doorway, however—once we had passed under the arch and by the stilled Tuscan fountain—there was a disturbance, a fluttering and tangling with the bell chain, so loud that the old beast stamped in his stable. The prowler, come perhaps to intercede for the prisoner, was caught by the owl and, with fury and pointed ears, he sat upon her head, slowly raising and lowering his wings as a monk his cowl. He dug into her scalp, circumcising the brain. Her tresses were gathered against his dirty tail and he tugged as if he would carry her head up into the air. The owl labored and beat upon the woman, rasping through his gray hood. She tried to run, but he was fast to her and flapping, and the beat of his flooded wings slowed her.

I relieved her, taking the owl to my arm and comforting him. Pucento whimpered. "Little Ginevra," I said, "for your sake, you had best return now to your father." She fled and held her hair and the wounds in her wild youthful hands.

After a long while the owl's wings began to settle again to place, stiffly, with reluctance, the stimulation and traction, once summoned, loath to leave his wings and allow them to lie furled in sleep. They continued to preen and rise irritably as with the urge toward flight, ruffled, mobile, his mode of propulsion uncontrollable. But I wet and smoothed the feathers under the triangle of his beak with my tongue and he regained himself, once more folded into his nocturnal shape, and only the eyes did not relent. I gave him a large rat and slept near him the night.

And I dreamed of the universe of the tribunal. It was a

closed sleep and a closed dream in which the tenacity of elements parted layer after layer to spaciousness. I dreamed of a brilliant morning and—I was remote, standing away—I saw the three turrets of the fortress rising each from its peak, and the mountain of Sasso Fetore off there was a pale green.

From each tower flew a small white standard, constant and square in the wind. It was a dream of the three white flags which were suitably the ensigns of Sasso Fetore, starkly bleached and deliberately unadorned with the hangman's owl. Their white was mounted briskly above the green. The country was no larger than the flags and as perfect. The road was a bright red line winding to the three precipices and the capital of rigid existence. And the flags were moving, fluttering, the motion of life anchored safely to one place.

A soundless wind. Then some silent battery commenced a cannonade from a distant point in the light of morning—not a figure appeared on the battlements—and a silent invisible grapeshot tore at the flags. The white standards were pierced and began a silent disintegration until they were no more than a few shreds beating solemnly against their masts in the blue sky.

And out of the blue sky came Monco's voice, wily and cold across the plains and fortresses, concealed in the rays of the sun: "The fish are running well. The fish are running well, Master," with mockery in his voice.

THE PRISONER ESCAPES

"When shall we meet again, Hangman. When shall we meet again?" whispered Antonina, the belle, as if she would have the moment exactly.

Her body and her character were her contracts and she called me by name, Il Gufo. She had firm passions and firm words, and I felt the responsibility of her declaration made so clearly, and the question asked simply in the word of parting. *Appassionato!* She was white as the Donna these days and hourly grew taller as her love increased, and her passion was of moral seriousness to a woman who was herself a covenant. Even a woman such as she, descended from fourteen dames of wealth and modesty, might make her words sweet and sentient in her stand, the shape of her throat, the tone of her voice which was always of the clarity and deliberateness of the fire that could but burn so bright. Yet it consumed all there was. Absolute, dark-haired Antonina, her arms were thin, neither fairs nor family had trifled with her complexion. Under a green tree in a black field she read her sister the *Laws of the Young Women Not Yet Released to Marriage*—and in none of the laws was there heartbreak—while, her jaws moving, she cast inside herself the terrible beam of introspection. Hangman!

Quando potrò riverderla?

Little Ginevra was younger; Lucia and Teresa also were younger than she. They had not known the waiting. Their bridal purses were not as hard as hers, their heads not so high. Nor could they look upon the hangman and his equipment without shyness, and they aroused the owl. Antonina would have grown old loving the bleak rose campions and myself. She wrote no letters to the dead, but sometimes after I passed, she walked among them. One would have looked for her white gloves to reach around her darkest years, one would have thought to meet her at the green arbor. A stately, infatuated woman, she carried a love poison and a shawl for her neck and shoulders to the summer fair. At the fair she was met by Sasso Fetore's sisters, walking in pairs as if they had already ventured too far from home, coming from opposite directions bareheaded, unescorted.

Down the cliff they came, down the road like black angels, and I heard their whispering, the complaints of goose flesh on their arms. Hardly a woman or girl was left behind in the thin black streets of Sasso Fetore, vacated as they would be at the end of existence. But the field below was filled with the noise of feet that would kill the crabgrass, and I saw how few childbearers remained for all the pleasure they seemed to be taking and despite their demands for husbands.

From a clump of nearby bushes the old fathers of Sasso Fetore began to strum the viola da gamba.

It was now midday; the sun beat upon the field. Garlic was on their women's breaths, their appetites were sated with the macaroni that might make them milk. Little Gineva was there too and wore the matron's wimple that covered her torn skull. They stumbled, the swaying shanks of hair, the flaming red scarves binding torso or hips and the cantilevering, the maneuvering of the skirts. Newly shod and gowned, the purple and green of earth and sky became warm in their presence; all that was female, unnatural in congregation, came into the open air walking as geese who know the penalty awaiting the thief who catches them.

Antonina had dark eyes. There was no girl's foolishness in her bosom. She was accompanied by her mother whose great square cheeks were white as salt. One dark and one white they passed, a tall one and a short, posting their two figures against the hagbush overlooking the field.

The fair was pitched directly below the fortress, in good view, and for the benefit of the prisoner up there. The black schism of the fortress fell thrice across our ladies' heads. In the silence of the hilltop, in the window, was the eye of him alone who could not join them. And I too, at that hour, felt the urge to climb again into the city. The owl and the prisoner remained and the women showed themselves freely, their voices drifted high and were suddenly clear.

History had forbade the fair, a guise for flirting and the dissatisfaction of a sex—the fair invoked only when the measures of fathers failed. I listened to the festival, the ribaldry of the viola da gamba, the concert of bushes. How could it be anything but an ill omen, the distraction and the gaiety of woman preceded the fall of man. Women could not be quiet when men met and stripped back the skin from their arms and presided over the bare bones of inheritance. What a time for the tithe of pleasure, as if the sun must assert itself before eclipse and radiate before bursting into the fens of winter.

For most of their days the women were threadbare, garbed for seclusion in gardens that were high-walled and bloomed only with a few sullen leaves. These faces were not classic, but in the charity of the fair one suddenly seemed good as the next, a dispensation granted to each with a large nose, eyes that were too large, and manners that were not proportioned. Like a useless cadre, the twelve Mongers stood in a line at the south limit of the fair, the brims of the twelve black hats touching and inseparably joined.

"If it pleases you, look at my daughter Lucia. Her mother has dressed her in brocade for the day." And there were more and more daughters; they promenaded on this slope where the lay brothers had fought with fists, and rope girdles entangled like fighting bucks, so long before the season when the field became spread with green.

"Mamma, I will carry your train. Un momento," spoke the very young, having forgotten the goats in the stable. The proclamation was wet upon the north wall. They had gold rings in their ears and other luxuries hung to their bodies. At just this fair in the past some were got with fornication and games, in the time when there were men to hang and those to spare, with clemency for neither.

"Attento, attento!" started the amusement and in the almond color of noon Pucento the lictor came upon the field. The women quieted and did not crowd beyond the small white markers but watched each beside her neighbor.

"To the hind legs!" Pucento shouted and proceeded slowly toward the center of the green. His walk was stiff, slow, itself determined by the beauty of the aged provincial combat between man and dog, the mastery of training over the temptation and distraction that plagued the low species. The women peered from the four sides, some scowling, some thrusting forward their cheeks withered as nuts, some smiling as if they alone were devoting themselves to a glassy pleasure at the sight of my ward high stepping and lean. The young girls watched covetously.

"They suspect something," murmured Signor Barabo and held Antonina by the waist, confidently. And where he stood also stood eleven Mongers more, their wind-troubled sombreros cut at different angles from amidst bodices, old women and their daughters.

The tempo of the viola da gamba increased, but there came only the soundless winging of the musicians' bows, the silent press of the female hundred, and the stilled orderly panorama of the fair. The olive faces, the roses, the chameleon breasts were ranked and slightly moving under the hemispherical silence of Sasso Fetore. The noon tilted overhead. Antonina seemed not to feel the binding of the arm about her waist and did not watch Pucento for long but looked directly away and to the east, steadily. "Adesso," came the movement, the will of her lips.

When the dog turned, they turned, and the oldest and most grudging, with lace upon the brown of their chests, paid attention and swung the great fans atop their skulls windward, frowning through malignant black eyes as if they would not be fooled.

The streaks of the gowns against the earth, the moving flecks of the man and dog, the liveliness of the noon and the windy pasture below him were the last that he in the fortress would see of mankind, womankind. Each minute the grade up to the fortress became more steep and the music only a toneless drift from the strings soon to die.

The dog was muzzled. To the tip of the muzzle into a ring fastened at the end of the snout was hooked the leash which Pucento and the animal kept taut between them, a thin rein of brilliant red. Pucento held his arm, the fist gripping the cord, straight as long as he and the dog maneuvered together and the one obeyed the other. Pressure about the head controlled the animal; two leather cups on the muzzle hid his eyes.

On their leaning instruments the musicians played the seldom heard 'March of the White Dog.' This whole breed had once been deprived and whipped, tied ascetically by the lay brothers on the slopes. The bitches were destroyed. And the rest, heavy of organ and never altered with the knife, day after day were beaten during the brothers' prayers, commanded to be pure unmercifully. The dogs tasted of blood given in mean measure but were not permitted the lather, the howl, the reckless male-letting of their species. Beaten across the quarters, they were taught by the monks the blind, perfectly executed gavotte.

The sole remaining dog moved and balanced as the first packs, flawless, the long wail of refusal still in his throat and still denied him by the muzzle. The dog followed Pucento on the end of the tight rein, a heavy animal, the white coat become tarnished and cream with age. The women could not see how Pucento sweat, himself straining to duplicate the measure, the ruthless footstep of the past. Welts were knotted across the dog's hide, causing the hind muscles to be tough as if the leg's tendons themselves had been drawn upward and bound across the spine. The joints were round, distended, polished to silver, thick though the legs were slim, worn and delicate with the hours of balancing. But the meat, the shoulders and loins—tempered by the monks—were broad and considerable so that the animal might endure the requirements and travel long distances without touching the front paws to earth.

The old dog did not once attempt to snap through the muzzle. It changed the rhythm of its gait perfectly and moved sideways with ease, crossing one set of claws over the other. All the desire, the reflex to kill, was still there under the white coat, inside the white skull and embedded the length of the spinal column, but Pucento had no need of the thick cane, no need to thrash the animal in the formality, the difficulty of the devilish dog's fandango.

First the two completed a square, then a circle, then the dog twisted and arched its back. Drawing down the quarters, it puffed and deflated its chest in one place, the leash pulling always the primitive long jaws and the restrained skull horizontally forward uncomfortably from the neck. But in this position the animal's silhouette was best.

"Attento, attento," they murmured again after silence and Pucento stiffened his arms, man and dog frozen on the green. Pucento spoke. The dog shuddered and swung backward in brutal symmetry, lifted, stood on two legs, then leapt, once, thrice, and each time a single leg only touched the earth, quivering, burdened, unnatural. On the one leg, the dog propelled itself upward again without falling, and the bones pressed through the fat. Even Antonina's mother did not regret the sight.

The dog stopped. As bidden, its front paws came to rest lightly upon Pucento's back on each side of the neck. Thus they remained rigidly, heads damp, white, lifted into the sun, while the musicians dragged their viols onto the field and the girls raised and silently shook their clutches of rose campions.

"Antonina," said Signor Barabo, "take your sister's hand."

But Antonina was gone and his arm was hooked only about his old wife's hip.

We climbed rapidly, Antonina and I, clinging to the steepest ascent. We pressed ourselves into the declivities of the cliff. The undergrowth, as it scraped the hand, was warm; now and then we moved upward through the devil's mace and were stung by the lonely nettles. Antonina took the path first and did not pause. She seemed to climb with her narrow shoulders, and there was spare straight movement under the twelve skirts. The music from the fair still reached us persistently up the bed of a mountain brook, la, la, la, la, so that we hurried. The women below trod across the green, a few disappearing off the edge of the slope.

Who has not wanted to climb on a warm day, up again toward the bare hills? We passed without thinking of the trickle of dispassionate water from the fortress. The air was clear and almost free of Sasso Fetore's garnishing odor of rust and yellowed tomatoes. I drew closer to my companion. Antonina made herself known, and we climbed again.

The whiteness of the underskirts lay against the rock and

coils of mountain grass. I heard my own boot slip and start, and I was behind her lest she fall. Antonina's pale hands touched the calcium encrustations of the rooks, and the wind took her face and clothes as if she had mounted those leaning steps to which the faithful will not return. Perhaps in her heart was good conscience for all her years.

Only that morning, so soon, she had distributed the contents of her bridal casks along the embankment to sun. After sunning them, she had made several bundles, tied them with cord, and carried them up the wooden ladder to the dark space beneath the roof, knowing they would not last there and that she would not need to take them down again. Her father would not speak for her.

And yet the thorn pulled at the leg, a trailing of her shawl was snagged in that steep place below the fortress. She swayed and proceeded to climb as if there would be more trysting. We were hidden by the glare reflected from the cliff, high where not even sheep grazed. In her hurry, her determination, she moved as if to absorb her indiscretion into the blood of her good family. Now she laughed.

At last we reached the ledge and stood side by side, then face to face so that I could not mistake her, Antonina. Not from weariness she leaned against the lowest walling of the fortress morticed agedly into the cliff. Already her breast was rising and the noon fled. We had no need to whisper, not even the birds were within rock's throw. But the wind was in our faces and we were temporary, though Antonina did not look as if her heart were sinking. The world this high creaked around us and, standing with no sure footing between the day before and the day after, she touched her bosom done with lightheartedness, spoke to me in the wind's way:

"Honorable Hangman. Carino. Il Gufo. It is you I love. I know what women do, and I have no fear of it. I have heard my father. I will be no belated bride. 'Not him,' they say. But it is you I love. I have seen you ride your jangling ass toward the rope readied and hung down from the sky like thunder. I remember the superstitions; I am old enough to remember them and you. 'Not him,' they say. But it is you."

And Antonina held to the leathern flanges on my hip, there on the cliff, among reed and empty eggshell. The fair was done; the waiting of rags done. I put my hand on her bosom and my hand met the two small silver hearts of a fine lady.

Antonina rolled stiff on the brown hilltop and the skirts loosened, lifted by the wind. She pushed her fingers into the bent grass and dragged her hair on the silt and stones. Her slender belly thrashed like all cloistered civilization among weed, root, in the wild of the crow's nest. I reached into the sheltered thighs touching this bone and that and felt for what all women carried. High and close to her person, secreted, I found Antonina's purse which she had hid there longer than seven years, that which they fastened to the girls when young. What was there more?

There was the prisoner. Having found his way from the room of four hooks, through the base passages, he climbed until he could go no further, bent and blinded by the light, clamoring into the air and to the stone above us scaled by no ladder or foothold. Now he freely cried *Guai!* Lifting his roving eyes away to the roofs, the spaces through the city, he seemed to fill his eyes with the distance to the borders. His was the rage of prisoners who climb quick as they can to the rooftops, who are caught in the tall trees—there was hardly that to steady him or give balance—reaching at last this windy free space. Perhaps the fair, the sudden quiet, the loneliness, made him understand that he could not escape the way he came. He was transmuted and prepared for the dizziness of the high ledge; the sun, the air currents, caught his face. I looked up at him and raised my hand to hold him.

The prisoner was covered with great feathers, pin feathers and flat feathers, pieces of wire and tin swelled his chest. The wings hung far down as arms and even below the hands, swaying, and were fastened across his shoulders. He crouched heavily, but his waxen feathers, his flying skein billowed angrily in the wind. His head stuck over with red wax turned loftily. Then he tested the wings, looking at the sun unbelieving, taking a cautious step closer the edge. The wings hung down and buried the arms inside; almost to the length of his feet, the tips waved like the lengthy, extra feelers of the dragonfly. The ends of the wings were wet, they motioned under the power of the primary feathers, the crudely fashioned wing with its sharp trailing edge. And when he filled the wings, they moved, lifted once, again, curving down and menacing. His half hidden chin jutted and thrust with the effort. He spread his legs and drew tight the red flying surface between them, so that he was a mass of machine and bird for the wind's picking. He appeared heavy as stone.

The wings caught, and he burdened the wings, the wax, and the red cowl from the rusty forehead. The skull and crossed bones were buried under the brown breast. He sapped the wings and his shod heels lifted, the knees flexing and ready to hurl him off. The eyes grew small in that headgear, birdlike, as if free they could distinguish only black and white and the long distance, in any direction, that there was to fly. None before him had thought of it, none fabricated such a means of escape. And his head raised, the urge to leave the earth and gallows, the very hilltop of Sasso Fetore, lightened the drag of the feet.

He tore himself away. He poised himself on the great stone and tried himself, peering aloft and away for some landmark by which he could travel and survive. The face was criss-crossed with red lines, he had discovered even the crop of the bird. The tail—for he would guide himself—spread out. Still clinging to the stone he wheeled once, then back again and pulled the feathers, not hesitating, merely tightening the tufts in the wings and drinking at the air. Behind him I saw the top of the low tower and the blue atmosphere. The wind blew up stronger and clear.

The wings beat slowly down. Then as if to break the bones in his arms, they were horizontal, sweeping a little windward. He brought his knees into the pit of his stomach and climbed toward open sky. The prisoner hovered, turned awkwardly, swooped close over our heads—he kicked the air as he dove!—and sailed in a long arc up again, around, about to disappear across the witch's huts and chimneys of Sasso Fetore now darkening with the night already close. I saw him lastly fly defiantly through the smoke of Monco's deserted fire and into the red sun that sank and drew him down over the edge of the earth.

HE HANGS

Finally the night enforced quiet. The tunneling cicadas, the cicadas taking the moonlight on patches of snow, were still. The shadows maneuvered, the eternal flanking movements and frozen sorties of the night were taking place. The brook ran cold, and the mountain slopes, so far and of silver, marched upon the rain, absorbed the moonlight like black cloth the sun; houses were deserted at dark when the four-legged animals, not many, hung their heads. The fortress imprisoned only the empty hooks. The ice span told no time. There was the webbed fern, the rafter, the proclamation's promise, and the iron doors ajar—the bishops and gaolers done convening and taken to bed until morn. The galax opened its sharp leaves to prick the prowler, and there was an odor of night's roots.

The owl was awake, he swelled his chest, breathed restlessly, and made himself known in the dark as if it were not deep enough. He was dissatisfied with the still lingering light and kept to his corner. Now and then, slow and purposeful, he eased himself from the pitch and moved in front of the window, his claws biting the ledge, his outline contesting heaven and plain, tree and pillar. He looked and the bare window was driven behind him, or blinked and was awake, frowning at the fortress and murmuring skies beyond the cliff. He looked so violently he heard nothing. Insects darted in and out of his feathers and they were nothing to him, so long did he stare to see that all was in the night as before, and before that. He looked steadfastly at the universe, then turned his back and proceeded to chew, pick, beat his cold heart, rustle so imperceptibly active with continuous life. Revengeful was he toward that which made him turn his white face and look into the dark.

He was old, scabrous at the window, he regarded the night from his stone and branch and all the night was preoccupied with some stretching of tissue or memory deep within the feathers, while rectifying the vision of the world in his owlish eyes, watching it as he might something that dared not move. He silhouetted himself and from that glance the night could not shrink into hiding in the atmosphere. He gripped Antonina's purse in his claw and now and then shook it, already it was ripped and musty as if it had been his forever. At times it fell to the window ledge and he kept near it.

Back and forth he went, continuously at work, conniving and busy within his feathers or lice eggs, watching the dark, flitching, flickering. He cut his bill on the stone, preened disinterestedly. Once, with slow effort, with a great plying of nerves and muscle he slowly shut his eyes, down, down, and obliterated the shadows, the space, and it ceased. Then, look, the dilation and they were round again, greater, the horned moons. He moved across the rim of his nest, Sasso Fetore, at the window. He outlined himself again and, face into the night, his head began turning so little, but sharply, right, left, and this was his alertness, something of all he saw aroused this speculation, something fallen upon that eye stirred him.

The owl carried Antonina's purse to the window and shook it. And the leaves in the scrub tree shook also. One claw was missing, another cut off blunt and short, at every feathered layer he was scarred and covered with old wounds that penetrated him like the grain of wood, his fiber, the old markings of the forest. But he had never cried with the pain, the scarred face, the face enraged and bloody, always anesthetized with the cold enormity of the eyes, the sudden circumference of the eyelids protecting him, making him insensitive.

Light began again to rise steaming from the earth, and from the owl's eye, slowly, lighted the knowledge of the day to come. He stiffened, watching the cicadas stop, and all about his motionless body the hoary piercing feathers rustled in the breeze as if they were no part of him. He glanced at the frosted shadows, the warped tree laden with a winter provision of dead mice, at the cold pump. It was morning, but only he could see through the blackness yet heavy to the light that was kindling. And he hooted, warning that someone was approaching up the winding road.

Signor Barabo came from the mist and halted near the window. He was wet, having come at this odd moment to take the owl's attention.

"Il Gufo. Boia?" he whispered, stooping and white. He looked up and bowed his head. He on the ledge waited. Signor Barabo stooped under his burden.

"I had not expected, Master . . ." turning his mouth on its side, whispering, squinting out of the frost. "For her I could not have asked you. Boia . . . Barabo's good fortune, I would not have missed it. Principale, I would reach up to you. . . ."

On his back he carried a black trunk, rounded and banded at the ends. Wet black hair fell from under his broad hat, the face of whiteness and dark lines hung there, smiling, the neck bulged with labor. He had walked all the night.

"You must pardon me, Altezza," grunting, wryly twisting under the load, "two men could not be found. So I have come alone. Half the treasure is here, Boia." Once he raised his voice, "Dowry," he exclaimed. He stood at the edge of the cliff and his fingers clamped the brass handles. The black lines of the face, sweat-strewn, slyly peered upward. He had discarded the cummerbund and his ankles were thick with mud. "It is a pleasure, Boia, for me to bring this heavy load myself." Since sundown he had carried it.

And suddenly he dropped one shoulder, swayed as if he could bear it no longer, and the cask was loose, fell out of sight and split wide on the first rocks, smashing, and its collection of coins showered down the slope until all was quiet again.

"Ah, sfortunato!" His eye cut narrowly and he wiped his nose. Signor Barabo turned on a heel and, his voice coming as through the rain-drenched forest, "Hangman. Follow me." A gust of wind carried his hat also down the cliff, and with that, again he fixed upon the owl his night-worn face.

Pucento saddled the donkey. We set off in single file down the morning rim of the quarry of Sasso Fetore. Pucento walked at the donkey's head, limping, pulled the damp halter. All about was the stillness that follows fugitive action, and we proceeded through that time of dawn when the werewolf gives up his feasting and the assassin lifts his hands from the jugular vein of history. We met the first citizen in a doorway awaiting our approach.

"Triumph to your day, Hangman," and the citizen fell in line behind us until we met the next, shivering, and more after that, sentinels suddenly coming alive from the low entrance to the caffè and along the down-winding route, those who with their hands and feet, their persons, making no noise, pointed the path that we should take.

"Is it the same?"

"It is, Signor Barabo."

"They have not wakened perhaps in my absence?"

"They have not wakened, Signore."

So Signor Barabo questioned each. These men, as they swung one after the other from niches and cold casements, out of the walls, followed us scenting and long-legged and sleepless, wet with uncomprehending vigilance. Over their brown shirts they wore short black jackets strapped high to their white throats.

"Power this day, Il Gufo," they murmured, surprised that I had come, and were gladly relieved.

The donkey braced his feet on the stones. It was not yet morning, the bells marked time coldly. No one peered from the windows, none proffered fowl or wine as we passed in single file. A gargoyle hid its face in corroded hands. I marched down through the people's hutch, thatch, sleep.

"Who lives here?"

"An old woman, Boia. She is asleep."

Even I had not seen this yard before. Under the hollow tile was an iron wall disappearing without vine or air hole into the earth. Leathern feet crowded and stirred upon her property while she slept, and the gate to her yard was open, pulled from its wooden hams. One had mounted the stones avalanched between wall and privy; silent, motionless over the others' heads, he watched the approach from the hill below. Another with large stride paced off the width of the yard and tapped his head grimly to remember it. There was tarpaper over the old woman's window, a trough filled only with a bed of fermenting straw, and the back step where she took the sun, all become cold and removed, visited by the dawn Mongers and the inquisitive strangers, because of the event perpetrated on this spot.

The deputation filled her yard like black chessmen thrust into the dampness and sands of ruin. The bony ponchos and black hats hovered to and fro, staring at the corpses in the idle chill.

The prefect was on his knees. His eyes protruded, the kepi was at his side. Signor Barabo sat down near the prefect on the trough of stinking straw. Traces of light began to flow onto the horizon with the roar of wind.

"Can you tell when it occurred?"

"Perhaps, Signore. Perhaps they have been here a few hours. Or more."

"And they are dead then?"

"Dead. They are cold, Signore."

The prefect's four ganders lay at the base of the iron wall and their white bodies were frost covered and gripped in the weeds, to be seen at the prefect's knees with all their dismal inertness and roundness of breast sparkling and portentous. They appeared white through the feathers, through the flesh, and to the earth. Their eyes lay like black berries half in the sand; through the bills the nostrils were bored with blue augers as worn holes in wood.

"Four hours at least, Signore."

The long-lying feathers were immaculate, though the wing of one bird was crumpled—fanning, uncomfortably jointed—against the black wall and hung there hazardous and spread as if it would defy the upsweep of air, no longer temperate, in Sasso Fetore. Otherwise, in the small space, they geometrically marked the four points of the compass, unruffled, exact creatures as they were left after death. The prefect did not touch them, he merely leaned further forward, put his hands upon the dirt near their circle and bowed so that the smoke from his cigarette burned his lip. He peered at the ganders who would no longer invade the impossible cliff top and campanile of Sasso Fetore, bedded down now emphatically in the place they would not have chosen to protect themselves from storm.

Not turning, with the smoke still branching and forking back from his lowered face, the prefect whispered: "Do you see the murderer?"

The one on the rocks hesitated. He opened his eyes wider, examined quickly the architectural slope and the ferns, and shook his head.

Signor Barabo's mouth fell as if to exclaim, but he remained silent. And one after the other the black figures rotated, stood a moment at the prefect's shoulder to look.

The ganders would no longer march through the steep places of Sasso Fetore, circling upon ridges, gables, spiked walls. No longer would they search the flagons—search the tall lady's piazza, the fortress, the field of dead foot soldiers—for the cliff and kernel of Flemish seeds, for a crack in the ice, for the remnants of dark days.

"They are dead, Signore, I feel it here. These are the lumps in the neck, there is a hardness under the bill, Signore."

And the prefect withdrew his hand, spitting away the smoke and tobacco.

The ganders had been felled carefully, symmetrical and clean. The long necks, straight, each perpendicular to the next, were crossed one over the other near the heads, the necks touching and torn, left in their severed lines and with their cold windpipes in this intimate, unnatural pattern. The ganders, whose eyes gleamed logically, whose march was rhetorical, surmounted the prisoner's sudden inspiration to kill them and survived his warped and cunning urge to lay their bodies in crudely artful fashion.

The donkey rang his bells dumbly and none heard. The straw fermented. The guard on the rockpile lost his eyes into the mist and gave no alarm. There was no sign of the one who fled. Pucento, with tentative finger, felt over and over again the slashes imprinted on the earth by wingtips and fierce talons. Another stood waiting, and, from the wooden saddle, my feet slanting as iron and one fist upon the tin tattooed horn, I motioned them away, signaling that they leave their posts and wet odor of the yard. I pulled on the rein sharply.

The dawn became the color of the pear's belly. And not long from that time the prisoner's discarded, tall, half-broken wings were found abandoned against the whitewashed sidings of a stall. The straps that had bound them to him hung stiffly. In the mud his footprint was recognized where he struggled free. Before the Sabbath labors began, the citizens of Sasso Fetore saw for themselves the old woman's yard and filed past to stare at the wings by the barn where they were rumored to be. When darkness came again, the wings were illuminated with the flare of two torches and were visited even then. The children looked for signs of his toes in the wet sand, they whispered upon hearing the bell that was struck hourly as long as he was free.

And he was not free for long but was returned to the cell from which he had escaped, to the four hooks and put upon them. No one gathered at the fortress, satisfied with the announcement that he was there. His wings were splashed with kerosene and burned where they stood. In a matter of hours his cries commenced again, and peaceful anticipation possessed the owl. The citizens listened quietly as they stared at the pool in the grass, now empty. And the sun set. The crowd dispersed from the smoking wings that cowered, withered, fell to ash. Some days later—the prisoner was still suspended on the hooks—the skin was drawn away from his belly in one piece and stretched across a drum that was beaten through the streets while they stopped work and listened.

The Pentecost was past. The prefect, as was prescribed at this time, fasted and shaved his head. He was ready, imprisoning himself with the condemned until he should be brought to me. All of Sasso Fetore returned to read the proclamation with more care. The drumming upon the prisoner's flesh continued, sometimes the drummer was followed by women and the Mongers, sometimes he beat alone through the steady rain, and he took the old courses of the ganders, going nowhere in particular but marching and tapping the drum so that all would hear during the day. Sometimes the cries stopped and that too was heard. The old men waited in the caffè and they no longer spoke of Lucia or Teresa.

"Listen, Signor Barabo. It is past."

"Yes. And listen, thou, do you hear him hammering?"

"Yes. He is coaxing his noose and knot."

"Il Gufo."

The owl waited for the drummer to come, and each time bestirred himself so that he might watch. He sanctioned the herald to stop and to strike four extra beats for the owl and move on.

The millet grew ripe and hampers of blood apples were left in the hangman's piazza. A stone of bread was left also. Those in the caffè waited and made no move to kill the lizards that came from their caves in the fireplace; the bent grass sprang up again near the wall in the old woman's yard; the rooks flattened themselves in their nests on the cliff. The fox came into the streets but was not noticed, traveled up and down my road. Pucento brushed the donkey's black trappings, the monarchial owl stared about the proximity of the execution. The prefect buried the ganders, and Sasso Fetore had nothing else to think of, nothing else to prepare for.

One morning the drumming ceased. The fox hastened back to his hole. The bells ceased. Monco did not fish that day, and the fish remained deep in their pools. The cicadas were hushed. The cries were hushed in the fortress, the prefect giving the prisoner water from a tin cup. That morning Signor Barabo saw nothing of his wife and daughters. The fortress towered its three parts over the city and nothing stirred.

The yellowhammers appeared and flew into the sun, and the rose campions speckled the hillock, the path by the headstones. Sasso Fetore was raw with the sun that fell headlong upon the unoccupied streets and before the campanile, the waiting city. Bright, clear, reddening the cliff, the sun rose and spread down across the unlabored fields. There was silence. None came from their shelters while the shot of the sun tore at the white flags raised on the bare masts and shone upon the ascending slopes with their briar, a few huts, inviting the spirits to come again to that empty plain. All day the sun warmed the copper in the eyes of doors and dried the tall lady in the piazza.

"Listen," murmured Signor Barabo, "it has stopped." And they listened, not venturing from the dark. It was a day during which the citizens sat until they must change a knee or arm and whispered while the sun swelled the streets with the light. No meals were prepared, but now and then they drank small quantities of spumante or rosolio. They had not forgotten the long, white, and crossing necks, nor perhaps their daughters. They had not dared to right the Donna. The Mongers themselves could not escape the superstitions, even when the sun whetted the gardens and filtered to gleam upon the wine presses.

The crabgrass grew again. The old men did not attempt to seek their neighbors; those who were already congregated when this day came remained so, waxen within the cellars or the caffè. No one gave thought to attiring the young women in hammered silver and lace. The council of crisis and the occasion of tragedy reached them during daylight hours and when the sun was high, Sasso Fetore was lighted the whole day and filled with the ferment of the sun rays. The day passed.

Only at dusk did a soft murmuring, the dialect and talk, start from the houses. Then some tried to remember the prisoner's face and they haggled over who had touched him and who not. The old woman who had proffered him the roasted fowl declaimed that she had retrieved it whole again, that he had not a chance to bite into it. The fathers would not speak a word to their daughters.

When it was dark Pucento carried in the kegs of grain, the bowl of blood apples, the pail of dissected chicken, the spice and paste and fish packed in leaves, from the piazza. He built a fire using the tinder and flint intended for the Donna. He cooked until midnight and heaped the brown pieces of meat and the strips of white fish on the stones and the fat drained into the fire, crackling and hissing. He brushed the earth from the blood apples and steamed them until they were soft and strong of odor. He cooked black twigs that tasted as chicory, and the water boiled in the pan, the bones fell from the fish, the skin and meat became tender and dropped loose. Now and then he returned to the court and discovered another homage food deposited there, perhaps a vegetable the color of rattan. And this he cooked. He found a bucket of eggs no larger than walnuts. He boiled them. And he replaced the eyes in the fish heads. He stirred, snipped, built up the fire, and we drank cognac. One small bird he roasted and this he stuffed—showing his teeth and pushing his thumbs—with a handful of green grass pale and fresh. He burned his arms and did not notice, he worked his knife on the block and he bled; the blood apples broke their skins and he took them from the rumbling water with his burned fingers.

How different from the Mongers' fragile fish or the square dark loaf and water! The pewter was filled, the flat leathern platters smooth as wood were filled, and the chicken stones, the sticks wet with fat, the hearts like cherries and the joints, the twists of bread, were devoured, heaped up and then eaten. The owl sat long with a large and savory chunk of white meat in his bill. The smoke backed into the grate and was filled with the moisture of feasting. Pucento scooped at the black fish roe; I ate the sickle-shaped sections of a fruit and the fire lighted our red hands. Pucento sat with his elbows between his knees, his cheeks wet and his eyes heavy. Until the meal was done and the intestines could not move.

The donkey's freshly polished harness hung on the wall; the casket containing the rope was ready.

"I shall see little Ginevra, Gufo."

Yes, and the rest of them. And the meal, torn from the anatomy of conscience, sat upon us, from the quantity found and cooked so seldom there came the effulgent memory of execution, step by step, dismal, endless, powerful as a beam that transudes our indulgence on the earth, in Sasso Fetore. There was suddenly the morrow, the way the brain sees death suddenly, and there was the penalty that could not be stayed. Lastly we chewed mint leaves.

In sleep there were the fantastic shapes of the food, the sensation of looking forward, searching ahead into the rubrics burning upon the slopes of the rose campions. Gathered about my bed were the hangman's articles. The gloved creatures of dreams paraded all night and a hundred times I settled the noose before dawn, and straightened it and turned it.

And the eye opened to find it cold, partially light, silent; the windows were open, all pushed a crack or flung wide, and the door was off its latch; the cold had come early and lay about the rooms. I rose, strapped a wide belt around my flesh. The stones were cold. I saw the ledge, empty and small, wet, from which the prisoner jumped. Pucento slept in his clothes and the lips were pulled back from the teeth. I shook him and he waked, clutching at my chest, and said: "Is it over, Il Gufo, is it finished? Have you hung him without me?" Then leapt from the bed and brought my cap and cape.

The crowds were in the piazza before us, ranked on four sides of the tall lady and pressing close to the gallows of white hickory. The empty arms, the cold hands, were folded and skull touched skull. I climbed to the top, the platform, and Pucento crept to the bottom, into the small space where the prisoner would fall. My footsteps crashed above Pucento's head and down there, out of sight, he crouched back against the wood and hid his face, trembling, sick as upon sea water, cowering in the darkness lest he be struck by the descending feet.

I stood. I might only have been searching the countryside from the low tower or kicking a splinter of glass down to the rooks. I looked over their heads through the slits. The soft black horn atop my hood curved forward and shook slightly in the wind. And the red cape, the collar of red, was short and left my arms free. The gallows faced the fortress. Not an old man, woman, and child but what was here and stooping in his brown shirt, gray cloth, and thinking of the book from which their hangman knew the terms and directions, the means and methods to destroy a man.

The wind blew and there was the odor of the hemlock at the border. The bare firmament of the cliff was hidden behind the heatless crumble of Sasso Fetore. The cold and dripping hole waited in the tall tree. My ward, of all of them, was sick under me. With my fists I tore the eyeslits so that I might see further and see them from such dilated eyes. I passed, shaking the horned hood at them and stopped.

The prefect brought the prisoner quickly from the fortress, under the portcullis, down the rampart, through the winding street, past the colonnade, between the crowds which opened, and into the piazza at last to the tall lady. The one and the other walked quickly and with single purpose, hair blowing, one official and one man walking as if they might not reach the gallows after all. The prisoner's greatcoat was open and it beat about his ankles; he walked now, came foot to stone.

And then there was no further for him to walk. The two of us stepped to the center of the trap, that board which shall be fastened so that it be firm at the proper time and fail at the proper time, leaving the foot nothing but emptiness. The muscles at the corners of the prisoner's mouth were hard like welts. There was not a minute more. He made a gesture as if to remove the greatcoat. But I bound his wrists, strapped the ankles, pulling the thongs tight. I put the hood upon him, down over the ears. I lifted the noose—higher, with both hands, lifting—and fixed it more easily than I dreamed. Then he stepped off the trap.

And that one noise of machine and man echoed and re-bounded against the four sides of the piazza, against the cam-panile and the low tower, and disappeared down my winding road. Then in the silence the trap banged several times like a door. I stood at the edge of the pit where the rope before me descended quiet and taut, tugged steady as some line dropped through a hole into the center of the earth.

And in the crowd, back near the wall, I saw Antonina. Al-ready her hair was gray and her complexion altered, the lips compressed, the temples shiny, and her habits and her charac-ter so true and poorly tempered that no man would come for her and the rest of her days would be spent with the manual for the virgins not yet released to marriage.

And then there was the air damp and cold and the owl exert-ing himself into flight, beating through the top branches now, shutting his eyes and crashing through the twigs to the drip-ping hole in the trunk, settling himself and sitting inside the bark for summers and winters, and he stayed thus, peering out of the warmth, the tenure of silent feathers in a cold tree.

Thus stands the cause between us, we are entered into cove-nant for this work, we have drawn our own articles and have professed to enterprise upon these actions and these ends, and we have besought favor, and we have bestowed blessing.

The Goose on the Grave

The priests on three white donkeys descended from a cloud and down the walls came into the steeper end of Castiglione's city. The beasts were for once unsure of footing and without a halt turned their white heads toward the top while little black pointed boots laced furtively into the short-haired flanks. The blackbreasts made a single file, one above the other, tightly skirted and silent, sunken into the end of a dusty journey. Chains were disarranged at their sides, the riders having been stopped far back on the road by thieves. These heavenly picadors now stuck against the white roof of the city; then turned, high as the bell tower, and without pity picked over the tiles below. Down there moved the decked-out sinners, beating across smokeless chimneys. The priests arrived from over the mountains to the toning of the morning call.

Under the sign of the winged cock chopped in relief from the door arch, butting its broken stone-tip out of antiquity, the dismounted priests made their own sign: against the past's brazen statuary, against the secret parts of the dead hung from the house walls like abnormalities perpetrated upon the loins of faceless cherubin with the power of flight. The stone was pink, the salmon color of long inactivity, out of which dropped the gray heraldry of half the populace, the hindward spectacle of meeting dogs.

In went the priests. Striking the door, they stepped to the side of Adeppi's mother. Adeppi, sitting in the darkness with the scattered litter of his brothers and sisters crying upward from the floor, watched them cross, lift, and carry her off.

The donkeys stepped out gamely with the load slung between and again picked their way up the steep, nosing the shaggy thighs of strangers.

Adeppi remained for a time where he was, kneeling and silent. Dust and the upflung sheets settled again to the bed; he heard the children fall about each other. Adeppi, one of Italy's covey of fragile doves, rose, stole out to the sunlight and in the opposite direction from the donkeys, ran down over the heated stones despite the cries that followed from the mouth of the abandoned cave.

A bakery and a hospital joined at the end of a narrow street blocked with carts upon which casualties lay in the sunlight. Ovens and operating benches merged beyond lake-blue plaster walls. Adeppi smelled the still-wet antiseptic blankets and the rising loaves. He sat on the hospital steps and watched the puttees green with mold passing up and down. The litters rolled to the gait of the boots scratching the dust and the flattened twigs spilled in the road. His haunches cooled on the stone and the sun fell across his back. From the darkness behind, Adeppi heard the ringing of bloody pans. At an angle to himself the baker's women came one at a time to the doorway, peered into the sky and at the slow movement of the injured into the Ospedale.

During the state's year of dissolution, the chains across the city gates were smashed and smoke rolled in from the sea and across the mountains. Hardly awake, the baker's women in the morning brushed flour from their bosoms, out of their hair, and the white sack dresses bagged slackly over nakedness. The dough they pulled in the daytime soured at night, but another day blossomed in the starving kilns. The pure brown flour itself was smoothed as between palms in near empty, mill-sweet bins, smelled faintly by the citizens as it drifted from the baker's whitewashed chimney. Adeppi's mouth was dry.

Two men entered the iron-patched yard of the church—its nave was filled with the wounded—and stooped to the weight of the stretcher they carried with handles across their shoulders, like an African queen carried on humps nearly drained of water; they stopped at the smooth blocks rising toward stained glass. Unable to climb further, the one in front slipped from under his load, rested the end of the stretcher on the stones. He began to smoke while the rear bearer stood in traces, arms pulled toward the ground by the sway of human gravity.

Adeppi crept close to the soldier who lay on his back fixedly staring into the sun. Nino had been sick on the blankets packed thickly and drawn close about his wounded neck. Adeppi shaded the eyes with his hand. The first carrier turned around, snuffing the cigarette on his puttee, and watched the boy breathe into the severed face. Then from his belt the carrier unhooked a heart-shaped water bottle and leaned forward, at the same time pulling at his bandanna with which to wipe the drinker's mouth. Adeppi saw the water splash and a few drops roll from flesh to cloth; and the tongue, greedy, unconscious of pain, dart suddenly and glide across the lips. He heard the loaves pushed from the baker's window on a board to cool. When they started again, he followed. Holding to the edge of the stretcher, his fingers caught below the blanket. Adeppi trailed into the cool darkness and asked for his mother.

Three priests turned and hid behind the altar.

This stretcher was propped on two sawhorses, and he stood beside it in the dark. An officer at the head of the stretcher, another stooping over the middle, pulled the blankets from the soldier. With razors they cut away one of the green legs of the britches. Adeppi looked at the brown limb, clothed on top, booted on the bottom, and looked down the rows of men settled on the floor. The knife slit harmlessly, without sound, across the leg. And the other way, in the direction of a cross, burning a thin line down the skin. Adeppi reached out his hand and touched the unfamiliar warm flatness of the thigh, for only a moment, as if both hands had come against the breast of a fallen animal in a ditch, his own feet bare and ankle deep in roadside water. The sun issued evenly from the flesh under his hand. But, frightened, he looked at the doctor and quickly pulled his fingers away, lest they too fall beneath the blade.

"Little boy," a voice echoed from the farthest soldier quietly bedridden on the stone, "sing for us!"

Adeppi had come into the world's platoon of broken lances and even while he smelled the iodine, he heard the far-off cries of women as the hot crusts burned their palms.

When they blew out the light, he crept from soldier to soldier, sitting cross-legged between the bodies. Behind the church the sky turned pale with darkness, luminously blue beyond the balconies, and the cypress in the graveyard glistened, as did the steeple.

Seville, Venezia, the voice of sunken cities and for the love of a woman—he tasted the first few notes and the chin lifted, feeling for the octave like a gypsy reaching out, upward on his mandolin, marking time in the air. Still Adeppi could not sing. Nino watched him sharply, kept him close by, and waited for the shrill notes to ring with the bells. Nino was finally able to use his leg, though the wound on his neck was unhealed and a gradual swelling gave him pain. He did not rejoin his regiment. Instead he stayed about the hospital. The months were fragrant and a few grapes behind the hospital on the graveyard vines began to twitch in the heat.

Nino took Adeppi with him at night. Soldier and boy sat under the partially bearing vines. They did not speak, but Nino tried to sing while Adeppi watched the movement of the lips. Laughter came from the bakery, the slapping of fists into bags of flour. But from the castle-shaped heights of the city, not a head peered down. Nino could not carry a tune, yet snatches of slow song, on a terrible raw voice, continued to the patient beat of the soldier's finger. Adeppi learned these songs from him who, with puffy throat, low soft teeth and curling hair, throwing out his chest, sang with hampered rumbling desire. In the middle he would break off himself and finish the song by the waving of a finger, shaking it at the boy.

There was wine as well as bread in the bakery. For weeks Nino visited there, going just at dusk and returning before dark. On these visits he drank with Edouard and did not speak to the white-smocked girls. The first time Nino brought Adeppi, Edouard met them at the door. There was straw hanging above Edouard's head, a feather dried to the stone and cobweb. He smiled as one smiles from a ruin in the evening, a particular pleasure in spying a church window on the edge of a place of hiding and at dusk. Egg scavengers, thought Edouard, are climbing through the rubble in the condemned fields, making for, lifting their eyes toward, the same golden dome.

Hand in hand they stood in the yard. Adeppi held his cap tightly. A starving guinea hen perched on the rim of the hooded sealed well, the setting sun streaked across the clay. Outside man and boy stood in the shadow of ancient buttresses.

"Older than you think, Padrone," Nino murmured. Without waiting for an answer, he slid forward and squeezed past Edouard into the cool, wood-smelling darkness.

Edouard searched the cupboards and after a time put a liter of wine on the table. Adeppi smelled the heat dying from the ovens beyond the wall. The three sat without a light.

"Shall we leave the shutters open or shut? Shut them." Edouard sat down.

"Salute," said Nino. He leaned forward with both arms on the table. Watching Edouard, he closed one eye and drew down the eyebrow, wrinkling the cheek. Still Edouard would not notice the boy. The bandage around his neck began to throb. He clasped his hands and, with two stubby fingers together built a steeple to amuse Adeppi, then collapsed it. He wiped his mouth on his sleeve.

Edouard looked at him. "Five," he whispered, "each with a

petticoat." He reached across the table and clapped Adeppi on the shoulder. Nino's long hair curled into his eyes.

Finally Edouard lit a lantern, and picked it up. The two men discovered that Adeppi had left the table. They saw him, barefooted, small, crouched at the door that led upstairs, his nose and staring eyes pressed into the jamb. Edouard, twirling the lamp, turned to Nino. "Flagrante delicto!" he said softly and laughed. He began to whisper.

"Not tonight," shouted Nino. And then carelessly: "The boy," he added, "it's time he went to bed."

They did not enter the hospital but sat on the steps where they first met. They watched the dew that had started from the stone. Windows were quiet behind their wooden mantles.

"After a minute," Nino patted the boy's head, "we'll go back."

Adeppi could not speak; he clutched at Nino's trousers.

"Wait," Nino smiled broadly. "A minute yet, ragazzo."

He kept a steady watch on the bakery, smoked quickly. Once he stole into the hospital and returned, knowing well the supply chests, with a fresh wad of cotton stuffed in the bandage about his neck. Again he took Adeppi's hand and they crossed the few paces of moonlit square. As they walked, Adeppi pulled and the soldier held him tightly.

Nino robbed Edouard of his guitar. With a hand clapped over Adeppi's mouth, holding the boy noiselessly off the floor, he crept back into the room where they had drunk wine and lifted the guitar from its peg on the wall. Outside, he slipped the cord over his neck, regardless of the wound, and as he walked the instrument hit his side. Unstrummed, it issued a hollow sound.

No one saw them. In front of the bakery, close to the shadow, Nino struck his feet far apart and caught Adeppi by the collar. He positioned the guitar. Then, with a jerk of the wrist, he swung the boy to his shoulder. Frowning, with only one hand, Nino began pecking out a song. He said nothing, but he squeezed the child's legs and watched the window.

Adeppi threw back his head and suddenly drove his fingers into Nino's hair. He swayed from the shoulder as a mad bird on a perch. The soprano voice, through one song after another, soared and the lungs puffed under the chin, the clear notes pained his nostrils. There was the lapping of waters, dark, flowing between the house of love and the Ponte Beffa, a cape skirled in an archway. Adeppi's eyes were wide, his tongue darted, he too watched the window.

It creaked when it opened. He lifted his hand, slowly, to his rising voice, shifting under the arm braced across his knees, and saw the dim shaggy head of hair. He screamed from his egg-shaped mouth, stood up, reaching for the window.

She listened for a moment, leaned out, lowering the gown. Then softly, her voice audible despite his cry, she said with a quickening: "Avanti! Avanti!" and withdrew.

Boy and guitar were flung to the ground.

The next time Adeppi sings the room is full, well lit by lamps. Edouard, seated with knees close together, holds the guitar, its great frog-like dusty bell rolling in his lap. He watches Adeppi. All of them listen, the five women, the men with heavily sunburnt lips, and Nino.

Nino holds the woman he courted so craftily on his lap and runs his finger over the cool inside of her thigh. No longer does he have to speak at all. His bandage is discarded; the woman's hair comes down upon his shoulder.

There is the smell of tomato over the urn of ashes. They have called Adeppi and he stands in short pants cut off high near the top of his legs, and no shirt. Stocky shoulders are held back, firm, hands in fists are at his side. And his shaved olive head is pointed at the rafters, his face alone works with the effort of the muscles around his gullet and moistened lips. Grown fat, smaller, isolated in a glaze of medieval lyricism, sweating and working at the song, he forces himself to voice those ecstatic melodies to which so many countesses have met and sinned, so many wolfhounds bayed.

For the exit of a few batteries of cannon, officials dropped the chains that pinched off the leathery slopes of the city. Adeppi was there with the rest to wave his cap at the passing of the guns that were ridden, like land-impaled porpoises, by the artillerymen whose torn trousers flapped astraddle the iron of the breeches. The powder-borne weapons heaved slowly to the south. Clanking, the mauled unit passed, the black-burned naked heels of the soldiers striking like tin against the sides of downward-aiming guns. Several times a day Adeppi came out of the shade to watch, back down the winding open stairways when he heard the crash of chains. Then he was gone again, trilling in Castiglione's town houses and drawing up to those who smelled of smoke.

He climbed the town's vertical walls alone. At the fountain the water carriers smiled at him as their shawls swung in the dust, and they held first one bucket then another heavily against their breasts and under the spout. At the foot of the campanile, outside the coffin maker's shop, or under the window where the countess toileted, at these places he stood sentry amid the rumbling of the carts and sang, the fishlike outline of his mouth wide open in his sunburnt face. He napped under a madonna's head that stared from a sun-streaked wall at the harness of donkeys and a clear sky filled with the shot of hovering birds. Nino's wounds had healed; the guitar warped on its peg.

Adeppi preferred the crowds, the old women who never drank twice at the fountain, each one of whom had borne two soldiers, one thief, and a daughter in Rome. They plucked at the skirts of priests and bled under the fruit trees by the grave, now shaking their own skirts, leading nameless passers-by to the rooms of venery. When he followed, the old women turned agilely about and shook the black skirts between their hidden legs. And he would hide in the recess of a wall and count the coins that had been tossed him.

He peered into sleeping rooms that opened upon the cobblestones without the shield of hallway or antechamber, in view of all who walked. In the evening he found his own voice

drowned by the church's choir. Heat issued from his body as
it had from Nino's leg and once, in the noon crowd, he was
hugged quickly and heavily by a woman who picked up the
basket she had dropped and disappeared before he could see
her face. A moment later three priests passed, dragging after
them asses with heads outstretched on the ends of jerking
bridles.

To other children, loitering on the steps of the governor's
palace, he sang snatches of the songs with which, later in the
hot night, he quieted babies carried aimlessly by night mothers
or set out amid empty demijohns on the brown balconies. The
darkness itself labored up the steep landings and incline of the
city, or fell swiftly down the tiles which, held without mortar,
dropped through the night their sound of breaking porcelain—
phantom vandals darting at the pedestal of a saint.

One night, having sung to the coffin maker asleep over his
boards, having passed on to wander in the women's portion of
the town, catching them as they opened or shut a door, tired
and cramped in a dream, Adeppi returned to the bakery. A
hundred steps from the entrance he stopped. Then, stooping
double, he shoved his coins beneath the belly of a weather-
beaten sheep that lay in the rotten straw of a crèche inside the
wall.

Edouard blocked the door and, in the darkness, leaned forward and braced his hands on his fat thighs, so that his face
was on a level with the boy's. He squatted, listening with another sense to the night gossip through the grillwork and,
wide-awake, would have a good deal to tell his intimates by
morning.

"I've been waiting for you," Edouard whispered, "I've been
waiting for you to come back."

Adeppi put his foot on the stair and climbed into a light
smoking overhead. The chalkstone was cool and smooth, the
narrow shaft filled with the odor of leavening. A few dried
bulbs and herbs bristled thinly, the women came from their
rooms to watch.

"Maria," they whispered, "be kind to him!"

In this close hallway under the eaves, Adeppi found Nino helpless, dressed only in his army tunic, tight, shrunken. It did not cover his waist. Out of reach, her hair loosed, trembling with laughter, stood Bianca Maria. Her back bent against the low beams.

Edouard peered over the women's heads.

"Edouard," they cried, "Edouard, cover him up!"

Nino struck a liter, empty and yellow, and it rolled away to return rattling to the tilt of the floor and lodge against his ribs. He looked straight at Edouard and the boy and cleared his throat. "Bianca Maria, your hand." It was a loud croak, Adeppi saw movement in the scar under the jawbone, and the woman shook her head happily, pressing backward a step. Nino was affixed to the floor; they stood over him with a lantern shining on his black-haired haunches.

"Maria, only your hand," whispered Nino.

Below his knee, in the thick of his calf, was the declivity of his second wound, the flesh white and pinched unevenly as if it had been sawed from the tooth of a wild hog. Edouard looked at the scar, then, taking breath, gazed at the waiting girl whose fingers played with the hanging firewood that turned into acrid smoke.

The soldier began, without smiling and in monotone, to imitate the song that Adeppi had sung beneath her window. And, with a single energy, he lifted his hand from the floor, suspended it limply without support, outstretched from his body in hypnotic endurance, so that those who watched leaned forward, feeling the heaviness of flesh and bone and the tingling in the fingertips.

"Dopo, dopo," Maria whispered over and over, seriously and with feeling, as if she did not want Edouard to hear.

"Take his hand," he said, slipping among the women, and slowly, face averted, Adeppi obeyed. He sat cross-legged, his fat brown chest perspiring. "Quick!" urged Edouard, and reaching up, the boy took hold of the soldier's hand and slowly drew it to his lap. Maria watched him closely.

Nino shut his eyes, rolling his head.

Edouard pressed a Florentine florin into Adeppi's other hand.

The children are at the windows late in the night, peering into dry canals and at frescoes flaking on Roman walls. These sleepers cry for food over the roofs of lava, mothers roll and thrust away the child. In the streets the beggar thrusts the bottom of his foot toward the moon. Cats cross now on the Bridge of Straw.

Leaning out the narrow window in the sunlight, Adeppi rubbed his fingers in his shorn scalp, watched a motor ambulance fit itself into the entrance to the court. Then he drank a cup of warm water and went down to the well yard below. The guinea hen thrust her scaled head into the sun bright on the handcart-rutted clay, and the women dipped the buckets one by one from the well. Black hair was uncombed, their working smocks spotted from the dampness of the stones. One was pregnant, and she too smoked and talked of the night that had just passed. Adeppi sat on the rim of the well and watched their faces that faded in the darkness until now, as they wiped water from their eyes with sackcloth, a sleepy belligerence lay on the flesh and they were older. Around the windlass and mended rope they talked like men and, pulling up the flat skirts, felt at bruises on their upper legs.

Stone and plaster, white mortar, tile and slate, crumbling, slowly the backs of the houses emerged from shadow and sweated in the sun. The women dropped their cigarettes down the well and prepared to work. Pale thin strings of smoke rose from the enormous chimneys, as a handful of twigs curled in small iron burners on the hearths.

They were milling in the yard, the child's face as expressionless as the women's, when Nino appeared in the doorway followed by the crashing of his boots. Below his tunic, still without trousers, he wore a short canvas undergarment, hastily tied. In his hand he waved a pistol, not a military firearm but an old weapon come by illegally, once the possession of a noblewoman. The guinea hen dashed behind a pile of manure.

Nino ran straight to Adeppi. The soldier did not touch him, did not put a hand on his arm, but placed the muzzle against the boy's temple. The gun was steady.

The women shouted for Edouard.

"Stop the noise," commanded Nino. The pistol was pressing against Adeppi's ear, he stared ahead shamefully, bewildered. Still aiming the gun, delicate, menacing, Nino began to rub his flat jaw. Absently, he opened the tunic.

Had the short scarred finger pulled the trigger, there would have been a flash, a leaping of the silver gun in the air, and a sharp noise echoing away among the ruins. The shot would have crossed the ancient tiles and disappeared. Nino's wild figure stood quivering by the hooded well, his feet deep in the dust, and at that moment the blast of the bullet would not have come unexpectedly: a man so excited in the early morning, clad only partially in a uniform, could have killed and not disturbed the early puttering of the old peasants in their yards.

Then, as if trying to remember, Nino laid the pistol on the well rim beside the boy. A worn medallion hung outside his tunic. He fingered it and his left eye closed narrowly.

"Nino, come up here, Nino." An early morning breeze swept Edouard's blond curls.

The women waited as the soldier walked slowly, buttoning his coat. Then they too trailed off to work, smiling. The pistol splashed down the well.

Adeppi pushed it, a quick movement, and it was gone. All morning he stayed in the silent yard. He wandered about the low walls as if waiting for Nino to come at him again, or sat crouched in the doorway. Several times he worked with the rope and bucket, trying to retrieve the gun. He remembered the nights he had sat beneath the trees with Nino and explored the soldier's kit.

Once he called out, but there was no answer. Only the hidden women kneading loudly. The sun rose higher, white on the moistened roofs, teeming across the airless turrets, and, as the day filled with noise, Adeppi felt more and more alone, confined to the sheltered yard. But as he waited, there came, not from the second floor but from the third, up under the roof, the light whine of the guitar, and voices, in unison, attempting to sing above their laughter.

At noon, sobered, Nino reappeared with all his bags and equipment. His trench knife was in place, his thick britches wrapped neatly in puttees.

"I'm going." he announced. "Adeppi, wish me luck."

They shook hands. "Arrivederci," said Adeppi and bowed. He stepped back and watched Nino fastening himself with straps. And, for the first time that morning, to see him off, Bianca Maria came into the yard. She wore a gray spangled dress, no stockings, no jewelry. She smoothed the sides of her skirt and kept glancing at the angle of the sun, constantly walking and with only a quick smile for Adeppi. Now and then Nino looked up to admire her.

From his soldier's great roll of musty gear, he pulled a large wooden camera, a tacked-down box that had a slow-shutting, enormous lens. He held it in front of his face and peered through the slot, stepping in blind, artistic half-circles. Fumbling, he pushed forward toward the girl who faced him now, motionless, in the sunlight. Adeppi stood behind her and to one side, leaning against the wall. Maria looked over her shoulder.

"Adeppi, come. Be in the picture." He shook his head.

Nino braced the camera against his chest. Bianca Maria posed with her eyes toward the stork-nested chimneys, with her hands to her throat, and once on her knees clutching the old guinea hen to her breast. She drew closer and closer to the photographer. Nino said nothing, perspiring in his heavy uniform. Adeppi could see nothing of the girl's face, her back was to him, knew nothing of the expression, color, or contour that met the opening lens.

Then, squarely in front of the camera, she stooped and lightly caught up the hem of her dress for the departing soldier, and drew the front of it above her waist. The skirt hung like parted wings on the dusty air. Through the transparency of the single thickness, Adeppi saw the outline of her legs.

"Goodbye, goodbye," called Nino as she ran into the bakery. "Walk with me to the street," he said to Adeppi and, the army straps in place and all his belongings tied across his back, they started sadly toward the gate.

They parted in the middle of the road that climbed straight up from the village and descended swiftly to the low country. A few old men and women, from their perches in the walls, watched the two separate: Nino upward leaning on his staff like a pike, Adeppi downward. Nino, unshaven and stiff, carried his rootless treasures to the distant fields. The episode of the pistol disappeared into the youth of the street singer, but, thereafter, while he counted upon the return of his companion, he was armed.

"Arrivederci!"

There was a corner on which Adeppi liked to stand; and it was to this spot that he ran, pushing through a caravan of children in slouch hats and ragged shirts. The Bocca di Piazza, often empty, was overhung with the blades of shops and littered with silent baskets from which the doves had been sold for sacrifice. Now it was full with silent forms squeezed one by one through the seven-foot arch as if some secret ceremony had ended. Bright scarves fluttered about the dark heads; there was no weight to the parcels on their backs. Slowly they entered and left the square, while those who had gained the center milled, knocking against craven stones. Across the piazza on the steps of the boarded-up opera house small boys fought with folding knives.

This was the silent portion of the city—Adeppi remembered the sudden gesture of the woman and the skirt against his mouth—and he found his way around three sides of the piazza before he discovered once more the exact spot where, under the eyes of the small madonna who gazed upon the harness of ghostly burros, he liked to stop. Adeppi leaned against the head of a gargoyle with a ring in its teeth. The strange crowd grew heavier.

The madonna was unusually small, a wooden figurine in a box covered with broken glass. Her colors were faded. But the woodcarver had made up for the small size by excessive clothing; two eastern cloaks and a heavy sash wrapped her around, thick crude wooden creases obscured the chin and the feet. The madonna peered fiercely from this weight, suffering in the sunlight. Mysteriously burdened, she gazed with enamel face across the city and held up her empty arms. The thick skirt and wear of the weather hid nothing, the woodcarver had sculptured his madonna still with child, to look down on this square of small boys.

Adeppi looked up at the wind-beaten statue. The sun tinted the cowl and few spikes of the halo, a worn-down eight-day candle burned invisibly in the light. One of the crowd paused behind him and with an arm reaching over his head, dropped a coin against the madonna's pedestal. Before Adeppi could move, the hand, withdrawing, knocked him on the ear. He heard the rattle of musket and heavy bayonet, and Nino disappeared into the stream, for a moment tipping his rifle in salute.

2

At the Caffè Gatto, Edouard leaned forward and kissed the top of an old man's head pitted in the crook of his arm. The old fellow's free hand swung out. But the primo camiere had already drawn back and was untouched. The crier whispered it was midnight.

"Giovinastro!" shouted the drinkers. Edouard wet his lips and, glancing over the room, kept his eye some few inches higher than the heads of the tallest dancing men. Now and then he stepped from the box hidden behind the bar, bent double to rinse a glass in the bucket of green water at his feet. He was dressed for night: a shirt without sleeves or collar, a red tie around the neck, and a black band on the forearm. The back of his skull, reflected in the white-framed mirror, was sharp, a piece of Roman stone. Around the mirror were pasted photographs of sallow men in straw hats. And Edouard's own picture was among them. Leaves of mercury discolored the glass.

"Edouard, the cat, Signorina, I am he, beautiful Signorina. I have a tail," he told women who visited the Gatto for the first time, having come perhaps from Umberto's sleeping chamber. On the opposite wall was a portrait of two enormous Siamese cats, painted close together, one atop the other, conveying the heat climbing upon the night, and the two faces seemed to be pressed into a single growth of whiskers, too starved to fight. There were no other cats in the Gatto; only the sardines which Edouard lately placed on every table, the smell of cat hairs on the wood, the archness of the dancers' feet.

Edouard took another sip of the vermouth. His chest itched as if it were covered with hair. Jacopo watched him.

"Basta, basta," muttered Adeppi but Jacopo only stretched his accordion again, until it had taken a full breath, and played. He leaned back, crossed his ankles, and watched Edouard. Adeppi took a breath and again sang "La Gelosia." He walked a few paces, put his hand on a table, a few more paces and stopped again. His voice was louder than the accordion, shrill. He pushed through the dancers. When he came near the bar, Edouard looked at his watch. "Another hour, ragazzo." He laughed and put a coin within reach.

Adeppi did not answer him but put the soldi in his pocket and loudly made his way back to Jacopo, squatted and sang at the accordionist's feet.

"Pussy cat, pussy cat, Jacopo," Edouard called.

Jacopo turned the bellows of the accordion in his direction and peered darkly over the top of the instrument, dropping many notes from the music. Again he looked to the bar.

"Get up," he said, "Edouard wants you to walk around."

For a moment the accordion choked. Jacopo concentrated on seeing Edouard, all of him—the yellow and black hair, the whiteness in the eye, the sharp fall of the shoulders, and behind him the straw hats. On opposite sides of the room, Jacopo and Edouard faced each other and did not move. But the accordion followed the provveditore, though Jacopo held it tightly about the throat, and repeated "La Gelosia" over and over in the rhythm of a death march.

Jacopo wore a short gray jacket on his shoulders—it had begun to rot the summer before—and from his ears, cut into the lobes, hung two square crystal earrings that once belonged to the women of his family. He had a habit of sticking out his tongue, though his fixed eyes forbade that strangers laugh or smile at him.

Edouard twisted the end of the red tie in his fingers. He waited. Suddenly he tucked it into his shirt and picked up the glass in both trembling hands, saluted Jacopo, drank. The vermouth smelled of cold skin.

Around him the young men ate cheese and eggs in the late night, but they did not bother to glance at the singer over their forks. Adeppi, the color of a fried fish, moved among the tables. For a moment he heard Edouard gaily humming the song behind him. Edouard never tired; he trimmed the hair out of his nostrils at sunrise and then slept.

Jacopo clapped the accordion in and out, pushed the stops on the pipe organ of the continent. His tongue was pointed. He had danced with Edouard in Brussels. In an Alsatian cemetery he had played his accordion softly for the burial cf Edouard's first partner, a dwarf. He had come down with fever soon after Edouard in Trieste. Both of them had been found in the waters off Marseilles and taken for dead. But, one spring, they had ridden through the center of Berlin in a black hansom, before Edouard dyed his hair and before he himself grew thin. Now they were without fortune; he dreamt of Edouard's face, Edouard standing with cane and straw hat, Edouard throwing him a coin in Il Valentino.

Adeppi's forehead was wet, his feet bare and flat. Jacopo waved him away; he stood against the white wall, the music heavy upon his chest, his hands automatically pulling at the wooden keys. Air hissed from the pasteboard bellows. Now Edouard was motioning, suddenly flicking his wrist above the heads. He was old for such a worried smile. Jacopo began to play a waltz, watched through half-closed eyes to see the change on Edouard's face. For his own part, nothing could be different: he remembered Edouard describing frescoes that depicted the creation of the world, and he was unmoved. His arms hugged the song, but in a cold catacomb he watched to see Edouard's collapse.

"Edouard has changed his mind," whispered Adeppi. Jacopo nodded. He rested his head against the wall. For a moment the music, though reedy, was anticipative, preoccupied. However, he continued immediately with a polka. The dancers struck shoulder to shoulder.

"Ciao, ciao," bowed Edouard. And if he saw a strange face: "Psst, what is your name, Giovenco?"

Jacopo played another stanza. "Plauso! Plauso!" exclaimed Edouard, rising as of old. He clapped his hands. At his soft enthusiastic shout, the dancers stirred uneasily and glanced at the quick brutal cats on the wall. Jacopo refused to finish the song; he was not convinced when the man called himself a grand 'provveditore' and vigorously shook a glass which he had pulled from the dirty pail. Jacopo stuck out his tongue; Edouard despised the sight of it. The accordionist pressed his fingers down, the screws were falling from his accordion. People talked to the sound of his music—Adeppi's singing made them talk with their hands, catch each other's hands in exclamation—and the metallic passages seemed to liven their white faces like a Viennese orchestra, turned the caffè, the park, or the blind street into a garden of buried remonstrance and love song. Alone, hair faded at the temples, Jacopo was central Europe's aged violinist among empty tables. He was not of the crowd—thinking, plotting, remembering behind the smoke and the beckoning of the instrument—a worn, thinned, narrow-eyed renderer of wine-cellar music.

Edouard slipped through a side door to the alley behind the Gatto. He took a candle with him. On moonless nights, in village after village, the accordionist had seen him shielding a precarious pure candle rigidly over the undrained stones, quickly lest the insects come to it. He returned. The wick was red. He was shivering, no match for the night clouds, the flacons of the canal, the tread of lonely boots. He poured a small bit of brandy into his glass.

The old man woke. His face, covered with spittle, turned slowly up from the bar. With a sudden flattening move he caught the end of Edouard's tie. Head on its side, the old man grimaced. His arm retracted steadily bit by bit and slowly pulled the provveditore close. They stared with horror into each other's eyes. The dancers, pair by pair, stood still.

"Discrezizione, discrezizione!" whispered Edouard sternly, trying to loose the red knot. "I beg you . . ." He choked and pretended to cough behind the back of his hand. Jacopo was out of tune. "Really. I must insist . . ." and the whisper glided up, inaudible. The arm jerked, the head responded uncomfortably.

"Oh, ah, keep them apart, shame," murmured the dancers softly. They stood on their toes. The accordion was conscious only of its own chromatic preoccupation, its blinded chords.

Edouard's eyes grew paler each year and now, wishing no help, he tried to hide their starting from the watery sockets. His raucous, excited breathing pained his own ears. With effort, reddening despite the blood already stopped in his head, he raised his arm fitfully and began, not as smoothly as he might, to stroke the other's wrist. He attempted to turn himself away from the crowd and toward the mirror, the photograph. Best wishes to Edouard. "You will . . . wrinkle my tie," he managed to whisper at last.

"Bah! You mostro!" shouted the old man and, falling from his stool, fled, knocking them aside.

Edouard panted. Then he smiled and motioned with both hands up as if to reassure them. He took three deep breaths. And, exuberantly, he caught the street singer in his arms and swung him off the floor.

"Bimbo," he laughed in relief, "bimbo, bimbo," and hugged

the boy from side to side, swinging the bare feet. He was dancing himself, breathing through his mouth.

Jacopo slipped from the black straps, rested the accordion against the wall. His shoulders ached.

EDOUARD

He found himself early in the century. It was of a sudden, in an Emperor's garden a few moments after it was opened to the public that afternoon, when, looking up from some children romping stiffly, he saw a rider astride a horse with rump broad in the fashion of those times and tail grotesquely bobbed above it; the horse, the sportsman, the plunderous hooves appearing heavy and uncertain on the fresh path, the beast walking like a dray in livery to the fretful ticking of the chopped and twisted stump of jet tail. This mammoth apparition passed but a few steps away, stirred up the earth after the morning's shower, and shook the blossoms of the peach trees immediately over Edouard's head. The rider hesitated, then reined his animal and kept its threatening hind legs from splashing Edouard's checkered trousers, as if in a glance he had thought better of muddying one who avoided stepping on the golden fruit at his feet.

Long and triumphantly he remembered the decisive moment when the horseman gave his signal, mysterious, with knees, wrists, or whatever, remembered the Black turn submissive at the coaxing of its master—count or chevalier—and pass, its staggering rear crowned by the tail in crupper gone at last into the misty horizon of the garden, the pink and green. Distinctly, the horse had bowed to him.

And the horse, prancing and light-boned or barrel-buttocked, sightless in black blinders, or breasting the fog with red eye, became the animal he too could ride so far forward on the withers in tailored uniform or make lift her front legs with one hefty loop of his stinging whip. Carriage horses, stock horses of Belgian soldiers, fillies and colts slim in starvation, there were mounts for Edouard across Europe's glittering paddock and slyly he fed sugar from a yellow glove to the four-legged pedigreed denizens out of Arabia.

He introduced himself as a horse trainer, he took his walks where the best of the breed paraded, and grew to know this all-curried and handsomely saddled world of pleasure by the colors of nearby stables. At one time his favorite was a purple stallion, at another a homely sorrel ridden by a lady in a veil and small black boots, and again he admired a pony kicking its groom. He dreamed of a fortunate trio of whites dancing round and round a pavilion filled with the smell of sawdust and roses and the brass trumpeting of a Netherlandish orchestra. The horse was his aristocrat, their belly bands were cummerbunds of rank, and to the height of his early career they practiced their five gaits each afternoon before his keen sense of form and flesh, and he met well, received well, patted his luck at arm's length, and got about the city well, without ever trusting himself to the saddle. Still, he had hoped one day to return to the Emperor's garden seated upon a horse. And had failed.

Now there was only the horsefly. The stall was in ruin. Outside the caffè, testing himself tentatively against the wall, there was not much to ask of the night or of the flies at his neck again. And the candle, the piece of glass, the disappearing soap cake secreted in an iron hand grip—he suspected street children of using it behind his back—all were nothing compared with the silver brush upon whose curve a fox and 'Edouard' had been engraved. Then stolen. He was wearing his nightcoat, holding it aside.

Blood fell on the newspaper. His shoelaces would become too wet again to dry by morning. Returning, how the guards' horses—small, dusty, ribbed—had shamed him at the gates of Vatican City, and how the horseflies had shamed him there, finding him so readily, settling upon him with such familiarity, Italian, as if smelling at once a friend with sweeter sugar and horse hair on his jacket. His country's domes, the Venite, the avenues with troughs used only by birds and children, were reduced to a constant recollection of dysentery.

Long had he been driven back to the country of flies like blue ticks, thrown back perhaps only hours before the Grand Steeplechase, as neatly as if he had been tossed off into a muddy ditch. He brought with him a pair of opera glasses for the field and Jacopo who was no equestrian. The old world took the bit in her teeth and stood still like an ass. He was accustomed now to the toilet in the street and waited for the buzzing to approach, grow loud, and become a sudden irritant feasting with mouth full between his neck and collar.

But he still donned his striped trousers to cross from the bakery to the Caffè Gatto, now pausing—an eternal cheapside pause—before setting off for the church's spot of feasting. He was in search of the red Riviera, how long it was since they had been to the Turkish baths or cycled together through Balkan capitals. And they had been detained at that last entrance, inoculated on the outermost docks in sight of Naples with its beds of contagious seaweed, as if the two of them were old parrots carrying some tropical disease. Though since landing, they had not been entirely without their flirting with amusement—until the country had nothing more to offer.

The flies walked up and down his nightcoat. He bled, drop by drop; it was late and here he stood, hanging to the handgrips in an iron maiden, apparatus of shield and spikes. He was plagued by the ghosts of small and famous jockeys, heard their dim bowlegged steps through the weeds at night.

"Jacopo, is it you?" He looked straight up at a shadow wide as the round head of Il Duomo, and beyond it into the stars lumining the grave's end, wrapping a few fretful saints. Then he peered over his shoulder. "Watch where you step," he murmured and saw the earrings sparkle.

Suddenly his left hand was torn from the grip, as by a pump sucking irascibly its wreckage, and thrown back against the tin; he was turned half around by his shoulder, drawing to the corner, waiting, wishing to close the nightcoat. There was hardly room for two. With dismal anticipation, he hoped he would not fall on his face.

"Jacopo," hazarding, "have you forgotten the Palazzo Pesaro?"

Perhaps in the days to come, he could pay the child to unclog the drain. For surely his footing would be lost and he would be left to lie in the water. "I hope," it was hard to talk, "you haven't . . . lost my soap. . . ."

He concluded after some minutes—vaguely the thoughts rattled about inside his head—that since Jacopo hit him with the upperside rather than the underside of the hand, it was the nails he felt on his cheek and their stinging that remained when the arm swept each time to the end of its half circle in the dark. It was true, his eyes did flash, and at one of the more painful blows—it grazed his eyelids—he took heart because he loved color. And now the light of his own paining pupils ran up and down the lavatory walls, quickening with red and silver the sweaty iron. He could see the place and realized that when struck, former sights were driven from the eyes, jarred from the walls of the retina unexpectedly, loosed to swim perversely down the system of optics in brilliant discoloration. From his left eye, beaten but still open, he saw Jacopo without benefit of the narcotic colors: only close, too close, and he allowed it to shut in the swelling grown like a compress upon his cheekbone.

He continued to try to talk in the dark of the attack. But Jacopo was always hasty, and after these years his breath was bad. The time came, he let himself flounder forward into Jacopo's arms, nightcoat dragging, and then Jacopo pushed him away. In the moment of consequence like the bending of a saw blade, he remembered a work of intimate draftsmanship, a harem of classical nudes packed together white and featureless like eels. There in the dark, white, featureless except for sexual distinctions, posing uncomfortable, abundant, in the airless dark. One model sat for all, he saw their cluster of similarities, the white details repeated over and over, and as he let go and fell he saw them the more clearly. He wondered, touching the cold of the etching, who might disturb the prohibitive blacks and grays of their tiring watch behind the faintly Egyptian door.

He fell and rolled over, squashing in his pocket a piece of Romano cheese.

Waiting, afraid to move, Adeppi stared at the spot where Edouard lay. He heard footsteps climbing from the weeded canal and another who watched, rattling his equipment, wet, stole to the victim. Fumbling hands poised over the fallen head, a cautious look. Satisfied with the loneliness, the black figure stooped and, catching hold of the shoulders, dragged the body under the quai.

Jacopo ran, the coat flew off his back. When he was out of sight, his relief echoed down in laughter. And Adeppi smelled the top waters of a farther canal, heard the swimming of sated rats. From up there came the sudden 'sciar' of colliding boatmen.

INTERVIEW WITH THE ALPINI

Several miles from the Gatto and a few hours before morning, Nino finally quit the jurisdiction of this city. Boarding a small-gauge train of three cars, he found himself after a time pulling up a low range of mountains from the ridges of which he could see the ocean, a bird-breast blue, flat, in the morning haze flitting with Venetian sails. The black cock's feather curled like a sickle from his Swiss cap, the helmet at his side was filled with grapes. He tapped his cleated boots on a muddy carpet, hugging about him his rifle, pick, and canisters, and watched for signs of the next village. One other in the compartment seemed also not to have slept that night.

The priest Dolce looked at Nino with eyes that retreated on either side of the white bridge of the nose into embittered catacombs and which, now sharp for the truth, now soft as dusk, held the beholder's glance as if, in a moment, they would divulge some bit of personal unfortunate news.

Dolce slipped the cross into the folds of his gown and, suddenly fastidious, lifted his arms and ran the fingers of both hands delicately along the edges of his thin hat, smoothing the brim. He looked out of the window, straight of spine, folding his hands in his lap. As he did so, the three segments of the train struck a curve in the Apennine tracks, glass rattled, chandeliers smashed bottom up against the roof of the cars. Dolce fell in a corner and a sharp tooth came through his lip. There was a trembling in the string that tied the thin hat to his collar. The whistling stopped, and from where they sat they could hear the stoker laboring his shovel.

Nino's helmet had been upturned and grapes rolled through the compartment, back and forth, as the train sped up the mountain. By the attitude of the priest, half on his side and chin pressed against his breastbone, a slight pulsing at the temples and a harsh, wide expression to the eyes, Nino dared not touch him but took his seat again to wait. He felt that the priest had been speaking all the while.

Nino stood up, holding to the sash.

"Secrets. And I suspect," Dolce's words came cold and accusing, after a moment, "no saint to guard your nights."

Dolce did not move. Then one hand drew from under the robes a handkerchief with which he daubed at the puncture on his mouth. He watched Nino persistently, wiped the wound, stared and half smiled as if the soldier had surprised him with a blow. The carriage rolled and the priest with it.

Nino sat down, pushing the tassels away from his knee. He whispered, "I'll tell you, Padre. The secret. It was a bad night." Leaning close his wide mouth and frizzled moustache, "Put away the handkerchief."

Now the priest's head began to jerk toward the speaker, away, near again, and Nino put his hand on the chest of the furtive listener. There was a pounding on the loose glass, and over the turning of the wheels came the sounds of the train master, shaking the handle, screaming at them the obscure name of the approaching town. The sun probed into the priest's corner.

"Adeppi," shouted Nino, "one by the name of Adeppi, Padre, a small boy."

Dolce was up, and before the train could stop, had climbed briskly to the ground. His feet moved rapidly, invisibly; his head was down. As he passed beneath the soldier's window, without looking up, his face hidden under the brim, he lifted his hand curtly—he shielded his gesture with the other sleeve —in the sign of the cross. And he continued on to the station hut, kicking the dust with his little black-pointed boots.

3

. . . The Ponte Beffa, short of span, high of arch, crowned with flowers and a lady riding on a pillion. Part of its battlement is in decay; it is crossed by many. A troop of eels doze beneath in a pool and their dull electrical tails disengage, then sink in the mud. Adeppi gives them a kick with his toes. The edges of his trousers have unraveled in the summer and his belt become tight. His mouth is dirty, in seclusion he has been sunning himself on a rock and sleeping under the bridge, preferring the Ponte Beffa to the Gatto.

But now he hears the sound of wandering feet and watches the head bobbing just visible above the curve of the stony half-moon. The accordionist trudges up over the canal and stuffs the last of his cigarette under the lady's pillion. He is unshaved. Each day he has crossed at the same time, followed by no children or rats, approaching from the west one day, the east the next. On top of the bridge he opens a knapsack, then continues. Jacopo's earrings flash in the sun. He dares not speak to the young girls waiting their turn at the bridge.

Directly overhead, the sounds caught in the city's draining cavern, Adeppi hears suddenly that the accordionist is playing a reedy tune to walk by, faintly, with one hand. The hand goes over the keys as a man absently fingers a few coins in his pocket. Adeppi shuts his mouth firmly, looks away, down at his shadow curled into a ball at his feet. "O Sole Mio"—but even this cannot make him hail his friend.

He disappears.

The bakery walls continued hour on hour their bluish molding, and the boy listened for the emerging of mice. Now and then from under the window Adeppi heard the slapping of sandals as pairs of young men passed, or the irregular, indifferent gait of a limping soldier. Beyond the city came the soft thousand murmur of troops in transit, quartered on the ground, asleep in the fields. On his breath was the smell of anchovy. The boy's knees were drawn up as he settled himself. One of the small, formless hands hung over the side of the bed, swinging back and forth, reaching for the tops of boots or whatever crouched coiled under the ropes stretched for springs.

"Edouard," he whispered, "wake up, Edouard. Bondi, Edouard, bondi! Do you wink at me, old man? Wake up there!"

Without lifting his head from the pillow, Adeppi turned sharply, restlessly, in the opposite direction, his other cheek to the musty cloth. The chest and knees were kept rigid, their stiffness for the appearance of sleep. His eyes were large in the darkness. An empty market smell of mortar and carter's grease, wicker, and warm geraniums came from the city moored so long on the hillside. Below them, the madonna lay buried in her case and, further down, the femurs of entombed monks grew chilled. Summer prowled the unnumbered doorways. Adeppi smelled the greenness of a few vats of wine and the scent of thieves now rousing themselves with basins of cold water. He began to scratch his scalp. Far away he heard the bending of the gondoliers at their midnight task, calling passengers.

Suddenly there was a noise in the street, a lone figure on his nightly way came into an unidentified square across which drifted the smell of sack-stuffed mattresses and the hissing of a small fire extinguishing itself on the open, watery floor of the gabinetto. Adeppi heard him pause, swing around, and fall up short against the door, weakly, with expelled breath. He could feel him look up unsteadily at the trussed window and steep roof, searching after the burning chestnut. With a rope, he would hoist himself to the balcony, a kick at the shutter, and then death for Edouard, too ill to stir.

More steps, the man stumbled in the darkness. There was no dog to drive him off, chase him who had with new energy ventured upon the streets. Adeppi got out of bed and crouched at the foot. An accordion struck up like a gramophone deep in the tombs and cellars. Then the boy, taking a breath and shaking his fist at the shutter, "Via!" he dared call weakly in his high voice, "via!"

The music stopped short. None such had been heard since the closing of the Gatto, no such frightening sound as that of music moving across the barricaded off-quarters of a silent city, across the back houses, gardens, and chimneys. The boy flung out the shutters, crept onto the balcony and, lifting himself, leaned over. "Via, via!" he whispered softly again but did not move. He was not agile, he trembled in the chill, the short low forehead stared down from the balustrade at the bellows of the accordion, the invisible fingers on the keys. Jacopo stepped forward and held out his hands until Adeppi, who finally climbed to a seat on the ledge, dumbly pressed his palms to his chest and jumped into the outstretched arms.

Two carabinieri emerged from around the corner at a trot and, running close together, shoulder to shoulder, gesticulating for silence, they approached and stood fanning themselves with leathern, cockaded hats. The accordion sagged.

"Buona sera," said one of the carabinieri and nudged his companion. They were short with heavy brows and tight black eyes and on the forehead of each was impressed the red markings of a Napoleonic hat. Their tunics were stained with the oil of canned fish. They winked at each other, swinging the rifles.

"Over here, please," ordered the carabinieri and retreated. Jacopo walked with bent knees, the fingers tattooing against his thighs, thin, looking over his shoulder toward the accordion. The carabinieri closed upon him, one reached out and touched the earrings.

"I am too young, Caporale, and sick. Someone else, per favore . . ." Jacopo pulled the coat up on each shoulder, half fallen forward, rested against the wall. The carabinieri stood but a hand's pace in front. Jacopo paused. Beaten back against the tiles, eyes averted, he whistled quickly between his teeth. "The winter," he added, "I would die in it."

The men threw back their heads, laughing, bent down to lay their rifles in the street. Their hands reached out together a muscled arm, a graceful gesture, stumbling in the shadow, and one of the pendants was torn from Jacopo's ear. The soldier dropped it into his trousers.

"Once more, Caporale, don't touch me." Softly, speaking to the ground: "The child would not see me go."

The prickly beards close together, they turned so that the flat stripes on their trousers twisted in the moonlight. "He must look the other way then."

Jacopo covered himself from the weight of their tufted sleeves. "Infermo," he cried as they herded him, kicking with their boots, "infermo!" Dropping his arms, Jacopo attempted to slip past the carabinieri with breaths of white tobacco and the sweet stewed meat of cats captured about the prison. Suddenly they freed him.

"He cannot serve," admitted the first.

"Fievole. Enough." The second nodded and straightened his uniform.

The carabinieri stared with curiosity into Jacopo's face. They picked up his coat.

"No harm, Signore?"

They gestured with open palms, shifting about. They clawed apologetically at the fleas in the sweatbands of their hats. A street dog crept to them, beating its tail, and licked one of the white ankles.

"Your dog, Signore?" Drawing away his foot, "He has a cold tongue." They laughed, showing the spaces between their teeth.

"I am Guiglielmo," said the first.

"And I Gregario Fabbisogno," mumbled the other.

Jacopo was silent.

They coughed, took up their rifles inconspicuously, and hurried away.

Three crude women were scratched in charcoal on the stones of the first portion of the aqueduct and under the drawing in childish script were the words, "Salve, Salve, Salve." In the night a wolf or dog had rubbed his quarters against the Roman watercourse and blurred this sign and its inscription which was written low near the ground. The broken butts of the aqueduct, like sepulchres, were visible across the olive hills; from them came the sound of falling pebbles and the sound of rats walking the tunnel on their long way to Rome.

In the valley a band of figures, stepping on the ties of the small-gauge railroad track, returned from saluting the statuette of the madonna at the Bocca di Piazza. The men carried their coats over their arms.

"Let them pass," said Jacopo and they huddled forward together, trailed by a cowed dog with a basket in its teeth. They dropped from sight behind an embankment, shielding the flames of their candles.

When the valley appeared empty, Jacopo and the boy hurried down the hill, skirting a windowless farm behind which, on a rope, a khaki blanket hung in the sun. Someone shouted at them from the blackness inside the hut, but they ran on. The tracks across the lowland turf were clear, the bare rails which attracted stragglers twisted on their thin bed of coals in the ravine and high on the other side collided with the whorls and fragments of the aqueduct. Lichen crept along the rails, racing the iron. Wind had blown the light ash to the right and left of the tracks and here grew newly scattered yellow flowers.

"Jacopo, where is the train? Have they put down a new road for it?"

They walked forward through the country of solitary animal pens and refuse fallen from brake boxes; straw and oil baked under an expanding sun that turned in the heavens like a boar on its back. Presently they reached a crossing and on this spot, stooping, with his rifle across his shoulder, they met a lonely guard. In daylight Gregario Fabbisogno stood even smaller, his bones were of medieval armor. He looked about hurriedly, as if for his companion the Caporale, and jerked off his tri-cornered hat—with this gesture the mussed black hair fell almost to his back—and bowed. The carabiniere laughed. His toes came through the boots.

"You will have to halt," he declared. And then, seeing Jacopo's earring, "Concittadino!" he exclaimed and patted his shirt front.

Jacopo walked stiffly around the soldier, clucking and nodding his head. He stopped behind him, and the carabiniere wiggled his baggy uniform, not daring to turn. "Your stomach hangs low, compatriot. But your eye is good, it remembers. Fabbisogno? That's right, I remember, too." And Jacopo, with the edge of his hand, struck the back of the policeman's neck.

Slowly the carabiniere got to his feet, disturbing the dust, and kept his eyes on his empty hands which caught the trickling from his nose. The cocked hat lay bottom up by the tracks. He spoke into his hands, "I am on duty."

Jacopo made no move to take back the stolen earring. He looked closely at the carabiniere's unbuttoned uniform. Lightly, carefully, he put his shoe on the man's toes, and from tight lips: "A question, Fabbisogno. When does the train pass? The child would like to see the train."

Gregario Fabbisogno shrugged. He put a finger over his mouth, then pointed to a small enameled medal on his breast. He looked up at the sky and flexed his baggy arms as if he wanted only to be left alone and to stand slouched at attention.

"An answer," said Jacopo, "quick."

And the other, guardedly: "There are days when it does not appear at all. Have you been told it will pass today?"

"I don't ask for myself," Jacopo gently pushed him, "but for the boy."

The carabiniere shook his head. "No train today, bring the child some other time. If it was expected, I'd put that bar down on the crossing. You see I don't."

The sun rolled over them. Under a single stunted cypress leaned a black and white sentry box, upended like a coffin, and inside, heavily shawled and hiding her face, stood Fabbisogno's mother who had carried his lunch from the village. Adeppi ran to her.

"Old woman," he shouted, "when does the train arrive? Will we see it soon?"

She made no movement but to shuffle her feet and draw the shawl closer over her face.

"When will it whistle, woman?" Adeppi struck the wood, peered into the little station, the floor of which was covered with rocks and particles of travel. "Come out. We will look the other way."

"Infermo, infermo," was the faint answer as she clutched at her shawl.

"She is old," said the carabiniere, hanging his head.

Fabbisogno's mother, struggling, turned her back to the door and bruised her hands, feeling for the latch, in her attempt to escape through the rear wall.

The train burst into view a kilometer down the track, and every moment or two its whistle reached high in the air while smoke gathered slowly above the insect engine. Pieces of black tin were bolted to the cars, with funereal caution it approached, looking for obstacles or secreted explosives wedged in the tracks. Fabbisogno ran for his road block, picked up his hat. Jacopo took hold of his collar.

"Signore," begged Fabbisogno, twisting his eyes wide, "Signore, I guard the road!"

The first car, the second, then the third rolled past, the couplings asway like shackles, the passengers sitting straight beside produce and damp munitions. The fireman waved a blistered hand.

"Signal ahead," he shouted. "Water, we must have water at Monte Motteggio."

Jacopo, Adeppi, and the carabiniere pressed as close as they could to the rushing of the wind, the sparks, and smelled the travelers' cold bottles of rosolio.

The train goes out of the valley and once again the afternoon is becalmed, settles moodily to foot. The sky, colored blue as the inside of a shell, is cleaved by a hairline from the distant, lofty, and several heads of the aqueduct so that between them appears an immeasurably thin glimmer of the after-heavens, the clear vacuity beyond the orb. There is no one caught out of the farmyards. It is country without the activity of shoot or sprout, without shadow.

The vendors continue to hawk china molded on the thumbs of Michelangelo over the mountain where the renaissance has failed. But the tartars smuggling from coastal port to port are away and here only an abandoned sundial passes the hours. Two harpies flap uneasily to a haymound, peer about the rose-covered fortifications of the valley, the catholic slopes, the wind shaking their wings, the sun their beaks.

The accordionist and boy leave the carabiniere rubbing his mother's hands with his scratchy claws and turn in circles on the white path, shading their eyes against the glare. Once more Adeppi trails. As he walks, the water rolls in his stomach.

"Who are we going to see now, Jacopo?" he calls and thinks of all who might meet them on the blue floor of the valley. He chews his fingers, looking out for a new face descended from the Longobardi. Adeppi expects every traveler to know him. He waits to be recognized, holds his hands over his head against the sun and is disappointed.

4

La Casa della Contessa, with orange out-buildings, a recent grave which the Contessa would not admit lay on her estate, and an empty aviary, belonged to the old lady and was her fortune.

The Contessa stayed in her room but was remembered by her woman, Arsella, as sitting before the fireplace for an hour each of those days past, wearing a wide green Florentine hat of velvet, face white with the cares of a doge. In that room a diplomat, hurried to the south and a little distance inland from the sea, had been shot before the empty blackened fireplace. The Contessa now kept in her unheated chamber the discovery, which she upturned in cards, that his soul and a wisp of his waistcoat stopped the flue.

Behind the villa, on the ground floor of a small building in which lived Arsella, her mother, and Pipistrello, was a cow of slatternly gray hide. The earth was her pedestal. Her horns were hollow. She had turned gray wading across the fields and now lay with back caved as if under blocks of stone, two delicate forelegs doubled beneath her breast in the straw. Several small chests, covered with dung, were stacked around her. Her whole face was swelled about the tongue which grew large, as did her haunches, while she guarded the stucco and statuary of a milkless past. There was a stain on her side where a liter of red wine had been spilled.

Arsella herself had the bare corroded legs of the cow, thin, white, mature as if she had borne children, and feet that belonged to the field. Year in and out the flannelette skirt was open to the winds that caught her above the knees, a skirt which in its weave had become part of the countryside along with the legs that rubbed against the animal in its dirt. A rosary was gathered at her waist.

Her husband, Pipistrello, was blind; at his wheel, he listened for the shape of the pottery that he turned. Arsella's mother sat beside Pipistrello, and from sunrise to night, held her ears as his clay grated the wood like sandstone. All day, with lips drawn back, she imitated the noise of the wheel, cursing as it ground against the hours. These two, the eyes of Italy, sat to the cow's rear on the other side of the wall, their hair blowing in the heat, waiting for news of the Contessa's death.

Arsella's mother led Pipistrello to his wife's room each
night. Then, through the darkness, the old woman would go
to her own bed and in the chill, undress. That night Arsella
seated Adeppi on the floor of her mother's room. The old
woman removed her short jacket, her narrow skirts, until
she stood in nothing but a sleeveless hair shirt, old and worn,
a thin brown penitent garb that clung to her body. And
Arsella's mother looked down at it on her chest and, before
kneeling upon her bed, pulled it aside and scratched. Long
ago it had been stitched unevenly up the front and little
punishment remained in it. She had come upon it thinking the
hair belonged to the disciples. In winter it broke the wind.

"Why do you wear that coat?" asked Adeppi. He sat against
the wall with his legs straight on the floor and stared at the
mouseback when she caught the light of the moon. He heard
Arsella and Pipistrello fluttering in their half of the building.

"Protect me!" cried the old woman, "protect me!" She put
her hands over her breast. "Arsella, he questions me!" She
tapped on the wall, but there was no answer. She pulled at
the shirt and burrowed into the bed.

"Are you going to leave me here? Madre, the animals!"
Adeppi got up and looked out of the window upon rows
of knotted, miniature tree growths that disappeared silently
with their misty branches into the darkness. The hair shirt
smelled like ash, the old woman fretting her sorry horse-
hair, the same who had chased him, shaking her underskirts,
screaming, "Signorina, Signorina," spitting and descending the
crooked streetways.

Arsella's mother had had sons illiterate as she. One in his
youth had fled with a green-complexioned actor not to return;
another died at birth; one more was stabbed upon a rock
after a far swim in the Adriatic—the old woman barren now
of recruits for either wolves or lambs, flat on her back with
only her daughter, a simonist, near should she be picked again
for castigation by the powers of night.

Outside a whelp began to bay, a political signal for inbred

dogs and hungry factions. Its voice was dry, almost a squeal. "Concittadino," it faintly howled to the small boy, "coraggio!"

Adeppi took hold of the old woman's water pitcher, put it to his lips and began to spit like a Tuscan fountain. He lay down under a stick from which spaghetti hung in white threads.

ADEPPI'S DREAM

Nino on a windy corner. Behind him a wolf, with pups still dragging at the dugs, laps the rain. A long indistinct coat falls from his throat to boots. For a moment his face contorts as if, come purposely back to a distant village, he sees what he is looking for.

Nino, the fatherless. Escaped, only to take up this post begrudgingly. At times the wind pushes him around the corner, but he reappears. He pulls at the bottom of his coat, bares one knee and a round of bandage. He glances up, then proudly points at the wound, brushing stupidly the black hair from his eyes. He cups his hands, he is calling into the darkness, the Italian autumn, the hoarse whisper through the storm in the city.

"It will not heal! It will not heal, fratello mio. . . ."

He is lost in the formlessness of the unruly coat, he forces the guitar inside again. "Bene," he mutters and nods his head. The black stones ring lightly, as a goat walking its quick pace. The narrowness and irregularity of the masonry of sixteen arches bitten by the teeth of centuries close above, the shuttered façades of private house or bordello offer no entrance, pooling their rain in a common spring into which he steps to the ankles.

Nino limps aggressively, walking on the strength of his wounds which in his country are congenital; he stops at every off-shooting passageway, his face close to the walls, musette bag at rest by his feet, and reaches his hand against the wet stones, peers, attempting to find a street name painted there:

Via Tozzo, Via Saccheggio, Via Santa Maria della Salute.
He is baffled by what he reads.

At every corner it is the same, the piazza is gone, as if some
trenchant martyr has lifted a stone to the hole. Shut in with
the rain. Nino lowers his head, moves rapidly, darkened with
the Mediterranean tan that will never fade. It is like Nino to
take shelter, expecting death.

Nino leans down, his lips begin to rise and deflate. The
bag in one hand, the pistol in the other, he stoops further and
thrusts his face along the muzzle. Then: "Peccatore, tell
Edouard 'Nino sends his love!'"

He shoots.

At dawn Arsella found Adeppi sleeping between the cow's
front legs. Sunlight brightened the yellow of the horns. He
lay on the first morning, sore and innocent of the manner in
which he as the child and the cow as the Bible's mistaken sheep
mocked the nativity of the crèche, asleep on the thin and
sacred straw which Arsella herself had pitched to the animal.

She stepped outside, and as the sun wrinkled the skirt across
her buttocks, began drawing her long hair into a bun.

"Get up, get up, Pipistrello," shouted the old woman above.

Pinned to the back of Arsella's door and the only decoration in the room was a bleeding heart with brambles, printed
on a piece of curled parchment the size of a playing card. The
arteries, cut close, were painted flamboyantly and crowned
with gilt; the thorns, a mustard green, went deep. Each
morning Arsella put her lips to it. Pipistrello kissed nothing
and wore a medallion down his spine instead; nevertheless, he
kept something for himself in the darkness.

Arsella's was a room in which a blind man and his wife
might well sleep. It was narrow, and except for the bed,
empty like a cubicle kept over the years for hire with a cold
floor and a price on the space in which two might lie side by
side. At the corners were four rude beams, in the sunlight
caught afire, and only the wood, bronze as the planking in a
stable, marked the room as distinct from any to be found in

the lower courses of Rome, stripped bare and convenient, awaiting occupation. The hand-illuminated heart hung from its nail in place of coat hook or calendar. It could be seen only if the door was closed—this part of the body hung like a lung extricated from its mass—and so bared, displayed the frightening inaccuracies of the imagination. Adeppi with his first glance learned that thorns grow inside the chest.

"Perchè, Arsella, perchè?" and added, "I don't believe it."

"God the Father," she answered from the bed, "anything is possible."

Arsella was born in a vineyard, was found to be a girl by an old man nearby and was carried in her mother's arms— a throng met them in the village—to the steps of the church, not inside. Her teeth grew cutting upon bits of bread wet in wine. Her flesh was brown and the heels heavy; she grew sanguine quickly and with hardly a trace of the dark madonna about the eyes. She married Pipistrello near the spot where the poet was burned on the windy shore. The ceremony took but a short time, was followed by feasting.

Thereafter Arsella stayed as much as possible in her room at La Casa della Contessa. Pipistrello kept below with his wheel, glazing away endlessly his vessels, the crooked spouts and bowls. From late morning through the afternoon to evening Arsella stretched flat on her stomach, sometimes in sunlight that came through a window at the head of the bed, day air into a monastic cell. She did not pray, lying as the monks could not. There was a twitching in the flank which she did not feel and with head bent there came over the room the sound of immodest breathing.

"Arsella, did he eat the brambles?"

Red, white, and gold, the heart looked full, a crimson mussel without foot or face. Adeppi watched; his eyes were small, close set, the gum in the front of his mouth was bare, his fingers clasped the bed irons. Then he shrugged and turned away.

"Turn him out, Arsella!" shouted the old woman from below, picking at the blinded Pipistrello.

Arsella kept several sacks under the bed. As the days passed, Adeppi drove his hands into the hard weave and grasped what appeared to be the arms and legs of dolls. And he spent days seated on Arsella's mattress in which the woman hid her stomach and chin. His only chore came at dusk when it was his turn to empty the cow's water, dragging it outside in a great tub, wide-rimmed, full as sponge.

Arsella, her eyes close to the mattress, stared through the open window. Adeppi too, with mouth hung open, looked impassively at the cropped earth and hemlock beset by parasites. They smelled the old men burning hay. And as Arsella and Adeppi roosted in the upper story, basking under a sun which made the roof creak, he passed his hand over her shoulder, down the back, sometimes still near the pit of her spine, until it lighted upon her buttocks, beginning to turn and wheel with the humming of the sun and dust high as her hip and low as the falling off of the flesh.

On a late afternoon Arsella pulled one of the long-necked sacks from under the bed and slipped away. She and Adeppi, the bag between them, blinked again in the sunlight. Pipistrello leaned near, smoking a cigarette. He lifted his face to tell the time of the sun.

"Arsella, un momento . . ." Pipistrello mysteriously waved the bit of cigarette, came toward them. His brow was severe with an effort to open the round lids. "Un momento," he ordered. He wore a leather jacket gathered close to the waist and on the arm a black band. There were flecks of feather and pollen in his hair, the hands were stiff and horned from his potter's work. On his feet he wore only a pair of light stockings. In the noonday sun he caught Arsella's shoulder and roughly, his fingers strong, felt her face, chest, and behind her ears under the hair, at arm's length the brusque exercise by which he knew her. Silently Adeppi took the sack.

She eluded him, and Pipistrello did not attempt to follow, turning after them abruptly and standing still, his skull so tilted and the chin lifted that, had he been able to see, he would have been staring over their heads and into the olive clouds. He brushed at the shadow under his eyes.

"Prudenza," he called while she could still hear. "Prudenza."

Arsella went first down the path. It was rocky and a white distance to the nearest shade. The neck of her shirt was cut as low in back as in the front. There, and at her knees, Adeppi could see the white line of her single undergarment. They passed stakes to which animals were no longer tethered. Now and then they crossed over reddish barricades of barbed wire by climbing on stones that had been heaped to serve as stiles. Arsella walked as if she were pushing a great load; her toes were black.

At the bottom of the hill sat an old man. He smoked a scalding hooked clay pipe which glowed brightly up to the stained reed of the stem. He had removed his shirt and draped it over his head as a sun hat. His arms rested in his knees and almost entirely hid the chest skewered with age. A goose with a broken neck lay against his foot.

"Arsella, wait. That man, there, the man who eats brambles!"

"Can't you see," she answered, "he has a goose to eat."

Before they could continue, the old man dropped his pipe, caught up the bird, and hugged it to his chest like a thin dog clawing a moth. The pipe lay smoldering in the grass. The goose's body—it was enemy to rodents and the pups of wolves —smeared blood from the old man's fore-flank to his collar-bone.

"Via, via!" he shouted as loud as he could.

They passed. There were a few farms and the dung heaps contained great holes, gouged nightly by wily jaws. The earth looked as it did the first day it worked itself up from the sea. Not a laugh rang out across a country still deep in its half-century siesta.

Arsella's sack was light, yet now and then she let it drag behind her feet on the loose path. Once she stopped, took off her rosary, and gave it to the boy.

They reached the hut at the same moment a priest approached from the opposite direction, down the hillside, beating his skirts. He was breathless and fanned himself with his black hat. His cassock was wrinkled, having been drawn close these nights against the chill.

"The village, Signora," he enquired and flapped the dust. "South, my child, or north?"

He did not look at Adeppi. Arsella pointed and Dolce sped away, swerving further from the forked meeting place of the hut.

Adeppi recognized the hut, the same from which he and Jacopo had been hailed on the day they hunted for the villa. Up one side reaching from the debris to the roof top was the pale imprint of a twice life-size cross, all that remained of the crucifix which, like a damaged chimney, had been torn down. The hut was small but it contained eight rooms, two by two, one pair behind the next. There was neither a door in the doorway nor glass in the windows. In the first room a small child, yellow-skinned, knelt upon a narrow bench with its peaked face forward over a tin saucer of wine.

"Brother Bolo," called Arsella.

The child glanced about, unable to run, then drew its body down even tighter to the bench. After a moment it dipped one of its hands into the wine and began, squinting its eyes at Arsella, to lick the fingers and palm. They did not enter. The next pair of rooms were empty but around the walls were hung a few alms cups. The floor was brown and yellow, the tile tracked with dirt and a fine sifting of trampled pottery and veneer. In the third pair the fresh ashes of a fire lay beaten in a corner. There was a cold current in these shadows that could rot the hardwood; the breech of a small rusted weapon sat on its tripod under the window in a draft of sunlight. In the last pair they found him. Bolo filled the left-hand room, bounded by the sides, top, and bottom of his cell, all parts of him swelled to the partitions buried within the hills and canal-cut plains of the dark country that did not comb its hair. He wore a coat with high buckled collar, close together and prominently he carried his small hands, which, tapering of finger, were clean and soft to the touch. On his left hand was the sacred seal.

"I return your greeting," said Brother Bolo quickly and reached for the sack. Arsella handed it to him, pinched Adeppi's arm.

Bolo untied the strings. He felt to the bottom and then by a wing drew forth a cherubim that had flown over the heads of the Volto Santos in the hour of prayer.

"Oh, holy, true, and golden cross, which was adorned with his body and watered with his sweet tears, by thy healing virtue and thy power, defend my body from mischance, and by thy good pleasure, let me make a good confession when I die." Brother Bolo took a breath. Carefully he laid the cherubim on the table. He leaned forward and blew the road dust from it.

"If you ever get to St. Peter's, Pipistrello's wife, you shall see him, safely hanging again from his wire. But at a price." The cherubim's knees were drawn up so that he might run in the air. "If you look closely you'll know him at the hour of vespers. Notice the broken wing, Pipistrello's wife."

"It's nothing, Bolo," she answered.

"Fifty lire for that wing. To be deducted." He put his fingers under its arms and lifted. Bolo hung his sharp eyes sleepily and began to pick at the gilt with a fingernail. From the hut's first rooms came the sound of the child humming a wordless song.

"Adeppi, shall we part with the little angel?"

"Yes." But he was listening to the child's wandering voice.

Away from the beatific font and in Bolo's grasp the cherubim weighed less than a kilo.

"How much for it?"

"Your pleasure, Brother Bolo."

"It will pass through other hands than mine before Rome sees it again; and if it is ground for mortar before then, well, it will bring little. . . ."

"Bolo, each is a dove. . . ."

"The golden holocaust, Pipistrello's wife. Each is a bead that has been cast off in prayer."

"Signore," Adeppi interrupted and flung off Arsella's hand, "I know where there is a madonna, in the Bocca di Piazza, a madonna, Signore!" And reaching up, he gestured, once more exclaimed, "Madonna!", urged Bolo to follow and struck the good wing so that the cherubim fell loose and broke on the floor.

"O sacrilegio, sacrilegio," cried Arsella softly and drew back from the pieces.

It is dusk when Gregario Fabbisogno comes upon the edge of the hillock and crouches with his rifle at port arms, fearful and with noisy ear, having deserted his post to the owls. His beard has grown in the last hour, he must make a place for himself in the grass. Is it not too late to discover the trench ringed with bloody sticks? No one will take him in tonight. He has not been commissioned to build a fire. Below, his mother is mad at the crossing. Fabbisogno's trousers balloon; he remembers they have been called his face and spits through his wide teeth. He protects himself with the gun as the dew comes and he sees the shadows of foes gathering behind the hut. He keeps pulling his mouth awry and listening for the tread of donkeys loaded with cannon and packs instead of bells. It is a night to challenge skeletons bound upright to the tops of haystacks or to kill the geese dancing upon the graves.

Fabbisogno takes his stand before the hut.

"What is moving there!"

The cold of the earth passes into his boots and he looks within a hundred paces of the outpost of sated crows. Exclaiming, "I am on duty!" he shoots at the shadowy figure, starts as the bullet imbeds itself in the chimney stone. Brother Bolo clasps his hands and falls; the child carries him a cup of wine.

Gregario Fabbisogno runs, with a frown that by its ignorance and solemnity covers his desire to shoot again, dark as the moon against which he leans for breath.

5

Christ had a sharp face. Dolce knew every line of it. All the quixotic notions of suffering and the guard-watched severity with which that heavy head lay to its side were bounded in limitless compensation as dignity upon a few beams.

Down the length of the vinegar peninsula, in a country that made much of the birth and worshipped more the bearer, Dolce was peculiar for his transfixion upon him who, a man and by a mob of men, was crucified on the ground and hoisted into the air. If he had walked in this village on this evening his face would have worn a further and befitting sign of a black patch across his eyes. As it was, wearing only benevolent stains, he was remembered by his nervous priest Dolce to be pitiful in awe-striking thoughts of windy illumination. Dolce's passion was known to the Brotherhood as devotion for the face itself and the agony contained in the brown eyes. Dolce carried this exact expression where he went, showing to strangers only his own insignificant suspicion, a trembling chin, meanly concealing the images of wind-beating locks and thorns.

Thus Dolce arrived. After a hard trip he appeared in the city some kilometers below La Casa della Contessa and went directly to the fountain. An old woman ladled him a cup of water. He drank, wiped the dust from his face, and blessed her. He noticed the woman—she lowered her head three or four times backing away—with the same eye that caught the birds at that moment hurrying to roost. Around the square they dropped to the open galleries, following one on the other under the narrow and florid arches darkening to the public spectacle. The old woman hurried behind him and he sat to rest, unaccosted, on the fountain's damp rim. He vigorously proportioned out the city, leveling it so that he might search it, piercing the uniformity of its dusty guise.

He appeared and sat in the Bocca di Piazza well after its hour of crowds. Two hundred feet ahead, his eye in passing found the small shadow-swept resting place of the miniature madonna, posted on the wall like a bird box, and at this distance he recognized her, made the sign. But his attention went to the combs and footways that climbed inward from the false opening of the square, conceived to belie the narrowness beyond, in which those who knew each other might move closely to their purpose. The last bird rose as Dolce snapped his hands at it, winged painfully toward a ledge, veered and fell safely behind a rooftop. All the noise from the inner caves of the city fell short of the square.

The old woman had left her cup and he drank again. He saw on the bottom, glittering under the last sipful of water, a few begged soldi, and he dropped it. He was warned. But he did not leave the sound of the water's continuing splash in its public font. Until he could sit no longer.

Chin jutting in subordinate holy profile, he moved now upon the city that could escape no further, caught intrenched at the end of its own tunnel. He took his steps carefully, not to miss any of the snares spread for him. At dusk, trailing his blackness, he freely exited from the placid, unfamiliar piazza and stole into the avenues of burros bunted with the stretched and rigid shapes of vegetables long hung by twine from the walls, toes inward. The bridge where the stony blue lady sat her pillion was hardly noticeable, the span shallow and the arch slight, squeezed between great sidings of the slaughterhouse. A single woman, without word or excitement, turned her body and face to the wall until he passed.

Dolce pulled sharply at his black brim, tipping it in dismissal. He felt the throat-pinching emotions of the stranger with his scant foreign baggage and dusty britches who, not knowing the way, may thrust himself into good quarters or bed and on this first night see with an immunity not completely sure against false steps and falls. That sense of being loose in a city similar to the one left, but without memory, offering itself or resisting investigation—its short chambers, kitchens, and roof touching roof—all before morning. About him were the secular playgrounds of the boys, the shrewd originations of young men and their entertainments, and old men. To be strange in such a place, it stirred God's cleric in excitement; he stopped to count the beads.

He continued until he found the unobtrusive entrance to a small church and its dismal surrounding silence. Here he could pause. He stepped cautiously into the center of the narrow street to peer at a small tangle of iron on top—the winds had whirled it—a cross which lay high like the skeleton of a nest fled by the rooks. Dolce admitted it, a sudden prayer for the magnanimous brown eyes, at death raised and looking through the breasts of the stoners to clouds beyond.

Dolce, without guidance, on a crooked branch of the street and through the darkness, found his way to the Gatto. After walking twice past it, he turned and presented himself at the door, thinking of the pension above for the night. The proprietress did not let him into the caffè but took him around the outside to an opening meant for exit and up the stairs. She climbed quickly and Dolce followed at last and despite fatigue into a hallway above.

Several doors opened a head's width on darkened rooms, and Dolce heard a man, two men mutter; but the proprietress took the placard number from a door as if, numberless, it was his. She went in before him and brushed away an old pair of trousers, swept some coins into her bosom. Her dress was fastened at the shoulder by rosettes and had no sleeves. She stepped aside and Dolce entered; eyes on him, she breathed heavily.

"In the morning, Holy Father," she said, "open the window." She took the light.

He discovered a candle on the bottom of a drawer pried loose from the commode. The image of the woman was before him, her luminous form impressed on the darkness, hands on her slight and transparent hips. Fitting, for Dolce thought of cities as old buildings superintended by women, giving shelter without comfort—as one might be taken into an almshouse—and harboring those from the street merely for the experience of a strange face and strange demands which they could exact themselves to meet with laughter or fear. He wondered what sins the proprietress had assumed for which there was no punishment in this city.

The candle by one heel, Dolce sat on the bed which sagged to the floor and untied his shoes. The room had a narrow air of unoccupancy, the sleepers who had come to it took away with them the soiled linen. Still he smelled an odor not from the wood alone. He put his hat on the pillow next to the gray spot where he would rest his head. Putting the proprietress out of mind, he rose in stockinged feet. He rubbed salt on his teeth and splashed his eyes with water. He gathered up his skirts, leaded about the hems so that each step brought a remindful blow to his ankles, and knelt, one knee then the other falling into place. His hands were white in the clasp. He put his forehead to the wall and began to talk, quite loudly.

He was in the darkest corner and kneeling as low as possible to the floor. If they should burst in upon him suddenly, bringing the curious light over his shoulders, he would not be seen at once nor his privacy violated before he could unclasp his hands and order them away again. He spoke loudly so that they might not think to listen, and the decoying candle, mounted on the farthest wall, burned as if he had just stepped out. It was his habit to so prostrate himself: all the more, since to leave his bent back unprotected to the openness of the room increased his nervousness until he was sick and longed to look around. He feared the sudden shout. And while he talked, he coughed, paused, cleared his throat, the confidence of his voice keeping him rooted and able to contend with the anxieties of a communion which doubled him over like one insensible.

This day he had taken only water. Dolce prayed and confessed on water, a few drops rigidly devoured. The dogs would not drink when he approached, and he went dry if the animals had been at the pond before him with their heads down and muzzles drawing from the still surface by tongue and through nostrils. Dolce was one for the edge of the forest, his clearings were crossed only on the bridge of a shadow, he could not drink without disturbing the water and making the mud rise.

In confession he crouched biting at his master's heels. Dolce did not confess the omissions and grievances of a few hours before—these present reflexes of wickedness went unmentioned until their turn should come after consideration. He concentrated instead upon smashing the most innocent days of earlier years. He saw Christ patiently impaled in a high-backed chair.

At last he went to the bed. He took the hat from the pillow and lay in its place a plain fraternal medallion that had been chained on his girth. He slept, and his hand was raised above the head and cupped defensively as if to catch some weight hurled out of the heavens through the roof.

THE CONFESSION

In the novitiate we were cruel. Jesu Christe Saviour. There was an old woman who came every day to the low wall around our monastery and begged for instruction. No other women walked so far. Near dusk she watched as we without hair took exercise in a circle. She carried a tall farming rake which she stood against the wall like a tree split dead and sharp by lightning.

"What had Christ to say for the old woman?

"What comfort for the defenseless?

"Let me walk with you."

These things she shouted, and if none of us raised our heads, she was likely to catch up a handful of dirt and throw it at us novices. But if the little bell rang—it was a soft mournful sound not heard any distance from the monastery—she hobbled off, dragging the rake.

"Chastise me, chastise me, you priests."

I can hear her yet. I did not pity her. Jesu Christe.

She appeared first in winter without a word, and we thought her the mother of one of us, come to beg us back, to claim us from the icy grip of the Order. If there was a last ray of sun, she would lean her elbows on the low stone and begin to nod her head up and down in approval or encouragement. A lone figure, she participated so foolishly and so regularly. When the winds blew in the darkness, she was there listening for our monotonous footsteps. On winter mornings the road took her below the monastery, and pulling her rake as a sledge—a tin of frozen milk was her load—she waved at us though none answered. By night she returned with the rake swinging across her shoulders like a great scythe; hardly lifting our eyes, we saw the wood cutting the snow until she dropped it to the ground, an old and brittle foot falling on the ice.

Toward spring she began to cry so that we should hear, and as if this were a sound we novices would understand, thinking the voice of misery our voice, our fate, as a hunter knows his hounds. When the briars beyond the wall divulged a few thin rabbits and new shoots broke beneath the rake, she unwrapped her head. In her youth she had not been beautiful. But we forgot her cries when the showers drove down our heads and filled the bowls sooner than we could eat. Jesu Christe Saviour. Many of us sickened in those months.

Spring came.

"Domine Jesu Christe, sancta cruce tua apud me sis, ut me defendas.

"Domine Jesu Christe, proveneranda cruce tua post me sis, ut me guvernes.

"Domine Jesu Christe, probenedicta cruce tua intra me sis, ut me reficeas," we chanted aloud, no longer chilled and walking through the puddles of a green thaw. And at these words the old woman first began to interrupt our prayers, to talk to us as if we might break our circle and crowd around her like boys, with questions or comfort. Receiving no answer, she took to following the prayers.

"Domine Jesu Christe, Domine Jesu Christe," as she stared at us over the wall, lagging a phrase or two behind. None of the holy fathers ever saw this woman. There was no one to send her away. I remember how, old as she was, it looked as if she might dare to climb in amongst us at any moment, just as she shouted down our evening ritual. What shame, Jesu Christe Saviour.

She was not easy to ignore, having began at odd fearful times to beat one fist into the other to the rhythm of our walk, the motion of justification, uninterrupted, constant, a movement of backs and without rhythm at all. Our eyes were closed, yet there was no escaping her inspection. She watched us with mouth open, then a frown, then beckoned, and we looked alike to her. We came to know: in the morning she waved from a distance, fenced off from us, by evening she was distrait on our right hand. We recited the prayers less frequently. Consumptive with sin, flesh of the devil, an old woman burning worse than ever though temptation was long done, and the church would not turn around to try her.

Jesu Christe. She provoked us. She came before the monks— for her sight were the leather robes—and exclaimed that she was old and of another sex before their cloister. Deaf she was to our silences, and we took a step with hands outstretched to each other's shoulders.

Heaven forbid, Jesu Christe Saviour, but it was the day of visible ascension before we mustered ourselves to put up with her no longer. We stopped. The brown wheel hardly knew how to cease its turning.

"Woman," our spokesman said, "this is the hour!" and raised his arm upright so that the ragged sleeve fell from the bare bone.

"Grazie, grazie, grazie, grazie . . ." and she hurried as fast as she could to the gate.

We led her to the stable. Brother Bolo, not I, furnished the pelts. One of us pushed her, undetected in the night. There were no horses in the stalls to whinny an alarm or swing their haunches against the planks. Brother Bolo began pulling his pelts from the beams, in generous handfuls destroying his collection of little hides. They were uncured. He had trapped only in the first months of spring.

Two held her arms. We put the lantern at her feet. She was undressed to the waist by another while we spoke Latin. Our bare toes and heels stamped on the straw that remained. From a high rafter overhead and this late at night—he climbed up there when he was free—one of Bolo's traps rang out. The capture made it fall from the wood, and trap and rodent swung in rotation on the length of cord. We hurried.

"You can see for yourselves, you can see for yourselves," murmured the poor woman.

The first pelts stitched together were held immediately in place covering the dugs. They were laid on with the fur turned in to the body. We knew the hides would shrink over the years. Brother Bolo counted as he gave them up but he held them himself while they were sewn. The swing was awkward though the old woman was not pierced. A great seam grew up the front. We made much of our work and cut away the pieces that did not fit, snipped off the tails and claws. The woman was told that the pelts were being sewn with their heads down. Our shadows fell backward, tall and sharply gowned on the rough boards, and she looked at these, calling them one at a time by the names of the disciples.

Finally but a shoulder remained, and this we covered quickly. What suits do bodies wear beneath the clothes! What evil fitters to trim this shirt for her without the demand of God and the authority of the Order, a few rat skins pieced together in a stable by one novice fat and one thin. The poor woman's face grew radiant as if we had pronounced that henceforward her children's children would go free of sin. Breathlessly we carried her beyond the monastery grounds and put her on her feet.

That night we agreed that more like her should wear the shirt. Forgive me this thought.

Dolce awoke several times and felt a sore—he was not tender with it—which had started and begun to pain his lip since the few hours he had left the fountain. He must learn better not to eat or drink. He blew out the candle, scraping the wax from his fingers. Each time he awoke, he listened and heard nothing. Tomorrow he would surely fling open the window before mass.

6

It was summer. The sun bleached the tiles to deeper shades
of red, the sound of a young girl's voice carried far over the
hillocks—with the singing even the grinding of the oxen's
shoulders could be heard—before fading. Adeppi lifted his head
and listened, though his lips curled. Each day's passing brought
a new accumulation of dust white as hair to the vines and
leaves, their hemlock color was not seen. Adeppi continued to
stroke the woman before the open window. Children run to
pat the donkey's haunch or throw their arms around its neck,
and he, like the rest, would have clapped after the little animal
as it trotted through the grove dropping its new dung. La Casa
della Contessa had only its forty-stone cow and the throat of
this animal was infected with boils. Adeppi preferred Arsella's
room to the stall below. Sometimes without a word she shifted
under his hand and then he climbed down at the window,
watched for a raven or some other winged boy-fowl to tumble
across the blue spacious sky, until he returned to her. Or he
went to the door and waited. "Permesso?" and if she did not
answer, he was free to descend and take the path into the
field and shallow pit. She might shout to him there if he did not
hurry.

These days they slept from noon to the hour of vespers, the
boy lulled away from the urge toward activity, Arsella's constant position making her head nod. She blew on his eyelids
until their hands dropped open and they were asleep. The
mouths fell loose, trembling to the breath of the unconscious.
Their clothes grew damp. Adeppi would wake sullenly and
be sent for water. The sun worked upon them while they
slept and tired them. "How old you look, Arsella," he would
say when they awoke in the shadow. The face changed hourly.
The skin was wrinkled where for a long time the fingers had
rested under the cheek. And the boy's forehead also, above the
eyes, had thickened and become enlarged with the cells that
grew randomly in the course of sleep.

The villa lay atop the conventional terraces of the country.

They were littered with the broken chips of Pipistrello's unsuccessful pottery; long ago the planted bulbs had died from these terraces. Here too were buried the discarded pieces of the cherubim. When his sleep was thinned away, it was to the seven artificial levels that Adeppi came, breaking down the rims with a bare foot as he patrolled them.

There were colonies of insects that toiled on or fought for the terraces: the two-heads, as long as his finger and deep black. If the shells of the jointed body were split, they were found to be hollow and yet able to keep alive even when so ruptured and filled with sand. The living weight of the two-heads was carried outside the shells and to the front in the double appendages. During battle, they fought to tear through the globular mass of these heavily connected lobes. As long as the heads remained together sharing ducts and tissues, there was no need of the body. Though without the shells which carried their legs, they were unable to walk.

Adeppi disturbed the two-heads' natural torment. He held them to the light and they were translucent, some had raveling holes in their black sides, and he strung these together on a twig, on sharp skewers. They were a locust species, transmuted on the grounds of La Casa della Contessa, hordes that had turned against themselves. He sat watching them or lay on his belly watching them, like a cat that has lost part of its senses through a wound in the eye and sitting upright, waits wondering with the other. Sometimes a handful of earth came down and destroyed them, as they were not wormlike and could live only above ground.

Attempting to pass from one terrace to the next, the two-heads killed each other by striking tenaciously at the doubly large target of the face. They lay in the sun, black, dry as kelp. Unlike most insects, a fall from a ledge to a bit of soft earth below could injure them; many were barely able to drag themselves to safe ground and took days to heal. They had forgotten how to denude the olive trees and their afternoons were confined to scaling the terraces, that miniature cleft landscape whose borders were treacherous and stripped of pebbles.

"Look how they crawl, Arsella!" he tried to say, eyes fixed on their efforts which were only to keep themselves marching in the sun. He spent hours on this terrace watching the bugs move in circles that would not keep their order as an old garden sank to decay. He covered his knees with cinders and dug his feet into the low vermin outline of the insects' fortresses. These somber in-between hours he spent surrounded by the creatures of his fourteen hundred days passing and repassing in smoking expeditions. "They have no wings, Arsella." But she did not answer, only put an arm over her eyes.

By sunset Adeppi, Arsella, Pipistrello, all were on their feet, the recumbency of the afternoon was done, and they began to drag over the stones and caked surface of the well yard; in the coolness, working. All three could be seen pulling the cow from its bed, wiping at it with a great quilted rag, picking the parasites from its ear. At last it was beyond the door, twitching its stifled hide to the open air.

"Breathe," Arsella commanded, "breathe!" But it had not the will. So night came to the scraping of the two-tongued fork, the poor dull-witted animal finally guided and beaten into place by the blind man, woman, and boy tugging upon its soft horns.

"A load of wood, Pipistrello. If you please."

Arsella's hair was undone by dusk and it swayed unkempt as she retreated again up the leaning stair, hands across her breast, climbing once more into the unlighted rooms.

It was a night for the hounds to run. Adeppi could hear them fleeting through the baleful mists with bellies and chests compactly forward. Such a hot night for coursing, outdistancing those who followed in ancient velveteen, their epees electrified. No mastiffs these, but the inbred packs whose prey, when run to ground, came to no harm. He felt them circling the villa, giving chase to the great rat tails distended rigidly from the bones of the quarters, damp and never winding, keeping to one exhausting path unless distracted by the far-off horn. The night smelled of the phantoms, what a squealing if one were lost! The gray dogs, in pursuit but not marauding, ran through this summer afterdark; slowed to a sudden trot, they stalked across the empty trysting places, then off again, jowls fastidiously dripping ground meal and bone. Atop the aqueduct they did not lose their footing, scaled like flesh-eating sheep the walls of a monastery, now scolded and called back by the weary whippers of bad spirit emerging from the bog. A lost warning, in the darkness unable to see, a man and hound perspiring and snapping expectantly: when women were behind walls and the hand-hammered latch. He heard their blood running fast and cold, their long lines bounding past time-telling statuary and into shrubs that tore their hides. He heard them panting as if there would be rain. The dogs of unrest—those that held their whining and would not stand for chains—were hard by. Ears flat, brains dry, plummeting over stilled fields like birds with wings drawn in, searching—but there was no infant left out of doors. The canescent animals were loose. The prints were fresh in the dew, the low shoots shaken. Woe to them crouched in the rushes; the hound was out.

Adeppi stayed close to the villa. Back and forth he marched, never beyond sight of the prow of the roof beam glistening like a cliff's tooth through the fog bank. He paced his child-hood's raided buildings, bareheaded, now and then staring above as if he had never been inside.

He carried the black pot of the mandolin against his chest. Every few minutes he stopped, spread his feet wide, and as best he could swung arm and mandolin upwards and outwards toward the window that had no balcony. He was glad for the mists which drove away the wanderers and left him alone, wishing for loneliness and a land covered with sea-smoke so that he might wake her from below on the tumultuous green and she, from the high familiar room, look down to find him posted, attendant, in the company of sharp stones and the nightly well-plumed owl. *Avanti, avanti.* But he would take good time. He expected that she would listen without smiling, then thrust head and shoulders into the darkness and give her nightdress to the touch of the fog. Only the mandolin would be found by morning beneath the window.

Even the ferns themselves were fending off the dogs with their sting, and he watched to see the yet undiscouraged animals mounting the cloud banks as stone stairs, rats faithfully thronging the mist's deserted incline, ending in fall. Behind them, the men were out, challenging each other as they hurried to their selected trees. All except Pipistrello who was asleep in his black cap.

At last the fog was moving. It too was impatient and rolled high against Arsella's window, then collapsed and fled, every quarter hour torn with hurry. Adeppi looped the mandolin cord twice round his throat. The instrument, weightless, darkly lacquered, swayed as he brushed wet leaves and stumbled, muffling the strings, the fretted neck, until he should allow its music to start with the loudness and desire of three viols.

The first stanza was simply to be sure no jealous ear was listening. A few notes—far apart as if the fingers were too short to strike all the strings at once—and a hasty silence. The next stanza was hummed for his own pleasure. He had decided to kneel, and his head was still bent in case of interruption and a thoughtless, vicious blow. It was in this position, his eyes burning, that he saw the single column of insects winding slowly outward from the terraces, over the dew. One he crushed with his fist and the rest halted. He hit another and the two-heads turned back, blindly leaving him the ground under the window. Again he took the mandolin in his arms.

Now he sang, and this stanza was meant to bring her from the bed. The stringed instrument and his voice, yet soft, sounded foreign amidst the dark, the white, and the earth smelling of undersoil and shallow graves.

"Who is it?" She heard with ears more ready than he expected. But before he could answer, she cried, "Via costà con gli altri cani!" The mist that had been rounding and rounding the house now suddenly darted and disappeared, sucked into the open window past where she hid.

How serious she was. He fell, separating himself from the

prickly shadows, and ran midway to the glistening wall, held up the mandolin in both hands.

"Arsella. Do you see me?" He turned sharply, waving the instrument, seeking to part the fog.

Letting the mandolin hang free, he rubbed his fingers, short and wide-spread. In the next silence he heard a sound of bare feet; she had stepped from one side of the window to the other. Never had she listened so closely.

"Perchè mi schiante?"

It was a low bloodless phrase that made his fingers light again on the frets, otherwise he did not move. She had pulled the tongue from the flower. And he saw her. She leaned from the window—so far that he could see the round of her back— and her arms stretched down, pushing the stone, the two ends of her shawl hung down.

"Perchè, Adeppi?"

He bowed, there could be no answer. She had dragged a sheet from the bed and, flung around her, still a corner flapped out of the window. Against it fluttered the dark tails of the shawl. One and the other, they were alone. He knew that at this moment the courtier's horse stood peacefully. He breathed full like a partridge. He sang loudly now, lost in a wood, until he heard Arsella turn suddenly from the window and proudly shout, "Mamma. Hear, Mamma? The monello sings!"

They had a light. There were the three of them squeezed at the opening and swinging the lantern over the gray whorls below. Pipistrello was in the middle, even Pipistrello had been awakened for the enjoyment.

"To the left, husband. Move the flame to the left. I saw him. How small he is!" Arsella reached for the lantern herself. "Hear how he trills!"

"Arsella," whined the old woman, "let us sleep."

He ran. He did not look around to see how those in the cramped gallery fought each other but, as far as the terraces, he heard Arsella's shouting, "Ancora una volta, ancora, an-cora . . ."

The dogs were gone.

Adeppi left the mandolin floating on a shallow pond, and when the sun touched the upended neck, the sight of it startled the waking ganders.

At dawn he crept from under one of the aqueduct's great arches and stared upon a countryside which the sun smothered in false fire. Far below, water evaporated from the roof of Brother Bolo's empty shelter; thistles were laid waste before the field mice stirred. All was saturated—the hut, the vineyard, bird nests long fallen to the ground, the irregular train tracks —and the spongy sun grew as if there had been no night. But it was a sun that tides storm or accident in uncertain, backward latitudes where the first secrets of science are vaulted up with the sacristan's greasy anchovy. In the early morning, Adeppi leaned against the towering silent aqueduct, rubbing his eyes, a small figure at the base of the sculptured and sighing pipeline. In the vicinity of the charcoal drawings, he watched the lower paths for the first woman to appear with hair reaching her waist and make an accustomed toilet in the privacy of a corner of one field. But only a gray lamb with red lips called faintly through a noose which choked and tethered it above the sleeping place of the dead shepherd.

An odor of Brother Bolo's black fire was still on the air, an old and abrasive smell as if all hearth fires, put out by pail, returned freshest in the morning, drifting again from the copper spears of the antiquated kingdom's compass. The fire of old alchemists, kitchen keepers, and monastic stokers turned to ash and from ash to ink which dried on parchments secreted in the trunks of trees, a raised city of life lost over plundered and extinguished valleys. The doges were warming their waxen hands again.

Amidst this stretching sea, quiet, steaming, vacated of leathern carriages and gun carriages—only the sun was on its scaffold—stood but one living and visible on the hillside: Adeppi, blood-filled, indolent, with bones sore from a sleep on the rocks. His heart was beating innocently at the side of the sunburnt neck, there was a darkening on his upper lip. He yawned like a small animal of prey contented a few hours after being whelped, sunning itself helplessly between the paws of its dam.

No one stooped to work the fields, the dry brilliant austerity of the morning was untroubled. He descended. But on the edge of the grove he met Pipistrello emerging hesitantly from between the trees as if he too had spent the night in the open. Adeppi stopped and began to make a clucking sound with his tongue against his teeth, threw a stone far to the left, then took deliberately slow and stealthy steps ominously cracking the twigs. All this while he grimaced, sometimes opened his mouth wide and waved his short fat fingers in front of him. Pipistrello waited without question, standing fatefully as he always did when hoping for some foreign mover to pass him by. Finally Adeppi ran at him so that Pipistrello, keeping his face toward the noise, reached behind him for a support in the nearest slender tree. Adeppi caught his arm, then spoke.

"Were you afraid, Pipistrello? I could not speak, friend, this plum silenced me."

The blind man felt quickly for the boy's other hand.

"It is swallowed already, Pipistrello. Mi dispiace. But we'll find you one before noon. Can't you say good morning?"

Adeppi kept fast hold to the blind man, smiling, winking, staring, for Arsella's curled piece of parchment with its bright hues was pinned crookedly upon the man's breast.

"I will lead."

Adeppi held the blind man's cloth at the elbow where it was loose under the joint, pulled and pushed fitfully as if avoiding the lime pit, a hanging branch, the cowcatcher of an electric tram silent as death. Arsella, or even God's wizened, silver-skinned angel, could not better have marked Pipistrello for the boy. All rituals had been stopped, the earth itself stilled with the light, hot and clear. The blinded walked loosely and severely, having taught himself to put his foot forward quickly. Such could walk off the edge of the earth despite the sun. There was no danger for him, only a day by day tempting of disaster and the door that might not be open.

"No tricks!" Pipistrello suddenly exclaimed and wrenched free. The parchment flapped; he did not notice it.

"There is only a hill ahead, elder. It is empty. It looks safe to me." A timid answer, once more taking the blind by the halter of his arm. And Adeppi did look around him to be sure.

But on top of the hill toiled two small figures hardly visible against the heaven. The hill was steep, straw-colored and smooth, so often baked and picked by cultivation that its altitude of sand seemed held on the incline only under the delicate pressure of the sun. The top receded like the peak of a white tent seen rising in the distance. There was nothing for Adeppi and Pipistrello to stumble against, not a cleft stone or root. Still their progress was slight and they climbed slowly. The hill was wide of front, its shoulders obscured far beyond either edge of the curve. The higher they went the less was their inclination to stop and face back toward the descent. Sometimes Pipistrello slipped and Adeppi faithfully lifted him again.

On the summit where a cart road threaded across the plateau for the passage of a few travelers, the minatory creatures labored with a rude lever and pieces of hempen cable thick as tusks. The men could be seen only by the waving of their wide, grass-like hats. They worked to move a boulder intended to mark a station where journeymen might pause and pray. *A Roma.*

Adeppi shaded his eyes. They up there were missing the dust around the rock. They had discovered the sheep, for a bleating came from beneath a ragged summer coat with which they kept it from the sun.

"Do you hear a lamb crying, Pipistrello?"

Wind blew across the hill's middle steepness. It was a breeze that lengthened the slope in a small country. Man and boy, like a thin kite and its young, struggled to keep their feet as the vaguest movement gave sound to the depths below. When Adeppi lifted his eyes to peer up at the pair twisting the boulder, he trembled with the light sensation of falling backward.

The lever had already ground to bits a few lilies placed at the bed of the rock. The old men did not stop for a moment but continued to assault the stone as if being on the summit filled them with obstinate vigor. It was a monument which,

when perfectly positioned, would make the approaching donkey and its rider shy, then kneel, though from below it
looked like some stationary speck of cannon shot.

The wind and the effort of climbing intensified Pipistrello's
blindness. His face showed exertion, the mouth opened, it was
the head of a man climbing quickly as he can and on those
features rode uncomfortably the shadows of the inactive eyes,
a dark band that constantly attempted to right itself on the
bridge of his nose. An odor of millet swept by; the earth
tilted endlessly higher. Adeppi—there was a taste of blood in
his throat from the climb—began to pull on the black sleeve.

"Pipistrello. Let us go back by the road."

Pipistrello only shrugged.

They ascended the sun-lit mountain without turnstiles or
wall and in the height loomed the impersonal wind, a faintly
sweet-smelling vastness offering no protection.

Pipistrello laughed. "Porcellino, think of the dizziness of a
fall from here, how the hands and heels of even a saint would
roll!"

"Watch your step then, Cieco."

The summit rumbled. On the sunny slopes it was more
audible, and for a moment, stopped still, they listened without
feeling while the boulder turned its first few revolutions on
the long way down. Gray, tomb-heavy, it came over the brink
like a stone wheel. Adeppi saw it. Pipistrello heard and shook
free of his guide.

The stone grew twice in girth while it was still far enough
away to admire. It began to whistle as if there was a hole in
its snout. Fifty ill-fitting church steps could be extracted from
it. The hill, ever widening to the blue skies, now showed itself
covered with stubble and impedimenta, and the boulder rose
several feet into the air, thrown from its course and from the
ground by the claw of a buried spring or head of turf. Again
and again it leaped but returned to earth bearing upon them.
And suddenly, dragging brambles and smaller stones, it was at
hand.

"Which way? Which way, child?" screamed Pipistrello, too late.

Adeppi watched the white card of the sacred heart fluttering on the black half-twisted breast, still affixed though the blind man thrashed in his tracks. Until it vanished. There was a rush and it was past, that which shook the ground gone, leaving no trace. Already it was descended to the lower depths where there were only a few last trees to bar its flight. *Salve!*

7

The tides are high at night and in the peak months of summer, and Adeppi finds they have risen in his absence to surpass the watermarks left the year before on the piles. The substructures have sunk and there is clear water atop dark. The stately gondolas are light, each occupied by a single pair who float behind drawn curtains smelling of seaweed. Half the city rides, having given no directions and at the mercy of gondoliers, burly men, masters of their decks, who now relax the oars. Adeppi need not ask them permission though as he jumps from prow to prow, one then another of these boatmen stops his oar entirely and peers at him through the darkness.

He slips, one leg plunges into the water; there is laughter. Nearby the water has just climbed over the last step into a ballroom and spreads across the marble until it reaches the further wall. Ladies run lifting their grandaunts' embroidered skirts. A taper falls and splashes. But the musicians do not get wet, and the stranger water disturbs the festa only a moment. "Ancora, ancora," the boy dares to shout as he sees the men climb off their chairs and brave yellow stockings to the high tide.

A long gondola approaches from the opposite end of the city. He waits, then jumps, and rides once more past the palace where the lackeys, arm to arm, now drive against the rank few inches of sea their great brooms. And the water is rolled back so that up and down the canal a faint rocking possesses the dark flat-bottomed craft.

The totemic arms rising from the bows of the gondolas are striped around with bands of gilt and red paint, necks of the headless swans festooned by once rich color, pale and flaking as the groined vaults of a church with its peeling decoration and ancient quarrels. The gondolas have been hired for an evening on the lagoon bordered by apses and limpets dating centuries. Adeppi joins in the merriment and, for a night, is anonymous, as if he too is no more than a whelk glued among lichen and fern on the lower butts of a bridge, any moment in danger of being sheared away by an over-anxious oar blade.

A gondola passes more severe in line than the rest. Its passenger, a priest, sits with curtains rolled tightly so that all may see he rides with his hands folded and alone. He tries to study the stone vines and inscriptions in the dark. He shouts, "Ferma!" But Adeppi's rower leans forward, without a command, and they are away.

Midnight is tolled by the collision of two of the pleasure boats. They ram, shake, list, and sink. A corked wine bottle and cushion rise from the debris and float toward the crevices where sewerage escapes between the stones. There is splashing as the parties attempt to disengage. Out of the lesser canals come continuous cries of warning, the 'to the left,' 'to the right,' and 'sciar' of other gondoliers still moving without accident, close by. Up on the quai, those who have been saved from drowning begin their apologies. Even the boatmen are solicitous, panting for breath.

The city clears her tortuous channels, then once again they fill with the unlighted sweating flotilla that will lie becalmed by daybreak. A robbed man's pantaloons and ruffle are weighted, slipped over the side, and sunk. An old man, still pensioned to cry the time, peers cautiously down, spits into the water, and shakes his bell. Beyond the cathedral, the town house and chapel that rocks as a sea bell near the head of the lagoon, a silver porpoise is seen to approach and is driven off by the water rodents that swim knowingly at a depth just below the bottoms of the gondolas.

From three or four channels, late in the night, the city receives her indefatigable benediction and continues to slumber upon her fair winds and foul seas which in summer are high and pestiferous.

8

Some few days later Adeppi was caught by Gregario Fabbisogno on the Via Saccheggio and beaten.

The coffin maker watched unmoved, not lowering his eyes until the whipping ended. It was dawn, the church nearby echoed with the exhortation of the first mass chanted since sunrise, and the coffin maker, who had no taste for the sacrament, put on his spectacles the better to witness the punishment meted out not ten feet from him. The old man held his head before the scene with yellowed fixity—he was old but his temples were shaved high—until the expression changed and his mind carpentered some further death-like pleasure at the sight of the soldier struggling with the boy over a heap of dung. Fabbisogno could not have picked a better place than this—between the church covered like a lighthouse with the white of rooks and the shop hiding its row after row of incomplete coffins—to apostatize by the ministering of pain. Adeppi's shouts were a bridge in the silence from the misericordia to the ancient paused now in the fashioning of caskets without a vow in his throat.

Gregario Fabbisogno beat the chrism into Adeppi's buttocks as if in a stupor, a soldier driven from his drunken, ill-pitched tent in the morning. The sight of a mad donkey—Mary had humbly ridden her—bloodied his eyes and he caught up the boy in his left arm. Cain was not more violent; with difficulty the coffin maker returned to his bony bench and nimbly squinted down the plank. And grimaced, noticing a curvature in that wooden spine. Those across the street had said barely fifty of the beads multiple as berries, and disappeared.

Only an hour before—it was the same moment that Dolce flung wide his shutters as he was bidden—Adeppi walked safely into the deserted haunt fronting the hospital and thought to beg breakfast from an old friend or his women.

But the crèche was no longer in its place and the small square, half in shadow, the upper half in new sunlight, was vacant, open to the sky. Vehicles, trucks, and motorcycles had decamped, hurrying southward in a retreat whose smoke still lingered above the smell of tires and gasoline siphoned into a knapsack.

One had been left behind. He seemed to lie in the surety that they would return for him. Adeppi recognized the litter and the water bottle at its side. Flat and deserted, the expanse of dust to the right and left, the body, though it was all that remained, shrank as he approached. The sun fell full in the darkened face. He lay an image of burned-out peace, all disaster come and gone. His thin form lay perpendicular to the steps and centered below the hospital doors which gaped as if they had just opened to eject him. Adeppi's footsteps did not startle the crossed arms. One trouser leg had been severed high as the belt, disclosing a knee and bones above and below which radiated the secret sun.

Adeppi stopped. But already, before he could turn and run, he was the discoverer of this stark, unmistakable survivor. The tops of the surrounding slanting roofs let through the light in irregular holes left by some olden, portentous damager; far below stood the bareheaded child, facing the prone creature that was diminished as a Bishop's sharp-chinned effigy atop his tomb. Now and then the boy heard a single unresolved musical note sounding over the still-standing, brittle chimneys of his city. Lesser scratchings upon the air, the trickling from an upturned demijohn or the strangling of birds in the few overhead wires, were gone.

The hospital, its saline pits refilled with sand, offered an interior vacant as a routed, partially burned cathedral. It had long been inhabited, long abandoned; in front of it Adeppi would have removed his cap. But the way was blocked by the stranger on his back. Morning was the time for such a meeting, as the city was oldest after dawn. Here was a man, a treacherous curve to the claw and yellow upon the lips, in detail complete—thirteen ribs, a gray shirt, mouth open two fingers' width and in it, hardly visible, the tail end of a bandage. A body that grows heavier on the Italian slopes and is ringed round with bloody sticks.

At this hour Adeppi might have joined Urbino's younger children to kill carp in the canal. Instead: "Scusi. Come si chiama? Gianciotto? Gianni? Giovanni?" he asked. But immediately he became quiet.

About the stretcher was the odor of salt. The hospital was made of salt, the streets were white with salt, and Gianciotto, or perhaps Gianni, was tan on the belly and wrists where the garments had shrunk, a tan of the seashore, mountain, or still piazza that dressed the flesh and forced it back to the color of corrosion. The sea was still beyond the city walls. The body cast no shadow. Adeppi wanted to stay by it, guard it, yet the more he watched, the more he feared it. The inertness of an idle scythe in a field at the sea's edge, the formidableness of the body adrift, the look of the dead.

Adeppi backed to the stretcher, took hold of the handles, lifted and pulled. He began to sidestep, turning it toward the shade. Ahead, he caught sight of a foul-smelling alcove and strained. In this country each of the fallen has a child to stumble upon him; from among the trees and irregular streets the boys call, waiting to hook themselves to those about to die. The stretcher resisted, shook, then slowly followed him, grating the dust and pebbles deposited Holy Year after Holy Year. It was not easy though the weight in its emollient costume yielded, and the boy grunted, hauled forward his wagon heaped with marrow and stones. The procession walked on little legs across the piazza. It was time for mass.

The exposed gray leg began to bend, wrinkling with the tension, the thin knee rose as if the sudden feeble onset of motion had loosed one last instinct under the bony cap. Adeppi continued to pull. Then the cleated military boot, belonging to some marching step of the past, drew back, shot up, and kicked the boy.

Adeppi did not turn, but as he escaped he loudly wailed: "Fratello mio, oh, fratello mio . . . disastro!"

The white donkey was tied before the church which in shape and ornamentation was a copy of the Basilica di S. Pietro. After a restless night and while its head hung stiffly in the halter, the donkey buried its character of servility in a noise that climbed high as the pinnacle. As the boy himself appeared within distance of the contracted nostrils and crooked ears, the beast became frenzied beyond control.

"Ahi, ahi!" shouted Gregario Fabbisogno and leapt from under the hooves.

Mary's small donkey lunged imprudently, lathering her white coat in ripples and bold waves down the narrow sides. She thrashed against the hunching figure of Fabbisogno who snatched now and then at the bridle, the wads of cloth wrapped around his bare feet paddling like the musty draggings of an executioner. Little of his face was visible, only the leathern elbows, the bandoleer, the arms shaking the chevrons up and down. A rider would sit this animal side saddle, face covered and holding limp hands in her lap. A pale pair, clicking safely along beneath the evergreens. She was thin, placid of gait, was protected from carrying loads heavier than the small woman who sat lightly near the rump. If Fabbisogno had confronted them, he would have lifted donkey, rider, and halo off the path in his two arms, cradling them, turned around and around, and shouted with rage.

The coffin maker, recognizing the cries of the donkey, came to his door and swept the shavings from a black apron. Then he watched, licking a finger he had crushed with a primitive rasp.

Adeppi, between man and donkey, cast up his round face to the frenzy of both. The animal beat her hooves and brayed when she seemed most out of breath, her stomach was loud and the very muscles added to the noise of each spasm.

There was blood on the backs of Fabbisogno's hands; he quailed, for at that moment he heard the woman behind him enter the Via Saccheggio and enquire after her mount, shook when he saw the donkey lift her nose and become calm. Adeppi stood up, surprised in the silence, and had time to notice the suspension of the dust they had driven into the sunlight. He saw the donkey nod her head as if about to drop it unconcernedly to the roughage trapped in the cobblestones —her eyes were turned from Fabbisogno. The three of them panted, Adeppi stared at the statuette of the donkey with drenched white coat, Fabbisogno crouched ready to fall upon the beast. The coffin maker cleared his throat.

"Ahi! Ahi! Ahi!"

Gregario Fabbisogno took one step, another, stooped and quickly as possible pointed the rifle downward, holding it but a few inches from the white skull. He would have wished to kill her in the stable of grace, perhaps as she was reaching through the mild dusk for hay from a crude rack, lightly flicking the hocks with the slender tail. He would have wished to raise the rifle to his shoulder and destroy in a shot the peace of the animal among her icons. He would mingle the smell of gunpowder with her thorny dung and see her bump once, twice, to the burnished planks and roll over.

Adeppi was cuffed to his knees and Fabbisogno's fist began to rise and fall. It was open, sometimes closed, as he beat he swung from side to side, abandon carrying him in a slow dance. Fabbisogno thrashed him for the donkey. The city roared at him and the boy more loud than the rest. Gregario Fabbisogno sweated and peered down the Via Saccheggio. But suddenly he stopped, swayed, and sat back. He loosed his arms and Adeppi rolled from him.

They emerged softly into the sunlight after mass: the masons to the endless reconstruction of Il Duomo, the clerks to their courts, a few loiterers to the benches above the sewers. And with them, lastly, came Dolce who had just given up this town's unfamiliar censer to its bag of ashes.

Dolce did not hesitate. He approached and laid his hand on Gregario Fabbisogno's head. He waited and, as the man remained dumb, gently shook him by the hair. When the carabiniere opened his eyes, Dolce stooped and made the sign. Once more, swiftly, with slight affection, so that he might comprehend. And the priest allowed the black eyes to close again.

Without even this formality Dolce took Adeppi by the hand and led him away, avoiding the donkey and the crowd.

The body before the hospital had disappeared.

Up and down the Via Saccheggio sounded the drudgery of the crooked hammer and crooked nails.

PALMS

Two fat coadjutors and a thin—Dolce, Brother Bolo, and a lay brother—do not allow their asses a moment's lag but ride them without relaxing the rein and watch the rocks slipping underfoot, the gallows approach and pass. Brother Bolo has a red face and thick brown hair that shines with the paternosters of his seclusion; he travels balancing a heavy stone upon the low center of his donkey's spine. Dolce is empty-handed, mendicant; the elderly woman rides with him. The three are followed by a wing of yellow bees that answer roughly in the heat.

The graces' donkeys look as if they have just been beaten from the bushes and appear quickly, hard driven, round every turn in the road, baleful under Thomist ejaculations. Dolce's mount, the smallest of the three, trips now and then, having been lame as long as he can remember. The woman's feet are uncovered; he holds her waist. Brother Bolo and Dolce abreast grunt to the jogging of the animals. The lay brother trails silently. The trio wear black smocks upon which are painted rough white stripes, bones, false ribs. They pass a tall water wheel turned only by the wind, and from its dark buckets peer the bodies of children wrapped in vines.

Gray dogs come out from their dens, from under haystacks, from white abbey and villages, to sniff silently their train. The religious travel more slowly now and Dolce clutches the woman tightly lest she be snatched away. Watchers along the way wait to proffer stumps of candles, toss handfuls of eye teeth in their path.

In their arms, against their bellies, the women with sores carry sacks of flour that have been dropped for them. The clothing is torn from their bodies wherever the scabs lie, no matter on which limb or whether front or back. The abrasions, each time verified with a kiss, long judged unremediable and painful, are exhibited noiselessly and listlessly. She there, studying her fallen hands, bore a dog with a torch in his mouth; behind her, a girl canonized at the age of seven. Even the toothless have the sweet smiles of the beatified. In the enclosure of the nunnery, matrons wearing white Flemish caps urge them aside for the entrance of the donkeys.

Dolce and Brother Bolo present themselves at the gate. The nuns do not rise. They continue on their knees, working up and down the corridors, pulling the iron pails, and the Prioress too bends across her brush. The donkey bearing the woman is led into their slippery cloister, onto their white stones. Spread-eagle in each tall window is a black angel. The donkey drinks from one of the pails, then lifts its head and smells the smoke in the court.

Beyond the nuns, in a small grill-covered space, a young girl, flapping her sackcloth apron, tends the fire. She is the only woman inside the convent on her feet. She does not pray and sleeps under a half-roof against the wood, her legs toward the pyre. Her arms and hands are blistered and her face marked with soot. Dolce pushes the white donkey close to the flames. The girl does not look up at once but pokes and digs at the fire which leaps above her head and reddens the coarse rods in the grill.

Bolo assists him, but the girl is strong and swings the burden to her shoulder and from the shoulder off, away with one sweep as the religious beat the sudden firebrands off their skirts. It is done. Theresa, Adeppi's mother, goes headlong into the pile, breaks through the red perishable tangle of illuminated twigs, falls to the live coals in the center—to flame her stocking, bodice, and shawl.

The smoke suddenly grows thick.

Three days Dolce prayed for him. The boy stood in a corner, without clothes, turned toward the wall so that he might not see. At times it appeared that Dolce was not speaking on his behalf at all. Nor did the priest speak to the boy. Now and then Adeppi tried tapping on the wall, thinking that someone might hear him. In a fashion he too was praying.

The priest, unquenchable, wore a white shirt and thought sanctus, sanctus, sanctus for the benefit of the flesh hardly more than infant. The shutters were fast. Adeppi spent the hours watching the inhuman descent of a small red spider riding its loose intimate strand of web late in the oppressive afternoons.

The more fervently Dolce prayed, the hotter it grew. He seemed to have at hand an immeasurable rote of pious negatives that applied endlessly to the narrow shoulders before him. He would not sit, but in the heat that rolled over the city stood firm, a figure of black and ivory marching behind the naked boy through many entrances to absolution. Hat off, neck bare, no blessed medallion in sight, Dolce challenged the transgression of the child.

Dolce had not raised his voice, but it became faint. Now and then, at any moment and with no anticipation in the rest of his body, he would fling out his arms and allow St. Elmo's fire to dance from his fingertips.

Fabbisogno lay drunk below by the bar. "Vino, vino," he ordered but no one served him.

Adeppi had not known there were so many saints. As Dolce prayed, the boy saw them, their stooping bodies moving before the façade of a black cathedral. The Pontiff's thousand eyes looked sharp. For the last hours the spider refused to descend the thread, hovering above in its knotted nest. Dolce whispered. The severe neckline of the white shirt, the eyeballs, white, round, the black wrap of the lower garment, all things soft, soluble, transient, and dusty. His cuffs were frayed. He bowed his head and in shadow and under the sharp nose hid the movement of lips and gullet, losing sight of the boy.

While offering a prayer aloud to St. Francis, he fell into

a pale sleep on the third night. Conscious that he was allowing the boy a chance to escape, he tried calling out. Then he dreamed of a traveler and companion he had seen at the gates of Vatican City, the dissolute wearing a straw hat with a red band and in the sun, amidst the sober and sick, a suit of large checks; the other, with a great head of black hair, was using his shoulder against those who pressed near. The two slowly followed through the crowd a small bare-backed boy whom they urged to wail melodiously and beg. They were purporting to bring him, in a moment or two, before His Holiness. The crowd was diverted at the very threshold of the Sanctum and the most impoverished of them, those hunched on rude litters, were seduced into a laugh. Dolce groaned. The walls of the Vatican were whispering and in the distance he saw the popedom slowly recoil, forever beyond reach, close with the steady precision of an enormous flower rejecting the dark.

He fell to his knees. Several in the crowd began to dance. Past his eye went the twisting heels. One dropped a piece of spiced meat under his nose. To his helplessness there came the persistent secular singing of the boy. Suddenly there was a tugging at his back. "Pray for me, Padre?" whispered the singer himself, "pray for me?"

Dolce woke. He was lying with his face toward the ceiling, hands far flung, and his feet dragged partly off the bed; the bottom of his robe had risen and when he lifted his head he saw his legs, silhouetted, the many times mended black shoes sticking up and old, pinched. His head ached and he was unable to move. As he gathered himself, the door opened.

Edouard rocked back and forth holding the edge of it. The light came in over his shoulder, unwavering. The front of his nightcoat was blotched and one of the flies remained with him, spreading its blue wings to his death. Edouard peered in a moment too long from the threshold. With effort he lifted a hand to his hips—but he was about to fall—and stared into the disordered room. The veins had burst under his eyes, there was a disused black sling hanging from his neck, the cold fingers could be seen feeling his heart.

Then he lifted his chin, managed an old look of affection, laughed and reeled back, saying, "Scusi, scusi," trying to wink. But he was not able to pull the door closed after him.

Dolce ran into the hall. He stood listening with his hand to his ear and his stomach suddenly clenched in hunger. There, he took a step, there it was again, the dying man was whistling to himself. Then he sniffed, looked down, and discovered the boy at his side.

9

So Edouard lay back upon the coverlet. His straw hat tilted from the bedpost. Somewhere, within the yellow of his memory, he heard an old woman snipping branches with an iron shears. Once, from a third-class compartment, he had seen a village with imbricated tiles the color of rouge, and against a wall in the sunlight a young priest who hardly lifted his eyes to watch the train, the priest concentrating upon a toy, a game he held in his two hands, turning it that way and another way, shaking it, trying to replace the whiskers on the cat. Perhaps the cat still had no whiskers, this not having been accomplished in all of Edouard's lifetime. And yet he could not help thinking that they should have patience, and he hoped the priest had not moved a step beyond his village.

Edouard folded his hands across his breast. One leg slipped from the coverlet and hung irretrievably off the bed. He thought he heard the grating of death's gate, the plash of the oar, but nevertheless had hopes for himself. It was the survival of the least fit; and though he was denied a sight of Il Duomo, he recalled the endless columns of old women and boys passing one to the next the bricks and piling them. They would not let him go too soon, for decade after decade only those who were thin survived, all who remained thus faring on one less green leaf, on water the more impure. And the rivers crept across Lombardy and covered the toes of the dead.

The Sforza family was all but dead. The egg scavengers walked across the field at dusk. All but dead, but not dead for there was always one more who lived like a mythical monster in the maremma. And Edouard thought of the centuries to come with a drop of blood shared by a hundred, and the generations it would take for the sports to appear, when men would be dwarfed and withered of limb, when the weak, the sickest, and the abandoned would steal the figs from the archbishop's tree and inherit the plains wherever the wind blew.

He looked down at himself and thought, "How many bellies such as this one, how many legs like these, how many bones and ligatures like those cannot die. How many are wearing my coat tonight?" Gene after gene was untrue, trait after trait ill-advised, and there remained the intemperate, starving, treacherous, cold demeanor of those who could not be trusted into limbo. And he would not have changed the tide at night, nor halted its backflowing. His own life now depended upon listening, upon hearing the coming of discomfort, daydreaming of uncharitable children. No, they could not afford to lose Edouard. And he smiled, thinking of the slow retraction of heat and light—in each of them—making the blood bad that the tall grass of the maremma and the dust of the cities might surfeit them. It was peaceful to return, to ask of the crows where the men were and be told and to climb the hill and find them.

Who was there to despair for Jacopo? Who was there to despair for himself? "Bene." He could not roll over. The Grand Hotel was burning.

It rained. The hills washed down into the groves and the clay ran white. A sluggish rain slid from the backs of the buildings, the water rose and drowned the reeds in the marsh. By morning the cobblestones were finally clean.

"Signore," Adeppi rubbed his eyes and enquired of a stranger, "what day is it? If you please, Signore." The man caught him by the hand and led him through the Bocca di Piazza, under the arch, down the steep and past the well yard to the edge of the city. There a crowd was gathered at the foot of a hill, pressed far as possible from the last segments of the wall. The rain came down as a cup spilling. It was early, before the matins, and lightning bolted swiftly over their heads through the gray cloud, seeking its ground. Adeppi pushed among the popolari, clawing at a woman's cloak.

The field was soft, rangeless, clay, he could not see its boundaries where it sank into the fog. Behind them were the forgotten chains and the emptiness of the Via Tozzo. The alarm had spread among them and they had come to the open, into the rain and under the natural electric startling of the heaven. Dolce stood a few feet in front of the crowd, behind him they awaited his sign. Over the hills in the aqueduct the rats lay down stealthily until the way should be clear again.

Dolce took the censer proffered him and began to swing it, dull and silver, smoking to the right, to the left, sounding as the swing of a gate, this ritual performed at the edge of the bare field to protect them so that they put their hands upon their breasts. Dolce fed it the beating of his heart.

"Patience, patience, temperance, patience," said Dolce. Firmly with the other hand he took hold of Adeppi's shoulder, all the while swinging, smoking, watching.

The eyes were upon the body in the clay beyond them. Only Adeppi glanced up to see the crow flying. The silent figure turned in the white mud. Dragging itself, slowly animated, hardly visible, bones of the fingers resting upon the rot of the helmet filled with mud, its bare head lifted and was unable to catch breath in the rain.

He ran, darted, and sank suddenly into the beginning of the plain upon which no city could be built, sloughing through the forgotten furrows, against the restraining priest and crowd behind him. The moment passed and their breaths were no longer at his neck. The boy raced and the body in the field flung up his head. The priest held back the crowd, with his arms wide stopped them, but he could not stop their cry. "O sacrilegio, sacrilegio!"

The earth was cold.

At the breaking of that day, high in the mountains, Nino huddled with his head biting the crossed arms and lay close to the earth chopped from the entrenchments in the black cliff, Nino cold, bearded, and deaf to the turn of the world drifting up from the sea below. The wind touched the hair and pulled listlessly at the greatcoat upon his back, but disturbed him not as did not the howl of the sentries and the gulls. Under his hands, behind the face, deep inside the dark sac of the brain, he dreamed of them and it persisted, a continuous dream, warm and without waiting and despite the presence across the valley of the enemy.